Counting Raindrops

The Streets of Cardiff Seri

Book 3

Anne Main

Counting Raindrops

By Anne Main

The Streets of Cardiff Series

Book 3

Chapter 1

1953

Father Edmund, Arthur Roberts was dying.

The cool, crisp white walls of the church sanitorium glowed with a pearlescent sheen as the winter light faded and grey shadows lengthened. It was the time of day when night and day became one, a tipping point.

Father Edmund knew he was dying; his skin was like a papery husk; lips cracked from the openness of his slack mouth. Speaking was a struggle for him now. His hands bony and weak rested quietly on top of the sheets, only his mind was alive, restless, and free to roam in the silence of this dying room.

Edmund lay awaiting his fate in the small, white ward with five other men; Edmund knew they were all dying too, most were barely conscious sleeping their final days away, as the pain medication gently took away their fight to stay alive. How Edmund envied that calm rest.

The doctors told him it was the cancer eating away at him, sucking the marrow out of his bones, and worming its way into his vital organs, but Edmund knew he was dying of sin… and *that* was why there could never be a cure for his wretched condition.

Edmund lay in his simple bed next to the large window giving him a partial view of the garden and he waited for his own small death to come, as soon it must. He was only fifty-eight years old, and he knew he would not see another birthday.

It had rained all day, a soft gentle, noiseless rain causing fat raindrops to hover and shiver on the windowpanes, each drop shining, perfectly round and separate. In the passing, tedious hours Father Edmund watched the droplets grow and tremble, shattering the view through the window into a bleary Kaleidoscope, before inevitably they lost their grip and slipped down the windowpane.

Edmund pondered the inevitability that each glistening drop would eventually fall, gathering others in their wake, losing shape and individuality, its perfect, spherical beauty obliterated.

Out of the corner of his eye, Edmund lay patiently counting and watching the droplets dance across his window, following each one like a special child until it collected others to itself and disappeared into rivulets; spent and gone forever.

Edmund knew his own life had been like that; at first hopeful, shiny and new before he became lost. His youthful joyfulness fizzled out and came to nothing and now, just like the spent raindrops running off the window ledge it was all over for him- it saddened him.

Lying in his bed for hours watching his life and the rain slip and slide had concentrated Edmund's thoughts. He knew he must act before his own life finally dripped away into nothingness. The year was coming to its close and his life was ebbing away as surely as any evening tide… he did not have long. He could not die without doing the right thing.

There was no point now wondering why his life had turned out the way it had; there was no point fretting that, in the next life, a wrathful God would judge him and find him wanting; or that he would be dammed for all his selfish actions.

If the hospital doctors were to be believed, then Edmund would find out soon enough if he was doomed to wander endlessly in limbo for his sins, his time on this earth was coming to an end.

But none of these thoughts of eternal suffering terrified him quite as much as the thought of dying without letting the one woman he had ever loved know that he was eternally sorry for what he had done; to apologize for ruining her life and breaking her heart.

All Father Edmund could do now was try to make amends for his sins whilst he was still in in this life. He needed to speak to his sister Deidre before he lost the faint whisper he managed to push between his lips.

He needed to tell Deirdre the whole dreadful truth.

Chapter 2

Phoebe sat, glass in hand, with the remainder of a second bottle of stout next to her armchair, she turned over the events of the day in her head. She cocked her head listening for any sounds of movement coming from the upstairs bedroom. Mercifully, it seemed as if June had finally given up trying to get out of bed for the umpteenth time and had eventually drifted off to sleep. All was still in the room above.

The child had been unsettled by all the strange goings on and changes of plan. One minute she was staying the night with Nanna Betty and Bampa Gag and then the next minute she was being bundled on a bus and being taken back home again to spend the night with Aunty Phoebe. Phoebe had to admit it had been a very trying day for the little girl, it was no wonder June was being fractious and difficult about going to bed.

Earlier in the day June had been worried when Bampa Gag had sat for so long on the bench saying that he was tired, she had been cold and hungry waiting for Bampa Gag to feel well enough to walk her back home to see Nanna Betty. June had overheard Nanna Betty crying and she'd never heard Nanna Betty cry before and then as soon as June had finished her lunch, she had been bundled out of the house and rushed off to the bus stop as fast as her small legs would trot, only to be returned home to Aunty Phoebe like a lost parcel. There would be no bedtime stories and cocoa with Bampa Gag tonight as June had been promised.

June returned home to Wilson road feeling tired, confused, and crotchety. She wanted to hear Bampa Gag's bedtime stories about Father Christmas and his elves, she wanted to sleep in her special bed in Inkerman Street, and, to top it all, she had been promised fish and chips for her supper; the last disappointment was almost the worst to bear, and June wailed her disapproval at the top of her voice.

"I'm sorry to land you with June like this Phoebe," Betty pleaded, her nerves fraught with worry over Gerald's health. Betty could tell June was spiralling into a tantrum and she felt guilty poor Phoebe had to step in at the last minute. Betty was anxious to get back home to Gerald to check he was alright.

Phoebe flapped away Betty's concerns, she could see how on edge Betty was, *she'll be fine,* Phoebe mouthed.

"Don't worry Junie, Aunty Phoebe will go and get some fish and chips for your supper as soon as Mammy gets back home," Phoebe soothed. Ivy was expected back at just after five o'clock, so Phoebe had plenty of time to nip out to the fish bar on the Grand Avenue for June's supper.

Betty smiled with relief as Phoebe worked her magic on the fractious child and defused the tantrum threatening to overwhelm June. *Phoebe really was a miracle worker.*

"And how about Aunty Phoebe makes Nanna Betty a nice cup of tea before she goes to catch her bus, *and* you can have the crust off the loaf with jam and butter to tide you over whilst we wait for your Mam to come home?" It was a meagre bribe, but crusty bread was one of June's favourites.

"Yeath please Aunty Feefee," June lisped, her wide tongue edged to the corner of her mouth, dribble drooling down her chin.

June sensed something was up, all this rushing around and grown-ups whispering in corners worried her, she wanted to see her Mam. The promise of seeing her Mam and having fish and chips mollified her for a while and she pottered off to play with her dollies.

But much to June's bewilderment her Mam was all of a rush and fluster as well when she finally came home, whirling in with no time to sit and play with June after all… it was the final straw. For June, the day was just getting worse and worse; June felt anxious and fretful, caught up in a storm of emotions she did not understand.

Ivy had been surprised to find June back home with Aunty Phoebe when she crashed through the door fizzing with excitement about her day in Porthcawl and she hadn't expected her daughter to be waiting for her. For a brief, anxious moment Ivy jumped to the wrong conclusion that something dreadful must have happened to her Mam to cause the sudden change of plans. Only Phoebe's reassurance that it was Gerald who had a *bit of a funny turn and needed a bit of peace and quiet,* mollified Ivy enough for the girl to still to be comfortable about going out for the evening with Billy Thomas.

"It's alright Ivy love…. Gerald's just feeling his age a bit that's all… it's nothing for you to fret about… now you go and get yourself ready and I'll get the fish supper June's been promised…. We're all good here." Phoebe reassured her

"Mammee…. Mamee," June pleaded, she followed Ivy around tugging at her mother's skirt begging for attention.

"Not now June…. I'm sorry darling but Mammy can't play with you she's in a rush to go out," Ivy tousled the girl's hair and kissed the top of her head. "Aunty Phoebe has gone to get you some nice fish and chips for your tea, and she'll be back in a few minutes so there's no time for playing games anyway."

June started to grizzle; *the day was all becoming too much; everybody kept rushing off somewhere else leaving her behind.*

"Shh darling…. Please be a good girl June" Ivy pleaded. The door latch clicked, "look…. here's Aunty Phoebe with your fish and chips now." Ivy said brightly anxiously to defuse a tantrum she could feel brewing.

Phoebe came through the door with a fat parcel of fragrant fish and chips wrapped in newspaper, the tempting aroma filled the hallway. "Here we are June, come and help Aunty Phoebe with these chips and let Mam get herself ready." Phoebe said, she grabbed June's hand and led her into the kitchen allowing Ivy to escape.

Ivy tore upstairs to freshen up her appearance, she was meeting Billy Thomas tonight and she wanted to look her best. Ivy had so much to tell him about her day in Porthcawl; finding her father had been the most exciting thing that had ever happened to her, and she was desperate to share her news with Billy.

In the kerfuffle of explaining June's unexpected re-appearance Ivy had barely snatched five minutes to tell Aunty Phoebe more than a few morsels of information about her father James. But even in her fizzing excitement Ivy had noticed Phoebe seemed a little muted in her response to Ivy's good news.

June's insistent demands to "play with me Mammee," fell on deaf ears and with just a brief hug and a kiss and the request for June to *be a good girl for Aunty Phoebe* Ivy rushed back off out again to catch her bus, leaving Phoebe and June to eat supper on their own.

June was *not* happy, and even after the tasty fish supper was eaten and cleared away, she was still testing Aunty Phoebe's patience to the limit. All evening June had been playing up, edging her way down the stairs with her thumb planted in her mouth, her other hand anxiously twiddling her hair into a matted loop. Grizzling and performing when Phoebe took her back upstairs again, June protested her disappointment at the top of her voice.

"Come on Junie darling let's go back to bed again shall we?" Phoebe could see June had been crying. June's eyes looking red and bleary stared back at Phoebe and the child shook her head vigorously-she didn't want to go back to bed, she wanted her Mam. When her Mam had left to go out for the evening, as far as June was concerned, it was the last straw in a rotten day.

"Don't fret now your Mammy will be back later precious…. Now why don't we let Mr Sandman come and see you asleep, because he's a big friend of Father Christmas and he'll tell Father Christmas which little girls and boys have been good about going to bed." Phoebe coaxed. Reluctant to incur the wrath of Father Christmas, June eventually stayed in her room. Phoebe stood outside the bedroom door for a few moments until the sobs and wails subsided.

Phoebe crept downstairs and poured herself a much-needed bottle of stout; she sipped the dark brown brew and pondered the chaotic day. She didn't normally like to drink on her own but tonight she felt in need of something to settle her nerves and a glass of stout fitted the bill. Betty had whirled into the house like a storm just before three o'clock with June in tow before whirling back out again an hour later to get back to her poorly husband.

It was obvious Betty was upset, and all at sixes and sevens; the shock of Gerald's angina attack had shaken her to the core, the fact that he had concealed his aches and pains from her for some time had shocked Betty even more; the couple needed some time to talk about the future. His sudden fragility had sharpened Betty's focus; she was forced to face the reality that Gerald was a man who needed looking after. Phoebe would just have to look after June tonight, she had more important things to do; her husband needed her.

When Ivy left to meet with Billy for the evening and June had finally given in and gone to sleep, a reluctant calm eventually descended on Wilson Road. Phoebe could see that today had been a tipping point, the precipice had been reached and now there was no going back. Ivy had met her father and things would never be the same again.

Anxious to get back to see how Gerald was faring, Betty had left before Ivy came home from her visit to see James. It was Phoebe who was left to discover what damage had been done by Ivy's visit to Porthcawl, and in Phoebe's opinion damage had certainly been done.

"Aunty Phoebe I've had the most wonderful day with my father. He's marvellous, simply marvellous," Ivy gushed. She was overwhelmed by her emotions all day, a roller coaster of joy and sadness and now she wanted to share her day with Phoebe. "He's asked me to live with him!" Ivy gasped as she hurtled through the front door, her hair a tousled mess from rushing; eyes bright with excitement.

Phoebe was speechless-*had James Pugh really asked Ivy to pack up her things and move to Porthcawl just like that, they'd only met for the first time today? Her darling Ivy who she loved more than life to up sticks and go and live with a man she didn't know, a lonely, blind man in need of a carer and companionship.*

"Did you say he *actually* asked you to come and *live* with him Ivy?" Phoebe was aghast such a proposal should have been made so lightly.

"Well, not exactly," Ivy admitted, "but what he said was, that if I wanted to have a new life away from all the bad memories of Jimmy then I could always go and live in Porthcawl with him. I told him all about June and he's dying to meet her… he said I could take her there for Christmas if I wanted to…. June's never seen the seaside." Ivy chattered on, heedless of the impact her news was having on Phoebe.

The words were like hammer blows in Phoebe's heart. Phoebe had been looking forward immensely to having this Christmas with Ivy and June. She wanted to hear the rustle and excitement of Christmas morning as presents were unwrapped and admired, the childish delight and squeals of excitement after a visit from Father Christmas, and the fat stocking left at the end of June's bed.

Phoebe felt a tide of anger wash over her. *How dare James Pugh try to poach this Christmas from her by enticing Ivy away?* Phoebe knew Nanna Betty and Bampa Gag also expected to share Christmas with Ivy and June as well; she could lay a pound to a penny Bampa Gag would feel the same as Phoebe did about the matter if Ivy decided to go to Porthcawl for Christmas.

Phoebe knew James Pugh was a lonely man and with his own mother dead he had no family to call on for support, but he couldn't just barge in and upset their lives like this! Phoebe had wrongly assumed he might want to try to persuade Betty to come back to him, reeling his old love closer to him again, rekindling the romance they once had. But it seemed Phoebe was wrong, and she had been out manoeuvred, it was Ivy, not Betty, who might be tempted away like a child following a seductive tune from a Pied Piper.

It's not bloody fair, Phoebe muttered to herself.

 Ivy was just beginning to make a new life for herself now Jimmy was dead; she was growing closer to Billy Thomas and Phoebe had high hopes the budding romance would flourish. Phoebe prayed each night that maybe one day she would see her darling Ivy a happily married woman with a handsome young husband offering Ivy and June a brighter future. *She couldn't allow the ailing James Pugh to throw a spanner in the works.*

Phoebe moved heaven and earth and called in every favour she had to rid Ivy of her loathsome husband Jimmy Benson, to give the girl a second chance at finding love and happiness and now, thanks to James Pugh, it looked like it might all have been for nothing. James Pugh might want to inveigle his way into Ivy's life, but Phoebe wasn't just going to sit back and let him steal Ivy away from her to be an old man's companion.

Over my dead body you will, she muttered to herself.

Phoebe watched the embers dying in the grate, she riddled the cinders and banked up the fire with some small coal. It was gone ten o'clock and Ivy should be back home soon. Phoebe could not face hearing any more about the wonderful James Pugh, with the fire secured for the night she headed off to bed.

Chapter 3

Billy Thomas was waiting impatiently for the bus to arrive at the bus stop on the corner of Portmanmoor road. His coat collar was turned up in a vain attempt to deflect the biting wind whistling around the corner and numbing his face; he slapped his hands against his thighs to keep warm. *Where was that bloody bus!*

The bus was nearly ten minutes late and Billy fretted that maybe Ivy wouldn't come at all. Perhaps her day to Porthcawl had not gone as planned and she was too upset to spend the evening in a crowded room listening to the banal lyrics of Saturday night club singers?

Maybe she'd missed her bus back from Porthcawl? Maybe she'd had a change of heart about spending the evening alone with him? His heart pounded in his chest; Billy could not bear it if Ivy stood him up.

Now that his sister-in-law Alice was pregnant, his brother George and Alice wouldn't come out socialising and dancing in their usual foursome. Tonight, it would be just him and Ivy chatting and listening to music in the smoky fug of the Bomb and Dagger club. He stamped his feet and willed the bus to sail around the corner before he lost all hope.

Ivy had met her father James Pugh for the first time and Billy wanted to hear all about it. He knew how important it was for Ivy to finally meet her father, the man who she didn't even know existed until a few months ago, her mother's one true love.

Ivy had chattered about the impending visit to Porthcawl at every opportunity, he knew she was frazzled with nerves, anticipating so much and yet terrified of rejection by a man she'd never known.

Billy wished he could have gone with Ivy and held her hand, comforted her and told her it would all be alright, but he knew it would have been a step too far. To ask to go with Ivy would have been a suggestion too intimate, placing him in a role at her side she had not yet agreed to.

Ivy had not hinted she wanted company on her difficult mission to meet her father for the first time, if she had, then Billy felt sure he would have jumped at the chance to be at her side, but Ivy was determined to go on her personal journey of discovery alone, all Billy could do was wait.

Ivy's own relationship with Billy was still not on a formal footing; yes they had kissed, yes they had laughed, and they held hands but… but he still didn't know *how* she felt about him; Billy dared to live in hope that eventually he could call Ivy *his* girl… no, more than his girl…. his fiancée and then he could introduce her as such to anyone he met.

This is my fiancée Ivy.

Billy knew his brother George didn't approve of his growing closeness to Ivy Benson, but he was becoming more certain as each day passed he wanted to marry Ivy and look after her and to take care of little June. In his head Billy imagined that maybe after they were married then one or two more children of their own might come along to complete the family. Billy loved children and he felt sure Ivy did too, after all she doted on her only child June.

He knew tongues would wag, but he didn't mind at all that June was born a Mongol, she was a sweet natured, happy little girl who he enjoyed spending time with, he would gladly take her on if only Ivy would agree to marry him.

Billy *knew* whoever said *"faint heart never won fair maiden"* was right and he *knew* that he would need to screw his courage to the sticking post soon and declare himself to the girl he loved. But his nagging inner voice, the one which told him he was un-loveable, ugly and that she would probably say *no,* held him back…. *It was just a question of picking the right moment, a time when he could be certain she would say yes,* he told himself.

Another two cars swept past; Billy had to jump out of the way to avoid the spray from greasy puddles filling the gutters. Then finally, when nearly all hope was lost, in a blaze of lights the number 39a Cardiff bus swung slowly around the corner.

Through the steamed-up windows Billy could not see the faces of the passengers. Perhaps he had hoped foolishly she would be sat on the correct side, peering through the window, smiling, and waving back at him, as enthusiastic as he was to be meeting again.

Passengers alighted slowly in ragged groups, some pausing to thank the driver for their journey, others gasping at the rush of cold air after the comforting warmth of the bus. He craned his neck, desperate to get a glimpse of her, *please let Ivy be on the bus!*

She was there! *His heart flipped with excitement.*

Ivy had come… she was almost the last passenger to exit the bus, she alighted from the step in her gaberdine Mack, and a fetching navy felt hat.

"Hello Billy,…. I'm so sorry to keep you waiting on a cold night like this." She smiled and his heart melted.

He wanted to say he would have waited all night for her if he knew she was coming; that time spent standing out in the cold and the wind meant nothing to him so long as she was there.

He simply smiled instead, leaving his thoughts unsaid; he could see Ivy looked tired.

"Don't worry Ivy, it's fine, we're not too late either, there's still a few minutes to go before the music starts. Now let's get inside out of the cold before they shut the doors and find ourselves a seat." He pecked her shyly on the cheek, then he took her by the arm and led her into the club.

The evening did not go well. They were squeezed on to the last available table in an unfavourable position cramped up against the stage. Once the music started it was hard to hear each other over the band, conversation was stilted; she laughed when it seemed that each time she started to speak a trumpet or drum interrupted her.

At Billy's suggestion they danced a little because he needed to feel close to her and the soft warmth of her in his arms soothed him, but the strident chords and loud vocals meant it was impossible to talk to her. Billy cursed himself for his poor choice of a venue, for not checking the billing. He couldn't talk to her in here, if he didn't speak to her before the evening was out he felt sure he would explode.

"Shall we go now Ivy?" he said dejectedly as he led her back to their small table perched near the stage.

"We can if you want to Billy." Her eyes looked anxious, had she upset him? She knew she wasn't exactly being bubbly and talkative tonight, but it had a been a long and trying day on her trip to Porthcawl.

He bent close to her ear, "I must talk to you Ivy and this music is too loud, come on let's get your coat and we can talk outside."

He ushered Ivy to the door, they collected their coats and exited into the cold night.

"Brrr… it's bitter out here," Ivy gasped, her breath pluming on the freezing air. A crystal sheen was beginning to coat the pavements. Tonight, there would be a hard frost.

"I know… how about I buy us some nice hot chips. There's a bus stop nearby so we can sit inside the bus shelter and eat them out of the wind, we can talk there…. and you can tell me all about your day." He had to know what had happened on her visit to Porthcawl, it had been eating away at him all evening.

He wrapped his arm around Ivy's shoulder and hugged her close to keep her warm, she was shivering with the cold. In that moment, with Ivy tucked under his arm he felt the happiest he had felt all evening.

Chapter 4

Deirdre Roberts collected her things in readiness for her visit. She settled her sensible hat firmly on her recently permed grey hair, she buttoned up her warm winter coat to keep out the December chills, donned her best leather gloves, and checked she had her house keys. Always prepared for all eventualities, Deirdre had a note pad, pen and a clean handkerchief safely tucked in her handbag.

A brief glance in the mirror confirmed she was presenting a smart, no-nonsense appearance to the world. Deirdre was a firm believer in the perfection of God's creation, and she did not feel the need to gild the lily with lipstick or powder or indulge in the use of perfume; the clean scent of Life Buoy was all the adornment Deirdre Roberts required to make herself feel presentable. She was a plain woman, and she knew it, any youthful prettiness she might have once possessed was long gone.

Deirdre lived alone now in the shabby house which had been her family home all her life. Number 2 Alma Road had all the comfortable familiarity of an old pair of slippers and the tatty appearance of having seen better days. Now that both their parents, Edna and Cecil, had passed away, she had more time to tend to the various jobs which needed doing around the place, but the trouble was Deirdre had her ailing brother Edmund and all her other commitments to think of now. Each day the house diminished a little more.

When their parents were alive Deirdre and Edmund grew up with the fussy figured wallpaper and checked hall tiles. As children, they barely noticed the rattling windows and doors so draughty there were fifty ways for the wind to get. All the other houses in Alma Road looked the same, terraces of modest Victorian villas with a bay front window, three small bedrooms and a tiny garden at the back. Now after decades of use, the same fussy wallpaper was losing a battle against the damp and struggled to cling to the walls. The biting draughts whistling through the house, seemed far worse than she ever remembered. Some days she felt bone cold.

Since their parents had died Deirdre was beginning to feel the draughty house was a bit too much for her to cope with. If Edmund had been in better health she would have raised it with him, but she wouldn't worry him with such trivial problems now. A small corner of Deidre's soul hankered after a nice little bungalow on the coast at Barry or maybe even Porthcawl, but it seemed more than heartless to discuss such thoughts when her brother lay on his deathbed.

Not given to moaning about her lot as a spinster, Deirdre always counted her blessings and *if* ever, in an idle moment, she thought a move to the seaside might suit her then she remembered all the ties that bound her to the old house in Alma Road. And the biggest tie of all was Rita.

Deirdre only had to think of her former neighbour's daughter Rita, now a handsome, grown woman with children of her own, who she had watched grow up all her life, to realise that she could never bear to leave Cardiff. Rita had only recently moved back into number 4 Alma Road with her husband George Prosser and their two children, Frank and Jennifer. At first Rita was only there to look after her ailing mother Phyllis Richards, but when the old lady finally passed away and the old house was left to Rita, the whole Prosser family decided to move in for good. Deirdre was delighted to have Rita living back next door again, it was just like old times.

All Deirdre's life she had been known as Aunty Dee Dee to little Rita and now she was stepping into the shoes left by the late Grandma Phyllis Richards as far as baby sitting was concerned. Deirdre might be a single lady who had never known the love of a man, but she had known the love of a child… young Rita Richards.

Deirdre switched off the hall lights and started out on the familiar short walk to the Catholic sanitorium where the sick and the elderly saw out their last days; frail men being tended to by the compassionate nursing Nuns of St Saviours.

Deirdre was fiercely proud of her brother Edmund for responding to God's call as a young man and embracing the priesthood, it was such a shame that his own life was coming to an end at such a young age, when he still had so much to offer.

Deirdre knew it had been an unspoken disappointment to her parents that neither she nor Edmund had ever married or given them grandchildren, but she knew they were immensely proud of their only son for embracing his priestly vocation. They had followed Edmund's progress avidly when the church had sent him into various parishes to try to build up ailing congregations helping them to flourish and grow. Edmund had soon built up a reputation as being a fisher of men.

And, in equal measure, they loved their plain, sensible daughter who looked after them so devotedly. Deirdre was a dedicated carer in her parent's old age, and they had died content in the knowledge that both of their children had brought credit to the Roberts' family name.

Deirdre was now a dowdy, sixty-year-old spinster who believed in doing her duty by God and man. She regularly helped to collect money for the foundlings and orphans of St Saviours, she made scones and cakes for the church fetes, and she could be relied on to organize the flower rota for St Paul's church… and three times a week, every week, without fail, she took it upon herself to visit her ailing, younger brother Edmund in his hospital bed.

She knew Edmund did not have long on this earth, but she wished, hoped, and prayed he could be more at ease with his passing from this life to the next. It troubled Deirdre that Edmund could not find peace in his dying days, his mind so aggravated by thoughts which would not allow him to rest easy in his bed.

Deirdre like to think her regular two o'clock visit gave her brother some comfort in his hour of need, sometimes she just sat with him and held his hand, other times she reminisced about their carefree childhood days spent playing in the wild gardens of Roath Park, but his constant restless agitation disturbed her.

Edmund was a priest, a man of God, a holy man devoted to the service of others, if he could not find peace in meeting his Maker then who could? Deirdre had tried to seek out what was troubling him, coaxed him to confide in her but he seemed unable to let the words come.

Deirdre did not consider herself to be a chatty, voluble sort of woman and she recognized Edmund's illness meant his power of speech was failing him, words struggled to leave his mouth, and on a bad day she had to step in and interpret what he had to say. It pained her that at the end of his days her brother could not say whatever it was he needed to say to ease his troubled mind.

As Deirdre walked down the soulless, antiseptic corridor towards Edmund's ward she offered up a silent prayer that she would find her brother in better health today. Edmund was all the family she had left now, and she would do anything to help make his last few weeks or months on this earth easier.

Perhaps today would be better. Perhaps today he would find the strength to tell her what was preying on his mind before it was too late.

Edmund heard the click of Deirdre's heels on the linoleum corridor. The church clock had chimed twice for the hour; he knew it would be her, Deirdre was always punctual.

He had spent the morning carefully honing what he wanted to say to his sister in his head. Edmund knew his voice was weak and likely to fail him, so he needed to be economical with his words. He could not afford to get emotional and overwhelmed trapping his words in his throat, sealing them behind sobs… there would be time for tears later. Deirdre needed to listen, and she needed to act on his wishes before it was too late.

"Good afternoon Edmund," Deirdre bent across the crisp sheets to give her brother a peck on the cheek. She thought he looked particularly frail, his eyes looked cloudy as if he were half dead already and his sunken face had a greyish tinge which spoke of a man who did not have long left on this earth.

"And how are you feeling today brother?" Deirdre said brightly, she drew up the chair and positioned herself near his head to catch his soft, rasping replies. The patient in the next bed was fast asleep but Deirdre still wanted to give Edmund a little privacy as they talked, and his voice was so weak now.

Edmund fixed her with a stare and raised his hand to still her chatter, he knew his sister would launch into a long description of the weather, or some chit chat about the neighbours if he didn't stop her before she got in full flow.

"Deirdre…" his voice crackled, "I must tell you something…." His agitated fingers scrabbled on the edge of the crisp sheet, scritching and scratching as if he was trying to claw some strength from the rigid cotton.

"Yes brother… of course I'm listening," Deirdre gave a silent *thank you* her prayer had been answered, perhaps her brother would unburden himself today of whatever it was he needed to say and find peace?

"You *must* help me…" his eyes implored her to help.

"Of course, I will Edmund… please don't go upsetting yourself," she could see the agitation in eyes. Small beads of sweat were starting to form on his brow with the exertion of speaking.

"Just ask me Edmund… anything." Deirdre tried to soothe his agitation, he was not strong, too much stress might do untold damage. *If she could help him then of course she would.*

I've sinned against someone Deirdre…." Edmund gasped. "I sinned against a blameless woman… a woman I loved." A tear trickled down his cheek.

He knew what he was about to tell his sister would crush her, he could not fully see Deirdre's face, but he could tell from the sharp clasp of her hand his words were hurting her. Raindrops hammered on the window hospital window.

Deirdre groaned; she had had no idea of the early scandal in her brother's career.

The Church had conspired to keep Edmund's transgressions covered up, they had blamed the vivacious, pretty Phoebe Horwat for being a temptress and agent of the devil for seducing a handsome young priest away from the path to God.

Edmund was absolved and forgiven, Phoebe Horwat was not. For years Edmund had buried his sinful actions deep within himself, complicit in a lie and he could bear it no longer.

Edmund knew must confess his sin to his sister, but even more importantly he must confess to another sin, a sin he had kept hidden from everyone. A sin that was *even* worse than his crime of seducing and abandoning the young, pregnant Phoebe Horwat all those years ago.

A sin only he knew about, a sin so huge that it was torturing his very soul.

And now Edmund needed his sister Deidre's help to try and make amends whilst there was still time. He willed her to forgive him and to agree to undertake the difficult task he was about to lay on her shoulders. A task which may cause untold heartache in so many lives.

She watched him beg.

"Please help me Deirdre," he pleaded.

Chapter 5

Phoebe Howat never missed going to evening mass on a Sunday. Without fail the young woman sat, rosary in hand, on the hard church pews at the sparsely attended evening service and performed her devotions. The young woman looked ethereal under her ornate chapel veil covering a glorious mane of dark blonde hair; her exquisite, delicate features peeping from under the black lace. Every Sunday evening, she could be found sat with her head bowed in prayer as the soft rhythms of the Latin service implored the faithful to pray for their sins.

Sometimes Phoebe would attend the popular midday service with her mother and father, and occasionally she would appear at the busy morning mass accompanied by her three handsome sisters Lisa, Carol and Katrina. But it was only ever Phoebe who represented the Horwat family at the quiet contemplative evening mass service held at the church of St Saviours and it was pretty Phoebe Horwat who had caught Father Edmund's eye.

Phoebe had a gentle grace and shy seductive smile which captured the young priest's heart; a heart that should have been reserved for God alone.

Father Edmund Arthur Roberts was not exactly sure what colour Phoebe's glorious hair was. The dark patterned, lace head piece obscured all but the smallest, tantalising glimpses of the young woman's crowning glory. When Phoebe knelt with her head bent at the alter rail beneath the image of a sorrowing Mary and a crucified Christ, Father Edmund tried to decide if it was dark blonde or light brown with golden highlights. In the soft glow of the church lanterns, he could never be certain of its exact hue, and it vexed him.

When Phoebe raised her bowed head with her lambent brown eyes closed and her soft mouth open expectantly to receive the Holy sacrament he struggled not to stare at her beautiful up-turned face, to not imagine kissing her soft, pink mouth. The intensity of his infatuation with the young woman, who he had not even spoken to, grew by the day.

Occasionally when Phoebe was accepting the holy chalice a light brown tendril escaped from the edge of the veil and curled delicately around her ear, at other times a dark golden whisp caressed her forehead and when Edmund saw them, he felt sure they were there especially for him.

The anxiety Father Edmund felt when he was following the two other priests in line to administer the Holy Eucharist overwhelmed him. The young priest could feel himself counting the parishioners to see where his presence would land in the priestly order administering the Holy sacrament. If Edmund's calculations showed he was to present the chalice as much as two parishioners away from her, then he felt his heart pound and race with annoyance; cheated of that one intimate moment with her, denied those few seconds when he was allowed to gaze into her lovely face and observe her.

Father Edmund was hopelessly and recklessly in love with the beautiful Phoebe Horwat, and he knew for certain he was living in a state of mortal sin. Every morning the vestiges of his torrid dreams where he caressed her delicious body and his damning, firmly erect penis accused him of such and throughout the day he could think of nothing but her. Every perfect inch of her obsessed him.

At night his beautiful enchantress, Phoebe, commanded his dreams and in the daytime without him even consciously thinking about her, before he knew it, she was invading his thoughts, dragging him away from prayers, and blocking his silent contemplation of the Bible. Everywhere he looked and went he thought of Phoebe.

If Father Edmunds didn't know better he would swear Phoebe Horwat had bewitched him with her golden-brown eyes and her seductive smile. No other woman had ever had such an effect on him.

Father Edmund knew how he felt about Phoebe was wrong, and he knew, in his heart, the girl had given him no cause to generate this passion in him, but whether she knew it or not, Father Edmund was her devoted slave.

That the fault was *all* his wasn't in any doubt, but he couldn't help himself. Slowly but surely, Edmund knew he would never rest until he had made Phoebe his and his alone… despite all his sacred vows, Edmund grew certain in the belief that he had to have her, to possess her body and soul or he would go mad.

Father Edmund had tried to find a resolution to his state of perpetual sin. He confessed to having impure thoughts in the sacred confessional, but the saccharine advice from Deacon Andrews that Father Edmund should *pray for strength and turn his thoughts to God* left him

21

hopelessly unprepared for the tidal wave of passion which engulfed him each time he saw the divine Phoebe Horwat on her knees before him at the altar rail.

Father Edmund tried to quench his ardour by wearing a hair shirt cilice; every morning as he stood in his spartan room before his small mirror in an obvious state of sinful arousal, he dragged the vicious, scratchy hair shirt over his head in a vain attempt to conquer his lustful thoughts.

The hourly harassment of his skin by the scratchy, itchy fibres disrupted his devotions and simply served to remind him of why he was wearing the hateful garment in the first place… it was all because of the captivating, bewitching Phoebe.

Eventually Father Edmund was forced to admit defeat, he buckled under the certainty that the only cure to his wretchedness was to be found in the arms of Phoebe Horwat.

"Good evening Father Edmund and thank you…." Phoebe said softly. She extended her hand towards the handsome new priest as he stood on the church steps bidding his parishioner's a safe journey home.

Father Edmund had recently joined the parish and yet in just six months his warm demeanour and inspiring personality had impressed the reverend Bishop and drawn worshipers to the church services. It was whispered that, with the correct guidance, young Father Edmund Roberts would go far.

 That evening Phoebe was one of the last to leave the service, she had paused for a few moments to light a votive candle in memory of her Godmother Alys who had died the week before, two days after Phoebe's twenty second birthday.

Father Edmund observed Phoebe slip off to the lady Chapel for a few moments of quiet reflection whilst the other parishioners queued up to leave the gloomy church and shake his hand…. *Perhaps she was in need of spiritual comfort?* He yearned to follow her instead of waiting for her to re-emerge.

"Good night Phoebe," Father Edmund smiled a warm smile; the skin crinkling around his sensitive blue eyes, he took her small hand and held it between his-*it was as divinely perfect as he imagined it to be.*

"I noticed you visited the Chapel of our Lady tonight Phoebe… do you have some special request for the holy Mother I might add to my own prayers?" Father Edmund held her gaze, willing her to ask for his assistance, slender fingers locked in his own.

And so, it started, little by little Father Edmunds gained Phoebe's trust and eventually unable to resist the subtle overtures of love and devotion, Phoebe started to return Edmund's affections. At first she felt guilty when her thoughts turned to lust for the tall, dark, handsome priest with the glinting blue eyes, but eventually she was convinced she had fallen deeply in love with this pure and selfless man and that he loved her in return.

Phoebe knew that her parents would be horrified if they thought their devout, well-brought-up Catholic daughter was indulging in such wicked, wanton foolishness with a man of the cloth, a man who had renounced all the pleasures of the flesh and the worldly ability to have a wife and family. But like Edmund she felt unable to the resist the pull of their mutual attraction and soon Edmund's ardent pursuit of Phoebe was bearing fruit.

Phoebe's honour was kept a closely guarded jewel by her watchful parents Pavel and Anna. Like her sisters before her, Phoebe was not a girl who was allowed to stay out late and flirt with boys. Phoebe's fierce Polish father, acted as a robust deterrent to any thoughts of premarital hanky panky when a young man walked any of his four daughters back home from an evening dance.

Pavel, a burly docklands stevedore with flashing brown eyes and a quick temper, was certain all four of his handsome daughters would eventually make wonderful wives when the right man came along, but until that day he would guard them with his life… Horwat women were pure and virtuous *and that was the way they would stay*.

Whilst Pavel was waiting for the right suitors to come along, he was determined no ne'er-do-well would creep like a fox into his chicken yard and steal the most precious commodity he had- the family's good name. A polish Tata, or father, was a fierce some prospect for any young man seeking a woman to court.

Despite their humble home in the shabby terraces of Adamstown, Pavel and his long-suffering wife Anna had brought up their four daughters to be hard working, God fearing young women who could cook and sew and keep a house to Pavel's exacting Polish standards.

In Pavel's opinion any woman who could not cook like an angel and keep an immaculate house was next to useless as a wife, if she happened to have a pretty face then that was a bonus. In Poland the land of Pavel's birth, the virtues of hearth and home was like a religion to him, and he carried his values into his adopted homeland of Wales.

Pavel's two eldest two girls had already embraced married life with decent, hardworking Welsh lads who had received Pavel's blessing and soon, God willing, Katrina and Carol would give him lots of good, strong grandchildren to bless his old age.

The only two fledglings yet to fly the Horwat nest were his youngest daughter Lisa and his favourite child Phoebe. Phoebe was the only girl to inherit his flashing gold-brown eyes and dark blonde hair, which on the fair skinned girl was a most striking combination. Pavel often saw young men giving Phoebe the eye, and he had said to his wife Anna, on more than one occasion that, *"Phoebe was too pretty for her own good and needed watching."*

In everyday society things might by freer and more permissive now the Great War had ended, but things had not altered one jot in the conservative Horwat household. Whilst Phoebe was under her father's roof she would accept her father's word was law and keep herself virtuous for her wedding night.

The heady, excitement of clandestine meetings and whispered sweet nothings with Father Edmund had completely overwhelmed an unworldly lass like Phoebe. Whilst Phoebe knew what she was doing was wrong and fraught with danger, she believed the young priest when he professed the purest kind of love and when he reassured her he would do anything for her… anything… Phoebe dared to live in hope*, surely Edmund would eventually leave the church and marry her, or else why would he pursue her so ardently?*

Of course, Father Edmund had sworn her to secrecy. But as their snatched trysts became more frequent and more urgent Edmund threw all caution to the wind and became reckless.

So many of his friends had died in the war, so much misery had been inflicted on the world was it really such a great sin to seek love and comfort in the arms of a woman he loved?

Edmund's holy vows of celibacy were but a distant memory for him now, when Father Edmund was near Phoebe all he could think about was her and the sheer bliss of possessing her delicious body.

In Phoebe's presence he was no longer a celibate priest, he was a man in the full flood of unbridled passion. Edmund knew there could be no turning back now, he had courted her, albeit in an underhand secretive way, and he had won her heart, now he had to possess her…. body and soul…. Nothing else would do.

"Of course, I love you Phoebe," Edmund murmured as he smothered her face with kisses and slipped his hand under her skirts. "Please let me … I must have you…. I must…trust me my darling, it will be all right, don't worry," he reassured her when he had entered her for the first time. His breathing was urgent and gasping in his rush to know her body, the perfect body he had explored so often in his head.

Phoebe's little cry of pain when he stole her virginity seemed to inflame him even more, "Oh God… Oh God," he gasped.

Phoebe wasn't too sure if it was a cry of ecstasy or despair.

"I love you Edmund," Phoebe said shyly pulling her skirt back around her hips. They were huddled in a small dark back office tucked away in the dark recesses of the church where the spare kneelers, church candles and bees wax cakes were kept.

Edmund felt a rush of guilt; he had committed the ultimate sin. He knew he could not marry the girl and yet he had selfishly taken the most precious gift she had to offer her husband.

Phoebe looked at him expectantly. *Was he pleased with her? His face looked flushed from the act of sex.*

"And you know I love you too, Phoebe, but you must go now," he said urgently. He kissed her briefly on the top of her head, he dared not kiss her on the mouth or else his desire for her would build again. She must go now. Soon the choir practice would be arriving, she could not be found here with him…. it was too dangerous.

When Edmund said his prayers that evening he begged God for help…. *"Please Lord, help me to find my way back to my calling… dear God bring me back from this sin…. Help me…."*

Then at night he went to bed and dreamed of Phoebe, caressing her, loving her, possessing her. In the pale light of morning his stained sheets bore testimony to Edmund's lustful, erotic dreams and yet again he was destined to spend a day in agony.

For months this bitter-sweet torture consumed him until Edmund felt he could bear it no longer; he resolved to confront her. When he was not with Phoebe he felt stronger, his courage to resist her charms grew, his fragile faith supported him and urged him to repent and renounce her, but in her presence he was lost, totally and utterly lost, a drowning man with no hope of rescue.

Edmund had not seen Phoebe for several days and the absence allowed him to gather all his resolve to resist Phoebe's seductive charms when he next saw her. With a heavy heart Edmund made up his mind that the love affair must be well and truly over. He told himself he would speak to her after evening mass, beg her forgiveness, plead for her to see reason….to set him free from her spell.

Then to his surprise at the next Sunday morning mass Mr and Mrs Horwat bade Father Edmund a cheery good morning and asked if he would pray for their daughter Phoebe. Apparently Phoebe had been feeling rather *under the weather* for several days and her parents hoped Father Edmund might add a little spiritual assistance to their own prayers for Phoebe's recovery to good health. The ailment meant Phoebe would miss attending the evening service and Edmund, without the irresistible pull of her presence, felt the cord of his desire slacken a little more. He felt it was as if God was giving him the space to escape her enchantment, removing the temptation from his vision.

In a moment of resolve and remorse Edmund hardened his heart and vowed to all that was Holy he *would* tell Phoebe there could be no future for them; they *must* not see each other anymore… it *must* end for both their sakes and the following Sunday he would sever the ties which bound them together and return to the righteous path.

Satisfied he was at last escaping the fog and madness of his obsession for the first time in a long time Edmund slept soundly and did not dream of Phoebe.

The following Sunday they met as usual in the cramped back office. Edmund was nervous, turning over the phrases in his head, trying to find the words to convey the finality of his decision without sounding too cold and heartless. He knew Phoebe would be distraught, but he couldn't buckle and bend in his resolve to end this madness. He had searched his heart and prayed until his knees ached and he knew his mind was made up.

Edmund vowed to tell her today, they would not have sex, he would not hold and kiss her… today it would be over, and he would never ever see Phoebe alone again.

"Phoebe…I…" he held her hands between his, his eyes searching her beautiful face, the face that he knew in a few moments would be blotched with tears and pain. Pain caused by him.

"Please.... I must tell you something first Edmund." Phoebe blurted out before he could speak another word. It had been six months since they had started their love affair and Phoebe had grown to love Edmund more deeply than she could have ever thought it possible to love another human being.

"I'm expecting *our* baby Edmund," Phoebe said shyly, a small, uncertain smile played on her lips. She knew her parents would be furious to discover she was pregnant, but she felt sure that once the initial shock was over Edmund would quit the church and marry her and all would be well... after all he had professed to love her so many times what other outcome could there be?

"But you can't be!" he dropped her hands as if they were burning him.... "Oh God Phoebe.... Oh God no, this can't be happening... No!" Edmund felt as if a grenade had gone off in his head, scattering his thoughts ripping out his ability to speak. *Phoebe pregnant!*

Phoebe backed away from him, horrified at the furious expression clouding his handsome face. "But you said you loved me Edmund," she wailed, tears rolled down her cheeks.

"Shh.... People might hear you," he was irritated by her pale expectant face, her mouth forming a small "o" of shock and misery. He was looking at ruin in the face, the end of all his parent's hopes and dreams, the disgrace, the ignominy.

"For God's sake be reasonable Phoebe, we can't possibly have a baby together... I'm a priest!" He jumped up out of his chair.

"And I'm pregnant!.... so, what are we going to do now Edmund," Phoebe moaned, she felt a tidal wave of panic rising deep within her, in her naive *happy ever after fantasy* she had imagined him clasping her in his arms and offering to marry her, instead of which Edmund was regarding her with all the horror and disgust as if she were a dog turd caught on the bottom of his shoe leather?

Edmund paced around the small office agitated, desperately trying to martial his thoughts. *The sordid truth, if it were ever to get out, would be the ruin of him, the parish would be scandalised, his parents devastated.*

"Are you absolutely sure?" He gasped.

Phoebe nodded her head miserably, the early morning retching and missed bleeding told their own story. She was in no doubt a precious new life, their own baby, was growing within her.

"What will *you* do now?" He demanded sharply.

In his panic and shame his voice sounded cruel. All sorts of appalling scenarios crowded his thoughts; perhaps she might denounce him to the Bishop, maybe Mr Horwat would demand Edmund was defrocked?

"I…I…" Phoebe could not even splutter out a reply. There was no *we* in his thoughts, she was disgraced, and she could see he was casting her adrift. Phoebe sat with her head hung low and wept.

There's still time, perhaps the pregnancy might fail? He thought frantically…. Perhaps she was panicking over nothing?

"Phoebe you mustn't breathe a word of this to anyone… not a word until I have had time to think…is that understood?" Edmund grasped her hands and urged her to hold her silence.

Poor Phoebe nodded, she sat wringing her hands, bitter tears were rolling down her cheeks, her brown eyes were red-rimmed and puffy, and her heart pounded like a steam train in her chest.

"Here…" he handed her a large fine lawn handkerchief with his initials embroidered on it. the set had been a present from his mother when he had been accepted into the church, "here take this and wipe your eyes, you can't be seen looking like this, people will suspect something is up," he snapped; panic caused bile to rise in his mouth.

Phoebe hiccupped and dabbed her eyes.

"You'd better leave by the back door Phoebe," Edmund nervously guided her through the storeroom and ushered her out into the passageway running behind the church.

"Good-bye Edmund," she said softly, she stood on tip toe to kiss his cheek, he stood stiff and rigid, he did not bend to meet her and so with the merest graze of her lips on his cheek she turned and left with a heavy heart.

He could see the misery he had inflicted, and it tore at him, but in that hateful moment he knew he would not leave the church for Phoebe Horwat.

He heard the clip clop of her shoes pattering away down the passageway as Phoebe disappeared into the evening dusk. Part of him hoped he would never see her again.

Now he must beg the Church to forgive him.

Chapter 6

For six miserable days Phoebe dragged herself about the house, trying not to raise suspicions with her bouts of retching, she had no idea what Edmund was planning to do now he knew about her pregnancy. She fingered his initial handkerchief over and over as if it was some sort of precious link to him. *Surely Edmund would do the right thing and marry her?*

It worried her he had seemed so cold when they parted, he didn't even kiss her goodbye. And he had sworn her to secrecy and forbidden her to try and see him before their usual Sunday meeting, the only exception to his instruction was if her bleed had come and her scare was over, then and *only* then she could contact him, otherwise she must stay away.

Edmund said he needed time to think and now all Phoebe could do was wait for their Sunday liaison; the torture of the waiting was crippling her. She yearned to see him; the days dragged so slowly it was as if time had stood still. She needed him to hold her, to reassure her that things would be all right; she felt so frightened and utterly alone; it was like a hideous nightmare she couldn't wake up from.

At night Phoebe tossed and turned for hours willing some restful sleep to overwhelm her, but all her thoughts were of the baby growing inside her. The crippling guilt and shame nagged away at her and drove all hope of sleep away. In the early hours of the morning when weariness finally overwhelmed her, she dreamed of her poor mother weeping and wringing her hands, telling Phoebe her life was ruined, and that the whole family was ruined too. Phoebe woke up and knew she had been crying in her sleep.

What had they done? What would become of her?

"Are you sure you're all right Phoebe?" Her mother Anna regarded Phoebe anxiously, her daughter looked distinctly peaky, in fact she had done so for days. Anna watched Phoebe trailing off to work every morning with a face so long it was pitiful, pale skin and dark circles under her pretty eyes, something was not right. *Perhaps the girl was sickening for something serious.*

Usually, Phoebe had a smiling happy demeanour, leaving the house with a bounce in her step as she set off work each morning, now the girl looked like she was being led off to the gallows.

"Are you still feeling off colour my love?" Anna had never seen Phoebe looking so flat and exhausted before.

Perhaps she should have insisted Phoebe had seen the doctor when she started feeling unwell ten days ago. Pavel said they could afford to pay for it, but Phoebe had been adamant she didn't need a doctor, she told her mother that it was all fuss over nothing.

"I'm alright Ma, thanks," Phoebe lied, she grabbed her waxed paper packet of bread and beef dripping sandwiches and headed off for her job in the Royal mail sorting office.

Pavel had been so proud of his daughter when she had secured this job three years ago. With so many men off serving their King and country all sorts of jobs had suddenly became available for his clever daughters, jobs which didn't involve skivvying and spending all day on their hands and knees scrubbing floors, jobs with better pay and prospects until they settled down and had families of their own. Pavel wanted a good life for his four pretty daughters.

All Pavel's girls could read, he had insisted on them practising their letters as children, he was determined they should have a better life than the one he left behind in rural Poland where boys worked until they became broken old men and girls became careworn old women worn out with large broods of children and a life of hard graft.

Pavel's strong arms and a brawny back had served him well working in the busy Cardiff coal port, but he hoped his four girls would do better than spending their working life skivvying and cleaning like their mother Anna once did.

Phoebe Horwat was popular at work, and she enjoyed the happy go lucky, bustling atmosphere of the huge sorting office. The busy Cardiff depot was filled with young women chattering away as they went about their work, nimble fingers flying through the packets and letters, and Phoebe had quite a few friends amongst the girls who worked there. Phoebe's best friend was a short, dark-haired girl called Bronwen Jones.

Nineteen-year-old Bronnie was the darling of the sorting office. Like a little dynamo, Bronnie's slender fingers worked more quickly than any of the other women in the depot and she flew through her tasks like a hot knife glided through butter. Garrulous and good tempered Bronnie hummed and sang traditional songs in her native language as she sorted through the post and the buxom lass seemed to exist in a perpetual state of chirpy happiness as she went about her day.

"Bore da Phoebe," Bronwen winked at her friend, she knew Phoebe found the Welsh language an impenetrable babble but Bronwen, coming from a proud Welsh speaking family, took delight in scattering her chatter with Welsh pleasantries and endearments.

"Good morning Bronwen," Phoebe muttered back, she was not in the mood for joking around. She wrapped her grey mail overall around her middle and hung up her coat.

"Well, it certainly doesn't look like you're having a good morning Phoebe…. What's up cariad?" Bronwen looked concerned, Phoebe's slumped shoulders hinted at a misery weighing her down.

"I've not been very well… I'm just a bit tired, that's all." Phoebe lied. She wished Edmund hadn't sworn her to absolute secrecy. Bronwen was such a good-hearted, down to earth sort of girl, Phoebe felt sure she could have confided in her, if only in a roundabout sort of way.

Phoebe felt like she was wandering lost in the wilderness, she so desperately wanted some advice about what was happening to her body about what to expect…*or more importantly if she still had cause to hope that all might be well, and her fears were groundless.*

As the eldest child from a family of eight boisterous children, Bronwen Jones was well versed in the art of looking after a large brood of brothers and sisters and Bronnie certainly knew far more than Phoebe did about sex, pregnancy, and having babies.

Phoebe kept hoping against hope there was still time for her bleed to come but every morning her hopes and prayers were dashed, and the sheets were clean. The queasy roiling feeling in her guts each morning was beginning to subside, but her monthlies still refused to come; Phoebe was certain a baby was still growing inside her. Soon her mother would start to become suspicious if there were never any rags drying over the airing rack.

Surely Edmund would find a way for them to be together. He had looked so angry when she told him about the baby, but she had convinced herself that it was just the shock of her announcement, nothing more. Edmund loved her, he'd told her he loved her on so many occasions, surely he wouldn't let her down.

31

She had to trust in Edmund, she would do as he told her and keep silent.

"Well, if you're certain you're alright Phoebe… but remember you can always tell me anything if you *ever* need a shoulder to cry on, I don't gossip, not when I'm asked to keep a secret" Bronwen shook her head she could tell Phoebe was keeping something from her, but if her friend wasn't ready to tell her yet, then she wouldn't press her.

Perhaps it was an affair of the heart, Phoebe had been awfully close about having any suitors when Bronwen teased her about it a few months ago, perhaps Phoebe had had her heart broken by a young man.

Phoebe gave her friend a hug, "thanks Bronnie-*cariad*"-she returned the endearment…. Sweet natured Bronnie was everyone's *darling*.

Bronnie's eyes lit up and she grinned…. "Well blow me, that's a first!…. Phoebe Horwat, I'll make a proper Welsh woman out of you yet!"

Father Edmund had spent most of the six days since he last saw Phoebe on his knees praying for a solution to the ghastly nightmare he found himself in. He was locked in a black misery which acknowledged the culpability for the ruin of innocent Phoebe Horwat and yet he didn't want to do the right thing and save the girl from impending disgrace. The dilemma was killing him.

He knew the only honourable solution would be to leave the church and marry her…. Which of course, would mean ruining himself at the same time. The disgrace would be huge, he might leave the church but, according to his vows, it would never leave him. He had promised himself to the church for life, with vows more certain and more holy than any earthly marriage could ever be, he was bound by sacred oaths he couldn't break.

When Edmund resigned himself to a life of serving Christ he also gave himself over the rule of the Catholic church, he knew that it was not as simple as just running off somewhere with Phoebe and making a new start. What ever happened next he must discuss it with Diocesan Bishop and throw himself on their mercy.

In his rational moments Edmund knew it was his fault, and his alone that Phoebe Horwat had found her way into his arms. He could recognize the times when he had engineered to catch her alone; the lingering touches, the seeking out and special attention which helped ensnare the guileless, innocent young woman.

Whichever way Edmund looked at it he was certain Phoebe would never have approached him if he had not led her to him, reeled her in like a fish on the line, so the fault must surely be all his?

But once that catch was landed she was as willing and eager as he was to indulge their passion so was the fault really all on his side, didn't Phoebe have her own guilt to acknowledge?.... She could have refused him, but she didn't.

As the gruelling days passed and there had been no hasty visit from Phoebe to tell him the scare was over, he began to see that his fall from grace was without doubt. He was a Catholic priest who had made a young girl pregnant.... Now the only question was what must he do next?

He must confess his sins to his superiors and suffer the consequences. Edmund knew he was about as far from the bountiful gaze of a loving God as any miserable wretch could ever be. Edmund was living a lie and he needed to make a clean breast about his weakness and transgressions to his fellow brothers in the church.

The question was, did he beg for forgiveness and absolution for his sin.... or did he beg to be released from his vows?

And yet the more his conscience wrestled with the dilemma, the more Father Edmund became convinced that somehow he had been acting like a man possessed... surely he had been suffering some form of madness, a delusion which had clouded his judgement and robbed him of his self-control.

Edmund eventually convinced himself he had no control over what had happened between them, the attraction had been electric, compulsive, an infatuation born of madness. As a man he had been tempted and he had succumbed- surely it must have been the Devil's work which transformed Phoebe Horwat into an irresistible temptress and the means of his destruction just like Eve had brought about the fall of Adam?

Hadn't Edmund felt bewitched whenever he was in Phoebe's presence, hadn't he felt compelled to seek her out, surely it was the result of workings beyond his control?

He began to wish he'd never met her, that he'd never set eyes on her beautiful face and golden hair. *If only he'd served in some other parish, then he would have kept on the righteous path and then neither of them would be facing this disgrace.*

Then in moments of utter remorse for his callous thoughts Edmund wished he was just an ordinary young man, free to marry a sweet girl who he'd fallen in love with. Because Edmund knew in his heart that if he were not already betrothed to the church then he would indeed be prepared to spend the rest of his life married to Phoebe, he would make an honest woman of her and spend the his days luxuriating the arms of a woman who adored him with children and a home to call his own.

Edmund had always loved children. His own parents had only ever had two children and he knew his mother had longed for more babies which never came. It had been a blow to his mother's heart when Edmund embraced his vocation, his Mam secretly grieved that her only son would never know the joys of family life and she would never be a grandmother.

Now there *would* be a child who could call him Dadda, the fruit of his loins which he was preparing to deny, *a child born of sin*.

He must pray for guidance.

In the wee small hours of the morning a soothing clarity finally descended on Edmund's troubled mind, it was if the deep murkiness of his thoughts settled like sediment in a pool after a storm.

Edmund decided to seek guidance, penance, and absolution from his superiors. And then whatever fate his Bishop decided for him, *that* was what he would accept. It would be out of his hands. He would submit himself once more to the yoke of duty and be obedient as his vows demanded.

His duty lay with serving God and he could only do that if he renounced Phoebe Horwat.

Of course, he must try to ensure the girl's welfare was attended to, there were homes run by the Church who could take her in, families who were desperate for a baby to adopt. If Phoebe's pregnancy continued then she would not be cast utterly adrift he consoled himself. But whatever happened to Phoebe now, Father Edmund saw with blinding certainty he needed to repair his relationship with God and the Church, and he could not…. would not, abandon those two precious loves for a life with Phoebe Horwat, no matter how tempting the prospect might appear.

He may have strayed from the path of righteousness but Edmund, after much soul searching, believed his God would welcome back a repentant sinner with open arms.

Tomorrow was Saturday, he would confess and seek forgiveness from the Bishop before he met with Phoebe again on Sunday and when he had confessed everything to the Bishop he would tell Phoebe of his decision.

Chapter 7

Phoebe felt more nervous than she had ever done before in her life, her mother and father attended the usual morning mass, accompanied by her sister Lisa. Alone in the house she had hours of torment and waiting before she could see Father Edmund.

Lisa had noticed Phoebe's pale face of late; she knew her sister well enough to know something 1was up, perhaps Phoebe would miss attending church again.

"Are you going to come to come church with us this morning Pheebs," Lisa was moulding her dark hair into finger waves as she sat at the dressing table they shared. Lisa slipped in some long grips to secure the wave in place. A pretty, young woman stared back at her in the foxed bedroom mirror.

 Lisa knew their father didn't approve of vanity, but she had to admit the new shorter hair cut suited her small oval face. A subtle slick of Vaseline on her eyebrows helped frame her slate blue eyes and enhance the angelic effect. At nineteen years of age Lisa had left her girlhood behind and the exciting world of men and romance beckoned. Lisa drew many admiring glances, and she knew it.

Phoebe was not yet dressed, she looked wrecked from another sleepless night spent tossing and turning, the guilty secret nagging away at her. Tonight, she would see her beloved Edmund in the back office, they would have some precious time together and she would finally know what was to come. She trusted him implicitly and now they'd made a baby together surely he must stand by her?…. The agonising waiting to discover their fate, would be over; Phoebe felt certain she could brave anything with Edmund at her side.

"I'm going to the evening mass tonight Lisa, so you'll be going with Mam and Tata this morning," Phoebe tried to keep her voice cheerful and neutral, her younger sister was a suspicious little minx who could ferret out a secret in a trice.

"Father Edmund is scheduled to take morning mass Phoebe, if *that* might change your mind," Lisa said mischievously. The handsome Father Edmund had many admirers amongst the ladies of the parish, even old Mrs Pritchard who played the organ was putty in his hands.

"What on earth do you mean Lisa?" Phoebe gasped, *did her sister suspect something?*

"Nothing," Lisa smirked, she patted her hair into place and added a slick of Vaseline to her lips. "It's just that you have to admit he's rather easy on the eye, and if he wasn't a priest I reckon he would have every girl in the parish chasing after him." Lisa rolled her eyes dramatically.

"Don't let Tata hear you talking such nonsense sis," Phoebe snapped "he'd have your guts for garters if he did!" Phoebe turned over in her bed, her back to her sister so she couldn't see Phoebe's troubled face.

"My, my, you are in a touchy mood Pheebs, I'm only teasing," Lisa felt a little afraid, Phoebe could be fearsome when roused. *She had certainly touched on a raw nerve.*

"Well, if you're going to stay a bed, then I'd best be off, Mama and Tata won't be kept waiting…. I'll put in a prayer for you whilst I'm there on my knees." Lisa joked as she pulled on her white gloves.

You have no idea how much I'm going need those prayers. Phoebe thought ruefully.

*

It turned out that Father Edmund did not take the Sunday morning service as expected. According to Lisa, it was Deacon Frederick Talbot who officiated, and Father Edmund was sat deep in prayer for the whole service. Even so, Lisa could still get a good look at Father Edmund's handsome profile as he sat in the choir stalls next to the alter, not that Lisa would admit it of course, after her tetchy sister had snapped her head off earlier.

The hours on Sunday ticked past with glacial slowness, finally Phoebe slipped out of the house and hurried off to the evening service.

As Phoebe sat at the back of the church with her head bowed she caught a glimpse of Edmund. He was sat on a pew near the altar rail, staring straight ahead, his hands clasped in prayer. *He would not be taking the service then this evening as she thought, there would be no lingering glances as she partook of the Host.*

Father Simon Jeffries conducted the service and Phoebe's thoughts refused to be marshalled to prayer, no matter what she did she could *not* think of God in her hour of need, she could only think of Edmund as he sat, tantalisingly out of reach, only a few yards away from her.

I love you…. I love you Edmund, she thought to herself repeatedly, as if by doing so she could somehow urge her thoughts into his brain, to let him know the strength of her love. She willed him to look at her, even if it was just a small glance but Edmund's face stayed fixed and turned away from her.

Eventually the service came to an end. Now she must slip around to the back office as they had agreed, she would be able to talk to him at last. Her week-long torment would be over. Phoebe needed him to hold her in his arms, to hear him assure her it would all be alright... to tell her he loved her.

Phoebe was to be disappointed. Two priests sat in the office waiting to greet her as she slipped through the door and neither one of them was her darling Edmund.

Later that evening Phoebe trudged home with a heavy heart and a sickness to the bottom of her stomach. The harsh words of Father Jeffries and Father Thomas had cut her to the bone and now she was abandoned and drifting towards the rocks as surely as any ship that had lost its anchor... Edmund had confessed to their affair and the Church had taken control of events.

"You have committed the most grievous of sins," Father Jeffries passed verdict, "and yet, even now, you seek him out like a shameless hussy, tempting Father Edmund to sin.... Skulking around in the very body of the church to indulge your carnal desires.... Have you no shame woman!" Father Jefferies snarled.

Phoebe had been shocked into silence when the two grey haired priests, with their steely eyes and grim mouths, dammed her with their caustic words. Her tears and anguished sobs failed to move them, her pleas to be allowed to talk to Father Edmund for one last time fell on deaf ears.

"You will *not* be allowed to communicate with Father Edmund... Father Edmund has confessed to his transgressions and sought absolution. He has recognized he needs help from the Holy Mother church, and he will be sent to serve God in another parish. He accepts he must not see you again and *you* must stop trying to pester him." Father Jefferies could not contain his disgust for the wicked creature snivelling in front of him.

Edmund was banished... and she was accused of pestering and seducing a priest... she was forbidden to see him, she was dammed. The words were like a knife in Phoebe's heart.

Devoid of compassion the priests lay the fault of the transgression at her feet. To their minds Phoebe was a woman who had tried to steal away one of their own. She was the agent of the

Devil who had ensnared Father Edmund with her flirtatious charms and seduced him away from his vows and now the church was defending itself from her vile attack.

It was made brutally clear to Phoebe that Edmund had chosen the Church and now the Church was protecting its own. They welcomed Edmund back to the fold on their terms and he must submit obediently to whatever measures they decided were necessary; measures which included never seeing the wicked Phoebe Horwat alone ever again. Phoebe was to be cast on the rubbish heap like a piece of broken furniture, destined to be the wicked, lascivious mother of a bastard child.

"The Church is not without compassion for the *children* of women such as yourself," Father Thomas held her gaze, his face impassive and his heart was cold. "If you decide you do not wish to keep this child of your sin, then you may wish to throw yourself upon the mercy of one of our houses for fallen women. The nuns of St Saviours know how to deal with women who find themselves in your condition," he glared at her, in his opinion women like Phoebe were not fit to raise a child. "after the birth they place the children in loving, God-fearing homes to be raised by *decent* people." Father Thomas waited for the judgement to sink in.

"In the past you have professed to love God and have sought absolution, your duty now is to cleanse your soul and ensure that this *child* is not cut off from God's love by your wicked actions. If you ask the nuns to take you in, then they will expect you to atone for your sins and to leave the baby with them. You must consider that, under the circumstances, any future attendance at this church by you is unwelcome." Father Jeffries joined the attack and piled on the agony.

Phoebe gasped each harsh word was like a hammer blow to her heart. To hear herself describe in such a way cut her to the quick. *Was that what she was now, a fallen woman… not the mother of Edmund's child, but a fallen woman carrying a child born of sin?*

In a moment of blinding clarity Phoebe realised her life was changed forever. She wept uncontrollably as the two priests stood, turned their backs on her and left the room without uttering so much as another word.

Chapter 8

Edmund sat in his room feeling like a broken man. He knew poor Phoebe would have been destroyed by his decision to stay with the church. The extracted promise that he must never see her again had been the hardest one to swallow.

"But I *must* tell her myself," he had pleaded to Father Thomas. "Surely it is too harsh to just abandon Phoebe without any explanation for my actions."

"A lascivious woman who has tempted and entrapped a priest is entitled to nothing!" Father Jefferies snapped. "You have admitted yourself to feeling a total loss of control in her presence, to acting like a man possessed, a man driven by lust… can you really suggest you should put yourself within this woman's malign orbit again?" Father Jeffries's eyes glittered with passion, he felt he was battling for Edmund's very soul against the forces of evil; the very Devil himself made manifest in the shape of the comely Phoebe Horwat.

"God and the Pope's terms are not negotiable, Father Edmund. You have sworn a vow of obedience to the church and now you must honour that promise…. You must never talk to Phoebe Horwat or mention this child again and that is our final word on the matter… Understood?" Father Jefferies would brook no argument, Edmund *must* bend to the will of the Church.

 Father Thomas gazed at the fallen priest; he was not without compassion for his plight. The man was young and handsome it was no wonder a foolish young woman wanted to capture his heart. Young women could be very capricious and devious in Father Thomas's opinion.

Edmund nodded miserably. He felt guilty for allowing Phoebe's name to blackened, but he could do nothing to save her now.

Father Jefferies continued to hammer home the argument. "If she is indeed pregnant Father Edmund, and it is a big *if*, for we have no proof of the matter, then it is *no* concern of yours now. It is only *her* word that she is expecting a child…. *your* child. Sometimes women like Phoebe will lie and scheme to get what they want; you cannot trust what she is telling you to be the truth Father Edmund. This is the devil's work. The matter will be dealt with in the appropriate way, you have no further part to play in this." With each poisonous word, Father Jeffries dammed Phoebe Horwat, blackening her name and sowing seeds of doubt in Edmund's mind.

"Like other foolish, feckless women who find themselves expecting a baby outside the honourable estate of marriage, she will be advised to seek help from the nuns of St Saviours. She's not the first woman to have thrown herself at a man and she won't be the last. If you ever visit the dutiful nuns you will see a whole building full of fallen women just like Phoebe Horwat serving penance for their carnal sins." Father Jeffries sneered.

Father Jeffries was only too aware of the harsh regime operated by the nuns of St Saviours, but in his opinion fallen women like Phoebe needed to see the error of their ways and work their way back to redemption. He didn't feel one bit of compassion for the harlots living inside the walls of St Saviours home for fallen women, they deserved everything they had coming to them.

"The blessed nuns are used to dealing with women like Phoebe. If this woman does enter their doors then they will find a good home for the child, a home where it will be brought up in the Faith. It will be raised in a Godly home with a virtuous family who will bring it up to know right from wrong. Every child is born without sin and can thrive in a good home." Father Thomas assured Edmund.

The act of confession to his brother priests may have cleansed Edmund's soul and placed his wobbly footsteps back on the righteous path but his heart was heavy beyond belief. He may have been welcomed back into the arms of the church, but in the process, he had lost two precious and rare things; the love of Phoebe and, most importantly the child which she carried, a child who he *could* have claimed as his own.

Unlike Father Thomas and Father Jefferies he was in no doubt that if Phoebe was pregnant then Phoebe *was* carrying his child, he did not believe her to be a promiscuous liar.

That evening Father Edmund would stay in his room and pray for his soul. The two priests would keep his assignation and deal with the knotty problem which was Phoebe Horwat. Things were out his control now and all Edmund could do was wait and practice patient obedience as he had been ordered to do.

Father Jefferies and Father Thomas would cut off Phoebe Horwat as surely as if they were chopping off a rotten limb, removing a cancerous appendage which posed a threat to the healthy body and good name of the church. They had made it quite clear to Father Edmund he would be sent to serve another church in another neighbouring parish with immediate effect.

Edmund was told that if ever Phoebe Horwat was to track him down and seek him out, then Edmund must refuse to see her or even acknowledge her. If he could not keep to this stricture then he would be sent overseas on a mission until the threat to his mortal soul was over. Phoebe's power over him was to be smashed to smithereens.

Father Edmund was utterly dejected as said his prayers...*please forgive me Phoebe.*

The next morning, in the eyes of both elderly priests, the malignancy had been excised completely.

Phoebe was sent away and told Father Edmund would never see her again. The nuns of St Saviours were told that if ever a Miss Phoebe Horwat turned up asking for shelter then she was to be gained admittance to the mother and baby home, but the nuns were to be watchful. Phoebe Horwat was considered by the church to be the most malign of influences. Any child born of this woman would need to be placed in a family with particular care. Father Edmund's role in the matter was never mentioned, in fact, as far as the church was concerned the matter was closed. The stain was excised.

Edmund was to be posted to serve the poor and disposed of Cardiff in Splott, he was to leave the cool hallow, ordered walls of St Saviours in Roath and be transferred to a ramshackle church which struggled to attract more than a dozen elderly parishioners each Sunday.

Home to visiting sailors and immigrants and settled on the edge of the dockland wharves the tiny, cobbled church of St Ignatius struggled to attract a regular following. The previous elderly priest had been shabby and down at heel, vestments grubby and threadbare, the death of Father Arthur had left a miserable gap which few ambitious young priests were prepared to fill. Now the challenge to rescue the ailing parish church fell to Father Edmund; it was his chance to redeem himself; to claw his way back into favour.

"Make something of this second chance Father Edmund, earn God's forgiveness with hard work and dedication," Father Thomas urged him. "You are always welcome to visit us at St Saviours but be mindful of your renewed vows." The unspoken concern over Phoebe Horwat was left hanging in the air.

The Catholic church had eyes and ears everywhere, Father Thomas had been charged by the Bishop to keep a watchful eye on Father Edmund and he would be doing exactly that.

A full report would be posted each month until they could be certain Father Edmund had returned wholeheartedly to the fold and certain Phoebe Horwat did not attempt to contact her former object of desire.

Father Edmund packed his few belongings and left St Saviours for his new ministry in Splott. Only one spark of rebellion remained in Edmund's soul, *he may not be able to have any connection whatsoever with Phoebe Horwat, but there had been no such conditions placed on the infant she was carrying... his child.*

Father Edmund resolved to find out all he could about this child. If things went well for Phoebe, then it would be born in a few months' time and Edmund would make it his business to know about it.

In the solitary stillness of his room a small spark of hope was growing within him, a germ of a plan which with any luck Edmund could bring to fruition.

Edmund would need to be vigilant.

Chapter 9

For days Phoebe wept and tortured herself with the knowledge she must eventually tell her parents about her condition. She had toyed with the idea of just packing her bags and slipping out of the house like a thief in the night, but she could not bear to treat her parents so shabbily.

It had been the hardest blow of all to be told she was never to see or speak to Father Edmund ever again, she could not…. she would not do the same thing to her parents. She was not a coward and they deserved to hear her story. Phoebe knew her parents would be furious and probably disown her once they knew of her condition, but she owed it to them to look them in the eye and tell them the truth. She would not run away.

Edmund was lost to her now, totally, and utterly lost to her. The church had snatched him away from her and would fight to keep him. The two Fathers had made it quite clear that Father Edmund would leave the parish immediately and be sent to another church out of her reach. They told her that if they heard her spreading malicious lies and gossip about one of their own, then they would publicly denounce her as a harlot and her whole family would be shamed in the process.

But what could she tell her own beloved Tata? If Edmund was any other man then her father would be racing around to his doorstep demanding he do the right thing by her, but Edmund was no ordinary man. Edmund could not be forced to marry her. The church could shield him and deny her Tata the justice he would demand

By Phoebe's calculations she had missed three periods. She knew she did not have long now before she would be forced to confront her parents and face the consequences of her actions, soon her waist would thicken and before long it would be impossible to hide her condition. As each miserable day passed and the baby grew inside her she became convinced that eventually she would be throwing herself on the mercy of the nuns of St Saviours and asking for their help; what else was there for her?

Whichever way Phoebe looked at it she could see no other way out of her dilemma, she could not keep this baby without Edmund by her side and without any money or support as an unmarried woman she could not raise it alone. It tore at her heart to think she would have to give her little baby away, she did not hate the child growing within her…. It was Edmund's baby.

Phoebe resolved to talk to her friend Bronnie at lunchtime, her head was nigh on bursting with all the thoughts running around inside it, she needed someone to talk to, someone she could trust.

Two weeks later on a bright, warm June day Phoebe seized her chance to talk to her best friend away from the watchful eyes and ears of the busy sorting room.

"Oh Cariad!" Bronnie threw her arms around Phoebe when she heard the sorry tale her friend had to tell. Bronwen hugged Phoebe so hard Phoebe gasped with the fierceness of her tiny friend's embrace.

"What am I going to do now Bronnie?" Pheobe said miserably, she would not cry. Phoebe felt as if she had had cried herself out over the last few weeks and now all she had left was a dull misery eating away at her like a cancer, there were no tears left to fall.

The two women were sat with their sandwiches in a quiet, favoured corner of the mail yard, they perched on two packing cases placed in a sunny corner by the ivy-covered fence. Clusters of lazy bees swarmed over the ivy hunting out nectar and on any other day the girls would have been gossiping, laughing, and joking in the sunshine. They only had half an hour before they must return to their duties. Phoebe would have to be quick.

She told Bronnie her tale of woe and whilst she would not name Edmund she told her friend how she had been seduced by a man of the cloth; a priest who had claimed her maidenhood and then cast her adrift. "I'm ruined Bronnie," Phoebe croaked, she could hardly swallow the thick crusty bread of her jam sandwich.

"There, there, don't fret Phoebe…. And him being a Catholic priest and all. The shame of the man! It's no wonder my Mam and Da attend Chapel, there's none of that high and mighty Roman nonsense there!" Bronwen was furious her friend had been treated so shabbily. *Yes Phoebe was foolish to let any man go all the way but a Catholic priest having his way with an innocent young girl and then him being let off Scot free was beyond the pale.*

"I've got to tell them soon Bronnie," Phoebe stroked her belly, she apologised daily to the child she was growing inside her for the shame she was bringing on it.

"I know they will throw me out so where will I go when they do? I don't have any money, apart from a few shillings saved up in my money box." This was the thorny question which had rattled around in Phoebe's head for days.

"There's nothing for me now but to throw myself on the mercy of the nuns of St Saviours," Phoebe said bleakly.

"Doesn't that just take the biscuit," Bronwen spat, "the Catholic church causes the problem and then they get to clear it up and hide it away, all the while lecturing *you* on the perils of sin!" She put a comforting arm around Phoebe's shoulder.

"That's if they'll have me… and they won't let me in straight away either Bronwen. I'd have to attend an interview with the reverend Mother and promise them I'm a first offender." Phoebe felt more and more like a criminal hauled up before the judge by the minute.

"Look I'm not promising anything Phoebe, but there's always my Aunty Angharad, she's my father's sister, she might give you a bed for a few nights if you do get thrown out…. You won't be able to stay any longer though." Bronwen added hastily. "She's a funny old bird my aunty and a stickler for rules. She might be a God-fearing single lady who attends Chapel three times on Sunday, but she's a kind-hearted soul and believes in showing God's love to those in need, so she won't see you without a bed for the night I'm sure of it…. I'll talk to her if you like?" Bronwen offered crossing her fingers her Aunty Angharad would come good.

Bronwen knew it was only a small crumb of comfort, but she was certain when her aunt heard a Roman Catholic priest had used her poor friend for a whore she would be moved to help Phoebe. Aunty Angharad's views on the papist conspiracy were legendary, the fact that she expressed most of them in fluent Welsh only added to the vehemence of her argument.

Phoebe nodded, if she did find herself thrown out on the streets then at least she would have somewhere to sleep for a few nights until she had secured a place at the St Saviours home.

"Thank you Bronnie, you are a true friend," Phoebe murmured gratefully, now at least she had one small glimmer of hope.

*

"What did you say!" Pavel Horwat's face was so pink it looked like he was about to explode. He slapped his meaty hand hard on the kitchen door and groaned a low guttural moan like the death throes of a wounded animal.

Her mother Anna stood beside her husband shaking her head, her usually smiling face hardened with disappointment. In that instant Anna felt she had failed in her duty as a mother and failed her husband.

Anna thought she had done her best to bring up her four daughters to be decent, God-fearing young women, made sure they attended mass and worked hard at school and now this disgrace!

Phoebe stood trembling before Pavel in the tiny sitting room. She felt sure the neighbours on either side would have heard her father's explosive outburst. Her sister Lisa had been dispatched upstairs to her room when Phoebe made her announcement.… *This discussion was not for her innocent ears.*

Phoebe caught her Lisa's horrified glance, her eyes goggling with amazement. *Phoebe was pregnant!*

Phoebe knew Lisa would be sat on the top of the stairs listening to the drama unfolding in the sitting room below, as little girls they never missed anything going on in the house when they sat on the top step, sounds filtered up through the bannisters with astonishing clarity. *Lisa would know everything.*

"I'm *so* sorry, Mam, Tata, really I am." Phoebe mumbled for the umpteenth time, she dared not meet their gaze. She knew they were shattered by her announcement, it pained her to hurt them, and she felt ashamed.

Her mother strode over to Phoebe and slapped the girl hard on the cheek, a stinging blow aimed with rage. "You're a stupid, stupid girl!" she hissed; Anna's hand smarted with the force of her blow. Anna had not smacked her daughter since childhood; light taps to correct childhood misdemeanours maybe, but this blow was meant to hurt… and it did.

Phoebe gasped and clutched her smarting face.

"How could you do this to us… to all of us?" Her mother blazed, her eyes flashing with fury.

"Who is he?.... Give me his name!" Her father demanded. Pavel's voice was not as angry as his wife's, he seemed to plead with Phoebe to help save herself even at this eleventh hour.

There could still be time to salvage the situation if Phoebe married the lad. Pavel was reeling with shock. *Phoebe was his golden child.*

Phoebe stood with her head hung low, her cheek flaming bright red from the vicious slap. She remembered Father Jefferies' warning that if she tried to name Father Edmund she would be publicly shamed and dammed, her family would be mired in her disgrace the subject of gossip and scorn.

"I can't Tata," Phoebe gulped, the fear of public disgrace, threats of hell, and damnation only too vivid in her mind.

With that her father started crying, huge fat tears rolled down his face, his body wracked with guttural sobs. Pavel sank to his knees moaning over the total ruin of his favourite daughter.

"Look what you've done Phoebe," her mother hissed as she sank to the floor to comfort her weeping husband. "I hope you are satisfied…. I hope you think *he* was worth it… you've brought shame and disgrace on our family."

Phoebe was terrified by the sight of her big, steely father sobbing on his knees, swaying back and forth in misery. She had always thought her father was so strong and now it was him wailing like a man possessed and her quiet amiable mother taking control.

"Get out Phoebe," her mother jabbed a finger in the direction of the front door, her voice was icily controlled, there were no tears running down her mother's face just a contemptuous, cold fury Phoebe would never forget. "You have broken your dear Tata's heart and I'm never going to forgive you for that…. Get out! … You're no daughter of ours…. Get out, do you hear me." Anna yelled, her eyes glittering with fury.

"I don't care what you do or where you go Phoebe…. You are no longer welcome here…. So, get out now!" Anna soothed and shushed her stricken husband, she knew it was the truth, her darling Pavel's heart *was* smashed to smithereens by his favourite daughter's fall from grace.

Phoebe fled upstairs to collect her things. She passed Lisa on the landing; the girl was white faced with fear; her sister Lisa had heard everything.

"Where will you go Pheebs," Lisa whispered. Downstairs all sort of crashing and banging was occurring, the sound of doors slamming echoed up the stairs.

"I don't know sis," Phoebe grabbed her few possessions and stuffed them in a canvas valise, everything pushed in a crumpled jumble, she didn't have time to pack, Phoebe was in a race to leave before she was kicked out with only the clothes she stood up.

Footsteps thumped up the stairs. "Mam's coming," Lisa gasped.

Phoebe kissed her sister hurriedly on the cheek, "pray for me Lisa," Phoebe urged. "I'm sorry I've brought this shame on you and the family…. Forgive me?"

Her mother barged in through the bedroom door, "any possessions that you haven't already packed will be given to the rag and bone man, now take your things and go." Anna surveyed the jumble of open drawers. "You've damaged Lisa's prospects, and you've squandered this family's good name… I hope you are satisfied Miss. You're not allowed to contact any of us ever again…. never! Maybe one day God will forgive you for what you've done, but I *never* will." Her mother's eyes blazed; her voice was icy with contempt.

Phoebe felt crushed, she had felt sure that her mother would have had some sympathy with her, she imagined her father in a towering rage but not this cold fury from Mam.

Anne pointedly turned her face to the wall as Phoebe slunk out with everything she owned in a battered canvas bag. She heard Phoebe's footsteps patter down the stairs and the front door clicked shut, then with a deep guttural sob Anna hugged her remaining daughter tightly to her bosom and wept floods of tears.

Anna's tears were not being shed for Phoebe, they were tears of bitter disappointment for her darling, stricken husband Pavel and her unfortunate youngest daughter Lisa. At that moment Anna hated her errant daughter for all the hurt and harm she'd caused them. She could not think about the baby or the fate of Phoebe now she was out on the streets; Phoebe had made her bed so she must lie on it. Her foolish daughter was dead to her now; all Anna could do now was try to repair the damage to her husband's broken heart.

Only Anna knew Pavel's secret. Only she knew that the reason he fled from Poland was to escape his own stain of illegitimacy in search of a better life, a life of hope and opportunity. The hopes and dreams Pavel had for his four pretty daughters to work hard and make good marriages was born out of love but out fear as well.

Pavel had an abiding fear his daughters might be trapped in a life of misery and poverty like his own mother had been when she struggled to bring up Pavel devoid of a father and a family to support her. The hateful names he was called as a child, the jeering, and taunts about his mother's status as the village whore. Pavel had wanted a better life for his own children and now his darling Phoebe had brought back all the old fear and trauma, cutting Pavel to the bone like a knife.

Anna would also have to tell her other two married daughters about Phoebe's fall from grace, a task that she was dreading. And all the neighbours were bound to ask questions, they were bound wonder where their pretty Phoebe had gone… what did she say to them? And how could she face going to Church again once the news was out? Anna was beyond fury her precious family was being wrecked by this dreadful event. How could she ever hold her head up now she was the mother of a tart. *She would rather Phoebe had died.*

Anna cursed the wretched girl for bringing the family low and heaping misery on her darling Pavel. When he had collapsed to his knees she thought the shock of Phoebe's revelation had brought on a heart attack. Pavel was her rock, and the love of Anna's life, she could not carry on without him…. It was him she must think about now, Phoebe would have to make her own way in the world.

Life would never be the same for any of them ever again… all thanks to bloody Phoebe!

Chapter 10

"So, you've come then… I thought you might," Angharad Jones appraised the tired, miserable young woman standing on her doorstep. Phoebe's large golden-brown eyes looked impossibly sad. Even so Angharad could see the beauty lying beneath the dark rings smudged under Phoebe's tired eyes. As her niece Bronnie had said, the girl was very pretty.

"You'd best come in then…. Make sure you wipe your feet now." Angharad pointed to the worn doormat.

Miss Angharad Jones lived in a tiny three roomed cottage which squatted awkwardly next to the river Taff where the river meandered its leisurely way through the area known as Riverside. The low, single-story cottage was spotlessly neat and only one room wide. Once through the front door it had one sparse bedroom to one side of the tiny sitting room and a low ceiling scullery led off from the other side; a low wash house stood outside in the yard. In keeping with Miss Jones's approach to life, the rooms were simply furnished, functional and devoid of any unnecessary ornament.

An embroidered religious tract hung above the fireplace- *"In the Lord I trust."*

Anxious to save every penny of her precious money, Phoebe had walked the three miles all the way from her home in Zinc street to Angharad's tiny cottage. To call the plain, traditional long house a cottage suggested a far prettier building than the whitewashed stone out-building which was to be Phoebe's refuge. The small house had once been part of a dairy and had been Angharad's home for the last twenty years.

"Thank you, Miss Jones…. Thank you so much for giving me a bed for the night." Phoebe stammered, she felt like a drowning woman thrown a lifeline in her hour of need.

Phoebe thought Angharad's Aunt looked fearsome with her stern eyes and plain black dress, but the kindly smile which lit up Angharad's face soon set her mind at ease.

"Come on in Phoebe, contrary to popular local opinion I'm not a witch and I don't bite," Angharad joked, she knew the young local lads were afraid of her, fearing Ty Gwyn was a witch's cottage, youngsters daring each other to play rat-a-tat ginger on her door knocker, and then running screaming if ever they saw her coming to answer the door.

"You'll be safe here with me for a few days. Bronnie has told me you're one of God's creatures in need of a bit of Christian kindness, so I'm happy to welcome you into my home for a few days.... But only a few days mind." Angharad said firmly.

"Of course, Miss Jones, I'll be away as soon as I can." Phoebe blushed she could see the modest house had little room to spare.

"And you'd better call me Angharad if you are going to be living under my roof. There's a cupboard bed behind those two doors next to the fireplace.... you should fit in there nicely and you can keep your things in there as well, so we aren't tripping over them every five minutes." Angharad knitted her fierce-some thick, grey eyebrows together. Phoebe would soon learn Angharad Jones had rather poor eyesight and this plain, thin woman was nowhere near as bad-tempered as she appeared to be when she knotted her brows to focus her eyes.

"Of course, Angharad." Phoebe corrected herself. "And thank you again for letting me stay, I'm truly grateful."

*

The following week Phoebe had a new bed to sleep on and it wasn't anywhere near as comfy and welcoming as the simple straw mattress in Angharad's cottage cupboard.

"You will sleep in the dormitory along with the other women until it is time for you to be delivered," the hard-faced Sister Mary informed Phoebe on her first day at the St Saviour's Mother and baby home.

"You will attend prayers at six o'clock in the morning before you take your breakfast in the refectory, and then you will work in the laundry during the day to earn your keep and then you will attend vespers every evening before returning to the dormitory." Sister Mary glared over the top of her steel rimmed glasses at the nervous girl stood in front of her.

So, this was the flighty Phoebe Horwat Father Jeffries had warned them about, she would certainly make sure the other sisters kept a watchful eye on this particular girl!

"You will only speak when you are spoken to, but no other talking is permitted at any point during the day. You will use your time here to reflect on the error of your ways, to pray for forgiveness, and to atone through hard work for your sins.... Is that understood Phoebe?"

"Yes Sister Mary." Phoebe was already dressed in the heavy, navy work dress worn by all the women working in the laundry, all the dresses were the same size and washed communally, there were no possessions in St Saviours. The serge dress was patched worn and shapeless, and it hung down to Phoebe's ankles but at least it was clean. The pleats at the front allowed for her expanding belly and the grey sacking apron protected the dress from the hot soapy water Phoebe would spend eight hours a day working in.

Sister Mary showed Phoebe to her workstation in the hot and steamy laundry, nine other women in various stages of advanced pregnancy stood behind huge Belfast sinks ranged along the walls. The girls did not even so much as lift their heads to see the new arrival they were all up to their elbows in hot soapy water washing and rinsing huge loads of heavy sopping linen and soiled ecclesiastical garments.

Apart from the rhythmic slop and slap of the linen on the wooden draining board and the creaking of the mangle as clothes were fed through the machine, the laundry was totally silent.

"You will stay at this end workstation until you are given permission to leave it, if you wish to relieve yourself there is a bucket in the corner you will use and as the new girl it is your duty to empty and clean the bucket at the end of each day." Sister Mary pointed to a large two handled pail sat in the corner of the room which served as the laundry lavatory. The galvanized bucket was already being circled by looping flies, the heat of the laundry room meant the lid did little to stop the stench of urine rising from the pail.

Phoebe nodded, the idea of taking a piss or voiding her bowels in front of these other women filled her with dread, *but then we're all in the same boat*, she thought ruefully. All dignity was stripped away in St Saviours house.

"These other women are all more advanced in their pregnancies than yourself, so when another woman leaves the laundry to be delivered, then you will all move along to the next workstation and then the next new girl will take over the task of emptying the latrine bucket, but until she arrives the job is yours." Sister Mary had a wolfish smirk on her face.

Phoebe had the overwhelming sense of being a an animal in a stall waiting to be led off to the abattoir. In the yard, just glimpsed through the high laundry window, she could see other pregnant women sorting laundry sacks and pegging out sheets on long lines looping across the yard. So many other desperate women just like herself and each week so many more would replace the ranks.

"Sister Angela overseas the running of the laundry, and if, at any time, you discover a problem with the laundry you have been given to deal with *or* if you think your baby is starting to come then, and *only* then, you may speak to Sister Angela, and she will tell you what to do. Otherwise, you are *not* to speak in this room at all. Is that understood Phoebe?"

"Yes Sister Mary."

Phoebe did not expect the vicious, sharp kick on her shins from Sister Mary's pointed shoe.

"No.... You obviously did *not* understand the rules Phoebe... I said you were *not* to speak in this room apart from the two specific reasons I gave.... *Now* have I made myself clear?" Sister Mary's hard steely eyes glittered; she enjoyed teaching the new girls the ropes and errant Phoebe was going to have Sister Mary's undivided attention.

Phoebe nodded, her shin throbbed from the forceful kick, her eyes brimmed with tears, but she would not give Sister Mary the satisfaction of seeing her cry.

After Sister Mary had left the laundry Sister Angela came up to Phoebe's workstation, the sweet natured nun gave Phoebe a small, gentle squeeze on her elbow. The young nun abhorred the mindless, vicious treatment meted out by some of the older, more bitter nuns to the fallen women under their care. In any small way she could, Sister Angela tried to show these poor women they were indeed loved by God.

Phoebe gave Sister Angela a watery smile of gratitude, the young nun's kindness touched Phoebe's heart. The nun inclined her head accepting the unspoken thanks and moved on. It would do Phoebe no favours if Sister Angela was caught showing any form of special treatment or favouritism to one of the women in her care.

Over the following grim, loveless months before the baby's arrival, Phoebe would come to love Sister Angela for all her small acts of defiance and bravery. Small acts of goodness made in the face of much brutal, unfeeling misery conducted by her fellow nuns.

For reasons unknown to Phoebe, she was singled out for untold spiteful acts by Sister Mary and her fellow tormentor the elderly Sister Faith. These two, unfeeling women made Phoebe's life a misery at every opportunity. For Phoebe, the gentle Sister Angela was one the small beacon of goodness inside the hateful walls of St Saviours' home.

"She's a cow that Sister Mary," Ellen Murphy muttered to Phoebe as they stood in line to collect their evening meal.

"Shh Ellen," Phoebe's eyes darted around to see if anyone was watching, even the slightest hint of gossip would earn a punishment. The last time Phoebe had spoken words out of turn in the dormitory she had spent all night standing outside in the yard in just her shift to pray for her sin of disobedience. All night Pheobe's teeth had chattered uncontrollably as she willed herself to stay awake.

Phoebe fretted her baby would come to harm in the cold May night air but by the time the grey morning light broke in the East and the nuns were up and about, Phoebe knew she had survived the ordeal. Phoebe gave a small prayer of thanks her baby was kicking furiously inside her to reassure Phoebe all was well.

In the morning Phoebe was summoned to the office and obliged to thank Sister Mary for teaching Phoebe right from wrong.

"Well, she is a cow…. and she's got it in for you," Ellen had learnt to utter words under her breath without moving her lips. Ellen always managed to avoid being detected. "Still, it's not long to go now… mine's due in six weeks then I'm off."

Sister Mary's gaze floated over to the queue, any excuse to punish Phoebe added zest to her day. She peered over the top of her steel rimmed spectacles in Phoebe's direction, Sister Mary thought she'd heard some faint muttering coming from Phoebe Horwat's direction. *She hoped she had!*

Phoebe kept her head low and moved a few inches away from Ellen.

Sister Mary had told Father Jefferies all about Phoebe and he had encouraged her to always keep Phoebe Horwat under firm control, to break the girl's spirit; it was a special job the hard-hearted nun relished. Sister Mary would not let Father Jefferies down. By the time Phoebe Horwat left the home she would be the model of cowed obedience.

Father Edmund had settled down nicely to his new parish, and as far as Father Jefferies was concerned Phoebe Horwat must be taught the error of her ways and with any luck she would not try to find the priest again once her baby was born. The quicker Phoebe Horwat disappeared back into the sewer where she belonged the better, in Father Jefferies's opinion.

But Father Edmund had not settled down quite as well as Father Jefferies had thought he had.

Edmund knew Phoebe Horwat was awaiting delivery in St Saviours. Kind-hearted Sister Angela had, in a moment of uncharacteristic disloyalty, happened to mention that some of the nuns were particularly strict in their dealings with one poor girl…. A girl called Phoebe Horwat. *His Phoebe Horwat.* Sister Angela had also said the poor girl would have her baby in the next eight weeks.

In eight weeks or even sooner his child would be born. Now Edmund needed to move fast.

Chapter 11

"Oh, Father Edmund it's so lovely to see you, I do hope that you aren't too busy, but I needed to ask you for some advice." Mrs Phyllis Richards had popped in from next door at number four, she was a woman on a mission. It had taken all her courage to decide to open her heart to Father Edmund about her problem, but she didn't know who else to turn to and besides Father Edmund was a trusted family friend.

"I do hope you don't mind me asking a favour, but it was your Mam who suggested I drop by when you were visiting next... so here I am." Phyllis looked nervous. She had confided in Edmund's mother Edna about her fruitless quest to get pregnant ages ago and when her husband Frank had finally relented about considering adoption, Edna was the first person she wanted to get advice from. Phyllis wanted to strike whilst the iron was hot and before Frank was persuaded to change his mind and tell her she couldn't seek out an abandoned baby needing a home.

Phyllis felt sure having a priest for a son imparted Edna Roberts with a degree of wisdom, and inside knowledge which Phyllis was desperate to gain access to. Edna had bristled with pride after Phyllis sought her advice on such a private matter and agreed her son Edmund was indeed just the man to help Phyllis with this rather delicate quest to adopt a baby.

It was Tuesday afternoon, and Father Edmund was paying his weekly visit to his mother. Phyllis felt confident with Father Edmund being a man of God and previously serving at St Saviours, he would know what to do about navigating the obstacles through the Catholic adoption process. As soon as Phyllis saw Father Edmunds go up the path next door she rushed around to her neighbour as fast as her legs could carry her.

Her heart was beating like a drum, with any luck she was about to start on her quest to adopt a baby... her baby.

Phyllis and her husband Frank had been married for fifteen happy years and despite waiting and trying, no children had arrived to enrich their lives. But Phyllis at the age of forty, was not giving up on the hope of motherhood... not quite yet. She hoped Father Edmunds could tell her a bit more about adopting a foundling or abandoned baby from the little angels left with the nuns at the St Saviour's mother and baby home.

Phyllis was a kindly, motherly soul and she knew she could love a baby, any baby, even if it was not her own by birth, all she yearned for in life was a child to hold in her arms and cuddle.

Phyllis was not a bright woman, and she dreaded having to go through a long and complex process to give an unwanted baby a home. Surely it couldn't be that difficult to rescue a sweet little baby and smother it with love? Phyllis felt certain that if anyone knew about the correct, and hopefully speedy, process to get a baby nestled in her arms, then surely it must be Father Edmund.

Worn down by years of Phyllis grieving each month for the baby who never materialised, Frank just wanted his sweet natured wife to be happy and fulfilled. After months of pleading, tears and nagging Frank finally agreed to allow Phyllis to try and adopt a baby but on one condition, Frank insisted it must be done quietly and discreetly.

Frank did not want it paraded to the world at large that he was somehow less than a man. They would never tell the child it was adopted… if the process went ahead then the child would never know the origins of its arrival into their lives. It would be the family secret. Desperate to have Frank's blessing, Phyllis agreed to his terms.

"So, you see Father Edmund, God has not seen fit to bless our marriage with children; Frank and I would love to adopt one of those poor children given away by their mothers." Phyllis blushed, first her Frank had raged about the possible defects of these cast-off babies, worried that the moral defectiveness of the feckless mother might somehow be passed on to their children, but eventually Phyllis had triumphed against all objections.

Frank was powerless to refuse his darling Phyllis the chance of motherhood before she became too old to take on the task.

When Father Edmund heard Phyllis Richards prattling on about her desire to adopt a child quickly and discreetly, he felt it was as if the stars had collided in the heavens. Phyllis Richards was desperate for a child to call her own and his *own* child would soon need of a home to go to. If Edmund could only engineer the process then it could all work to his advantage…. But he would need to move quickly, Phoebe's baby was only weeks away from arrival; he did not have long.

It might only be the occasional glimpse or morsel of news, but at least he would know about his child, it would not be totally lost to him even if he could never declare himself as the child's father, he would at least have secured it a loving home. And this baby, this only grandchild would be right on his own mother's doorstep if he succeeded in his plan.

It was the perfect solution.

"Mrs Richards giving one of God's children a loving home is a very noble thing to do," Father Edmund said sagely; thoughts were whirring in his head.

"Exactly!.... that's *exactly* what I said to my Frank," Phyllis beamed, delighted Father Edmund saw it from her point of view and was prepared to help.

"I do have contacts with the mother and baby home, and I do know one of the nuns-Sister Angela who takes a keen interest in all the girls. Sister Angela is very knowledgeable…. I'm sure she could help find the right child for you and your husband Frank."

Phyllis Richards felt she could burst with happiness and maternal joy. "Oh, thank you Father Edmund, I knew you would help us… bless you!" Phyllis grasped the priest's hands fervently.

"My Frank said he would prefer to adopt a lad and I of course said I'd rather it was a little girl, because they tend to cleave to their mothers," Phyllis prattled on," but I think either would be just wonderful so long as it's healthy…. After all nature doesn't let you pick and choose does it?"

"Wise words Mrs Richards, wise words indeed. If you are prepared to leave this with me then I'll make sure that Sister Angela finds just the right child for you and Frank…. Just think in a few weeks' time you could have a precious little baby nestling in your arms." Father Edmund smiled.

Phyllis Richards skipped next door to tell Frank the good news. She could indeed picture a precious little baby in her arms, and it made her heart want to burst with happiness.

*

Phoebe struggled to get the heavy, dripping wet sheet through the wretched mangle. All day Phoebe's back had been aching like Billy-o. The bending and stretching as she loaded mounds of sopping linen through the wringer was sheer torture. It was less than two weeks now before her baby was due but there could be no respite from the mountains of laundry which filled the room, she knew she must work until the day baby came. The only good thing was she was no longer on slop bucket duty, three weeks ago another poor, frightened girl had joined the laundry at the last sink position and that was her foul duty now; Phoebe's heart went out to her.

As she bent over the pile of wet washing Phoebe felt a sharp *pop!* A gush of warm liquid rushed down her leg staining her skirt and joining the grey soapy ooze gathering in the floor drainage channel. Phoebe tried not to cry out.

Sister Angela was standing by the new girl whispering a few words of quiet encouragement. With all the composure she could muster Phoebe walked over to the kindly nun.

Even though Sister Angela did not practice the petty acts of violence doled out by the other nuns she still had to enforce the rule of silence in the laundry. Phoebe would not embarrass the good-hearted sister by crying out.

"Sister Angela, I think my baby is coming," Phoebe murmured. The other women knew better than to turn around and see what any fuss was about.

Sister Angela gave a kindly smile, she liked Phoebe and was pleased her ordeal was coming to an end. The small spiteful acts and sly digs and pinches would soon be over. It wasn't fair Sister Mary singled poor Phoebe Horwat out the way she did.

"Bless you Phoebe, take this with you and go to the delivery room next to the covered walkway," Sister Angela handed Phoebe a slender navy-blue strip of ribbon with Phoebe's name written on it. The long ribbons were looped in a bunch and dangling from the leather belt circling sister Angela's habit. The ribbons acted as a tally system within the home, the blue laundry ribbon was Phoebe's ticket out and would be tied to the baby's cot with the mother's name on it before the child was placed.

"Give this ribbon to the sister on duty, you will be in her care now." Sister Angela gave Phoebe's arm an affectionate squeeze of encouragement. She knew Phoebe would have a long, painful ordeal ahead of her.

For the kindly nun there was some comfort in the fact that Father Edmund, from St Ignatius's parish church, had found a loving home for this child, a childless couple who would welcome the infant with open arms from the moment it was born.

Father Edmund was a good, kind-hearted man, Sister Angela felt sure he would have chosen the adopting family with care.

Sister Angela only wished she could tell Phoebe of the child's good fortune, but it was absolutely forbidden to reveal where the abandoned children were being placed.

Phoebe walked slowly to the delivery room, the weight of the baby pressed down in her pelvis, pains ricocheted across her body, she grasped her contracting belly and willed each foot to follow the other. Phoebe was scared by the ordeal ahead and for the first time, in a long time, she thought of her mother.

Sister Mary was on duty in the delivery room. Phoebe's heart gave a small lurch of disappointment. It was as if, for the last final torment and punishment of her miserable stay in St Saviours' house, Phoebe was destined to suffer once more at the hands of Sister Mary.

"I'll take that," sister Mary snatched the blue ribbon. If the child was born alive then it would be attached to the cot and a register made of the family where it was placed, if the child was born dead then its tiny body would be disposed of in the garden pit the nuns used for such purposes and the record ribbon would be burnt. All evidence of the nameless child would be gone, its life forgotten and un-mourned.

St Saviours did not waste money on funerals for the children of whores, nor did they bother keeping a register of their existence; unbaptised, illegitimate children had no place in a decent Christian cemetery.

"Get undressed and leave those soiled clothes in the corner, you will launder your own filth when you have been delivered. Before you leave us, you will scrub this room, this bed and this pile of laundry. Put on that linen smock." Sister Mary snapped her instructions, the nun pointed to a simple linen shift folded on the bed.

"Do not announce your sin to the world by screeching and shouting in labour Phoebe. God decreed after Eve's original sin all women would labour in sorrow and in tears to bring forth a baby, but my understanding, from working in this place, is that women who give birth in sin feel those God-given pains all the more acutely." Sister Mary's mouth was set in a cruel line she was enjoying seeing the fear in Phoebe's eyes.

"The rope tied to the bed will provide you with some assistance during the birth process and I or another sister on duty will look in every hour to see how you are progressing. When the time of your delivery is imminent the duty sister will stay with you until the birth is complete to collect the baby and then take it away to the nursery," with that Sister Mary swept out of the room leaving Phoebe to labour alone.

After ten painful hours Phoebe felt she was half dead with exhaustion. All through the night and into the early hours of the morning Phoebe writhed and strained in unimaginable pain with only the birthing rope to hold on to for comfort and support. Phoebe thought of Sister Angela as she battled the deep spasms wracking her body, Sister Angela was her one small comfort in this whole horrid experience.

Pheobe vowed that if this baby was a girl then she would name it Angela in her heart, in memory of the sweet sister who had befriended her; the only woman who had ever shown her a shred of compassion or respect in this hateful place.

Sister Mary entered Phoebe's room just as the cold grey light of morning crept over the courtyard. The sister recognized the final gasps of a woman in labour whose time had come, the sour faced nun looked at the exhausted, sweat drenched woman moaning on the rumpled bed and felt triumphant, *Phoebe Horwat had certainly felt the full sting of labour and it served her right! The strumpet didn't look quite so pretty now!*

"Sit up," Sister Mary ordered.

Phoebe used the rope to haul herself into a sitting position.

"Spread those sluttish legs and let this child come into the world." Sister Mary delighted in hurling the final insults, she would give this girl no comfort and assistance in her hour of need.

Phoebe groaned in agony; she felt as if she was being split apart and with one final tremendous effort she pushed her child into an unforgiving world. As the child came from Phoebe's body she heard the morning angelus bell calling the faithful to prayers.

Sister Mary scooped the greasy child from between Phoebe's legs and cut the cord, "I see you have given birth to a girl... let's hope she doesn't grow up to be whore like her mother."

"A girl! … Oh, please let me hold her Sister Mary… my little Angela." A rush of utter love overwhelmed Phoebe, she longed to hold the tiny baby in her arms.

Sister Mary was busy wrapping the child in clean white blanket. "I think you forget the agreement we came to when you entered this place Phoebe, this is not *your child*, this is *our child* now." She said spitefully, Sister Mary kept the baby's face out of view. "She is not called Angela or any other name of your choosing."

Phoebe groaned, each spiteful word like a knife in her heart, "please let me hold her Sister Mary…. just the once… Or at least let me see her," Phoebe pleaded…. to never even see the face of her own daughter was punishment too much.

"My advice to you is to forget all about this child now Phoebe…. she will belong to another woman, a woman who will bring her up with all the morals and values you have abandoned."

Fat tears rolled down Phoebe's cheeks, Sister Mary seemed determined to inflict as much suffering as she could.

"Please Sister Mary, just let me see her… I promise I will be good for the rest of my life…. I will do all that you ask of me…. But please, just this once, please let me see my daughter before you take her away."

Sister Mary walked slowly towards the bed, the baby mewling and squalling in her arms. A small spark of pity stirred within the nun's hardened heart, and she relented.

"It seems we have taught you a lesson after all Phoebe," the nun kept the child's face turned away from Phoebe. "Take one look at her Phoebe, because this is the first and *only* time you will ever see this child." Sister Mary bent low to the bed and turned the pink faced child to face Phoebe.

In the few brief moments granted to her, Phoebe could see her daughter Angela was perfect and beautiful. Without doubt Angela took after Edmund in looks, the baby girl had a fuzz of brown downy hair and piercing slate blue eyes. "She's beautiful," Phoebe gasped as she drank in the tiny starfish hands and button nose, desperate to imprint the fleeting image on her heart… "Goodbye little Angela," Phoebe murmured as if to lock the child in her memory…*this was her daughter Angela and whenever she heard the angelus bell ring she would remember her.*

Without another word sister Mary turned and took the baby out of the room. Phoebe turned her face to the pillow and wept as if her heart was breaking into a million pieces.

*

"Oh, she's so beautiful," Phyllis gasped. Phyllis felt sure that if she hadn't been sitting down she would have collapsed with sheer joy when the tiny sleeping bundle was passed into her arms for her to hold. "She's even got your brown hair Frank," Phyllis stroked the downy fuzz on top of the sleeping baby's head.

Sister Angela beamed with joy as she handed over the baby. Father Edmund had chosen well, Phoebe's baby was certainly going to a loving couple, she could see the delight on Phyllis's face. Sister Angela was certain Phyllis would make a wonderful mother and the soft smile of pride on Frank's face melted her heart. Sister Angela always rejoiced when the children of St Saviours brought joy into the hearts and homes of childless couples.

"I'm going to call her Rita after my grandmother," Phyllis announced, "and we haven't thought of a second name yet, but if you don't mind Sister, I think Angela is such a pretty name we could name her Rita Angela after you." Phyllis beamed with pride.

Sister Angela was touched, she would never have children to call her own, it was the heavy price she paid to serve her God. "Thank you Phyllis, I'm honoured you would consider giving this precious child my name." Sister Angela smiled.

"We can't thank you enough for choosing this child for us and we promise she will be well looked after don't we Frank?" Phyllis felt so happy she felt her heart could burst. The soft, comforting weight of the child in her arms had filled the void in her heart and she knew they would love this child as if it was their own.

Frank Richards nodded, he couldn't speak, his eyes were welling up with tears of joy to see his wife so blissfully happy after so many years of sadness and disappointments.

Frank was nearly fifty years of age now and who knows, he might not live long enough to see this child get married and have children of her own, but he could see it would be a blessing to them both to have this child to make their home complete.

Little Rita Angela had somehow found her way into their lives, and they would give her all the love her own father and mother could not.

This was their child now and she will want for nothing Frank vowed.

Within weeks Phyllis was rewarded with Rita's first gummy smile and as the baby grew and thrived Phyllis and Frank's love for their little daughter knew no bounds. Each tiny milestone delivered untold happiness into their lives, and for the first time in her life Phyllis felt like a complete woman, a wife, *and* a mother.

The couple's gratitude to Father Edmunds also knew no bounds either, they could not thank him enough for bringing about the selection of little Rita, and it gladdened their heart to see the kindly priest took such an interest in their child whenever he visited Alma road.

"Honestly Edna your son is an absolute saint for bringing us such happiness," Phyllis enthused over a cup of tea with her neighbour. A warm and milky Rita dozed in Aunty Edna's arms and Phyllis, as proud as any mother could be, gazed on the beautiful perfection that was her new daughter.

The older woman smiled, delighted to feel the comforting weight of a baby nestled up against her bosom, tiny translucent eyelids flickering with contented dreams.

"She's an angel this little one of yours Phyllis, and since it seems I'm not destined to have any grandchildren of my own now, perhaps you might let me borrow little Rita now and again."

Edna rocked the child gently.

"I feel she *is* a part of your family Edna, thanks to Father Edmund, if it hadn't been for him we'd never have found our Rita, I'm sure she's going to love having Aunty Edna look after sometimes…. And if your son wasn't a priest I'd suggest we call him Uncle Edmund…. but he might think that sounded improper…. What do you think Edna?" Phyllis pondered the conundrum of how to address Father Edmund.

Edna looked at the cherubic, sleeping child on her lap, and smiled "Oh I'm sure you'll have your Uncle Edmund wrapped around your little finger whatever you call him won't you my precious." Edna was proud that her own dear Edmund had helped this lovely couple find happiness, *he was such a good man.*

Chapter 12

December 1953

Deirdre gasped when she heard the enormity of Edmund's sin. The strain of confession had exhausted him, her brother lay on the bed with huge blue, saucer shaped eyes pleading for forgiveness. Not only had Edmund confessed to abandoning his vows to seduce an innocent young woman all those years ago, but, even worse, he had connived and plotted to get the illegitimate child adopted by the family living next door…. He had placed his child next door to his own mother and sister with all the cunning of a cuckoo choosing the comfy nest of a fellow bird to raise its young!

Her brother's own bastard was on his parent's doorstep living in plain sight and only Edmund knew it, he'd tricked them all…. It was beyond belief.

For years little Rita had run in and out of their home, calling her own grandmother Aunty Edna, for years Deirdre had cuddled and told stories to her actual niece whilst basking in the honorary title of Aunty Dee Dee.

"How could you do this to us Edmund?" Deirdre croaked; the magnitude of his lifelong deception left her almost speechless. He was a priest; how could he live such a wicked lie all his life? She wanted her brother to unburden himself before he passed away but now, in doing so, he had placed an enormous burden on her own slender shoulders. Only she knew this secret he said… just her.

This monstrous sin, this stain on the family good name could have died with him, could have been left for his Maker to pass judgement on, but instead, he had chosen to give his load over to his sister Deirdre to carry. *It just wasn't fair.*

In that moment Deirdre despised her weak foolish brother, he was using her, playing on her sense of duty and sisterly love.

How many lives would be turned upside down now if Edmund's terrible secret came out? How much hurt would Edmund cause in this final act of confession? Surely it would be better not to rake over this old wound again. Deirdre was angry he had extracted a promise of help from her when she didn't know what an awful thing he was asking of her.

Anything Edmund .... Of course, I will help you brother.... I'll do anything.

And what good would it do now to cause poor Rita Prosser and her family, so much pain and upset? To let Rita, know that the kindly Uncle Edmund she saw every Tuesday was her actual father. Deirdre was sickened by the thought of ruining so many lives if she helped Edmund unburden his conscience.

Deirdre was still reeling from the catastrophic revelations when Edmund gestured towards the bedside drawer.

"In there, look in there Deirdre," he gasped, each word seemed to weaken him further.

Deidre pulled out a small bundle of professional photographs taken by the studio in Wellfield road. The bundle was tied together by a long, faded blue laundry ribbon. Each dated picture had similar inscription… *To Uncle Edmund*…and signed *with love.* Many of the pictures were of Rita as little girl charting her progress through childhood to her first holy Communion, others were pictures of Rita and George getting married and then pictures of their own beaming children Frank and Jennifer smiling in delightful family photographs.

Edmund, secure in his guise of favourite "family uncle," had obtained a complete record of his daughter's life sent to him in Christmas and birthday cards over the years by a grateful Rita or Phyllis. Little mementos sent to man they held in the highest regard, a man they credited with their happiness.

Only one small black and white picture stood out amongst the rest of the professional snaps, it was of a young girl standing on a bleak beach. The moody child was wrapped up against a chilly autumn day in a knitted hat and winter coat with room to grow into. The girl was looking off into the distance, her face studiously avoiding the photographer.

Deidre had not seen the picture before, but she recognized the girl immediately, it was Jennifer Prosser, Rita and George's daughter… Edmund's own granddaughter. On the reverse of the picture the inscription said:

"We just had to send you this picture Uncle Edmund as Jennifer said she would not look at the camera or watch the birdie because she couldn't visit her favourite Uncle Edmund in hospital…. So please get well soon… Jennifer misses you so much and so do we…. You are always in our thoughts and prayers. Love Rita."

The picture was dated October 1953… the month Edmund entered the sanitorium, the month he'd been told he was dying.

"Find Phoebe," he croaked….. "Please, I'm begging you Deirdre, please find Phoebe Horwat for me. I can't go to my grave without letting her know where her daughter and grandchildren are." Tears rolled down Edmund's cheeks.

Deirdre stood before him wracked with indecision. Was it wise, or kind to indulge this pathetic need to bare his soul before her brother slipped off his mortal coil? She held the blue ribbon between her fingers. Deidre knew without doubt the grubby, faded ribbon was Phoebe's identity ribbon…. faint pen marks, almost rubbed away by years of examination, confirmed it.

She could refuse to do as he asked, after all, for years he'd allowed his own mother to be denied knowing her only grandchild… did she really owe Edmund this final sisterly act?

If she refused to act out Edmund's wishes, then so many lives would be left to carry on undisturbed, spared of the pain caused by the confessions of a guilt-ridden priest. And if she did agree to help him then it would be like tossing a colossal boulder into a calm pond, the impact would cause waves to crash onto so many shores, possibly ruining lives forever.

After a few moments thought Deidre came to her decision. She always tried to do what was right and all her life she had put others first. Today would be no different…. She had given Edmund her word and, hateful though the task was, she would keep it.

"I'll try do what I can to find her for you Edmund…. I can't promise any more than that," Deirdre collected up the photographs and the ribbon. If her brother Edmund wanted Phoebe Horwat to have these pictures, then she would ensure they were delivered into her hands. Of course, Phoebe might be so angry with Edmund and his deception, she would refuse to come and see him in his final days, but this was something Deidre had no control over. As his loyal sister she could only do her best to keep her promise to her dying brother.

Deirdre gave him a small kiss on the cheek and left his bedside with her heart broken into a thousand pieces.

At that moment she hated her lying brother Edmund, the golden child who had deceived them all, but she loved him enough to do as he asked. If she could help him find some modicum of peace before he died, then she could not deny him this act of mercy even if it cost her dearly.

When his sister left, Edmund felt as if a huge load had finally slipped off his shoulders, he had confessed and given Deirdre all the clues he possessed as to Phoebe Horwat's current whereabouts. With any luck Deirdre should find Phoebe within a few days.

He'd always known where Phoebe Horwat could be found, sometimes he lost sight of her for a little while, but she was never too far away. In the early dark days when his heart was heavy with guilt and grief, he worried about the girl he had abandoned in her hour of need. Edmund knew that as a devout Catholic Phoebe would never abandon her faith and sure enough when she turned up in the Tiger Bay area after she left the nuns of St Saviours home, he discovered she had gravitated towards the congregation of St Pauls.

Edmund had always kept to his solemn promise to Father Jefferies and Father Thomas that he would renounce Phoebe forever and never meet with her again, so he had kept his watch from a distance. Unknown to Phoebe he had observed her from afar on many occasions.

Edmund's own parish church was not so far away from St Paul's church, it was easy for him to keep track of Phoebe, sometimes she disappeared, but she always came back to the comfort of St Paul's, he felt certain Deirdre would find traces of Phoebe there. Someone would know where Phoebe Horwat lived or at least know how to get hold of her, he didn't feel bound any longer by his promise to Father Jefferies, his life was at its end. Edmund needed to see Phoebe one last time.

Edmund lay on his crumpled, sweat stained pillows and tried to sleep a little. He prayed his health would hold out long enough for Deirdre to track down the only woman he had ever loved. He could not bear it if he died before he could tell Phoebe how sorry he was for what he had done and to beg her forgiveness.

As his tired eyes watched the parade of raindrops slowly rolling down the window, Father Edmund drifted off to sleep.

Chapter 13

Phoebe was having a busy Monday afternoon getting June's angel costume ready for the Christmas Eve nativity tableau at St Paul's. The wire and tinsel halo proved particularly irksome. No matter how hard Phoebe tried she couldn't get the circlet to sit straight… somehow a wired halo listing precariously to the left didn't look quite as angelic as Aunty Phoebe hoped for.

June squealed with excitement when Aunty Alice had arrived with the costume and told her she could be an angel in the play, complete with tinsel wings and a halo. Now it was Phoebe's job to deliver the perfect angel outfit by Sunday. Phoebe wondered if a simple circlet of tinsel around June's golden curls might do the job just as well.

Phoebe's mind wasn't really on the job in hand, her thoughts were too busy whirring in her head after she heard Alice's tale about a mystery woman asking questions in church. Over the morning cup of tea with Ivy and Phoebe, Alice Thomas had caused a fluster and Phoebe still wasn't sure what it might mean.

"Little June is going to be the best and prettiest angel ever seen on this earth, isn't she Mam and Aunty Phoebe." Aunty Alice announced with great authority. Alice watched the church angel costume being altered and repaired for June to use. June was standing as still as she could whilst Aunty Phoebe took her measurements and pinned the garment to fit. Alice secretly hoped she was carrying a little girl herself. She so wanted to spoil and dress up a girl in pretty clothes, she knew George was hoping for a boy to carry on the Thomas and Sons family name, but a darling cherub all dressed in pink was Alice's heart's desire.

"I'm so please Father Malone said June could join in the Christmas tableau," Alice was delighted June was being made so welcome by the congregation at St Paul's. "Once Aunty Phoebe shortens the angel outfit you will look an absolute picture June."

June practised placing her hands together just like Father Malone had shown her to do.

Alice smiled, the long white smock was made for a larger child, a temporary hem would be needed to raise the garment off the floor if June wasn't to trip over the flowing angel robe.

After Alice and Phoebe had persuaded Ivy to get June christened, the kindly priest had done all he could to welcome June into his flock with open arms. Now Jimmy was no longer around to bully and dictate, Ivy was free to choose baptism for her daughter and Aunty Alice and Aunty Phoebe were dutifully looking after the child's spiritual well-being.

Phoebe had more than one reason to grateful to Alice that June was now part of the St Paul's nativity service on Christmas Eve, especially since not everyone was as welcoming to a disabled child like June. The appearance of June in the nativity tableau had effectively scotched any idea of Ivy disappearing off to Porthcawl to see her newly discovered father James.

On Christmas eve Aunty Phoebe, Nanna Betty and Bampa Gag would all be sat in the pews as proud as punch to see June acting the part of an angel and Phoebe knew Ivy wouldn't miss it for the world either.

After Bampa Gag's health scare, Betty was taking particular care of her husband these days and seeing June as an angel would gladden his heart. Ivy wouldn't want to deny Gerald the pleasure of seeing his June up at the alter with all the other little children by going to visit James for the day.

Phoebe did feel sorry James Pugh would be spending yet another Christmas day on his own, with just his faithful dog Nero for company, but she was secretly delighted June would be spending Christmas night in her own home. Now Phoebe and Ivy would have all the fun of stuffing an old nylon stocking full of surprises for June to discover at the end of the bed on Christmas morning and James Pugh wouldn't be luring Ivy and June away to spend Christmas day at his house.

"I know June doesn't attend St Paul's on a regular basis Ivy, but I'm happy to take her to service as often as I can, if you'd like me to," Alice suggested.

Alice knew her brother-in -law Billy was getting serious about Ivy, and Alice shared Phoebe's opinion that they would make a lovely couple. Alice didn't want Ivy shooting off to Porthcawl either if she could help prevent it. "After all, I am June's Godmother so if ever you can't manage to take her to mass Phoebe, then I'd be happy for June to come with me." Alice sipped her tea thoughtfully and then she dropped the bombshell.

"Oh, that reminds me Phoebe, I meant to say straight away…someone is looking for you."

Ivy's ears pricked up, *this sounded like trouble.*

"What do you mean someone's looking for me Alice?.... Who's looking for me?" Phoebe felt a cold shiver run down her spine.

Perhaps it was a member of Jimmy Benson's family seeking explanations or even worse seeking revenge. Phoebe knew Jimmy's death was no accident when he was locked up waiting to hear his fate in the Cardiff remand centre. Phoebe was as certain as anyone could be that Jimmy Benson had been strung up and hung like the dog he was, as punishment for his vile crimes against children. And the reason Phoebe was so certain Jimmy had not placed the noose over his own remorseful head and then suspended himself from the top bunk.... was because she had paid someone handsomely to make sure that the deed was carried out, life was cheap in jail especially for an animal like Jimmy.

"I really don't know much about it Phoebe.... All I know is that an older woman is asking around, wanting to know where Phoebe Horwat lived. I don't think the old dear comes from Tiger Bay though, somebody mentioned she was from Roath. Apparently this woman said it's a matter of some urgency she contacted you Phoebe, *life and death*, so she said. A few people seemed to want to help her so I'm sure she'll find you soon."

Alice cuddled June on her lap, she was sure someone had already given Phoebe's address to the woman. Someone mentioned Sean Riley's wife Eileen had been seen talking to the stern woman in the black hat after the service. Alice knew Sean and Eileen had recently moved into Wilson road so seemed quite likely Eileen might have passed on the information.

"Anyway, I'd best be off Ivy, George will be wondering where on earth I've got to. I'm sure that whatever this woman wants it will all come out in the wash." Alice put on her outside coat; buttons strained to meet across her expanding belly and adjusted her hat.

"I can't wait to see this little one playing the part of an angel, see you all in church!" Alice trilled, she kissed June goodbye and left the two women to deal with the wreckage of scraps of tinsel littering the floor.

Phoebe and Alice looked sceptically at each other as if to say they didn't share Alice's optimistic view; a stranger asking questions was never good news.

Ivy looked equally disturbed by Alice's news, even though her husband Jimmy was dead and buried, he still had friends involved in his rotten trade, *friends* who didn't take too kindly to the police officers knocking their doors asking awkward questions and frightening away the customers.

72

None of the low life Jimmy mixed with had welcomed a nosey sergeant disrupting their carefully crafted network of boys who acted as Jimmy's runners. The network of lads with bikes who distributed pornography across the city crumbled because of Ivy's information and some people bitterly resented her interference.

Ivy didn't want any trouble coming to her door. *Someone might want to teach Ivy a lesson for sticking her nose in where it wasn't wanted, it was well known that Phoebe Horwat was close to Ivy.*

Ivy knew she had made enemies when she turned Jimmy over to the police and she was nervous about some strange woman asking awkward questions, could this woman be something to do with Jimmy? People asking questions always meant trouble in Ivy's book.

Ivy still hadn't made her mind up what to do about Billy Thomas either, now that she would be staying home in Ely for Christmas. Last Saturday night when they had had left the noisy jazz club early and she had cuddled up to Billy for warmth her mind had been in a turmoil, she was torn in two.

Ivy had told him all about her father James Pugh, her Mam's long-lost love, she'd said how lonely and pathetic the man was stuck down in Porthcawl with only his guide dog for company. As they had shared a packet of chips in the bus shelter, she revealed her father had asked if she wanted to join him for Christmas in Porthcawl.

Ivy knew it would be a surprise to Phoebe if she went and she knew Mam and Gerald were counting on seeing June, but she had to admit she was tempted by the prospect of Christmas with her Da. Torn, she didn't know how she was going to make her mind up

It was then that Billy told her he loved her.

"Ivy it's only natural your father wants you in his life, and that he wants to get to know you… and he must…you must both take time to get to know each other." Billy took a deep breath… "But I love you Ivy and I want you in *my* life too." Billy had been rattled when she said James had suggested she could consider moving away from Ely and live in his house in Porthcawl if she wanted to escape all the bad memories and nasty gossip.

"I love you… and I love June…. and in time I believe I could make you both happy…. We could be a proper family Ivy….. Please don't go to Porthcawl for Christmas." Billy held her tightly, pulling her towards him, strong arms circling her shoulders. And he knew then with absolute certainty he wanted to marry Ivy Jenkins. *He loved her...he always had.*

Ivy felt her cheeks begin to burn; no man had ever told Ivy that he loved her before. *Jimmy Benson had certainly never loved her or June.*

"I was hoping I might introduce you to my parents an' all if you'd agree to it?" Billy said shyly, he knew his parents would draw their own conclusions if he took Ivy to meet them. He'd never introduced a girl to his parents before, visiting with the girl he loved on his arm would speak volumes.

Ivy knew Billy was serious about their relationship and she had to admit she had fallen completely in love with him too, but then he didn't know her dreadful secret; she could never have any more children, she could never give him a child of his own and she would have to tell him the truth one day... would that be the day he would leave her, could June be enough family for him when he knew the reality of marrying a barren woman?

Ivy's decision to stay at home for Christmas and then to see her Da on the day after Boxing day made the most sense when she considered all the options. Ivy could take June down on the bus to Porthcawl to meet her new grandad and to have some fresh sea air, she could even invite Mam to go with them; make a real family outing of it.

 Ivy could tell things were coming to a head with Billy and she knew he would expect some answers soon. Ivy would have to tell Billy the truth about not having any more children... she owed him that much before he proposed to her... if indeed he was going to propose, *and she'd lay a pound to a penny he was.*

The hammering on the front door in the afternoon made Ivy and Phoebe jump. The two women looked at each other; visitors were not expected. Phoebe put down the pins she held between her lips; the hem would have to wait.

"No... it's all right don't get up.... I'll answer it, Aunty Phoebe. It might be Norah wanting to borrow something." Ivy didn't believe it for a moment, her friend Norah would have tapped the front room window-this loud knocking on the door sounded urgent.

When Ivy opened the front door, she saw a nervous woman aged about sixty standing on the doorstep.

74

"Excuse me, I'm sorry to disturb you, but I was told Phoebe Horwat lived at this address," Deirdre Roberts could see the young woman answering the door was certainly not Phoebe Horwat, *perhaps it was Phoebe's daughter?*

"She might do…. Whose asking?" Ivy eyed the stranger suspiciously. The woman was plain but presentable, she reminded Ivy of a teacher she'd had at school; looks could be deceptive.

"My name is Miss Deirdre Roberts, please tell me if I can find her here. I have some extremely important information I must tell her, and I have to give her this parcel," Phoebe held out what looked like a parcel of documents.

Phoebe appeared in the hall behind Ivy, "what do you want," she said rudely. Phoebe had never seen this grey-haired woman before in her life and she never liked people poking their nose into her private business.

"Are you Phoebe Horwat?" Deirdre could see that *this* woman could indeed be Phoebe, she was about the right age, brown eyed with faded blonde hair and Deidre could see that at one time the woman had been beautiful before time wreaked its revenge.

"So, what if I am… and what's it to you anyway?" Phoebe said suspiciously.

"I've been asked to give you these… by my brother Edmund," Deirdre paused to see the spark of recognition in Phoebe's eyes, *she had found the woman she was looking for*.

"I'm Deirdre Roberts and my brother is Father Edmund Roberts. He said he *needs* to see you." Deirdre said hesitantly, she wasn't sure if the door was about to be slammed in her face.

"Oh, Dear God, are you saying Edmund has sent you to find me….. after all this time!" Phoebe's hand flew to her mouth, her legs felt so weak with shock she felt sure she would collapse at any moment if she didn't steady herself on the door frame.

"What's going on Aunty Phoebe," Ivy looked terrified. Hearing the commotion June came running into the hall.

Phoebe was moaning with shock. For years she had wondered what had happened to her beloved Edmund and now, out of the blue, a woman, claiming to be his sister turns up saying he wanted to see her. *What on earth could it mean?*

"Who is this woman Aunty Phoebe? Are you all right you look like you've seen a ghost?" Ivy was worried by Phoebe's deathly pale face; her aunt looked shaken to the core.

Sensing something was wrong, June started to cry, holding her arms up to be cuddled. "What's matter Aunty Fee Fee?" June wailed.

"Please may I come in. I don't think we should discuss private business on the doorstep," Deirdre Roberts said softly, she looked embarrassed by the upset she was causing, and she knew that once she had related the whole sorry tale, things would probably get a lot worse.

Ivy looked at Aunty Phoebe and Phoebe nodded her head, if this was something about Edmund Roberts then she needed to know what it was all about.

"I think you'd better come in Miss Roberts and tell us everything you know," Ivy said. She showed Deirdre through into the small sitting room littered with white cloth and tinsel shards. "Now I'll make us all a cup of tea while you tell my Aunty Phoebe what this visit is all about. Come on June, come in the kitchen with Mam." Ivy took June into the kitchen with the bribe of a biscuit.

"Go upstairs and play luvvie, that's a good girl and you can take an extra biscuit to share with your dolly Margaret." Ivy smiled to reassure her daughter. June often picked up on unhappiness, it was best June stayed out of the way. Through the closed sitting room door, Ivy could hear a woman crying…. It was obviously bad news about something.

Happy to secure two biscuits, June scooted upstairs to play with her dolls.

Ivy was worried, she had never seen her Aunty Phoebe look so upset. Phoebe was always so strong and calm; she was not given to tears and outbursts of emotion. Ivy felt a shiver of worry run down her spine. *What on earth could this woman want and who was this mysterious Edmund she needed to talk to Aunty Phoebe about?*

Ivy took in the tray of tea.

"But I didn't know any of this myself until last week Phoebe, honestly I didn't" Deirdre wailed. "I'm so sorry to bring this to your door Phoebe but I'm his sister… his *only* family now. I had to help him…. That's all I promised him, nothing more. The rest is up to you now." Deirdre dabbed at her eyes with a large white handkerchief.

Phoebe sat stony faced in the armchair opposite a tearful Deirdre Roberts.

Ivy passed her aunt a cup of strong tea, she didn't know what was going on but, Deirdre seemed distraught, and her aunt looked in shock, grim faced and miserable.

"Here Aunty Phoebe, drink this, you look like you need it." Ivy passed the other cup to Deirdre who sat sniffing in the armchair.

"I think you've said enough for today Deirdre," Phoebe's voice was measured and cold.

"Ivy doesn't know *all* my story so if you don't mind I'd like to end our conversation now…. I want to tell her everything myself and I need time to think about what you've told me today."

"Of course, Phoebe … I understand perfectly, I think we've both have a lot to think about." Deirdre sniffed. "I'll just drink my tea and then I'll leave you in peace. I won't stay any longer than is necessary, but I do need to know what I can tell Edmund when I go to see him tomorrow… I know he has absolutely no right to ask you to visit him, but he has things he wants to tell you before it's too late." Deirdre's eyes pleaded with the sad woman opposite to relent.

"Will you *please* see my brother Edmund before he dies Phoebe?" Deirdre waited for the decision.

Phoebe took a few moments before she gave her answer, her mind was in turmoil. At that moment she did not know how she felt about her long-lost love, she did not know what she would say to him even if she agreed to see him. She had trained herself to stop thinking about the handsome Father Roberts years ago, the wound was all but healed and now it was being split wide open again, as raw as the day it was made.

The things Deirdre had revealed that afternoon had broken Phoebe's heart, the photographs were bittersweet images of a life stolen from her; a happiness kept from her by the man who had once professed to love her.

How could Edmund do things he did… all the lies and deceit.

"I'll go on Thursday at 2'oclock… I think that after all this time I'm owed some explanations from Edmund." Phoebe could think of nothing else to say… she was promising this Deirdre Roberts nothing.

In Phoebe's heart Edmund meant nothing to her now, but this young woman in the photographs…. this Rita and her family did.

Phoebe wanted to know why Edmund had chosen to place her baby Angela next door to him when he could have left the church and been with Phoebe and they could have raised their daughter together. Why instead, did he choose to find a home for their child, keeping the girl close to him when he knew she was forced to give up the baby she loved? She could feel the anger bubbling within her… there was so much she needed to know and however painful it might be she was determined to get some answers.

Phoebe was prepared to run over glowing hot coals if it meant she had a small chance of finding her precious Angela again. She would have to be brave for Angela's sake.

Phoebe threaded the familiar, faded blue laundry ribbon between her fingers, painful, deeply buried memories came flooding back to her of that horrific day…. The day the nuns took her baby daughter away and gave it to another mother to raise.

"Tell him I'll see him," she said grimly.

"Thank you." Deirdre felt her promise to her brother had been fulfilled; she owed Edmund nothing now.

Chapter 14

When Deirdre Roberts finally left, Phoebe collapsed into floods tears, all her steely self-control deserted her. Surrounded by about twenty black and white photographs, Phoebe put her head in her hands and sobbed uncontrollably.

"How could he be so wicked?" Phoebe gasped looking at a picture of a cherubic Angela, dressed in her best dress aged about eighteen months. The photographer had captured a beautiful child with plump cheeks and dimples smiling for the camera, her cascade of ringlets held back with a pretty ribbon, tiny fingers clutching a velvet rabbit.

"Who is that little girl Aunty Phoebe?" Ivy said softly. Her aunt looked crushed, she collected up her precious pictures, her face a picture of misery.

"That is my beautiful daughter... *my* Angela," Phoebe said with passion. "My baby who I was forced to give away all those years ago, the baby who I only saw for a few moments before she was taken from me by the nuns and all the while he...." Phoebe started to gasp and sob uncontrollably, choking so hard the words would not come.

"Please don't cry Aunty Phoebe," Ivy hugged her, she loved Phoebe more than life, she hated seeing her aunt so distraught, if only she knew what she could do to help her. Ivy wished her mother Betty was here.

".....And all the while Edmund knew where she was!" She moaned. "Just like a bloody cuckoo he placed her in a nest of his choosing! Edmund deceived the family who wanted to adopt a baby into having *his* child and they called her Rita... this beautiful little girl is *my Angela,* and they called her Rita!" Phoebe showed Ivy the photograph, tears rolled down her face.

Ivy was stunned, there were no words of comfort she could offer her tortured aunt.

"Angela was utterly lost to me Ivy, but *he* became part of her life in a way that I never was...." Phoebe said bitterly, she looked totally bereft by the ultimate betrayal on Edmund's part.

"How could he do that to me Ivy?…It was just so wicked…. So truly wicked." She moaned in agony.

Over several more cups of tea Phoebe told Ivy the whole heart-breaking story of how she had given herself to Edmund and lost everything as a result, her family, her home, her self-respect.

"So, what will you do now Aunty Phoebe?" Ivy had tears trickling down her cheeks too, she had no idea Phoebe had experienced so much heartache in her life. She felt Edmund had treated Phoebe appallingly…. *To think that a man of God, a priest could act so deviously.*

"I need time to think about this Ivy, it's been such a shock." Phoebe was wracked with uncertainty about what to do next.

"I *will* go and see Edmund on Thursday, he's in St Saviours' hospital and Deirdre said he's dying so I haven't got long." Phoebe looked thoughtful, she only had a short time to question Edmund before he passed, it was a chance she could not afford to miss, much as it pained her, she would see Edmund before he died. "He owes me the truth Ivy… if nothing else, he owes me that."

"He certainly does Aunty Phoebe." Ivy said hotly.

"The more difficult decision is what do I do now about Angela… or I should say Rita?" Phoebe looked wracked with indecision and pain. "What will Rita Prosser think if I suddenly turn up in her life and tell her this whole awful tale? According to Deirdre Roberts, Rita doesn't even know that she was adopted by her parents!" Phoebe said miserably, she hated the idea that she might bring pain into her unsuspecting daughter's life.

Ivy felt shocked, so many secrets were coming out because of this brief visit from Deirdre Roberts. Ivy tried to imagine how she would feel if someone just turned up out of the blue and said she was adopted. It was traumatic enough when Ivy found out that her own father wasn't dead like she always thought he was.

"Will this woman hate me Ivy, when I tell her the truth about me and Edmund, and how he manipulated her life for his own purposes? And how will she feel when she knows how her own parents kept the secret of her adoption from her…. and how her parents were also deceived by the priest they called their friend?" Phoebe said bitterly. Hundreds of questions were ricocheting around in Phoebe's head, each new dilemma spawning a hundred more. The mere thought of all the possibilities was giving Phoebe a headache. She was utterly bewildered.

"And since both Rita's adoptive parents are now dead she can't ask them to give her any explanations either... it's going to turn this poor girl's life upside down if I tell her everything." Phoebe was furious she was being given such a terrible dilemma to resolve- dammed if she did and dammed if she didn't.

"Edmund might be dying, but when he leaves this world he will be leaving a huge mess for other people to sort out." Phoebe fumed.

Ivy could see the pitfalls ahead, but as a mother she knew it would be impossible for Phoebe to just let sleeping dogs lie. Now Deirdre had delivered the photographs as Edmund requested, Phoebe was left in an impossible situation and when she went to visit Edmund it might get even worse... who knows what other secrets might come out of the woodwork if Edmund made more death bed confessions!

"Edmund must have known I would want to find out about my daughter when I knew where she was living, or else why did he send me these?" Phoebe reasoned. "But will Rita want to find out about me?" Phoebe wailed.

"I might ruin her whole life if I tell her all this and she might curse me for it. I'm not exactly someone a daughter would be proud of." Phoebe sniffed miserably; she was only too aware what people thought about women like her who stood on the wharf for a living. The idea that Rita would be angry with Phoebe for crashing into her life and disrupting her happiness was torture. Phoebe would be crushed if after all this time Rita was ashamed to know her and turned her away, hating Phoebe for turning her settled, respectable life upside down; wishing her story and Phoebe had stayed buried in the past.

"Rita's not just my long-lost daughter, Ivy, she's now the mother of my two grandchildren Jennifer and Frank, children I'd love to get to know as well.... I don't know what to do for the best Ivy... it's such a bloody awful mess." Phoebe shook her head sadly.

"Is it *so* very selfish of me to hope that Rita might want me in her life Ivy?" Phoebe looked at Ivy, her golden- brown eyes brimming with tears. Phoebe wasn't a fool, she knew life had taken its toll on her, she had spent too many years standing outside on the wharfs of Cardiff docks, servicing desperate lonely men for a few shillings for it not to show on her face. What child in its right mind would want to acknowledge an ageing prostitute for a mother?

"I love you Aunty Phoebe and if I was Rita I would be proud to call you my Mam," Ivy wrapped Phoebe in her arms, it broke her heart to see her aunt so crushed, "you've been like a mother to me all my life and you are the bravest, most wonderful person I know. Rita would be lucky to have you in her life." Ivy said fiercely and she meant every word of it.

Phoebe kissed Ivy and held her face between her hands, "your Mam was so brave keeping you Ivy, you're the best daughter any mother could wish for… I only wish I'd had the courage to do the same with my own little baby… perhaps things would have been very different if I had."

"I know Aunty Phoebe and it must be so hard now you know all this information about Rita." Ivy said kindly. "But, *if* you had taken that decision then probably my Mam would never have met you, and my life would have been very different…. I'm so glad you *chose* to be in our lives Aunty Phoebe…. And don't you ever forget that."

*

The stress of telling Phoebe Horwat all Edmund's hateful secrets had caused Deirdre to feel quite unwell; all day she had been living on her nerves, she just wanted the day to be over, to hide herself away to forget the whole awful mess.

She felt unclean as if Edmund's grubby secrets had sullied her in the process. Above all she felt bitterly sorry for Phoebe Horwat, Deirdre's revelations about Edmund had caused the woman enormous sorrow and it grieved Deirdre she had been the bearer of such devastating news. *Phoebe must hate you for this Edmund.*

Deirdre dreaded she might run into her neighbour Rita Prosser and her children. She didn't feel as one Christian to another she could look Rita in the face if she happened to meet her now that she knew who Rita really was. Deirdre was convinced Edmund's guilt would be written all over her face for all the whole world to see.

Deirdre wasn't a natural dissembler; she couldn't bear the possibility of Rita asking her if everything was all right. Luckily, the damp gloomy December afternoon meant Rita should be safely tucked indoors. It would be dark soon and Deirdre just wanted to draw the curtains and hide away from the world.

Deirdre was still uncertain if Phoebe would ever contact Rita and reveal all to the woman she now knew to be her long lost daughter. The two women agreed that it was all up to Phoebe now, it was not Deirdre's place to reveal the secret of Rita's identity. If Rita was to learn the truth about her background and parentage it would be because of Phoebe, Deirdre's role in the matter was over, but it still hung over her head like the proverbial axe waiting to fall..

The trouble was that regardless of what Phoebe chose to do now, Deirdre would have to see Rita on an almost daily basis and not reveal the truth. Deirdre wasn't sure she could continue to live a lie.

One possibility starting to form in Deirdre's mind was that she might move away from Cardiff. Perhaps she should move to a bungalow by the sea, leave the city behind for good? She had always thought a nice little bungalow would suit her in her old age, perhaps it might be the solution to her dilemma? It would be an impossible daily torture to see Rita and all the while know she was keeping a shameful secret hidden from the trusting girl she had watched grow up…. The little girl who had kissed her and called her Aunty Dee Dee.

And if Rita did ever learn the truth, would Rita ever believe Deirdre was not party to her brother's dark secret, complicit in the lie? Deirdre felt utterly wretched.

One thing was certain her brother Edmund did not have long for this world and Deirdre knew he would never see his Rita again, the daughter he had loved, and kept secret from the world. *It was a punishment of sorts.*

It was all in Phoebe's hands now and Deirdre would keep her thoughts on the matter to herself, she was only glad her own parents weren't alive to see this humbling of their favoured child; the disgrace of it would have broken her Mam's heart.

Deirdre had kept her promise to Edmund and now her job was done. She would tell him she wanted no more involvement in the matter, she'd done her duty and delivered the photographs as promised and Phoebe had agreed to see Edmund on Thursday so he could make his peace with her. It was all out of her hands now and she wanted nothing more to do with the matter, just thinking about the injustice of it all was making her feel quite ill.

When Deirdre returned home from the trip to Ely she planned to have a little lie down, she didn't sleep well the night before, nagging anxiety robbed her of her peace of mind. The stress of all the lies and tears had taken their toll and exhausted her.

83

Deirdre's heart felt fluttery and at odds; a nagging, dull ache settled in her chest as if an iron fist was clutching her heart. The dragging pain was unlike any other she'd ever known, and she knew she needed to rest. Deirdre was not a strong woman, she was used to a quiet, ordered life, all this drama, emotion and upset had shattered her peace of mind and made her feel not herself.

Tomorrow would be another difficult day. Deirdre would tell her brother everything she had learned about Phoebe and inform him of the planned Thursday visit in two days' time. Deirdre knew Edmund would need to hear each and every detail of the meeting and the thought of the tortuous gasping conversation as her brother struggled for breath, filled her with dread.

She needed to rest to gather her own strength. Deirde could not even be bothered to make herself the simplest of meals before she went to lie down, she just longed to sleep and to forget the worst day of her life. As soon as her head hit the pillow she drifted into a deep and blessed slumber.

*

"I'm sorry but you're too late Miss Roberts," Sister Martha said with a kindly smile. "Father Edmunds passed away in his sleep in the early hours of the morning…. They've taken his body into the preparing room, but I'm sure we could arrange for you to see him if you wish."

"Oh no," Deirdre gasped. She was too late.

"As you know Father Edmunds had been in such a lot of pain and it had agitated his mind for a few days, but in the end his passing was quite peaceful. It's such a blessing he went in his sleep." Sister Martha crossed herself.

Deirdre stood in the ward next to the empty bed where her brother had once watched the raindrops slide down the windows and she felt like weeping. "Did he say anything before he went sister Martha…. anything at all?"

"The duty doctor had given him quite a strong sedative because Father Edmund had been in discomfort all evening, but just before he drifted off he did say one thing….."

"What did he say…"

"He just said a few last words, perhaps they might mean something to you. He said," Sister Martha composed herself…. Careful to get the words just right.

"He said tell Phoebe I'm sorry." The nun inclined her head and smiled.

Deirdre gasped. There was no message for Rita or herself, just Phoebe, the woman whose life he had ruined all those years ago, the woman he could never forget.

"Do you know who this *Phoebe* is Miss Roberts?" Sister Martha asked gently.

"Yes, I do," Deirdre said sadly. Now Phoebe would never get the explanation she wanted so badly.

"I'll make sure she knows Edmund's last words, Sister Martha." It would be Deirdre's final sisterly duty.

"He only had a few personal possessions in his locker, but I have put them in a bag for you to take away." Sister Martha handed over to Deirdre a canvas bag which was so light it seemed almost empty…*it was not much to show for a lifetime* Deirdre thought sadly.

"You may find his personal Bible of some comfort to you and there is also a small diary or journal Father Edmunds used to record his private thoughts. Of course, he stopped writing it towards the end… but up until the last few weeks he used to write in this book every day…. I think it comforted him." Sister Martha smiled; she had become very fond of Father Edmund.

Private thoughts!

Deirdre did not know if she could bear to know any more of Edmund's private thoughts. Perhaps she should just hand the journal over to Phoebe and let her read it. Maybe Phoebe would find some of the answers she was seeking inside the notebook, after all Edmund could not speak to her now.

"Thank you Sister Martha, I'll make sure they are looked after. Thank you for all you did for my brother." She said stiffly.

"It was an absolute pleasure and a privilege to nurse him in his final days, Miss Roberts…. Father Edmunds was such a good man." Sister Martha smiled beatifically and went about her duties.

With a heavy heart Deirdre turned to go home. Tomorrow, she must take another trip to Wilson road to let Phoebe know Edmund was dead and to hand over his notebook. Deirdre decided she would keep the Bible; it was one her parents had given Edmund for his twenty first birthday. She knew the inscription off by heart.

To our dearest son Edmund with all our love- you are a son to be proud of x

Deirdre decided she did not want to go to the hospital morgue to see the mortal remains of Father Edmund Arthur Roberts, she did not know the man they had laid out on the slab… the brother who she *knew* and loved had died several days ago when he had told her the truth about his secret life and the ruin of young Phoebe Horwat.

Chapter 15

It was the day before Christmas Eve and Betty was making mince pies. The kitchen was filled with the delicious aroma of cinnamon wafting temptingly through into the sitting room. Gerald was sat with his feet up on a footstool reading his newspaper in front of a roaring fire.

"Those smell delicious, Betty," Gerald called. His mouth was watering, and it was two hours before his lunch would be served; he was feeling peckish. Betty was an excellent cook, and mince pies were one of his favourites.

Betty stuck her head around the door, "would you like a nice cup of tea and a warm mince pie Gerald? …. Just the one mind." Betty was keeping a close eye on Gerald after his angina scare, she had cut down his portions, resulting in a loss of ten pounds and she insisted he sat down for a rest in the morning and in the afternoon without fail.

Gerald had to admit the new regime was doing him good, and he secretly liked being fussed over.

"Here you are," Betty brought in a small tray. "They are all out the oven now and cooling so I can sit and join you for a few minutes," she passed Gerald his tea and mince pie.

Christmas was always a busy, memorable time of year, but this year would certainly be one to remember on so many fronts.

"I do hope Ivy accepts him," Gerald said as he tucked into his warm mince pie with relish. "They will make a lovely couple and it's time the girl had a bit of happiness in her life… something to look forward to." He polished off the last buttery crumbs with his finger; the pie was delicious.

Gerald had been pleased as punch when Billy Thomas had turned up on the doorstep the day before dressed in his best suit and had asked Betty if he might have her permission to marry her beautiful daughter. In Gerald's eyes the young man was doing exactly the right thing to ask for the girl's hand even if Ivy was an independent woman living in her own home… it was a sign of courtesy and good manners and that went a long way in Gerald's opinion.

"I do hope so too Gerald, it's obvious he dotes on little June too. I'd be very happy to have him as our son in law." Betty sipped her tea. "But it will be awkward for Phoebe though if Ivy does get married again, I'm not sure what Phoebe will do when Billy and Ivy live together in Wilson road, it will cause a bit of a dilemma I'm sure of it."

And that wouldn't be the only problem on Phoebe's plate…. Betty thought to herself, she hadn't told Gerald *all* of Phoebe's dilemmas. Phoebe had turned up on Thursday in such a flap and a fluster with a tale to tell which had rocked Betty to the core. After Phoebe had left, Betty had only told Gerald the bare bones of it all. Gerald knew Phoebe had rediscovered her long-lost daughter, the one she gave away thirty-three years ago, what he didn't know was that the father of the child was the late Father Edmund Roberts, a serving Catholic priest…. A priest with lots of secrets.

"I can't cry for him Betty," Phoebe had declared over a cup of tea as she told Betty the whole sorry tale. "He got to share in the life of my daughter in a way I never could. I know he promised the Bishop he would never contact me again, but I can't forgive him for what he did. Edmund acted like a deceitful cuckoo tricking the Richards family living next door to his parents into adopting and raising his own child and all the while *they* thought the world of him; a hero for finding them a baby to love…. Mr and Mrs Richards could have had *any* baby from that maternity home, but he connived to make sure they had *his* baby placed in their home…. It's beyond wicked!" The more Phoebe thought about it, the more devious Edmund's actions appeared. It was certainly no accident her baby was placed where she was, Edmund had planned it all to perfection.

Betty gasped. Phoebe had often told her of the cruel treatment doled out by the heartless nuns of St Saviour's and now it seems the cruellest treatment of all was done to her by a priest who deceived everyone.

"And now Edmund's dead I can't get any answers from him…. I'll never know the truth or why he did what he did." Phoebe sniffed.

Betty was shattered to hear Phoebe's tale of woe; the simple narrative Phoebe had told Betty over the years was far from the whole truth. Phoebe had always believed she had met a young priest and that they fell hopelessly in love only to be torn apart from each other by the church and his vows…. But it was all a lie. Edmund had made some calculated decisions to save his own skin and at the same time he had callously broken Phoebe's heart. No wonder poor Phoebe was devastated.

Phoebe felt utterly drained, it had been the most turbulent of weeks, in a few short days her life had been turned upside down and she had been left with two terrible dilemmas.

The second visit from Deirdre Thomas to tell her that Edmund was dead and to give her his journal had brought everything to a head and now she must decide what to do next.

The problems to resolve lay at Phoebe's door, and she needed Betty's advice. She needed her best friend to hold her and tell her it would all be alright; to help her with untangling her twin dilemmas; what to do about Rita Prosser and what to do about Edmund's private journal.

In the end Phoebe decided to do nothing… *at least not yet.*

"I can't ruin Christmas by causing a huge fuss and a drama now Betty," Phoebe felt better unburdening her worries to Betty. "It's been thirty-three years since I saw my Angela, I can't just trample all over her life. She's Rita Prosser now, a married woman, with a husband George and two young children of her own, I can't just barge into her life and upset everything just because I want to."

Betty patted Phoebe's hand reassuringly, she felt sure that Phoebe was right to tread softly, Phoebe was a good, kind thoughtful woman.

"I need some time to think about it Betty…. at least I have these now," Phoebe patted the precious packet of photographs.

"I agree Phoebe…Let's just enjoy our Christmas… our first proper Christmas all together," Betty smiled, she was so looking forward to a happy family Christmas, free from tension and worry…. it went without saying about being all the happier because Jimmy Benson was no longer on the scene.

Betty gave her friend a hug. "We will see June in the nativity play on Christmas Eve and then we will see you on Christmas day for lunch, all together, just like a proper family should be." Betty smiled. Gerald had ordered a large turkey from Wilson's the butchers on the Grand avenue, it would be delivered to Ivy's house on Christmas Eve. A whole turkey would be such a treat.

Betty didn't envy Phoebe the job of cooking the monster twelve-pound bird for the family Christmas lunch; a plump succulent turkey with all the trimmings should make it a feast to remember. It was planned to be such a happy day; Betty didn't want any clouds hanging over the proceedings.

Phoebe smiled a small, tired smile, if Deirdre hadn't dropped her bombshell about Edmund, then her heart would have been skipping with delight at the prospect of such a wonderful family Christmas surrounded by all the people she loved. But now Phoebe knew she did have *other* family, her own flesh and blood, and she wouldn't be them seeing on Christmas day, it saddened her.

Phoebe resolved to try to be happy and carefree over Christmas for Betty, Ivy and June's sake. "You're right Betty, no more long faces…. Let's enjoy Christmas and then I can decide what to do next in the New Year… it's only a few days away, and June and Ivy deserve to have the best Christmas ever. Let's end this year on a positive note and then we can all look forward to the future." Phoebe said bravely.

Now to put the tin hat on it, poor Phoebe would possibly face having to look for a new home in the New year as well if it worked out between Billy and Ivy, still it had to come one day. Betty mused over her cup of tea pondering Billy's surprise proposal.

"Billy said he hasn't bought her a ring yet because he thought Ivy would want to have the fun of choosing it herself," Betty looked fondly at the band of diamonds sparkling on her wedding finger, *Gerald had chosen well.*

"I do hope that is the real reason Elizabeth…. I hope it's not because he thinks she'll turn him down," Gerald raised a knowing eyebrow, he remembered the butterflies in his own stomach when he had proposed to Betty not so long ago.

"Get away with you! They love each other to bits; anyone can see that." Betty laughed.

When Billy told Betty of his plans to ask Ivy to marry him her heart had skipped a beat. Betty was thrilled the kind thoughtful young man who stood in front of her with an expectant look on his face had asked for her daughter's hand and at the same time she was troubled. Ivy had confided in her mother on several occasions of her concerns about the future, she fretted any man would lose interest in marrying her once he knew she could never give him any children.

"Mam I'm enough of a damaged package as it is being the widow of Jimmy Benson. What man, in his right mind is going to want to take me on if he knows I am only ever going to be the mother of Jimmy Benson's child, and he'll never have children of his own?…. I'm not a fool Mam, once a man knows the truth I reckon he'll turn tail and head for the hills, and who could blame him." Ivy had said glumly, Betty knew it preyed on her daughter's mind that she could never have another baby and her heart bled for her.

When Billy announced his intentions, Betty decided to take the bull by the horns and tell Billy about Ivy's predicament *before* he popped the question. She didn't want Ivy rejecting Billy because of silly worries about him not knowing the truth of what he was letting himself in for. It was obvious Billy loved Ivy and he loved June; the couple were made for each other. Betty was sure she was doing the right thing even if Ivy was going to be cross with her.

"I'm thrilled you want to marry my Ivy; you certainly have our blessing Billy."

Billy grinned with delight.

"But before you do ask her I must tell you one very important thing I think you need to know before you pop the question."

Billy looked puzzled; he had hoped for a simple *yes* from Betty.

"I know you love my Ivy and I think you would both be incredibly happy together, but Ivy does have something that worries her, and I think you should know about it before you ask her.

Billy's face fell…. *What on earth could Betty be talking about, she certainly looked serious.*

"Ivy was very ill after she had June, in fact she nearly died," Betty took a deep breath, the memory of that dreadful time still raw, "so to save her life they had to take her womb away…. Ivy might only be a young woman Billy, but she can never have any more children." Betty choked back a tear, "I know she worries how another man might feel about her once he knows the truth."

Billy's face relaxed. "Poor Ivy…. It must have broken her heart to get such devastating news," he said kindly.

Betty knew then this was exactly the man who should marry her daughter and heal the hurt caused by Jimmy Benson.

"I love Ivy, Betty and if Ivy can't have any more children then so be it. I love Ivy *and* I love June and that will be enough for me. I'd be a liar if I said I hadn't thought about having a child to call my own one day, but I'd rather have Ivy any day with or without any more babies." Billy said loyally.

Betty gave Billy a big hug, "thank you Billy. I do hope she won't be cross with me for telling you, because I know Ivy always said she would tell any man herself before he asked to marry her. But at least now you know; you can ask her to marry you and she won't have any reason to turn you down. She does love you Billy, as her Mam I can see that. Good luck!"

Billy left the house a happy man, he had Betty and Gerald's blessing and every hope Ivy would accept his proposal of marriage. His own parents might not be quite so enthusiastic about having Ivy as a daughter-in-law, but they would just have to swallow it, this was his decision, and he knew in his heart it was the right one.

"Yes, I reckon we can hear some good news this Christmas Gerald.... I think we all deserve a bit of good cheer; it's certainly been a funny old year so far, what with one thing and another. Next year is bound to be a better one and Billy's proposal to Ivy will be the start of it, you mark my words." Betty smiled.

Chapter 16

Phoebe felt easier in her mind now she had shared her news with Betty. She would decide what to do about Rita and the Prosser family once Christmas was over.

Edmund's funeral was to be held on December the 28th in St Saviours church. Deirdre said it would be a small private affair with just a few friends and of course the Prosser family from next door who regarded Edmund as part of the family would also be there. She had grudgingly invited Phoebe to attend and pay her last respects.

Phoebe thanked Deirdre for her selfless kindness and made the brave decision to stay away.

I can't mourn the man in that coffin, if I went to his funeral it would not be to see him… but to see them. And yet I can't bear to see my own flesh and blood sitting only few feet away from me and not be able to speak to them. I want to meet them on my own terms, not in the shadow of Edmund's funeral when everyone is murmuring respectful platitudes about a man who has lived his life as lie.

Phoebe looked at the small, battered book which lay on her lap, the worn green leather cover concealing so much hurt and confusion… now she had read Edmund's innermost thoughts she felt she understood him a little better but hated him a little more.

Phoebe could only conclude that for all his protestations he had *never* truly loved her, she had been an infatuation, an experiment which had gone badly wrong, nothing more and nothing less.

Edmund wasn't the only one paying the price of his sin.

*

Edmund wrote his deepest thoughts in his private journal. He did not write every day and often it was just a word or a sentence too important not to observe or record, miniscule scribbles holding huge import, a perfect moment in time not to be forgotten. Sometimes his jottings amounted to dense paragraphs of outpourings, his aching heart spread across narrow lines and crammed onto small cream pages.

This second journal was Edmund's secret life, starting from his final months serving his King and country in the muddy fields of France before he returned to dedicate his life to serving God. His first notebook had been lost at Passchendaele like the lives of so many of his friends and comrades in arms.

It always helped to clear Edmund's mind to note the milestones of his life, it was as if the simple act of putting pen to paper made things a reality. Whilst random thoughts clattered about in his head, chaotic, jumbled not yet the truth, they were not who he was. As soon as his thoughts, hopes and emotions made it onto the paper for Edmund they became the truth which could not be denied. A truth which could be his undoing if ever it was brought to light.

A journal of his most intimate thoughts could be a dangerous thing.

The poignant entry for one momentous evening in December 1917 crystalised much of what Edmund had suspected, nay known in his heart to be true… he was passionately in love with a beautiful, gentle, noble young man called Piers Loxley.

On that one special night in 1917, when in a dark abandoned barn, his secret love for the beautiful Piers had been returned, the revelation had been stupendous. The fact that Piers died the next day as the result of a sniper's bullet had broken Edmund's heart, he'd lost a good friend and his first true love. But in one perfect moment, when two frightened men sought comfort in each other, Piers had revealed to Edmund who Edmund truly was and he loved Piers for it.

Piers Loxley had come from a wealthy, noble family with a country seat in Gloucestershire, a home in Belgravia and a profitable family business in Bond street. It had been easy for Piers to live a fast life in the gay and carefree clubs of London. But Edmund knew such a life could never be for him when he returned home to the settled rhythms of Wales.

When life teetered so precariously, and death was all around him in on the battlefields of France, Edmund had abandoned all fear and embraced his true nature before it was too late. Now he had tasted the forbidden fruit he did not know how he could ever go back to living a lie on the streets of Cardiff where the neighbours knew the ins and outs of everybody's lives and where he was expected to settle down and get married like all his schoolfriends had done.

It would kill his parents to know their handsome, law-abiding son was attracted to men.... a sodomite. A *Nancy boy,* as his father would say as he sneered about the deviancy of other such young men.

For Edmund to face ruin, ridicule, and perhaps even jail, by embracing the love he could not name, was too terrible to contemplate. He could not shame his parents in this way. They would never understand why he would choose a life which would involve losing so much if the truth about his inclinations ever came out.

His mother had always hinted at babies and marriage to a nice young girl when the time was right, the intervention of the war had interrupted those dreams, but he knew she would cherish those hopes for the future in her heart. Edmund decided there was only one thing for it now, if he survived this appalling war, then he would become a priest and take a vow of celibacy. In the nights after the death of his lover Piers, Edmund Arthur Roberts made a deal with God. If he was spared death on the battlefield then Edmund would dedicate the rest of his life to God and the service of others.

If Piers had taught him one thing, it was to be brave. He would have to quash any maternal hopes of grandchildren and marriages to a nice local girl; Edmund would become a priest and renounce the pleasures of the flesh forever; he would choose a path which left him beyond reproach.... No other man would capture Edmund's heart ever again like his beautiful Piers had done.

Edmund would devote his life to serving God and make his parents proud, the memory of Piers would live in his heart and in his private journal.

When Edmund first saw the beautiful girl, he later came to know was Phoebe Horwat, kneeling in the cool dark nave of St Saviour's church that fateful Sunday it was like a lightning bolt through his heart. Only Piers Loxley had ever stirred such longing in him before.

Edmund was totally unprepared for the *coupe-de-foudre* which overwhelmed him. For days afterwards he thought of nothing but the beautiful Phoebe Horwat. He obsessed about her soft wavy hair and her golden-brown eyes as he served her the communion cup, he lusted after her pink lips as she opened her mouth to receive the Host and he groaned to possess her body.

It was a kind of madness, and he knew it. He could not understand what had come over him. Never before had the sight of a pretty woman roused such emotions in him.

Certain young men had caught his eye and Piers Loxley had caught his heart, but never had any woman had this intoxicating effect on him. This intense desire to make love to a woman… to Phoebe Horwat, made Edmund question all that which he believed to be true. His mind was in spin… perhaps Phoebe had been the *"cure"* he was looking for.

It troubled him to contemplate the possibility that if he'd met Phoebe earlier, and if he'd never met Piers, then his whole life might have been travelling on a completely different path.

Edmund loved the church and honestly believed he had a vocation to serve. His pledge to God on the battlefield was bearing fruit and he had made his parents proud of him. Now Phoebe, through no fault of her own, had thrown a complete spanner in the whole works.

Phoebe Horwat came into his life like the ultimate temptation when he was least expecting it and Edmund, despite his best efforts, felt powerless to resist her charms. The pull of attraction to this woman intrigued and confused him in equal measure. It was yet another forbidden fruit Edmund was being tempted to try.

As the days and weeks passed Edmund began to question his calling, had he simply been running away and hiding when he took on the mantle of priesthood? Should he have tried harder to make his parents happy by waiting for the right girl to come along… to settle down to a conventional life of hearth and home with a nice girl… a girl like Phoebe Horwat?

Had his entanglement with Piers been born out of fear and loneliness in a battle torn country, or had he genuinely loved the golden boy with the sweet features and seductive rosebud lips?

After much prayer and thought, Edmund knew one thing with absolute certainty…. *For that one brief and perfect moment in time he had indeed loved the glorious Piers Loxley and he would never regret it.*

But Piers was dead, and no other man would ever come close to capturing Edmund's heart like Piers had. Father Edmund had been safe in his vows of celibacy because his heart had been dead to temptation…. He had found it easy to resist what he did not desire…. That was until he met the bewitching Phoebe Horwat.

At first Phoebe resisted him and later he came to question what might have been if she had been impervious to his first tentative approaches to win her heart, if she had had affections for another man who was wooing her, a lover who could have kept her away from him and saved him from his forbidden desires. Part of Edmund wished she had rejected him and saved him from himself, but could he really lay any blame at her feet for returning his advances, or was the fault all his?

It was almost as if Phoebe Horwat was the ultimate test to his priesthood and he had failed it miserably. The bitter irony was that when the scales finally fell from his eyes, and he had found the strength to give her up, to renounce her delicious body, and deny himself the touch of her lips, she had told him about the baby…. *and that changed everything.*

Edmund knew he could live without the joy of sex and the loving embrace of Piers or the seductive charms of Phoebe… but to deny the existence of his own flesh and blood was more than he could bear! Once he knew Phoebe had given birth to his daughter, he felt powerless to resist the call to be a father. The desire to help and watch over the abandoned child in any small way he could was irresistible.

Edmund spent pages in his journal agonizing over his final decision. If Phoebe had kept the baby herself then he might well have found himself in a different situation, but the minute the baby was handed over to the nuns of St Saviours, it was as if providence had placed the chance of keeping contact with this child within his grasp. It was the third and final temptation of Edmund and he failed it miserably.

Later as Edmund lay dying, too sick and weak to write his final words, it struck him that his whole life had been governed by three acts which had tempted him to sin; three acts which had caused him to abandon his vows… and just like St Peter, three times Edmund had failed to be steadfast in his faith when challenged. When the poignant photograph of little Jennifer Prosser arrived with its loving message and endearments from the whole family, it had the same effect as the biblical cock crowing did on St Peter, it was Edmund's wake up call to repent.

As Edmund's last weeks on earth trickled away, like the innumerable winter raindrops on his hospital window, he became agitated and desperate. Edmund knew he must repent and try to make amends, to beg forgiveness for the hurt and wrongs he had inflicted; to atone for his weaknesses.

He couldn't apologise to Piers, but he could apologise to Phoebe for ruining her life.

It would be Edmund's everlasting torment that he would never see his daughter Rita and his two grandchildren ever again and that they might never know who he really was. The nuns at St Saviours' hospital only allowed family to visit the dying in their final days…. *It was no place for a child anyway.*

Edmund knew in order to accomplish his final task of penance; he would have to take his loyal sister Deirdre into his confidence. With Deirdre's help he could die a happier man knowing he had made his peace with Phoebe, the girl he'd wronged all those years ago…. if only Phoebe would agree to see him one last time. He prayed Phoebe would find it within her heart to forgive him for what he'd done.

Edmund's last anguished entry in his journal was…. *Tell Phoebe I'm sorry.*

Chapter 17

Christmas Eve dawned icy cold with leaden skies threatening snow. Outside greasy, damp flagstones had turned into treacherous, slippery black mirrors. Thick frost glittered on the insides of the windows in Inkerman streets causing Betty to shiver and grumble. She turned over in her warm bed, pulled the bedclothes tightly around her chin and snuggled up to the comforting bulk of her husband Gerald snoring gently next to her.

In Wilson road June was racketing about the house like a coiled spring. Tonight, was the church nativity play and most importantly tonight was the night when Father Christmas would be coming down the chimney with a big sack of presents for a good little girl. June was beside herself with joy at the prospect of the exciting day and magical night ahead.

"I'm a good girl Aunty Fee Fee," June lisped when Phoebe came in to get the girl dressed. The pile of ice shavings scraped from inside Ivy and June's bedroom window lay melting in small puddles and told a different story. June stood on the bed looking guilty, the pristine frost inside the windowpane had been too tempting to resist and June's fingers had worked their magic showering the window ledge with rapidly melting frost sparkles. The rumpled and disturbed appearance of the double bed she shared with her Mam spoke of vigorous bouncing.

"Well, that doesn't look very good to me you little monkey," Phoebe tried to suppress a smile, she remembered creating frost pictures when she was a child and her father Pavel had told her off too. June looked crestfallen.

"I think we'd better clean up this mess before Father Christmas sees it *and* before it runs down on to the floor, don't you?" Phoebe raised an eyebrow and gave a mock frown. It was hard to be cross with June for long. For all June's little shortcomings because of her condition, such as the slowness of speech, lisping tongue and clumsy gait she was the sweetest most trusting child you could ever meet, her sunny smile lit up a room and her merry nature meant she found fun in everything.

June scooted off to fetch a bath towel to wipe away the evidence and Phoebe straightened the disturbed bedding.

Ivy was busy downstairs in the kitchen making sage and onion stuffing for the turkey and peeling mounds of vegetables ready for Christmas morning. Ivy had a damp, stained pinafore around her waist and her hair was a frazzled mess. A large, galvanized bucket was filled to the brim with vegetables and cold water to stop the potatoes and parsnips going brown overnight; a heap of sprouts and carrots covered the draining board waiting to be washed for the pot.

There was such a lot to do, a dinner for five was going to be a lot of work, especially if Ivy was to have plenty of vegetables left over for mounds of bubble and squeak on Boxing day, one of Betty's favourites.

The kitchen preparations were in full swing when a loud rapping came on the front door. Ivy's heart gave a small flip when she heard the vigorous knocking, the last time such rapping had heralded the arrival of Deirdre Roberts. *Surely not again?*

"Don't worry, I'll get it, Aunty Phoebe" Ivy shouted up the stairs.

"I'm just coming," Ivy called as she slip-slopped into the hall in a pair of old slippers. She wiped her hands on her grubby pinny and headed for the door…*Who could it be calling on Christmas Eve? It couldn't be the butcher…. Mr Wilson said he would deliver the turkey at midday, and it was only just half past eight.*

Upstairs on the landing, alerted by the knocking, Phoebe stood listening to hear who the visitor could be so early on Christmas Eve morning.

Ivy opened the door cautiously and peered around the edge. She was too scruffy to show her face to the world, her pinny stained from washing and peeling muddy potatoes.

"Billy!" She gasped. Billy Thomas stood on the doorstep with a large bunch of berried holly in his arms and a bagful of presents. He was wrapped up against the frosty morning, with a warm glow on his cheeks from the brisk walk in the crisp morning air. At that moment Ivy thought how handsome he looked.

Ivy was surprised and mortified he'd caught her in such a state, Billy might look a picture of glowing health and scrubbed good looks, but she looked positively grubby and dishevelled in her work clothes.

Upstairs Phoebe smiled; *Billy Thomas was always good news; she would keep June distracted upstairs to give Ivy a few precious moments alone with Billy.*

"Morning Ivy," he grinned.

Ivy opened the front door a little wider. "Goodness me Billy, this is a surprise at this time of day." She hoped it didn't sound as if she wasn't pleased to see him because she was.... but he had caught her on the hop.

"You'd better come inside before all the heat escapes.... And you'll have to excuse all the mess though, as you can imagine we're all in a bit of a state getting ready for the big day tomorrow," Ivy's hands fluttered to smooth down the stained pinafore; she thought of the messy kitchen. She opened the door to let him in.

"I've come bearing gifts, if that helps," he joked.

"Don't be silly... it's lovely to see you Billy, really it is," Ivy relaxed a little, she'd known Billy such a long time, she couldn't worry about him catching her in her scruffy old slippers and work clothes.

"I'll make us a nice, hot cup of tea, you must be frozen out there." Ivy led Billy into the sitting room. Fortunately, she had already riddled and made up the fire, it was always her first job of the morning; the fire was blazing nicely in the grate.

Luckily, it was too early yet for June to have covered the floor with her toys so at least the sitting room wasn't as messy as the rest of the house and the paper chains looping across the ceiling and Christmas cards on the mantlepiece gave the room a festive air.

"Shall I take your coat Billy; you won't feel the benefit else?" Ivy felt oddly nervous having Billy in the house, particularly at this hour. Usually, he said good night on the doorstep if he walked her home, he'd never called uninvited and so early before. Ivy caught a glimpse of herself in the hall mirror and wished she didn't look such a fright.

"Just for a few minutes Ivy, I won't interrupt the preparations for too long, but a nice hot cup of tea would be grand," he handed Ivy his heavy coat and scarf and settled himself on the sofa. "I can't stop too long Ivy because my father wants me to collect the Christmas order. I just wanted to drop these presents and this holly off. I thought it would be better than handing them to you this evening when we all go to the nativity." He placed the bulky bag on the floor.

"Thank you Billy, and I do love a bit of holly in a vase at Christmas time, I'll take this out to the kitchen and get that tea." Billy certainly was thoughtful, if she'd had to carry all those presents her arms would have been aching and June would have been impossibly excited by the prospect of opening them the next day.

Billy planned to go to the church and watch June in her first ever nativity play that evening, June had invited everyone she knew and indeed everyone she met to see her being a pretty, Christmas angel in the play. But he also had something he wanted to say to Ivy, and it wouldn't wait another moment. The idea that he must sit through the hour-long church service before he could speak to Ivy and even then it would be amongst a chattering throng of excited children, was too much to bear.

After his chat with Betty and Gerald, Billy concluded he needed to speak to Ivy on her own and this morning would be his only chance, the presents gave him a good excuse to call on her.

When Ivy came back in with the tea she'd combed her hair and removed her apron, she still felt she looked at less than her best, but Billy would have to take her as he found her.

"Here you are Billy," she handed him the cup, she'd placed a Marie biscuit in the saucer.

"Thanks Ivy," he sipped his tea and took a deep breath and took the plunge.

"Ivy, I've had a long chat with your Mam…."

Ivy's eyebrows shot up… *What business did Billy have talking with Mam?*

"Hear me out Ivy," Billy stilled her. "your Mam has told me everything."

"What do you mean Mam has told you everything?" Ivy spluttered. *What business was it of her mother's?* Ivy's eyes flashed with irritation..

Billy could see she was riled.

"Shh, Ivy, don't go flying off the handle!" He smiled. "I know about you not being able to carry any more babies and I want you to know it makes no difference to me…."

"Well, I'm pleased to hear it, Billy Thomas" Ivy said hotly. *She would be having words with her mother!* She had wanted to tell Billy this secret in her own good time, now it seemed her Mam had jumped the gun and got there first. Mam had no business going behind Ivy's back.

He laughed at her feisty reply, "what I wanted to say Ivy… before you interrupted me is… that makes no difference to me because.. because I want to ask you to marry me anyway. I love you Ivy and I want you to be my wife."

102

"Oh…" Ivy's mouth formed into a small "o," the wind had been knocked completely out of her sails.

Billy sank down on one knee, "Ivy… will you do me the honour of becoming my wife?"

He looked up at her beautiful face, a small, muddy smudge streaked on her cheek where she had pushed her hair away in the kitchen as she peeled potatoes, to him she looked beyond beautiful.

"I…."

"Please say you will Ivy, I love you and I love June. I would be proud to call you my wife and to call June my daughter." Billy held her hand as if he never wanted to let her go.

"Please say yes!" He looked at her expectantly willing her to accept him.

At that moment June came hurtling into the sitting room.

Phoebe could not contain the excited child any longer and June came rushing downstairs to see her favourite Uncle Billy.

June was surprised to see Uncle Billy kneeling on the floor; he did look funny.

"Hello Uncle Billy!" June laughed and jumped on Billy's knee. She threw her arms around his neck.

Billy and Ivy burst into laughter; the romantic moment completely lost.

Billy raised a questioning eyebrow; he wasn't going to let Ivy escape without giving him an answer.

"Yes Billy, I'll marry you," Ivy smiled, her eyes starting to brim with tears. Billy was a wonderful man and now he knew her secret he would be marrying her with his eyes open and she loved him for it.

Billy smiled with delight. He gave June a big kiss and a hug. "I can't wait to see this beautiful little girl tonight as a Christmas angel."

June beamed with delight.

Ivy had agreed to marry him and now June was going to be his daughter and Billy couldn't be happier. "I love you," he mouthed at Ivy. It was not quite the proposal he had imagined but it was perfect none the less, he had the answer he wanted…. Ivy was going to be his wife.

"And now I'd better leave your Mam to get on with all her jobs or else she'll be telling me off and I'll be on Father Christmas's naughty list." Billy pulled mock pout.

"I'm a good girl, Uncle Billy." June said earnestly.

"Of course, you are my precious…. the very best."

Chapter 18

Sean and Eileen were preparing to spend their first Christmas in their new home in Wilson Road. A few sticks of mismatched furniture filled the sitting room and a potted Christmas tree stood proudly in the sitting room window, presenting a joyful face to the world. Eileen had decorated the tiny spruce with great care, wreathes of sparkling tinsel glistened in the reflections of the windowpanes of the small bay window. Their first ever Christmas tree!

Sean watched proudly as his wife added the gauzy Christmas fairy to the top of the tree.

"It's perfect, just like you," Sean declared an easy smile on his face, only the slightest droop on the left-hand side of his mouth remained now. He wished he could do more to help Eileen about the house but since his accident on the East quay when the flailing hawser nearly robbed him of his life, he had to take things easy and build his stamina up.

Sean was determined to give thanks for every day of good health he had. Slowly but surely things were improving, and his wife Eileen gave him cause to hope the best was still yet to come. Walking shakily with a stick was a small price to pay; at least he still had the use of his legs and bit by bit his strength was improving so perhaps Eileen was right to be hopeful; after all he'd proved the hospital doctors wrong on many an occasion.

"You old charmer you." Eileen grinned, her green eyes flashing with merriment. To Eileen every day they had together was a blessed miracle. In the quayside tragedy which claimed two lives and injured many more, Sean had nearly died. She thanked God every day he'd been spared. His recovery might be slow, but she could see a little progress every day and it gave her cause to hope.

 Sean had suffered a stroke and it left him with partial paralysis in one of his legs, the other leg had made an almost full recovery but was still weakened. Months of physiotherapy meant he could walk again, but most importantly, they had discovered, much to Eileen's joy, he could make love to her.

When Eileen married Sean in the chapel of Rookwood Hospital four years ago, she had meant every word of her marriage vows… even if Sean had remained bed bound with slurring speech, needing help with washing, and feeding for the rest of his life, she would have married him anyway.

Eileen loved Sean beyond life and every day they had together she counted her blessings; if they could be blessed with a baby, then she would consider herself to be the luckiest woman on earth. For the first difficult years of their marriage when they rattled from hospital appointment to hospital appointment, the doctors warned her Sean's recovery may have stalled, that he may never recover enough sensation to make love to his wife. Eileen had taken the news in her stride and had continued to hope and pray for a better outcome.

And the doctors *were* proved wrong, at first it had been an impossible dream but now Sean was recovering his strength bit by bit and Eileen dared to hope the impossible dream might become a reality… one day they might have the child they both so desperately longed for.

"What time is your mother arriving today?" Sean had grown enormously fond of Ida, Eileen's generous, but bossy, mother. The feisty, good-hearted woman, *a pocket battleship,* as Sean once described her, had been their rock during his long recovery. Widow Ida Murphy had opened her heart and her home in Adeline street to the young couple when Sean finally left Rookwood hospital.

 When the stairs in Eileen's family's home proved impossible for Sean to climb, the couple had commandeered her tiny sitting room with their bed jammed up against the wall. Ida Murphy's home had become their home for nearly a year whilst they waited to be allocated a council bungalow on the burgeoning Ely estate, and Ida had never grumbled about it; not once.

Sean was delighted to be having his mother-in-law come to stay for Christmas in their new home… *I never thought I'd be looking forward to having a mother-in-law stay for Christmas but in Ida's case it's the truth.* Sean chuckled to himself.

"She will be here by two o'clock Sean, if the bus isn't late, you know how unreliable the buses are at this time of year." Eileen sat on the floor packing the last few presents to go under the tree. In her typical organised fashion Eileen was calmly finishing off the preparations and then all would be ready for a perfect Christmas day.

The plump capon was sitting in the larder, with a tasty thyme and parsley stuffing tucked in the crop; the giblets had been simmering all morning to make a rich stock for tomorrow's gravy and all the vegetables were clean and prepared ready to pop in the pan on Christmas morning.

Sean was proud of his gorgeous, capable wife; Eileen had stood by him when many others had drifted away. Fair weather friends like Jimmy Benson had just melted away, especially after Jimmy had moved to Ely into a nice new two bedroomed house. *Just like the one Sean and Eileen had hoped for before the accident happened.*

It had always irked Sean that Jimmy had pinched his idea to make the move away from Tiger Bay onto the new Taff Ely development, it had galled him even more when Jimmy's visits with his good friend Jack "Cappy" Thomas had dwindled away to nothing. Only Cappy had proved to be a true friend in those dark months when he lay useless and hopeless; a prisoner in his hospital bed..

But when Cappy told him all about Jimmy's disgusting trade in mucky photographs and subsequent arrest, Sean reckoned he'd had a lucky escape from Jimmy Benson. He didn't want his good name associated with the likes of a man like that. He'd been surprised to hear that if Jimmy hadn't been arrested and then topped himself in the Cardiff remand centre, he and Eileen might have been living only a few doors away from him and Ivy in Wilson road.

It certainly was a funny old world.

"I do hope that Deirdre woman I met at church found Phoebe Horwat," Eileen said as she wrote gift tags to go on the presents. "It was rather strange, she was asking all around for Phoebe Horwat, saying it was urgent she found her. I wonder what it was all about?"

"I remember a Phoebe Horwat," Sean said as he scoured his memory. "She used to hang around the wharfs in Tiger Bay, turning tricks. She was a nice-looking woman in her day, I often wondered why she ended up in Tiger Bay." Sean remembered the popular, buxom, brown-eyed lass who frequented the dockland pubs.

"Well, she's living at the bottom end of Wilson road now with Ivy Benson, apparently she's Ivy's aunt…. It's certainly a small world." Eileen mused. Since moving into the bungalow Eileen had met quite a few of the neighbours and she'd grown particularly fond of gossipy, Norah Ashworth who lived at number 7 opposite the Benson household.

Norah and her troupe of four noisy boisterous children had welcomed Eileen into the street with open arms. Norah's pretty, young daughter Karen hid shyly behind her mother's skirts as the two women gossiped in the street. It was obvious from Norah's rounded abdomen the woman was expecting another baby.

"When's your next baby due Norah," Eileen envied the woman's good fortune in having such a large family. Eileen's Irish Catholic roots meant large, chaotic families were ten a penny, now Eileen would settle for just the one child to call her own, if God ever saw fit to bless them with a baby.

"Whist!" Norah blew through her teeth. "Sometime in March if midwife Marion Spears is to be believed… but I reckon it might be before then though. I vowed not to have any more after little Karen was born, but my Jack just sort of catches me unawares." Norah rolled her eyes. "I'm crossing my fingers for another girl though, 'cos I don't reckon I can squeeze another boy into that back bedroom, they're like sardines in there as it is." Norah guffawed.

"Just remember Eileen, if there is anything you need just knock, and if you need my Jack to help you with anything just knock the door and ask, he won't mind… I could do with keeping him busy." Norah joked and patted her sizable bump. "Seriously though, we are only down the road if you need any help at all." Nothing escaped Norah's eagle-eyed gaze and she had seen Eileen's husband walking with a stick.

"Thank you Norah, it's very kind of you to offer." Eileen knew Norah meant well, and she might well need a man to call on if ever there was any heavy lifting to do.

"Well, I must be off I've a hundred and one jobs to do today… I hate Christmas Eve! I could do with a troop of those bloody Elves to help out in our house, I can tell you… what with all this lot to look after and the next baby keeping me awake half the night kicking like a rugby player." Norah ruffled Gareth's curly mop.

"And to top it off my eldest lad Lenny seems to be coming down with one of those winter colds that's doing the rounds, he's not been himself for a few days now. Poor lad he's all coughs and sniffles and as sure as eggs is eggs, I bet we all go down with it over the Christmas…. Gareth will you stop doing that!" Norah yelled as Gareth excavated a sizable snotty lump from his nose and wiped it on his shorts. Norah cuffed the lad gently around the ears. "Honestly, kids! There's always something to worry about, the last thing I need is a load of snotty noses and more washing… as if I haven't got enough on my plate as it is!" Norah rolled her eyes, as if to say *a woman's work was never done.*

Eileen could only look on enviously as the bouncy, motherly woman marshalled her children like a mother hen gathers its chicks together. Steering Gareth around a muddy frozen puddle which invited jumping on and taking Karen by the hand, Norah headed for home to tackle the mountain of Christmas chores.

One day, God willing that might be me, Eileen mused as she watched little Karen Ashworth trotting dutifully by her mother's side.

Eileen was determined to have a merry Christmas come what may and then hopefully in the New Year there might be a baby of their own. She would give anything to be a flustered mother of a large gaggle of healthy, lively children just like her neighbour Norah.

Chapter 19

The St Paul's Christmas Eve nativity tableau was a triumph. The sight of Joseph and Mary sitting on a hay bale surrounded by the glittering hordes of angels and the shepherds wearing tea cloths on their heads, brought tears to the eyes of all the proud parents in the congregation and the fact that Mary held the Jesus baby-doll upside down for most of the play only added to the smiles fluttering over happy faces in the audience.

June was so excited to be centre stage; she waved enthusiastically to everyone she knew for the entire performance including Father Malone. June was having a marvellous time, trying to catch the eye of Nanna Betty, Bampa Gag, Aunty Phoebe, Mam and Uncle Billy, whilst all the other angels were holding their hands together in prayer as instructed, June was waving merrily to the entire congregation.

Billy sat next to Ivy during the carol service and discreetly held her hand; they were both as proud as punch to see June joining in with the rest of the children at the altar. Thanks to Father Malone, June was treated just the same as every other child in his flock; she proudly took her place with all the other girls and boys from the Sunday school class.

Billy and Ivy decided to wait a while before announcing their engagement and before telling June she was going to have a new Daddy; a Daddy who would love her and be kind to her, not a father like Jimmy Benson, the man who had rejected her because she was different and had labelled her a *useless retard*. But for now, their engagement would be kept a secret.

Of course, her Mam and Gerald knew about the engagement proposal, and Ivy had told Aunty Phoebe... how could she not tell her Aunty Phoebe and Billy had promised he would tell his parents on Boxing day, *he didn't want to say the announcement might spoil their Christmas day, but Billy was under no illusions they would welcome his beloved Ivy enthusiastically with open arms, and he wasn't too sure they would be thrilled to have June as a granddaughter either, but he was happy with his choice and that was all what mattered.*

So, it was agreed the engagement would be kept a secret until new year's Eve when Billy would slip a ring of Ivy's choice on her finger and then the whole world could know that Ivy

Bensons would become Mrs Billy Thomas in the New Year. Billy wanted to marry Ivy as soon as possible; they decided to plan for a Spring wedding when the weather was kinder.

At night Ivy hugged herself with excitement, her wedding to Jimmy had been such a miserable, glum affair, this time their marriage would be a joyous and fun occasion and she could hardly wait to tell her friend Norah her good news.

Phoebe couldn't hold back the tears as she watched all the little girls sat in the flickering candlelight of St Paul's, sweet, angelic faces adoringly playing their part in the tableau. It struck her to the core that, yet another happy event was being denied her; she did wonder if her own little granddaughter Jennifer Prosser was playing some part in a church hall somewhere at the very moment she was sat in St Paul's watching June, and if she was, then Phoebe would never know about it. The hurt of years of exclusion threatened to overwhelm her, Phoebe sniffed quietly into her handkerchief.

After Christmas Phoebe would have some very tricky decisions to make if she was ever to have contact with her own flesh and blood. Edmund had connived to have a relationship with his daughter Rita and his grandchildren… would it be possible for her to do the same?

Phoebe also knew the engagement of Billy and Ivy would cause some decisions to be made which would inevitably affect her too in the coming months. Next year was going to be a year of change and challenge of that Phoebe could be certain, she could only pray it would all turn out for the best.

"Are you all right Aunty Phoebe," Ivy whispered anxiously, as she noticed Phoebe dabbing her eyes with an enormous handkerchief.

"Yes I'm fine thank you luvvie," she squeezed Ivy's free hand, "don't you go worrying about me, I'm just a little tired and it's so moving to see all these precious children, including our June, looking so happy… and I'm happy too, really I am." Phoebe sniffed.

With that Phoebe blew her nose loudly; Ivy got a fit of the giggles.

"I'd hate to see you unhappy then," Ivy whispered loudly and stifled a laugh.

The woman in front turned around and glared over her shoulder at the noisy offenders sitting behind her, "Shh!... some of us are trying to listen!"

"That went well Ivy," Phoebe said softly as she carried an exhausted June upstairs to bed. "It looks like June is dog tired with all the waving and jigging up and down she did in church. I think she must be the friendliest angel St Paul's has ever seen," Phoebe smiled and kissed the dozing child's head. Soon she would find June too heavy to carry like this, the weight of the child pulled on her back, Phoebe was feeling her age.

"At least she should sleep tonight though," Ivy said gratefully. June had had such a busy Christmas Eve, she had no energy to fight sleep in the hope of spotting Father Christmas, even the thought of flying reindeer couldn't stop June's eyes from fluttering asleep.

"Fingers crossed we get past six o'clock tomorrow morning then," Phoebe said with a grin as she laid June on the bed. "Don't send her in to me before then unless she's coming in with a nice cup of tea," Phoebe joked.

In the little two bedroomed house Ivy and June shared the bigger room and Phoebe had the smaller bedroom to herself, it had not escaped Phoebe's notice that things were about to change when Ivy and Billy tied the knot in the Spring.

Christmas day disappeared in a blur of tinsel, mountains of succulent turkey and a sea of wrapping paper. The four walls of the little house rang with laughter and merriment and outside in the street troupes of children ran up and down the road playing noisily with new skipping ropes, roller skates and foot balls until creeping darkness and calls for supper drove them indoors.

For Ivy it was the most perfect Christmas day she could have hoped for. The roast turkey was pronounced a triumph and June revelled in playing with Aunty Phoebe, Nanna and Bampa Gag all afternoon. June had the contents of all the crackers and magically she even found the lucky three-penny bit in her portion of pudding.

June so wanted to join in the fun outside the house with all the other older children running up and down, playing tag and letting off steam, but Ivy wouldn't relent June was staying indoors. The older children in the street weren't always as kind to June as they should be, and besides, June's special friend Karen Ashworth wasn't outside playing with her brothers either.

"You can play with Karen tomorrow luvvie, there will be plenty of time on Boxing day to show Karen all the presents Father Christmas brought. You can put your play clothes on after breakfast, and then you can go and knock her door tomorrow morning. It's best to stay indoors with Nanna and Bampa today." Ivy wanted this to be a special family Christmas, just the five of them, so June stayed inside in her best new dress and party shoes.

As usual the Ashworth children were amongst the last to leave when Jack Ashworth hauled his sons George and Gareth indoors for their supper; Lenny was noticeable by his absence.

By five o'clock the last of the stragglers had left and street was dark and silent.

*

"Measles!"

Jack Ashworth had knocked the door loudly on Boxing day morning, with an impatient triple rap.

Ivy could see through the sitting room window it was Jack calling because for some strange reason after knocking the door he went to stand at the end of the front garden path and waited. Ivy opened the door still clutching her dressing gown around her middle to find out what was going on.

"Did you say your Lenny's got a dose of the Measles!" Ivy gasped.

"Yes Ivy love, that's why I'm stood here, just to be on the safe side. I'm under strict instructions from Norah to stand well clear of all the front doors when I let people know." Jack explained.

When Lenny received the diagnosis of Measles on Christmas night, all the Ashworth family could do was make sure that the friends and neighbours in the surrounding houses were warned to expect the infection. Norah insisted Jack let the neighbours know about the virus affecting the Ashworth household.

Ivy secretly thanked her lucky stars June hadn't been playing outside with all the other children in the streets yesterday. Troupes of excitable kids chasing up and down, playing tag had all been in contact with the Ashworth lads. Perhaps June had a lucky escape on Christmas night.

"Norah reckons it's just a matter of time and all our others will get it too, an' if they do it's going to be bloody awful having four sick children in the house I can tell you... luckily I had it when I was a kiddy, so I reckon I'm safe enough," Jack said thoughtfully. "My Norah doesn't remember ever having it as a child, so we aren't sure if she's going to get it an' all. Lenny is that poorly, the little blighter is miserable with it."

"I'm really sorry to hear it Jack I do hope Norah isn't affected.... Is Lenny going to be all right, do you think?"

"We hope so, when Doctor Mason saw him last night the poor kid was plastered in a hot, red rash, all over his body it was; there wasn't a square inch that wasn't covered with it. The doctor said the crisis point was almost over though and said to keep Lenny cool and to put some calamine on it. It turns out Lenny never had a cold at all, like we thought he did. It was this bloody Measles all along causing the coughs and sniffles; he was at his most infectious in the few days running up to Christmas... coughing and sneezing all over the place he was.... Sure, as eggs is eggs the others are bound to get it." Jack grumbled.

Ivy tried to wrack her brains and remember when she last had any contact with Norah or other members of the Ashworth family in the run up to Christmas. "So how long before you know if you've caught it?" Ivy asked, anxious to get some information.

"I don't know exactly Ivy, but Dr Mason said we all might be carrying it and not know it and it can be days before the symptoms show themselves... So, all we can do now is wait and see what happens. We should all know for certain in the next few days if we've got any more infections, but until then we're keeping all our kids indoors." Jack rolled his eyes as if to say what a trial that would be to have three lively children rattling about the house waiting to see if they went down with the Measles.

Ivy looked worried, *perhaps she couldn't be certain for a few days yet if June had caught it or not?*

"Our Lenny sleeps head to toe with his little brother Gareth and in the same room as George so it's a racing certainty they are all going to get it, we can only hope it's not too bad... I just hope my Norah doesn't go down with it, especially with her expecting the baby. Dr Mason said adults often suffer more than the kids do when they get it, so I'm on duty with the kids until we are all out of the woods." Jack said ruefully.

"I'm really sorry to hear that Jack, let me know if I can do anything to help." Ivy could see Jack looked tired and worried.

"Thanks Ivy…. Anyway, I'd best be off. I'm under strict instructions from Norah to tell all the boys' friends to be on the lookout for this bloody Measles! Still, it's one way of spending my Boxing day going for a long walk all around the housing estate, I reckon this is going to take me most of the morning before I'm done!"

When Ivy shut the front door, her mind was running in circles, poor Norah!

The Ashworth family was so popular, all the local kids traipsed in and out of the Ashworth house on an almost daily basis and now this!

 If the Measles was half as infectious as Jack said it was, then heaps of unsuspecting families would now have the infection incubating in their homes. Jack said all anybody could do now was wait and see, the damage was already done, and nothing could stop you getting it if you had contact with the virus.

Ivy had planned to visit her Da in Porthcawl the day after Boxing day. She had promised to take June with her to visit James for the first time…. Would it be fair to take June down to see her new Grandad now if Ivy knew she might be carrying the measles infection with her?

Ivy knew her Da had poor health and weak lungs after his gas attack in the trenches; a dose of the measles might prove more than weakened his system could cope with if June was infected.

"What's up Ivy? I heard you talking to Jack Ashworth, is there a problem?" Phoebe pottered into the sitting room with a cup of tea in one hand and a slab of toast and butter in the other.

"Jack said Lenny has got a raging dose of the measles, and Dr Mason has said the lad's probably been infectious for days." Ivy looked worried. "Thank heavens I didn't let June go playing out in the street last night…but Karen was over here the day before Christmas Eve so we might have caught it from her. What are we going to do Phoebe?"

"I don't think there is anything you can do except cross your fingers and hope that June isn't going down with it." Phoebe said sagely. "I know you had it as a nipper and so did I so we should be all right, but it's pretty nasty if you get it as an adult, so I'm told." Phoebe added.

"That's exactly what Jack said Dr Mason told him. Jack said Norah doesn't know if she's had it so he's worried she might get it from Lenny."

"And Norah is pregnant too…. That is bad news Ivy. I've heard measles can cause all sorts of problems if a pregnant woman catches it." Phoebe said sadly. "Let's hope and pray Norah isn't infected."

"So, Aunty Phoebe, what do you think about me taking June to Porthcawl tomorrow to see my Da?"

"I'd almost forgotten about it Ivy… But you can't still think of going can you? I don't think you'd forgive yourself if you gave your father a dose of the Measles would you?"

"I know you're right Phoebe, but he'll be expecting us. He'll be so disappointed if no-one turns up to see him, and how can I tell him I'm not going?"

"How about I go instead Ivy and let him know what is going on and then you go next weekend after the risk of infection has passed. That way he won't be left in the dark wondering why you and June just didn't turn up and I won't be risking his health like a visit from June might." Phoebe secretly thought having a few hours to chat to James Pugh on her own might prove to her advantage as well.

"You could always write him a letter letting him know the news of your engagement to Billy and I could take it with me?…. I could even read it to him if he needed me to." Phoebe offered.

Ivy could see that it was an imperfect solution, but Phoebe was right, she would never forgive herself if she took the wretched infection down to her father James… and there were all the other passengers on the Porthcawl bus to think about as well.

"Would you Phoebe? It would be such a weight off my mind if you went instead. I would hate to let him down after I promised I'd go to see him and at least if June suddenly starts to go down with it she will be safe here at home." Ivy said gratefully.

So, it was agreed Phoebe would go to Porthcawl the next day to see James, whilst Ivy stayed at home with June.

Upstairs June started to wake up from a restless sleep; she had a headache, her eyes itched, and her nose was running. "Mam….mameee!" she wailed.

116

Chapter 20

Deirdre spent the quietest Christmas she could ever recall; the curtains were kept closed and she shut herself away from the world, cheerful tinsel and glittery decorations would not appear in the Roberts' home this year. She didn't even go to church, the very thought of people asking her how she was, filled her with dread.

She hoped people would assume it was the grief over losing her brother which caused her to shun the festive season and lock herself away, only she knew it was the enormity of Edmund's sin crushing the life out of her and bathing her in shame keeping her a prisoner in her own home.

Of course, the Prosser family kindly invited her to join them for Christmas dinner, for fun and jollity with games and laughter, but Deirdre couldn't stomach the deception; she made her excuses and sat home alone. Deirdre couldn't possibly sit opposite Rita and the children knowing what she knew, it was a huge, guilty secret chewing away at her, denying her sleep, and torturing her soul.

Deirdre felt worse as each day passed, she became convinced she wore a shifty underhand look on her face obvious for all to see, as if Edmund's stain was somehow seeping through her skin and branding her a liar. Unable to face the world Deirdre kept to herself as much as possible. She had, of necessity seen Rita several times since Edmund's death, little thoughtful gifts of cake and home-made tart were sent round with Jennifer obliging Deirdre to return the plate and stop a moment for a chat. Each brief meeting felt like a sharp pebble stuck in her shoe and she couldn't get away quick enough to stop the pain.

Frank brought around bunch of Christmas holly to cheer the room, but Deirdre didn't want cheering; she wanted peace of mind and to know if she would find peace in her soul ever again. She couldn't see how it could be possible to rest whilst she lived next door to Edmund's illegitimate child and maintained the lie. She knew the ugly truth and it was suffocating her.

On Boxing day Deirdre accepted a plate of sliced cold turkey so as not to hurt Rita's feelings but Deirdre's heart just wasn't in it. When Deirdre made herself some sandwiches the meat turned to dust in her mouth; she surreptitiously gave the leftovers to the skinny black cat from two houses away when it visited her garden.

Until the funeral was over Deirdre felt she could not swallow another morsel, food was simply a reminder of all she had lost. All her family was dead and her darling girl who called her Aunty must be a stranger to her too. Protecting Rita from hurt was more important than any desire Deirdre had to still be involved in the woman's life. Deirdre had experienced the joy of Rita's childhood, and nobody could ever take that away from her, but it was a small crumb of comfort for the dark times looming ahead.

It was decided with Phoebe that Deirdre was to be kept completely out of the picture from now on. If ever Phoebe told Rita the story then Deirdre's name was not to be in it. She couldn't bear Rita thinking badly of her, thinking that somehow Deirdre been complicit in the lie.

Deidre's ignorance of her brother's deception had been absolute up until the very end when Edmund confessed; Phoebe promised it would always remain that way, Deirdre was in no way to blame. Deirdre never colluded with Edmund in this appalling deceit to plant his child in a cuckoo's nest of his own choosing and she would never admit to knowing the truth, even if it was only for a few days. And if Phoebe never told Rita the truth, then Edmund's secret would go with Deirdre to her grave.

Rita was quite worried about her Aunty Dee Dee, she felt sure that Uncle Edmund's funeral must be preying on her mind and what the kindly old neighbour really needed was cheering up, not lots of time to think and brood on her own, locked away with the curtains closed. Rita had even offered to do the post funeral sandwiches, but Deirdre was having none of it.

Desperate to avoid a large gathering Deirdre had lied and said Edmund didn't approve of such things. The funeral would be a simple farewell at St Saviour's chapel and that was all. There would be no wake or post funeral fuss, no mourners back to the house.

Deirdre could not face the thought of countless platitudes and kind words said over cups of tea and cake about a man who she knew to be a consummate liar and a cheat. She hated the idea that men of God who wore the cloth might come to her home, shake her hand and pass on their condolences whilst at the same time they may, have helped Edmund conceal his sin and been party to the ruin of a naïve young woman whose only crime was to have loved her brother.

Deirdre's ultimate punishment was that she knew she must keep her lips sealed; she could never unburden her soul without destroying her brother's reputation or the Prosser family in the process.

As each day passed it became clear to Deirdre she ought to move away from Alma road. Any more than that Deirdre had not yet decided, but the idea that she could see Rita Prosser every day and keep Edmund's secret was like acid on her skin, burning away at her until she felt certain if she didn't do something to put some distance between herself and her neighbours then she would go utterly mad.

When their parents died, they left the house in equal shares to Deirdre and Edmund with Deirdre having the right to live there for the rest of her natural life. Now that her brother was dead she believed the house was all hers, but was it? Who knows what Edmund might have done with his portion in his will?

Deirdre knew Edmund *had* left a will and she would not rest until she knew what he had done about his possessions, including his share of the family home. A small, tormenting voice told her that maybe Edmund had somehow left her in the lurch in his will, and it gave her the horrors. *Who knew what Edmund was capable of?*

Deirdre resolved that once the will was read on the day after his funeral she would come to a decision about her future, a future which looked increasingly likely to be somewhere far away from her old family home in Alma road.

"You can't expect Deirdre to be the life and soul of the party when she hasn't even buried her brother yet, the woman has still got all her curtains closed for heaven's sake, just leave her be Rita" George chided irritably. He felt his wife's constant fretting over their elderly neighbour might be getting on Deirdre's nerves. "Just give her a while to grieve Rita, don't go bothering her every five minutes, I'm sure she'll come around once the funeral is out of the way. She knows you've offered to help, now leave it at that!" George harumphed, it was getting on his nerves too, if the truth be told.

"All I'm saying is that it's not like her to be reclusive. You know what Deirdre's like, always taking an interest in other people, wanting to be involved. I felt sure she would have come for Christmas dinner and join in a bit of fun... it's just not like her *that's all* I'm saying, and

119

it worries me!" Rita snapped and then flounced into the kitchen irritated by George's interference.

George tutted loudly and went back to reading the paper, he had no idea where his wife got her quick temper and sharp tongue from, her mother Phyllis had always been such a sweet natured woman and her father Frank senior never raised his voice, Rita could be a veritable spitfire when the mood was on her.

Women he would never understand them!

*

Deirdre decided she would take a bus trip to Porthcawl for the day. It would pass the time before Edmund's funeral, and it might soothe her heart to escape the daily sight of Rita Prosser trying to cheer her up.

It was a long time since Deirdre had last gone to the seaside; she fancied blowing the cobwebs away with some bracing sea air. It had niggled away at the back of Deirdre's mind that her mother and father had been particularly fond of Porthcawl; there had even been some talk of her parents moving to the little town a few years back before they got too elderly, but Edmund had talked them out of it.

Now she knew the real reason for Edmund's concerns; he wasn't worried Mam and Da might be lonely leaving long standing friends and neighbours behind if they moved, he *knew* that they would be leaving their granddaughter Rita behind, and more importantly, he wouldn't have a convenient excuse to see his daughter when he visited his parents in Alma road.

Edmund's treachery and deceit knew no bounds.

Deirdre thought a brisk walk along the promenade would help lift her spirits and clear her mind. A change of scene might do her some good. She hadn't anticipated bumping into Phoebe Horwat returning from her mission to deliver Ivy's letter to James Pugh.

"Well fancy bumping into you Deirdre, this is a surprise," Phoebe gasped. Phoebe could see poor Deirdre Roberts looked run down and fragile as if she had all the cares of the world on her slight shoulders, always a slim woman, Deirdre now looked positively scrawny. Phoebe was shocked to see the deterioration in the poor woman in such a short time.

Deirdre on the other hand, was relieved to see Phoebe Horwat on the promenade. Phoebe was the *one* person in the world who knew her secret, the one person she could talk to openly and honestly. "I could say the same," Deirdre half managed a grin. "Hello Phoebe… it certainly is a small world."

"Shall we have a cup of tea; I could do with a sit down before I head back to the bus station, my bus doesn't go for an hour yet, but I've finished my business here." Phoebe gestured to the small beach side café. The café had opened its doors in the hope that day trippers might be walking off the Christmas festivities and need a cup of tea. The two women headed inside.

Deirdre was intrigued to hear Phoebe had *business* in Porthcawl. Over tea and biscuits Phoebe explained about Ivy's father living the quiet life in Porthcawl and how he'd hoped to see Ivy, but the measles outbreak in Wilson road had put a stop to the visit.

"So, you see Deirdre I'm just acting as messenger, and getting a bit of fresh air whilst I'm at it,." Phoebe sipped her tea; she didn't mention she'd had a long chat with James to quash any vain hopes about encouraging Ivy to consider a move to Porthcawl. Phoebe couldn't allow Ivy to be prevented from finding happiness with Billy Thomas just because James Pugh was lonely.

"He's a nice man James but intensely lonely, what with his poor eyesight and his Mam and Da both passed away. He only came to Porthcawl with his mother for the sake of his health, he'd such a dreadful time in the War with the gas attack. Now his neighbour Gwynneth has had a stroke gone into a nursing home, so he's feeling a bit lost without anybody to keep an eye out for him. He's only got his dog Nero for company." Phoebe mused. "I think he really misses old Gwyneth popping in and out for a chat and a cuppa."

Deirdre's ears pricked up; she always hated the thought of a poor soul in need, especially since the man was obviously paying the price of serving his country. "That is a shame, where does James live?"

"He's got a nice bungalow at the far end of the esplanade, it's only a few hundred yards from here, and for some reason it's got a bright green, tiled roof," Phoebe chuckled, "It certainly stands out from the crowd!"

Intrigued, Deirdre thought she might take a stroll to see the end of the esplanade and pier, she wasn't in any rush to go home.

"Personally, I prefer his neighbour Gwyneth's little bungalow, of course it's up for rent now she's gone into a home, but I shouldn't imagine it will hang around too long. It's got the most glorious view of the sea from several aspects…. Winter is never a good time to let a house, but on a sunny day that view must look a rare treat from Gwyneth's sitting room window."

Phoebe checked her watch. "I'd best be off Deirdre, my bus back to Cardiff will be leaving soon and I don't want to miss it." Phoebe clasped the sad woman's hand, "good luck with the funeral tomorrow, I'll be thinking of you." Phoebe said kindly.

Phoebe didn't bear Deirdre Roberts any ill will, she could see the poor woman was suffering for the sins of her brother, it wasn't her fault so many lives had been messed up by the conniving Father Edmund.

Deirdre strolled slowly along the blustery promenade lost in her thoughts. She cut a lonely figure as she headed towards Ty Gwyrdd the squat little bungalow with the distinctive green roof. Inside Deirdre's head thoughts were whirling around; the vaguest outline of a plan was beginning to form, and it ignited a spark within her.

Maybe the hand of fate caused her to impulsively take a trip to Porthcawl that day and to learn about this little bungalow by the sea lying empty; perhaps this was where she was meant to be. Meeting Phoebe Horwat had certainly been providential. God did move in mysterious ways. Phoebe mused.

Deirdre saw a bright green roof in the distance, a solitary figure seemed to be keeping watch out of the bay window, *it must be James Pugh.*

Deirdre headed towards the white rendered bungalow belonging to his neighbour Gwyneth, a sign saying "Cartref" was fixed to the gate. She slipped through the gate and went up the front path. All the curtains were half drawn and in the front window of the bungalow an Estate agent's notice advertised, "House-To Let."

Deirdre tried to sneak a glimpse of the interior through the windows, what she could see of the simple organised rooms pleased her. She let herself through the side gate and walked around the side of the house to find the small garden neatly laid out with flower beds and a circular lawn boasting a sun dial. Even in winter, thanks to the mild coastal air, some of the shrubs were already showing signs of springing into life. The heady, musky scent of a small Daphne bush blooming in the bed by the French window stirred her senses.

In Alma road there was only small yard, it couldn't really be called a proper garden, there was barely space for a few bushes let alone a lawn. Here, she could grow flowers, and maybe even get a cat for company; she had always wanted a ginger cat. Perhaps she could dare to dream and hope again if she made a new start here in Porthcawl?

Deirdre felt her spirits lift, and just at that moment, the winter sun broke through the low grey clouds, and shards of sunlight kissed the bay. The glittering sea and the sparkling waves spoke to Deirdre's, heart, and she knew then, this *was* where she was destined to be. She *would* move to Porthcawl.

Deirdre didn't know the contents of her brother's will yet, but she did know she could afford to rent this tiny bungalow with the perfect view and a neighbour who would welcome companionship. She would have a new start and leave the house in Alma road for another family to enjoy. She felt "Cartref" was waiting for her.

Deirdre went back to the front of the property and made a note of the Agent who was managing the letting, she decided to contact them immediately to express her interest in renting the house.

Deirdre had made her decision; she was moving away from Alma road for a new life in Porthcawl and nothing would dissuade her. She knew it wouldn't be all plain sailing but at least here she would not have to live a lie every day of her life, she wouldn't have to scurry about avoiding her neighbours because she couldn't bear to look them in the face. Of course, she could see Rita and her family if ever she visited Cardiff, but at least she wouldn't be living her life in the shadow of Edmund's deceit.

It was as if the weight of the world she had been carrying since Edmund's confession, had suddenly slipped off Deirdre's shoulders and she felt more like her old self again. For the first time in weeks, she felt a sense of purpose.

Deirdre headed home. She vowed to put her plan into action as soon as Edmund's funeral was over and done with. Only one more dreadful day to be endured, before she could start the rest of her life.

Chapter 21

The day of Edmund's funeral dawned crisp and bright. Annoyingly for Deirdre, it was being ascribed by goodhearted mourners to God smiling on Father Edmund, several even observed that God in his heaven had blessed the funeral morning with such cloudless blue skies for one of his servants.

What tosh and rubbish, Deirdre muttered mutinously under her breath, *if only people knew the truth of the matter?*

Deirdre took a moment to imagine how glorious the sea front in Porthcawl must look today under bright blue skies, with winter sunlight reflecting off the water. The delightful picture in her mind lifted her spirits; the tranquil image would sustain her through the difficult day. Soon it would be *her* view in about six weeks' time if everything went to plan. She would no longer look out of her sitting room window onto a dreary, paved Cardiff street she would see the vast and glorious bay stretching ahead for miles into the distance.

Now that her mind was made up she thought about the little house by the sea constantly. In her mind's eye Deirdre had already planted some spring daffodils in the pots standing empty by the front door, she imagined colourful summer geraniums and cheerful lobelia planted in the flower beds.

The letting Agents had been surprised to get an enquiry about a seaside bungalow on a grey, late December day, they had warned Gwyneth's family that they might have to wait until the springtime to find a tenant for the modest bungalow.

When Deirdre learned the bungalow was still vacant, she snapped it up. It was agreed that the day after the will reading Deirdre would have a formal viewing of the house, but in her heart she knew there was nothing to deter her from agreeing terms on the property. She began to hope that maybe one day the bungalow might be offered for sale, and it could be her home for ever.

With a glittering blue sky and frost sparkles glistening, the air was like wine. Deirdre resolved to just get through the next two days the best she could, and then get on with the next stage of her life. She would not let Edmund drag her down.

Deirdre drifted through Edmund's funeral service with as much quiet dignity and composure as she could muster. She forbade herself to dwell on Edmund's wickedness as Rita wept floods of tears for the man she had lovingly called her wonderful "Uncle Edmund."

If only you knew, Deirdre thought as she watched Edmund's daughter sorrow.

Dry eyed at the lonely graveside Deirdre dutifully tossed in her handful of earth and left a wreath of seasonal Chrysanthemums. Her duty to Edmund was complete now, he would have no more call on her sisterly sense of duty.

Deirdre would always love Edmund for the brother he was when they were children, funny, loving and kind; she hoped in time she could forgive the flawed man he became.

Deirdre would not dwell on the past now; she would look to the future as her parents had always taught her to do and make a new life for herself away from all the memories of Alma road.

She murmured her thanks to the mourners for their support, she shook hands with elderly priests who remembered Edmund as a pillar of the Church and said her farewells. The hateful day was finally over.

As the light faded in St Saviours Church yard, it was both the end and a new beginning.

You can't change the past you can only change the future Deirdre; her Mam had said on many occasions when some disappointment afflicted her as a child.

Deirdre vowed to do exactly that.

*

The Last Will and testament of Edmund Arthur Roberts held no surprises, only the small handwritten letter included with the Will would do that. Cautious and discreet to the end Edmund's Will did not mention Phoebe or Rita. As Deirdre had thought, Edmund's share of the house had been left to her along with the contents of his bank account after all other bills had been paid.

"Mr Williams, if there is nothing else for me to attend to, if you don't mind, I think I should like to go home now and get some rest…. It's been a trying few days." Deirdre murmured, she folded her hands on her lap and remained composed.

"Of course, Miss Roberts, I quite understand. Funerals take a lot out of a person." William Williams, solicitor, sucked his teeth in sympathy, he folded the official documents into an envelope and passed them over to the composed Deirdre Roberts, *an admirable woman if ever he met one.*

"If ever you need our services, don't hesitate to ask Miss Roberts, we are happy to be at your service." William Williams inclined his head to one side, it reminded Deirdre of a beady eyed blackbird listening for the shuffle of an underground worm.

"Thank you Mr Williams. Now that the rest of my family has passed away, I may need to consider changing my own Will soon. The family house is too large and too cold for a woman of my age Mr Williams so I have made up my mind…I shall be moving when all the formalities have been settled." Deirdre said. Just saying the words made the move feel like a reality. *She was leaving Cardiff.*

Mr Williams' mouth formed into a small "o" *this was extremely good news indeed.* A new Will and a house move were good for business. "Of course, Miss Roberts, a wise decision, in my opinion, very wise indeed," he muttered.

"After I've read Edmund's last words, I shall give it some thought and then I'll make another appointment, to sort out my affairs sometime next week Mr Williams." Deirdre thanked the elderly solicitor for his services and left clutching the mysterious envelope to be read in private.

*

Deirdre opened the stiff envelope with trembling fingers. She recognized Edmund's confident bold handwriting in an instant, a little shakier than it used to be but still his handwriting, nevertheless. Her heart thudded in her chest.

Dearest Deirdre,

I'm so sorry for everything I have put you through, and I'm begging that you will help me one last time. If you can find it within your heart to do this for me then I shall be eternally in your debt, if you say no then I shall understand, I have no right to ask anything more of you.

You have always been the best sister a man could have, and I want you to know how much I loved you which is why my actions have been inexcusable. If I said sorry a million times, then it would not be enough.

I can't begin to justify what I've done Deirdre. Call it a weakness, call it a madness, call it what you will, but I can never explain, excuse, or apologise enough for the hurt I have caused you and of course the damage I did to Phoebe Horwat when I abandoned her.

By now you will know that I have left some two hundred and fifty pounds in my bank account and my share of the house to you, as is only right, and I wish you joy of it. It is all yours now to do with as you choose.

Try to forgive my trespasses and don't let my actions spoil the years we had together in happier times. Be happy Deidre, I do so want you to be happy; don't let what I've done rob you of the happiness you deserve.

I want to help Phoebe Horwat have a more comfortable old age if possible. Who knows what comfort and happiness she might have enjoyed if she'd never had the misfortune to meet me all those years ago? I could not put this in my Will or else the truth would come out, so all I can do is put this plea in a letter and throw myself on your mercy.

Over the years I have saved up some money not mentioned in the will. If you remove the back panel of the small cupboard in my old bedroom you will find the rest of my life savings of five hundred pounds tucked away in a leather purse.

If you can find it within your heart to do this Deirdre, then I am asking that you give this money to Phoebe as a small gift from me... if she will not accept the gift, or if you do not feel you can carry out my wishes then I shall leave it up to you to do with it as you see fit... no-one else, but you, knows about this money.

I know that whatever you choose to do Deirdre, it will be the right thing and it will be for the right reasons.

Always your loving brother Edmund. Xx

Deirdre sobbed bitter tears… *he was asking too much.* She read and re-read her brother's final words, he had obviously been in such torment, the confident, calm joyful life she always imagined he had enjoyed had just been an illusion, Edmund was a tortured soul and now he needed her to try to put things right.

Deirdre went upstairs to Edmund's room and found the loose back panel as he described; delving in the cobweb darkness she pulled out a soft leather purse containing fifty, large ten-pound notes rolled inside. She sat on her haunches in the quiet gloomy house and wept one last time for her brother Edmund.

Deirdre needed to think what to do now. She was reasonably, well set up with money left by her parent's. Always thrifty Deirdre had managed to pay her bills, look after herself and put a few savings aside; she was a woman who lived within her means. Not given to extravagance or excess Deirdre had lived a simple life with few wants; five hundred pounds was a huge amount of money- it could even buy a small house if spent wisely.

Deirdre began to doubt the wisdom of listening to letters from the grave.

Neither Edmund, nor Phoebe would ever know what she did with the money, she reasoned. He said in his letter it was up to her to decide to do what was best, he also said she could do what she liked with the house.

Edmund was trusting her to do the right thing for the right reason, she hoped she could carry out the spirit of his wishes and at the same time find the happiness he wished for her.

Deirdre's mind was whirring with possibilities.

Tomorrow Deirdre would see inside "Cartref," the little house she hoped to be able to call her home. Deirdre decided that would sleep on it before deciding what to do next about carrying out the last wishes of her brother Edmund.

Chapter 22

The Ashworth family had a miserable Christmas, Lenny, Norah's eldest lad had spent all Christmas Eve, sweating with a temperature which robbed him of his sleep, by Christmas day both George and Gareth started to feel unwell and by the next morning both boys were covered in the tell-tale pink rash, as the two younger brothers drooped under the infection Lenny started on his road to recovery.

"Thank the Lord, Jack our Karen hasn't gone down with it an' all," Norah stood in the kitchen washing soiled sheets, Gareth seemed unable to hold down so much as a cup of water without vomiting half of it back up again. Norah pushed back a strand of damp hair from her forehead, she felt tired and lumpen with the baby squirming in her belly she was unable to rest. It was going to be impossible to get all this linen dried at this time of year, the next time Gareth spewed up she'd have to turn the sheet.

"It's still early days love, but fingers crossed she'll be spared it... what a bloody awful Christmas this has been for them all," Jack shook his head. He worried about his Norah catching the virus as well, but so far his wife looked in the clear.

Dr Mason reassured them that Norah's pregnancy was at an advanced stage now so that even if she did catch the Measles then the baby she carried within her should be unharmed by the virus. Jack was trying to help Norah in any way he could, he could see his wife was struggling with so much sickness in the house and the housework piling up.

"George doesn't seem to have got it too badly Norah, but Gareth is feeling rotten today poor lad. He said he had earache bothering him all night." Jack was a loving father; his children meant the world to him, it pained him to see them suffering.

"I gave Gareth a bathe with a nice cool flannel this morning and there's not a square inch of him which hasn't got that blessed rash on him." Jack said sadly. Gareth's body was an angry mess of red blotches, Jack had dabbed some soothing calamine lotion over Gareth's hot body to cool the boy's skin.

It tortured Jack to see the poor mite lying miserable and sick in bed. Rascal Gareth was always the life and soul of the household, normally the lad was never quiet or still for a moment. The house was eerily quiet with all three lads confined to their sick beds. Jack was worried for his youngest son, he didn't want to worry Norah, but Gareth certainly seemed to have the worst of it… he'd talk to Dr Mason about it when he called in on his rounds.

*

Ivy so missed going to see her Da in Porthcawl. For weeks she had anticipated a joyful, special time with the father she dreamed of as a child. When Phoebe left to catch the bus in her place, Ivy's heart sank, but she knew she had done the right thing. Overnight June had developed the most appalling winter cold with a hacking cough to boot. The child was spluttering to catch her breath and a wheezing crackle came from deep within her lungs. Ivy's Mam visited the following day and suspected her little granddaughter might have a case of croup.

It might not be the dreaded Measles raging in the Ashworth household and half the other houses in the street, but Ivy had to admit June wasn't at all well and needed her Mam. As Phoebe pointed out James probably wouldn't thank her for giving him a cold with his bad lungs either. Much as Ivy wanted to go, she knew the only sensible decision was to let Phoebe go instead.

The Benson household stank of Vicks Vaporub and the bedroom windows were fogged up with the bowls of steaming hot water infused with lemon and peppermint oil, to clear June's blocked nose and chest. June sat with her head under a towel and inhaled the hot damp air to ease her tortured airways.

"Mam it's been an absolute nightmare for poor June, coughing and wheezing and awake most of the night," Ivy said as she chatted over a cup of tea and a finger of moist Christmas cake. The steam treatment seemed to be having effect and June, exhausted by coughing was having a nap upstairs; Ivy dared to hope the worst might be behind them.

The two women were sat in the kitchen preparing vegetables to make soup out of the turkey carcass. After three days of eating cold leftovers, the turkey had been pronounced well and truly finished, any remaining morsels clinging to the picked over bones had been boiled up for stock yesterday, so today the rich stock was destined to make a hearty soup once any bone fragments were removed.

"This should help build her up though when it's ready, a tasty drop of soup is easy to digest," Betty slid a pile of sliced carrots into the stew pot. Ivy was busy getting the grit out of the leeks.

"I saw Norah Ashworth yesterday…. Don't worry I didn't go close," Ivy added hastily as she caught her Mam's disapproving look. "She was stood on the front doorstep waiting for Dr Mason's visit and getting bit of fresh air… I think she must be going stir crazy shut in all the time, the poor woman looked completely done in." Ivy said sadly. Her friend looked a ragged, careworn mess; sleepless nights and worry had aged her, there were dark circles like bruises under her tired eyes.

"How are all the children faring?" Betty asked. Betty liked Norah; the kindly woman was good to Ivy when Jimmy was treating her daughter badly. And after June had been born with her condition Norah encouraged Ivy to stand tall and be proud of her little daughter, she welcomed June into the Ashworth family with open arms and gave Ivy a shoulder to cry on when times were tough. Norah was a trooper.

"Norah said her eldest Lenny was now on the mend, George, her middle lad only got a mild dose of it and luckily Karen hasn't shown any signs of infection at all, which is a blessed miracle under the circumstances… but it's young Gareth everybody is really concerned about." Ivy shook her head sadly. "Norah said Dr Mason is visiting the lad twice a day now and apparently if Gareth doesn't start to improve soon Dr Mason might insist the lad has a stay in hospital until he recovers."

Gareth was such a lively rascal at times, but the little lad with the cherubic features and mop of blonde wavy hair was now lying in his bed a listless blotchy mess struggling to hold down anything but sips of water. "It's been five days since the rash came out, he really ought to be on the mend by now." Ivy said.

"That's a real shame, let's hope he turns a corner soon. Norah must be out of her mind with worry." Betty finished dicing the last of the potatoes and started to clear the kitchen table.

"Are you sure you're happy to be left with June, whilst I go out for the afternoon Mam," Ivy felt in a turmoil, she had butterflies in her stomach at the thought of the afternoon ahead, but June was still not well and might need her. *Perhaps she should stay home, Billy would understand.*

131

"Of course, I am Ivy, now don't you worry about me, I am quite capable of being left in charge for a few hours, just go out and have a lovely afternoon with Billy" Betty smiled, her daughter deserved a bit of happiness and fun.

Ivy hadn't seen Billy since the nativity play on Christmas Eve, well not properly if you didn't count a few snatched words on the front path. Billy popped by the house on Boxing day but had to be content with a quick chat with Ivy outside in case June really did have the dreaded Measles. They agreed to meet in the city centre if June was well enough to be left for a few hours .... and her Mam was insisting that she was.

"Now go along and enjoy yourself, stop worrying June will be fine with her Nanna looking after her, especially now she's had a bit of a sleep *and* if you're not back in time for tea I can always give her something to eat. Now why don't you run upstairs and get changed, you'll miss the bus if you don't get a move on." Betty ordered.

Ivy scooted upstairs to put on her best frock and tidy her hair, she wanted to look pretty for Billy when they went shopping; today was the day they were going to choose her engagement ring. Ivy only kept wearing Jimmy's wedding ring to give herself the appearance of respectability, she wasn't having that ring on her finger a moment longer than was necessary. She would swap it over to her right hand as soon as she had Billy's ring on her left and once her and Billy were married she'd sell it.

"Bye Mam, I'm off then if you're absolutely sure... I've checked June and she's sleeping like a log so with any luck she might sleep all afternoon." Ivy buttoned her winter coat up to her neck and tucked the pretty silken scarf Billy gave her for Christmas over her hair.

"You look lovely Ivy. I'm so pleased to see you looking so happy, you and Billy make a perfect couple, he's a lovely man." Betty kissed her daughter on the cheek.

"I know Mam, I do love him." Ivy said shyly.

"Shew...Off with you!" her mother ordered as she glanced at the kitchen clock, "look at the time! If you miss that bus Ivy he'll think you've changed you mind, now get a move on," her Mam ushered her out of the kitchen like a farmer's wife scattering hens.

Ivy knew Billy wanted to buy her an engagement ring, but she also knew he couldn't really afford such an extravagant gesture. She'd argued a wedding ring on her finger was enough;

fancy engagement rings were not for the likes of girls like her. "I don't need an engagement ring Billy, really I don't!" Ivy protested.

 But Billy was having none of it. "Nonsense Ivy, I want you to wear my ring, and if I hadn't worried that I might have made the wrong choice it would be sitting on your finger already with no more argument about it. So, let's not squabble, I'm buying you an engagement ring Ivy and that's the end of the matter!"

It was the day before new Year's Eve and the shops still wore their Christmas finery. They agreed on buying a second-hand ring from a jewellers and pawn broker shop nestling in the Wyndham arcade. The glazed shopping arcade was filled with a myriad of tiny shops and attractive windows displaying, books, tobacco, and antique curios to tempt the eye. Mr Locking the jeweller had a good selection of second hand and unredeemed pledges in his window, they were bound to find something Ivy liked, and Billy could afford. Ivy was to meet Billy on the corner of the arcade at two o'clock.

Billy was early. He'd already scanned the window to see if they could afford something nice for Ivy, the nicer rings with diamonds even the second-hand ones were a lot more expensive than he'd thought they would be, they might have to settle for a semi-precious stone instead. He only had six pounds twelve shillings in his pocket for the purpose…. It was less than a weeks' wages, but it would have to be enough for a second-hand ring; Billy couldn't afford anymore, especially not after buying Christmas presents and handing his rent money to his parents.

Billy could see a few of the less pricey pieces were in the un-redeemed pledge tray…. perhaps they should start there. He noticed Ivy hurrying towards him through the crowd, her tiny figure looking lost in the crowd of shoppers. He waved.

"Ooh I'm all puffed out," Ivy fanned herself with her hand. Anxious not to be late, Ivy had rushed all the way from the terminus as fast as her gammy leg would carry her, she gave Billy a shy kiss on the cheek.

"You look marvellous Ivy, and the scarf really suits you," Billy had spent a long time choosing the silky head square for Ivy's Christmas present and the soft muted green and caramel colours really suited her colouring.

"Thank you, I love it…. You made an excellent choice Billy," Ivy blushed a little at the compliment. She was still shy with him, uncertain of herself.

"I certainly did… after all I chose you," Billy grinned as he put his arm around her, "come on let's look at the rings in the window, they aren't going to bite you. I'm sure we can find something nice."

Ivy was in agonies of uncertainty, not wanting to choose anything too extravagant, unsure what she ought to spend, wishing the whole ordeal was over-*why couldn't he have just chosen something he could afford and surprised her, having to choose was a torment for her.*

Ivy glanced at Billy patiently looking through the shop window. He wasn't saying anything to guide her towards any ring in particular.

Perhaps she should she ask him how much they should spend… it seemed sordid to mention money, but Billy only worked in his Da's fish and chip shop, he was not a man with money to splash around on luxuries like rings.

A frown crossed her face. Spending money had never come easy to Ivy, it worried her she was indulging in buying fripperies Billy could ill afford when times were hard. If they were planning on getting married then they would need all the money they could scrape together, spending a man's wages on ornament felt foolish and a waste, *but in her heart she did so want a pretty ring on her finger, she hated Jimmy's cheap wedding band with a vengeance.*

Ivy dithered on the shop doorstep reluctant to enter and allow a persuasive shop assistant to sway her into spending Billy's hard-earned savings.

"Why don't you choose for me Billy, I'll love whatever you choose honest I will." Ivy pleaded, her eyes started to brim with tears, she worried she might burst out crying, overwhelmed by the task ahead.

"Now don't get upset you daft 'apeth, it's supposed to be fun choosing your engagement ring, not torture." Billy grinned and chucked Ivy affectionately under the chin.

"No, I'm *not* choosing this ring, you are!" he said firmly, "if you are going to wear this for the rest of your life then it must be your choice Ivy, come on let's go inside and try some on…. What's the worst that can happen…. You might even enjoy yourself." He teased, he so wanted her to have fun.

Ivy trudged reluctantly into the shop, like a lamb to slaughter.

Mr Locking himself stood behind the polished wood and glass display counter, he noticed Ivy's wedding ring. "Good afternoon Sir, Madam, how can I help you this afternoon?" He said unctuously. Mr Locking was a short, grey-haired gentleman who had owned his shop for thirty years; he deemed himself a good judge of character. This looked very much like a young couple in love, even if the lass was already wearing a wedding band.

Ivy blushed and wanted to flee the shop... No-one had ever called Ivy *Madam* before.

"We are looking to buy an engagement ring, Mr Locking, and we thought we might look at some of the rings in the window." Billy pointed to the second-hand section of the window display.

Mr Locking nodded, at least this meant a potential sale not another pledge, too many people down on their luck came through his doors wanting to pawn wedding rings and the like. He'd obviously misread the situation. The young couple looked respectable enough, but he could tell from their dress they would not have a lot to spend, he surreptitiously turned the key on the display counter housing his more expensive items.

You couldn't be too careful when your back was turned on a customer in the shop, distraction theft was a perpetual worry in a business like his.

"Yes of course Sir, I'll bring some trays out for you and your fiancée to look at," Mr Locking took a large bunch of keys from under the counter and unlocked the window cabinet.

Ivy thought she would die with embarrassment. The glittering baubles were displayed to best advantage on the counter.

The pawn business had boomed after the war and now Albert Locking had a lot of stock he needed to sell on. He selected some of the less expensive trays containing some of his un-fashionable rings or unredeemed stock items which had lingered in the stock room. There was plenty to choose from whatever the budget. Garnets and white spinels tried to ape rubies and diamonds, dated turquoise and opal stones abounded and small diamonds enhanced with illusion settings tried to trick the eye, but many of the rings on the tray looked too big or clumsy for Ivy's dainty hands.

Ivy saw some of the price tags and gave a small shake of her head. *She couldn't allow Billy to spend so much money. It was foolishness.*

Billy's heart drooped he could not see many he could afford, each little white price tag seemed out of reach. One tiny ring caught his eye on the velvet cushion, it was a circlet of glittering white stones, so small they were barely chips embedded in the metal. The ring was so minute it looked doll sized, but under the lights it flashed prettily and stood out from the rest.

"Now that one is a real bargain, and those *are* real diamonds Sir," Mr Locking said as he caught Billy's eye examining the price tag, "It was a pledge and I've had it in stock for quite a while now because of its tiny size, it either fits a lady's finger or it doesn't, because it can't be altered due to its construction." Mr Locking explained.

Mr Locking removed the diamond circlet from the blue velvet pad and displayed it to Ivy. "See the stones go all the way round the ring," he twisted the narrow glittering band, so it caught the light to best advantage.

"I call it my Cinderella ring, "Mr Locking joked, "because it's a bit like the fabled glass slipper, it's only going to fit one special lady with dainty hands. Some might say it's more of an eternity ring than an engagement ring I suppose" he admitted, "but that's just a matter of opinion, and it is a little beauty." He placed the ring on the velvet pad next to Ivy's hand.

"Here why not try it on, your hands do look very dainty." Mr Locking smiled, his eyes calibrated the size of Ivy's fingers and felt hopeful he had found his fabled Cinderella.

The ring was tiny, but it slipped on Ivy's finger as if it were made for her. "There we are a perfect fit...now there's not many ladies who could do that I can tell you, my dear!" Mr Locking beamed. With a bit of luck, he might be able to persuade the young couple to take this ring off his hands, it had sat on his shelf for two years now and so far had fitted no-one who had attempted to try it on. The style was not of an engagement ring and its size meant most ladies had been fearful of even trying it on in case they couldn't get it off again. Even the promise of jeweller's grease, in the form of a bar of soap, couldn't persuade some girls to take a chance and try it on.

"It's very pretty," Ivy admitted. The ring twinkled on her finger in the place where Jimmy's wedding band had been, in the shop lights the tiny ring glittered like a rainbow.

"They are nice little stones in the ring, it certainly does sparkle well, and it suits the young lady's hand, "Mr Locking could see that Ivy was taken with the ring, he just needed to persuade the man to buy it. "It looks a treat... don't you think so Sir?" Mr Locking coaxed.

"It does look very nice.... But I'm not sure if it's what Ivy is looking for," Billy said hesitantly.

A few other rings, discreetly selected by Mr Locking for being within price range, were now being placed in rows on the velvet counter mat for perusal. The other rings were not as sparkling as the one currently on Ivy's ring finger, some even looked quite worn or unfashionable by comparison.

"Tell you what Sir, if the ring does suit your fiancée then I am sure I could offer a generous discount. As I said, there are not many young ladies who could fit that ring and I have had it in stock for a little while now, so I'm sure we could come to some arrangement on the price." Mr Locking was keen not to let the sale slip away, the tiny ring had been selected and rejected on many an occasion, *he'd begun to regret accepting it as a pledge.*

Ivy's ears pricked up… a discount? She did like the ring and was quietly proud of the fact few others had hands dainty enough to wear it, she also liked the fact that Mr Locking had described it as an "eternity ring," somehow it seemed more fitting for a previously married woman to have such a ring. She had fretted that engagement rings were for young girls just starting out when Billy had suggested buying her a ring in the first place.

It was as if this narrow ring with the diamond chips circling the edge had been waiting just for her. "I really do like it, Billy," Ivy smiled and displayed the white metal and diamond ring which sat so comfortably on her wedding finger.

"It *is* rather expensive though," Ivy said when she saw the price tag of six guineas. *She couldn't ask Billy to spend so much money* she started to loosen the ring on her finger to return it to the pad.

Mr locking noticed the motion and took decisive action.

"If you like Sir I could bring the ring in at six pounds… now that is a magnificent ring for the price Sir, I'm sure you will agree." Mr Locking said smoothly, anxious to secure a sale.

Mr Locking picked up another similar priced ring to illustrate what else could be bought for that sum, the well-worn three stone ring with illusion setting looked dull and lumpen beside the dainty band on Ivy's finger.

Billy looked at Ivy and nodded, six pounds was within his budget, and he had to admit it did sit very well on her finger, "what do *you* think Ivy… would you like it for your engagement ring?" He asked shyly.

"Oh yes please, Billy" Ivy gasped in delight and gave Billy a huge kiss.

Mr Locking discreetly looked the other way and started returning the rings to their velvet pads in the window.

At long last he had shifted that ring.

Chapter 23

Phoebe and Betty were sat drinking tea in the sitting room when they saw the ambulance take Gareth Ashworth off to St David's hospital. A weeping Norah stood on the step and waved Gareth off, Phoebe immediately shot across the road to offer any assistance.

"What's happening Norah love, we saw the ambulance arrive," Phoebe gave poor Norah a hug, her heart bled for the distraught woman, it was obvious Gareth must have reached a crisis point.

"Our Gareth is so poorly Phoebe," Norah sniffed loudly into her handkerchief, "he keeps complaining his ears are aching all the time, he's been absolutely screaming the place down with it. Neither of the other two had such bad earache... I just don't know what to think about it. Dr Mason insisted Gareth should go to the hospital for a bit of nursing and rest... I think he wants me to rest as much as anything an'all," Norah smiled ruefully.

Norah knew she looked completely done in and the baby she carried kicked and thrashed night and day... it was a joke when the midwife Marion Spears had told her that Norah needed to rest and put her feet up *a chance would be a fine thing now her Jack had gone back to work.*

"Jack will be home in a couple of hours, he's going to be shocked to know they've taken our Gareth into St David's," Norah admitted, "but Dr Mason insisted, he said Gareth might be developing complications, the rash is on the wane now, but Gareth doesn't seem to be on the mend as he should be, so the doctor said hospital was the best place for him."

"He's right Norah, hospital is the best place for him," Phoebe said sympathetically. "If you like I could come over for a few hours tomorrow to baby sit so you could go in and visit Gareth if that would help at all?"

"Oh, would you?" Norah gasped with relief; she had been fretting about how she would be able to visit her poorly son.... "You're an angel Phoebe. Dr Mason said we are out of the infectious stage now so you'll be safe in the house."

Norah trudged back indoors there were so many chores to do, and her back was playing up as well, she might only be thirty-five but today she felt like she was a hundred.

Deirdre sat inside the café on the Porthcawl promenade, the windows were steamed up with the warm fug from the café fire; two old men sat nursing a pot of tea as they waited for the rain to ease. Business was slow.

Deirdre was not put off by the blustery cold weather and the grey waves battering the promenade, it was nearly January for heaven's sake. She suspected the agent Alan Jones who showed her around "Cartref" had expected her to change her mind when she saw the inside of the bungalow in such dreary weather. Without a fire to warm the rooms the air inside the house was distinctly frigid, rain lashed the windows and the storm lurking out at sea had turned into a bubbling grey mass on the horizon. A faint odour of cat's pee caused Deidre to wrinkle her nose.

"Mrs Prosser's cat was left locked indoors for a few days I'm afraid," Mr Jones looked towards the yellow stain on the rug by the sitting room window, "the family have said they will get the rugs cleaned."

Deirdre jolted upright, "did you say that this house belongs to a Mrs Prosser?" Deirdre had only heard from Phoebe that the neighbour was called Gwynneth.

"Yes Mrs Gwyneth Prosser owns the house, but her son and daughter have found her a place in a nursing home nearby, the poor old soul can't manage on her own now since having a stroke. The family are renting the house out to help pay her fees. Mrs Prosser isn't willing to sell her home yet… I think she hopes she might come back home one day if she gets better." Alan Jones shook his head as if to say the family were simply humouring the old lady.

Gwynneth Prosser! What were the chances of that? It felt like it must be an omen of sorts! Deirdre was leaving one Prosser family behind in Alma road and now she would be renting a house from Mrs Prosser and her family in Porthcawl,

"What happened to the poor cat who lived here?" Deirdre glared at Mr Jones, his lack of sympathy for the abandoned cat left locked inside for days waiting for its owner to return home irritated her.

"The cat? Oh, I believe Mrs Prosser's daughter is looking for a home for it. But if they can't find a new home then I think it might have to be put down poor thing…. it's a big, old ginger and white tom cat, called Bobby. He was here the last time I came to see the property, but he is getting on a bit, he might not settle in a new house."

Alan Jones stood in the hall; the last time he came to appraise the property for the Prosser family he recalled the rather grumpy old cat with glaring green eyes perched on the windowsill regarding him with distain.

This viewing was not going well in his opinion. *The pungent smell of cat pee was most unpleasant, the family might need to buy a new rug, and he had a sneaking suspicion old Bobby had left his mark in several rooms as well. He did not hold out much hope for Miss Roberts accepting the house.*

"Thank you Mr Jones for showing me around; I think I'm finished here today," Deidre took one last look out of the windows and turned to go, there was nothing more she needed to see.

Alan Jones felt his shoulders droop a little, he was not feeling positive.

"I'll take the bungalow Mr Jones ….. and I'll take Mrs Prosser's cat. If the family could look after the animal until I'm ready to move in, I should be extremely grateful to them. Please tell the family, I expect all the rugs to be cleaned thoroughly, I'm sure poor Bobby doesn't want to be reminded of his mistakes… if you lock the poor thing in a house for a few days, what was the poor animal supposed to do," Deirdre said briskly.

Mr Jones stood gaping like a fish, "Of course Miss Roberts. I'm sure Mrs Prosser will be so relieved to hear Bobby can stay in his old home, her beloved cat was one of the things worrying her when she went into the home."

"I'll come along to the office and sort the paperwork at lunchtime after I've had a cup of tea and bite to eat. I'll see you at one o'clock Mr Jones." Deirdre turned on her heel and left.

Alan Jones scratched his head in amazement; he certainly hadn't seen that coming, *she was taking the smelly house and the smelly cat to boot!*

In the café Deirdre was forming a plan, well more of a business plan really. She was certainly moving to the bungalow in Porthcawl, but she still had the house in Alma Road to sort out and the remainder of Edmund's money with which to help Phoebe Horwat have a better life.

Edmund had left the ultimate decisions up to her about how best to help Phoebe and now she needed to speak to the woman and put her plan into action. Two things were certain: Deirdre would *not* be selling her house in Alma Road, and she would *not* be giving Phoebe Horwat five hundred pounds either unless she had to.

Deirdre tidied up all the legal loose ends in Porthcawl and agreed a moving in date for five weeks' time. Now all she had to do was have a tricky meeting with Phoebe. Deirdre decided she would catch the bus to Wilson road first thing the next morning and get it all over and done with, she didn't want the problem hanging over her for any longer than was necessary.

Tomorrow was New Year's Eve and Deirdre wanted to get this off her chest before the year ended. A new, confident no-nonsense Deirdre Roberts was emerging, and she quite liked the feel of her. She would craft her own destiny from now on and be beholden to no-one.

If Edmund had taught her anything in the last few months of his life, it was that it was possible to live a life of your own choosing.

When Deirdre arrived in Wilson road on New year's eve to speak Phoebe she found the house in a bit of a flutter. Betty was looking after June and Phoebe was on her way out to baby sit for Norah Ashworth. Phoebe looked irritated to see Deirdre standing on the doorstep yet again.

"Oh, it's you, "Phoebe said somewhat ungraciously when she saw Deirdre. "I'm afraid we are up to our eyeballs at the moment and I'm just off across the road to do some babysitting; Mrs Ashworth needs to go out to visit her sick son in hospital." Phoebe barred the door; she couldn't have Deirdre Roberts turning up on the doorstep every five minutes.

"I really *do* need to speak to you today Phoebe," Deirdre said firmly, she hoped she wouldn't be turned away.

"In that case Deirdre you had better come and keep me company over the road, you can tell me whatever it is whilst I'm there." Phoebe grabbed her coat and the two women left Betty looking after June.

Betty overheard the exchange from the kitchen, she was itching to know what this latest secret was all about. Whenever Deirdre Roberts came to call she seemed to bring some drama with her. *I wonder what it will be about this time.* Betty mused.

Chapter 24

"I love you Ivy," Billy gave her a tender kiss as they waited for Ivy's bus to arrive. She was so tiny she fitted comfortably under his arm.

"And I love you too Billy, and I love my ring too, it's just perfect." Ivy enthused; she could hardly believe the beautiful ring was really hers. "It feels like it was waiting for me somehow, just like Mr Locking said it was. I can't wait to show it off to the family." Ivy beamed with happiness, she had never owned anything so beautiful or precious before.

"Do you want to take the ring until tomorrow?" Ivy said hesitantly, she hoped Billy would not insist on making her wait for a New Year's Eve engagement as planned, the ring felt so perfect on her finger she never wanted to take it off.

"Of course not!" Billy hugged her, "we are engaged now, so there's no need to take it off. Now we've found the right ring, I want you to wear it."

Ivy kept glancing at the ring twinkling on her wedding finger all the way to the bus stop, she had placed her plain, gold wedding band on the third finger of her right hand for safe keeping. She would not wear the two rings next to each other.

Ivy noticed Billy had looked a bit nervous all afternoon, at first she thought he might be having second thoughts about getting engaged, then she fretted he might be worried about the money. Now she was pleased he seemed more relaxed and was enjoying himself. She squeezed his hand.

What Billy hadn't told Ivy, was about the enormous family row that erupted in morning and his pending engagement to Ivy Benson was at the very heart of it. He wasn't going to spoil Ivy's day because his parents were being bone headed over his choice of a wife. The deed was done now, so no going back. *Ivy was wearing his ring and they could like it or lump it.*

His father and mother had pleaded with him not to go ahead with his proposal. His Mamat cried theatrically and his Da had blustered and threatened, but when his Mam blurted out that it would have been better if Ivy had left June in a home so as not to ruin Billy's life with a Mongol to look after, Billy had exploded. He stormed out of the house threatening never to go back unless they accepted his choice and minded their comments about June.

He loved Ivy *and* June. *Ivy was going to be his wife come hell or high water, and June would be his daughter and they had better get used to the idea.* He seethed; the thoughtless, cruel comments cut him to the quick.

"We can show people the ring in good time, the main thing is you are going to be my wife Ivy and I couldn't be happier." He raised her hand to his mouth and kissed it, "thanks for loving me Ivy. When no-one else would so much as look at me because of my terrible spotty face you treated me kindly and made me laugh, I couldn't want someone better to go through life with and that's the truth." His voice cracked and the words choked in his throat, *if his parents wouldn't accept Ivy as the woman he loved, then they would have no part in his life anymore. If there was to be a choice, then he would be choosing Ivy.*

The red and cream bus trundled around the corner in a blaze of lights, the dusk was creeping on even though it was only half past four; soon it would be dark.

"There won't be any buses on New Year's day Ivy, so I'll walk over to Ely to see you in morning at about eleven o'clock to wish you and the family a happy New Year." He kissed her one last time.

Ivy was a little disappointed not to be seeing Billy the following day but with Alice pregnant, George needed Billy to help him in the shop and now they'd bought the ring he was needed to go back and help with customers.

"I'm working all day in the chip shop tomorrow; New Years' Eve is always busy. I expect we'll have queues halfway round the block," he joked. The chip shop was hugely popular, and business would be brisk on New Years' Eve. "Give June a hug and a kiss from me." He helped Ivy onto the bus.

Billy waved Ivy goodbye until the bus disappeared around the corner and out of sight.

Instead of taking his usual route home Billy looked in the direction of Caroline street and the family fish and chip shop. He decided he would rather stop there the night on the sofa with his brother George and his wife Alice rather than go home to a frosty reception from his Mam and Da. At least being on the premises he would be up bright and early to help in the shop.

Billy couldn't bear to see his Mam and Da that evening; nothing, and nobody was going to spoil his happy day for him. He had made his choice and there was no point in being harangued about it. He wouldn't take any criticism from his brother George either, if George knew what was good for him he'd not interfere.

Billy knew one thing was for certain though, Ivy's best friend Alice would be thrilled to hear the news about their engagement. He preferred the idea of happy chatter with Alice, to rows and recriminations with his parents.

Head down against the chill breeze, Billy quickened his pace towards the Tasty Plaice chip bar in Caroline street. He would not go home tonight.

Chapter 25

Norah Ashworth stood watching in the window with her coat on, she was waiting for Phoebe and anxious to be off. With the baby hanging heavy in her belly, she couldn't walk as fast as she used to; she couldn't afford to miss the bus to the hospital. Norah was frantic with worry about poor Gareth, she didn't have any time for chatter or gossip with Phoebe Horwat today.

"Hello Norah, I hope you don't mind if Miss Roberts comes and sits with me whilst you're out, she just popped by for a visit just as I was leaving to come here." Phoebe wasn't sure how to introduce Deirdre Roberts, *friend* wasn't exactly the correct term.

"Of course, Phoebe, help yourselves to a cup of tea," Norah grabbed her handbag, she was in too much of a rush to care who Miss Roberts was.

"I'm afraid I can't stop, or else I'll miss my bus. The children know not to bother you and they're upstairs reading and playing with their toys, so you should be fine... I'll be back as soon as I can," Norah left in a fluster and hurried up the road to the bus stop on The Grand Avenue.

"That poor woman has had such a dreadful time of it with sickness in the house and now one of her lads is in hospital suffering complications from the measles." Phoebe explained. "Here let me hang up your coat Deirdre and then you can tell me what this is all about." Phoebe was intrigued to know the purpose of this surprise visit on New Year's Eve. She hoped it wasn't more bad news.

Over a cup of tea in Norah's kitchen Deirdre revealed her plans, and Phoebe was dumb struck by the strange proposal Deirdre unveiled.

"I see... well, at least I think I do," Phoebe said doubtfully. Deirdre was in effect pushing Phoebe into a corner and she wasn't sure she could accept the unusual arrangement on offer.

"It's quite straightforward really Phoebe, but of course the choice is yours," Deirdre added hastily. "All I'm saying is that I would appreciate a decision soon, as I might need to make other arrangements about the house in Alma road. Whatever *you* choose to do, I am going to live in Porthcawl." Deirdre gave a little smile as she thought about the pretty bungalow with the sound of the sea and the ginger cat waiting for her.

"Thanks to that chance meeting with you Phoebe I found the empty bungalow next to James Pugh and it's going to suit me right down to the ground, it's just perfect. Whatever you decide to do, I'm leaving Cardiff for good." Deirdre's eyes glittered, she felt she had come up with a clever plan which would respect Edmund's wishes and make herself happy at the same time, she only hoped Phoebe would see the wisdom of going along with it. At the very heart of Deirdre's scheming was her overwhelming desire to ensure Rita's happiness

"If you accept my offer Phoebe then you will live in my house in Alma Road. You will be next door to *my* niece who is *your* daughter Rita and *your* two grandchildren Jennifer and Frank. In time you will get to know them and become part of their life as our family did." Deirdre watched as Phoebe calculated the deal.

Phoebe had been unsure how to approach the conundrum of her daughter and had decided to wait until the New Year before coming to a decision about what to do for the best. She so desperately wanted to see her lost "Angela" and to declare herself, but she also did not want to ruin Rita's life by upsetting the apple cart and letting all the sordid secrets come out. Now Deirdre was offering her a third way.

"Number two Alma Road has three bedrooms, so you can rent out rooms if you choose to and you could have a lodger for income to help you with the running of the place... I want nothing from any arrangements you might choose to make." Deirdre paused to let the offer sink in, everything rested on Phoebe's decision now.

Deirdre had decided she would use Edmund's five hundred pounds to eke out her own savings if Phoebe accepted her proposal, but if Phoebe refused her offer then she would give Phoebe the money and rent out the house to provide herself with an income. She could then walk away to a new life in Porthcawl and never see Phoebe Horwat ever again with a clear conscience.

Phoebe looked intrigued. Never in her wildest dreams did she think she would ever be living next door to the child she gave away in the wretched St Saviour's maternity unit.

"I shall tell Rita that you are an old family friend who is going to live in the house and look after it for me when I make my move to Porthcawl, and it is a lie you must go along with if this plan is to work." Deirdre paused for a moment before stating her terms.

"I only have two conditions Phoebe," Deirdre regarded the woman opposite her with a stern stare. The whole edifice relied on Phoebe keeping her word...*could she trust this woman*

who she barely knew, a woman who had a desire to declare herself as Rita's mother, a
burning desire which might trump anything else Deirdre might propose?

Deirdre decided to take the risk and lay her cards on the table.

"My first condition is that you do not ruin Rita's life by telling her who you really are Phoebe. You *cannot* reveal that Phyllis Richards, who Rita knew and loved as her mother, was not her real Mam and that Frank Richards was not her real Da." Deirdre wanted at all costs to protect her beloved Rita from upset and shame and if this deal on the table sealed Phoebe Horwat's lips then Deirdre's greatest wish would have been fulfilled.

Deirdre could see the shadow of doubt cross Phoebe's face. "I know you want to claim her as your own, but my neighbours Phyllis and Frank Richards were the best Mam and Da any child could have hoped for, they loved your child and cared for her when you couldn't. Just think what is for the best Phoebe, I'm *begging* you to consider what's best for Rita. In your heart you are her Mam, and no-one can ever take it away from you, but don't crush Rita by telling her that her whole life has been lived as a lie."

And Deirdre *was* begging… begging that Phoebe loved her child enough to let her go, that Phoebe would love and respect Rita enough to accept the crumbs on offer instead of pushing for more. Deirdre hoped the wisdom of Solomon would prevail again and Phoebe would love Rita enough to stop fighting to be declared the rightful mother and allow Phyllis to claim the mantle even in death.

"Just think Phoebe, you'll be able to live next door to the Prosser family and see them grow up…. and I'm sure in time, like me, you *will* find a place in their hearts… But my price is your silence." Deirdre's voice was choking up. She had told herself it would be for the best if she let Phoebe take her place as Rita's new neighbour, but it would be hard for Deirdre to leave behind the family she had grown to love, the family she knew were her own flesh and blood.

"And what is your second condition," Phoebe's voice was level and controlled.

Deirdre couldn't read the woman's thoughts.

"Would you write to me from time-to-time Phoebe and let me know how Rita is?…. I will miss them all so much, I can't bear to think they will feel I have forgotten them after all they have meant to me, over the years." Deirdre was starting to sob. It was taking every ounce of her strength to make this deal; it was tearing her in two.

"I know I can't live next door to them any longer Phoebe… I can't live Edmund's lie for him, and I will understand if you say you can't bear to live next door to them either under the circumstances…. I *know* I'm asking a lot of you," she looked at Phoebe with her eyes brimming with tears.

Deirdre was not a woman given to displays of emotion, but it was tearing her heart apart to say goodbye to Rita and her family, and this was the best solution she could come up with to avoid harming her beloved Rita. All other scenarios she had explored in her head did not deliver as much benefit as this one did.

But if Phoebe was determined to shatter Rita's illusions and tell the whole sordid truth about her brother Edmund, then there was nothing Deirdre could do about it. Her heart was pounding as she waited for Phoebe to say something. Everything was in Phoebe's hands now. Deirdre willed her to accept the terms.

Phoebe sat for a few moments and gathered her thoughts. Thanks to Deirdre Roberts who had taken the trouble to track her down, she now knew where her lost daughter was and most importantly she had snapshots of her daughter's childhood which she could hold close to her heart. If Deirdre had ignored Edmund's wishes then Phoebe would have had absolutely nothing. As Deirdre said, she *was* Rita's mother, and nothing could ever take that away from her.

If, all those weeks ago, Deirdre had refused to do as her brother Edmund had asked, then Phoebe would never have had this chance to live next door to her daughter, to see Rita and get to know her grandchildren. But could she accept Deirdre's conditions… was the price of her silence a price too high?

Soon Ivy would be marrying Billy Thomas and Phoebe would be obliged to find another home elsewhere. She couldn't throw herself on Betty's generosity for ever, even though her friend had offered her a place to live with herself and Gerald. The sparkling ring Ivy proudly displayed yesterday evening had made Phoebe face reality; soon she must leave Wilson road and, for a woman like her, the choices were few.

Now thanks to Deirdre Roberts as one door in Phoebe's life was closing, a window was being opened, and all it needed was for her to agree to Deirdre's terms

Deirdre was offering Phoebe a home to call her own, a home with room for June to come and visit, and a spare room she could earn an income from to help her in her old age and Deirdre's only price was that Phoebe must pledge to maintain her discretion and silence forever.

Thanks to the loyalty and generosity of Edmund's sister she would have a chance to open a new chapter in her life, a chapter which included her long-lost baby Angela.

Phoebe reached over and took Deirdre's hands between her own, "you are a very good woman Deirdre, and I can never thank you enough for tracking me down and bringing my daughter back to me."

Deirdre gazed into Phoebe's face and felt sure she could trust her.

"I know it will cost you dearly to leave your niece behind Deirdre, and I know you have been hurt terribly by Edmund's actions as well." Phoebe could see that Deirdre could have been an attractive woman once, but a life of self-sacrifice and denial had taken its toll and now the woman sat in front of Phoebe, looked faded and tired.

Deride had been a woman living in the shadows of other people's lives, the spinster daughter caring for her elderly parents, the dutiful sister looking after her brother and even now her love for Rita was driving her life choices. Now she was making the choice to sacrifice her own home in Alma road to a woman she had barely met. Deirdre Roberts didn't owe Phoebe anything and yet she was still giving so much.

"We both love Rita in our different ways Phoebe," Deirdre said softly, "so can we agree that my plan is for the best under the circumstances." Her eyes pleaded with Phoebe to agree her terms.

"We can, Deirdre." Phoebe hugged the kind generous woman sat in front of her, now they would have a bond between them forever, they would both protect Rita with their silence. Phoebe felt Deirdre's thin shoulders relax a little.

"Good, that's settled then, I shall go and see my solicitor next week and change my Will to reflect our agreement," Deirdre pronounced firmly.

"Your Will?" Phoebe exclaimed.

"If I die before you Phoebe then I will leave provision in my Will so that you may stay on in the house for as long as you desire. Then when you die or choose to move on, you and your estate, may keep half the house to dispose of as you think fit and the other half will then go to Rita as a present from the woman she always called her Aunty Dee Dee," Deirdre had tried to think of everything, it would all be tied up correctly by Mr William Williams when she visited him next week.

Phoebe felt choked by the unstinting generosity of the kind woman who sat opposite her.

In the space of a few weeks Phoebe had gone from being an aging prostitute living with her godchild and an uncertain future, to the prospect of being a woman of means living next to her long-lost daughter. It beggared belief how quickly her luck could change.

Who knew what life had would have in store for her now? Phoebe felt a warm glow in her heart as the possibilities were endless. *Surely her silence was not too big a price to pay.*

Phoebe had already revealed part of her story to Betty and Ivy when Deirdre first came to Wilson road with the mysterious packet of photographs, but Phoebe knew she could trust her friend with her life, and she would ensure Betty kept her secret, there was too much at stake now to risk discovery.

"I can't thank you enough Deirdre and I promise I won't ever let you down…. I'll keep my word." Phoebe kissed her saviour on the cheek.

"I know you will Phoebe… I know you will." Deirdre smiled; she may not have carried out Edmund's last wishes exactly as instructed but she felt in her heart she done the best she could. She had re-united a mother with her lost child.

Chapter 26

After Norah came back from her hospital visit to see Gareth, Phoebe's mood had plummeted. Phoebe trudged back across the road with a heavy heart. All the lightness, excitement and happiness of just a few hours ago seemed to evaporate when Norah had shared her shocking news.

Gareth was almost totally deaf.

The fever and pain of the measles had subsided, and the child was on the mend, soon he would be well enough to return home to be with his family. But the bad news was the virus had robbed him of his hearing and, short of a miracle, Gareth would never hear again.

The boisterous, noisy boy with the infectious laugh and mischievous ways would now live in a world of silence. The virus had damaged Gareth's hearing to such an extent the child was rendered deaf. The doctors had tried to offer Norah a few crumbs of hope that, in time, the lad might experience some limited recovery in one ear, but there was no hope Gareth would ever hear properly again. The dreaded measles had changed the lad's life forever.

Norah wept bitter tears as she cradled her bewildered child in her arms. She knew it would break Jack's heart to discover his special, golden lad would struggle to make his way in the world now that he could no longer hear like a normal child.

"The poor woman was totally distraught Betty; I didn't know what to say to comfort her, Gareth's barely seven years' old for heaven's sake, she's worried sick he's going to have such a hard life ahead of him if he never gets any hearing back." Phoebe shook her head sadly. Norah had cried her heart out as Phoebe tried, in vain, to comfort her.

"What is there to say Phoebe at times like these, all we can do is help her and the family as best we can…. It feels so sad to think that it was the lad's last Christmas hearing his Mam and Da's voices." Betty remembered the day when June was born and all the torment and worry about what the future might hold for a little girl born to be different.

"Thank the Lord June didn't catch the blasted virus," Phoebe crossed herself.

Ivy had taken June out for a walk, to give the child some much needed fresh air. Betty would need to catch her bus home soon; she would just wait long enough for her daughter to return so she could say goodbye to June. Phoebe would have to pass on the bad news about Gareth's misfortune.

Phoebe observed only yesterday how Ivy was positively glowing with happiness and the two women counted their blessings; the Benson household had the hope of happier times ahead.

"I need to have a quick word with you Betty before Ivy gets back from her walk," Phoebe kept a watchful eye through the sitting room window, she could never share the secret of Deirdre's deal with Ivy, but she needed to take Betty into her confidence before Ivy returned.

"You must swear that you'll keep what I'm going to tell you an absolute secret Betty," Phoebe said earnestly; she knew she could trust Betty with her life, but she had to be cautious now she'd given Deirdre her solemn promise and she needed Betty to help deflect awkward questions and smooth the path of her move to Alma road.

"Of course, Phoebe, you know you can always trust me, cross my heart," Betty was intrigued, she guessed it was something to do with Deirdre's surprise visit earlier that afternoon.

Phoebe sketched the outline of Deirdre's plan, and the more she thought about it the more brilliant it seemed.

"Phwe!" Betty whistled, "well who'd have thought it? I must say Phoebe, it's going to be a huge relief to Ivy to know you'll have a comfy home to go to…. I know it's been a worry to her ever since Billy proposed." Betty would never say a word to Phoebe, but Betty had been worried about where Phoebe would live too.

Gerald had made it quite clear that Phoebe could not live with them forever, a temporary port in a storm was one thing, but Betty's friend would need to plan on living elsewhere after a while, now Betty could go home and tell her husband the good news.

"I knew it would be a worry to her Betty, and I certainly wouldn't want to stand in the girl's way now she has found Mr right. It's only natural they will want to live here together, and they don't need me getting under their feet. My role here is over now and it's time to move on and leave Billy and Ivy to get on with their new lives together. Deirdre has given me an opportunity to make a new life for myself and I'm going to take it." Phoebe smiled; she was happy Ivy had found true love.

"So, when will it all happen and what is the official storyline you'll be telling anyone nosey enough to ask?" Betty's eyes glittered with excitement, Phoebe would be moving to live only a few doors away from Betty's old home in Alma road and only two streets away from Betty's new home in Inkerman street. The two women would be able to see so much more of each other in future, it would be almost like old times.

"Deidre has invited me to go around next week to see the house and then we are going to agree a moving date for the end of January. She will tell Rita and all the neighbours that I'm an old family friend who is looking after the house whilst she is living away in Porthcawl."

"I see... and what will you be telling Ivy?"

"I intend to tell Ivy the same, I'll say I've had a bit of a legacy left to me and that I can live in Deirdre's house for as long as I want.... Just think I can even have June come to stay over with me." In her mind's eye Phoebe imagined the little box room Deirdre had described being turned into June's special room, she'd also promised Deirdre the room would hers to stay in if ever she wanted to visit Cardiff.

"I think Ivy's too in love to be worrying about the ins and outs of my good luck," Phoebe smiled, after-all it was only going to be a small lie. "I'll need to find a lodger pretty quickly though as I won't be able to afford to pay my bills and run the house otherwise," the reality of managing a whole house felt daunting, but she knew she could manage with Betty to help her.

Betty gave her friend a hug, "I'm so pleased for you Phoebe, you deserve some happiness. It's the best news ever!"

"Oh, and I didn't tell you the strangest thing Betty... Deirdre's renting a small bungalow in Porthcawl and it's the one right next door to James Pugh... now isn't that an amazing coincidence!"

Betty had to admit the world was an exceedingly small place.

Ivy was coming down the path. June was skipping happily, reinvigorated by the fresh air, roses bloomed on June's cheeks and Ivy was laughing.

"It's time I moved on Betty, I shall tell Ivy my good news today, she needn't be worrying about me for a moment longer."

"There's too much gloom and doom in the world Phoebe, it's good we have something to celebrate. I'm sorry for Norah's misfortune, but let's just enjoy what we have… I promise I won't breathe a word to Ivy; your secret is safe with me." Betty grinned with delight.

*

When Phoebe told Ivy the good news about her "legacy" Ivy felt as if a weight had been lifted off her shoulders. The girl had been wondering how to broach the subject of future living arrangements in Wilson road now that she was engaged to Billy. Thanks to Aunty Phoebe's bit of good luck there was a solution which seemed to suit everyone. *It was such a relief.*

Ivy had warned Billy they couldn't rush the wedding date because she needed to give Aunty Phoebe time to sort herself out, Ivy couldn't put Aunty Phoebe out onto the streets even if Wilson road did only have the two tiny bedrooms. Now, thanks to some kindly old uncle Aunty Phoebe could live in a nice house in Alma road and she and Billy could have the house all to themselves. Ivy hugged herself with delight.

As soon as she heard the good news, Ivy vowed to go into the council offices next week to enquire about changing the names on the house tenancy once she'd re-married. It would be their house, hers, and Billy's. Moving in to Wilson road with Jimmy would be just a bad memory.

Ivy couldn't wait to give Billy the good news when he called in the morning. It was the best New Year's present she could wish for. They could get married as soon as they wanted to, there was nothing to hold them back now. To top it all, her friend Alice would be delighted as well. When Ivy married Billy, the two women would become sisters -in-law. It was perfect.

Perhaps Billy might want to introduce her to his parents soon. Now that they could make plans to get wed, she really ought to meet his family… she hadn't been introduced to Mr and Mrs Thomas yet and she wanted to make a good impression. She would suggest it to Billy tomorrow.

Mrs William Thomas certainly had a nice ring to it.

Chapter 27

Eileen and Sean had a delightful Christmas. Eileen's Mam stayed for two whole days, and the Riley household was a merry one. Ida Murphy positively twinkled with good humour and recounted family anecdotes making Sean rock with laughter.

"Mam!" Eileen gasped in disbelief as Ida told some long-winded tale about her father being caught with his trousers down around his ankles one day when his braces broke in the middle of Cardiff market. Her Da was carrying a pallet of vegetables above his head weaving between the stalls when his trousers trickled to the floor.

"Well, it's the truth Eileen…. And luckily it was on a Monday, so he'd had his weekly change of clean underwear in the morning." Ida giggled, she'd drunk two bottles of stout and felt quite tipsy.

Sean cackled with laughter, he felt the happiest he'd felt in a long time and thanks to Ida helping with the household chores Eileen had a delightful Christmas too. Luckily they'd not had any real contact with neighbours since they'd moved in, so there was no panic when Jack Ashworth knocked the door on Boxing day to tell them the news about the infection. The measles outbreak in Wilson road was shocking especially since some adults were affected by the virus too. The Riley family, at least, were safe from the dreaded infection.

Now Sean's strength was returning he could make love to Eileen more frequently. With any luck, and God willing, the couple might have some good news to share with Ida in the New Year. They both hoped 1954 would be the year they'd be blessed with a baby.

"Come here you," Sean patted his knee for Eileen to sit on. "Have I told you I love you today Mrs Riley." Sean kissed her deeply.

"No, you haven't," she breathed throatily, her breasts heaving with desire. Even though Sean still carried all the scars of his dreadful accident he could thrill her in ways she'd never dreamed possible. He was tender and caring and she ached for his touch in a way that made her feel wanton.

"Now your Mam has gone home perhaps we should take advantage of the peace and quiet and celebrate the New Year in style." Sean's eyes twinkled, he still found it hard to believe the beautiful angel sitting on his knee was his wife.

"I think perhaps we should," Eileen started to unbutton his shirt and lead him to the bedroom. She so wanted to have their baby and their lovemaking gave her such joy she would never refuse him.

Her Mam might have told her the act of sex was a woman's duty to her husband, an act to be endured; Eileen could only assume her Mam, who never ever admitted to being wrong about anything, for once in her life did not know what on earth she was talking about!

*

"Billy, come on in, I've got some wonderful news to tell you," Ivy blurted out the minute she saw him standing on her doorstep swaddled up against the cold.

"I think you can give me kiss first Ivy, before you tell me anything," he grinned and swept her up in his arms.

"Careful Billy, the neighbours might see!" Ivy giggled.

"I don't care... Soon you'll be my wife, so the neighbours will just have to get used to it." Billy grinned and kissed her on the lips. "Now how about a nice cup of tea Ivy, I'm parched after walking here all the way from Caroline street."

Ivy noticed Billy said he'd come from the flat in Caroline street where Alice and George lived above the chip shop, *so he obviously hadn't slept at home in his parent's house last night.*

"So, come on then Ivy, spill the beans, what's this exciting news you're busting a gut to tell me," Billy supped his tea.

"Aunty Phoebe is moving out at the end of the month!"

"Is that so?" Billy had to admit he was surprised; the subject of Aunty Phoebe was a tricky one.

"It is... but don't you see Billy it means we can get married whenever we like now... as soon as we can get the banns read of course."

Billy's heart sank a little. He hadn't told Ivy he'd been christened in the church of England, so he couldn't get married in a Catholic church, nor did he want to. He'd assumed since Ivy's first wedding to Jimmy was at the Cardiff registry office, she'd be happy to do the same again. With no date set for the wedding, and the tricky dilemma about Aunty Phoebe hanging over them, it meant they hadn't discussed how or where they would get married.

"I think we should start making plans Billy, now I know Aunty Phoebe will be settled elsewhere there's nothing to stop us naming a date. We can tell Mam and your parents once we've decided as I expect they'll want to make some plans an' all." Ivy suddenly noticed Billy's crestfallen look, *surely he wasn't having a change of heart.*

"What's the matter Billy, "she said anxiously.

"I'm not a Catholic Ivy, my family didn't really bother too much with the church, I was christened as a baby, but that's about it. So, you see, I can't get married in your church." He didn't add that he didn't want to get married in St Paul's with all the pomp and ceremony like Alice and George had done. He wanted a quiet wedding; and like as not his parents wouldn't attend the wedding anyway, wherever the marriage ceremony took place.

"Don't worry, Father Malone will let you fly a flag of convenience, lots of people do it," Ivy said brightly. "If you go to lessons for a few weeks, then they'll let us marry in St Paul's, that's what your brother did when Alice's Mam insisted she had a proper church wedding" Ivy could see Billy was not happy with the idea.

"Please tell me what's the matter Billy, I can tell from your face something is wrong," Ivy pleaded.

"I can't beat about the bush Ivy; I want to marry you more than anything on earth but…."

"But what?" Ivy's hearty was pounding in her chest.

"But my parents are dead set against the idea of us getting married."

"Oh…" Her Mam and Aunty Phoebe were so happy to hear the news of their engagement, it hadn't occurred to Ivy that Billy was facing a falling out with his family because of her.

"Don't worry love," he drew her into his arms, "I'm sure they'll come around in time, but I don't think they'll even want to come to our wedding."

158

"Do you still want to marry me then?" Ivy's eyes were starting to brim with tears, she couldn't bear the idea she was driving a wedge between Billy and his parents.

"Of course, I do Ivy…. More than anything else on this earth! I've told my parents I am marrying you come hell or high water, so they'll just have to get used to the idea. I've made my choice…I'm not a child they can boss about." Billy said firmly.

"Thank you," she whispered and kissed him.

"I just don't want a fancy wedding Ivy; I want us to get married quietly with no fuss and only those who love us attending. If my parents choose to cut their noses off to spite their faces then so be it… it's their loss" Billy said firmly.

Billy didn't add that he couldn't afford the added expense of a fancy wedding either. His father's parting words left Billy in no doubt his parents would do their level best to make Billy feel the pinch if he chose Ivy Benson.

"So…. the good news is?" Billy said, eager to change the subject.

"The good news is that Aunty Phoebe will be moving out at the end of January and then as soon as we are wed you can move in here and we can get the house tenancy put in *both* our names," Ivy grinned. "Billy I love you, and if you want to get married in a registry office with my face hidden by a paper bag, then that's fine by me." She hugged him for joy. She knew she was marrying a man who truly loved her.

"I love you Ivy and I hope in time my parents will come to love you too, but until then we have each other and that's enough for me." Billy kissed her.

June ambled into the room with her favourite dolly Margaret tucked under her arm. "Hello Uncle Billy," she grinned a wide gappy smile and climbed on his lap.

"Correction, *we* have each other, *and* I have you and June…and that's enough for any man. I suggest I visit the registry office in the week and find out what we need to do to get the paperwork sorted for the wedding."

"Can I be bridesmaid," June's ears pricked up, since she had been a bridesmaid at Alice's wedding every time she heard there was to be wedding she volunteered to be a bridesmaid. It didn't matter who was getting married June felt sure they would need her services as a bridesmaid. "I'm a good bridesmaid, Uncle Billy" June grinned, her eyes bright with excitement.

Ivy shot Billy a nervous glance, it was obvious June didn't know who she was volunteering to be a bridesmaid for, they hadn't told her they were getting married yet. June struggled to understand the concept of things happening in the future, June lived for the day. Ivy didn't know if Billy would allow June to be a bridesmaid after he said he wanted a small quiet wedding.

"Of course, you can be a bridesmaid my precious, it will be another chance to wear that pretty dress Aunty Alice bought for you," Billy kissed June on the head. He would not deprive the little girl of her fun.

"Who getting married," June lisped, the girl was jigging up and down with excitement.

Billy took Ivy's hand, "We are…I'm going to marry your Mam because I want to be your Da, Junie."

June stood still and tipped her head on one side, struggling to grasp the concept of Uncle Billy being her new Daddy. June liked Uncle Billy just the way he was, he was fun and took her to the park, she didn't want him to stop being her favourite Uncle Billy. June's bottom lip jutted out and started to wobble, her eyes filled with tears.

"Oh bless…. what's the matter June!" Ivy swept her daughter up in her arms.

"I don't want Uncle Billy to go!" June wailed; she buried her head into Ivy's shoulder, refusing to look at anyone.

Billy looked at a loss, he thought June would be happy.

The child started sobbing inconsolably. Loud hiccoughs came thick and fast as she struggled to gasp between breaths, "please don't go Uncle Billy." June pleaded

"Uncle Billy isn't going June, he's *coming* to live here with us," Ivy soothed. The tears stopped and June's face lit up.

Ivy shot Billy a look as if to say, *don't say any more for now*, she could see telling June about Aunty Phoebe moving out would not be an easy task. June hated change and in June's trusting little world she wanted to keep her friends and family just the way they were.

"Well, that's sorted then June, as soon as Uncle Billy can get the paperwork done he can come and live here with you and Mammy… won't that be fun." Billy ruffled June's golden girls. June nodded her head enthusiastically.

Chapter 28

The first day of the rest of Phoebe's life day dawned crisp and bright. Phoebe felt like her stomach was tying itself in knots as she set off to meet with Deirdre Roberts in Alma road. The bus left the sprawling Ely estate behind and rattled its way through the narrow Cardiff streets bringing Phoebe closer to her new beginning.

The nearer Phoebe came to Roath and the Victorian terraces springing out in uniform rows off the main roads, the louder her heart seemed to pound in her chest. Shoppers and families were out and about early, small children were clutching the hands of mothers laden with groceries and shopping bags. Bustling crowds going about their everyday business, Phoebe's eyes scanned the crowds looking for a face she hoped to recognise.

Every woman that she saw around the Roath shopping centre might be Rita Prosser.

At eleven o'clock Phoebe was meeting Deirdre Roberts in the house in Alma road, the house which was to be Phoebe's home for as long as she wanted. Sometimes Phoebe had to pinch herself to believe this piece of good fortune had come her way. Deirdre could have just rented out the house or sold it completely and forgotten all about the past; she wasn't obliged to sort out Edmund's guilty secret and yet she hadn't taken the easy route and abandoned Phoebe. The two women were now bound together for life with a shared purpose to protect Rita.

Roath was a different world from the chaotic, sprawling housing estate filled with troops of children playing in the roads, which characterised the Taff Ely development. Wilson road was at the heart of the busy new development full of families, a road she'd called home for the last three years. The houses here in Roath were older, jumbled in and amongst with busy shops, it reminded her more of the bustling streets of Tiger Bay. City road led directly into the busy centre and onwards to the mighty dock yard, Phoebe felt like she was coming home. It was easier to be anonymous on streets like these.

The prospect of being in her own home again was exciting enough but above and beyond any thoughts of exploring rooms and seeing the inside of her new house was the tantalising thought that she might, by chance, meet or see Rita Prosser as the woman went about her everyday business within just a few feet of where Phoebe was.

Phoebe steeled herself to think of the baby she gave away as Rita now… she could only call her Angela in her heart; she could never let on she knew the woman by any other name. The thought that Edmund's photographs would come to life before Phoebe's eyes filled her with longing and dread in equal measure. She must try her best to grow a relationship with the Prosser family, Phoebe could not assume they would suddenly welcome her with open arms as their new neighbour. She would have to work at it.

Phoebe had already thought of a few ways to try to win her way into Rita's life. Deirdre mentioned she often used to baby sit Rita as a child. As Aunty Dee Dee next door, little Frank and Jennifer knew they could always turn to Deirdre if they needed help or Rita needed a favour. If the plan was to work then Phoebe would have to slowly replace Aunty Dee Dee in Rita's life and the children's affections.

 It wasn't exactly a trap being set but Phoebe did feel it was rather like a sticky spider's web she was weaving to lure the Prosser family in, and today was to be the first day of her spinning. Spiders were patient and so was Phoebe.

The bus stopped in the bustling City road only a few hundred yards from her destination, the enticing turning into Alma Road lay ahead. Number two was the first house in the terrace behind the City road shop fronts. The long street stretched ahead of her, row after row of brick and stone houses with slate roofs, identical tiled front paths, and majolica tiled porch steps. Each house boasted a small sash bay window and a few still retained railings but most had lost them to the war effort. A uniform line of smoking chimneys stretched as far as the eye could see.

Phoebe strolled slowly towards the house, she began to wish she'd begun her journey from the other end of Alma road, that way she could have strolled casually past Rita and George's house; perhaps caught a glimpse.

Phoebe took a deep breath and approached the front door of number two Alma road. For a moment, out of the corner of her eye, Phoebe felt sure she saw an upstairs net curtain twitch in the front bedroom of number four. *Perhaps it was little Frank or Jennifer watching the comings and goings in the street, or maybe it was just wishful thinking.*

Phoebe knocked the red painted door with its gleaming brass work and within a few moments, Deirdre answered the door.

"Hello Phoebe, how lovely you're early…" Deirdre said brightly and loudly, "do come in and meet my dear friend and neighbour Rita just popped in for a quick cup of tea,."

Phoebe froze, she stood in the small, tiled hall unable to move or say a thing. *Rita was in the sitting room*! Phoebe could just see a pair of women's legs through the gap in the sitting room doorway.

"Here let me take your coat, Phoebe" Deirdre took Phoebe's heavy woollen coat and hung it on the hall peg, "I wasn't expecting you for at least another half an hour…. Still, it's lovely to see you, and Rita was just going anyway, we've had our natter."

Phoebe looked bamboozled, it was five past eleven, she was *not* early at all, they had agreed eleven o'clock.

Deirdre shot Phoebe a *trust me look,* and ushered Phoebe through.

"Come on through Phoebe, come through and meet my dear neighbour Rita Prosser. Actually, I'm so pleased you've caught Rita just before she left, because I was just explaining that you were going to be her new neighbour." Deirdre enthused brightly.

Rita Prosser stood up and extended her hand towards Phoebe. Phoebe felt as if her whole world was exploding, waves of disbelief washed over her. As she reached out to shake the hand of Rita Prosser, she could see her daughter staring back at her, the likeness was unmistakable. Apart from Rita's dark grey-blue eyes, just like Edmund's used to be, Phoebe could see the wide planes of Rita's face which reflected Phoebe's Polish background, the same dark blonde, almost light brown hair and the plump prettiness of Phoebe's girlish self, looked back at her.

For a moment Phoebe thought she saw a flash of recognition spark in Rita's eyes.

"Oh hello, how lovely to meet you, Phoebe, Aunty Dee Dee told me you would be living here whilst she lives in Porthcawl," Rita stared quizzically at the woman in front of her, and then laughed. "Do we know each other; because you do look *very* familiar?" Rita continued to hold Phoebe's hand.

Deirdre held her breath.

"No, no we don't," Phoebe said with conviction. She could feel tears welling up…. *her daughter had felt a connection too.*

"In that case I think I'd better make some introductions, this is my lovely neighbour, Rita Angela Prosser." Deirdre said as she looked straight into Phoebe's puzzled brown eyes.

It took all of Phoebe's self-control not to crumple to the floor when she heard Rita's full name. *Rita Angela.*

"Aunty Dee Dee." Rita laughed, "no-one ever calls me Rita Angela, not even my Mam did!"

"It's a very pretty name," Phoebe gulped, she was astounded to hear her daughter was still called Angela, the name Phoebe gave her baby all those years ago. *How could that be possible?*

"My Mam always said I was named Angela after a sweet nun from St Saviour's church she used to be very fond of," Rita explained, "I don't think I ever met Sister Angela, though." Rita Prosser mused. "Anyway, it was nice meeting you Phoebe, but I must get back to the children before they get up to any mischief, you know what children can be like … you must pop in and have a cup of tea once you have moved in, I've promised Aunty Dee Dee I'll take you under my wing." Rita smiled and Phoebe's heart melted.

"I told Rita you didn't have any close family around here so she's promised to help you settle in," Deirdre said and then she turned to Rita, "I've also made Phoebe promise to write to me and let me know how the old house is, and so I can also hear how you are all getting on without me." Deirdre used every ounce of her courage to compose her features into a happy smiling face. She could not afford to start getting emotional.

"Don't say that Aunty Dee Dee, I've promised Jennifer and Frank we'll come to see you in Porthcawl in the Spring. You are only a bus ride away and the children will love a trip to the seaside, they are dying to see your new house." Rita kissed Deirdre warmly on the cheek, "no-one could *ever* replace you Aunty Dee Dee, you've been like a second mother to me."

Phoebe stifled a sob and watched Rita scurry back next door to her children.

"Thank you Deirdre, that meant everything to me." Phoebe said softly, she sank into the armchair. Phoebe looked visibly shaken, all her hopes and dreams had met in that small sitting room in those ten minutes when her daughter Rita Prosser sat opposite her and held her hand.

"Come on Phoebe, sit down and I'll get us both a cup of tea, you look a bit shaken. I hope you don't mind the subterfuge, but I felt that if you knew Rita would be here, then it might have unsettled you. Now you have met her, it will be the most natural thing in the world to meet her again," Deirdre smiled kindly.

"You are so brave Deirdre," Phoebe gasped, she could see just how much Deirdre was prepared to give up so Rita could have a happy, untroubled life. After a lifetime of longing, hope and worry about what sort of home her baby had been brought up in, Phoebe had met her daughter.... and she could see Rita was happy. Deirdre was right Phoebe couldn't ruin that happiness now by wrecking everything Rita knew to be true.

"Nonsense Phoebe, when you love someone you'll do whatever it takes to make them happy... as a mother you should know that better than I do." Deirdre patted her hand. She knew then she had made the right decision, Rita's secret was safe with Phoebe.

Deirdre could leave Cardiff content Phoebe would do everything she could to make Rita happy.

*

Deirdre showed Phoebe around the house; she had started to pack her clothes, personal ornaments, and possessions into boxes ready for the move. The tiny box room was filled with the evidence of packing, piles of newspapers and old apple boxes waiting to be filled.

"I'm not taking any of the furniture with me Phoebe, the bungalow I'm renting comes fully furnished and it seems better these things stay here, some of these pieces of furniture have been here ever since my parents first furnished the place, so they belong here." Deirdre trailed her hands lovingly over the worn sticks of furniture which held so many happy memories. "Most of it wouldn't fit in the bungalow anyway and I'm sure you will need these more than I will."

"Thank you Deirdre.... I've only got my clothes, everything else in Wilson road belongs to my niece Ivy. I've precious little to show for a lifetime," Phoebe shook her head sadly. It was true, after she lost Edmund she never found love ever again. A series of bad choices and even worse men had left Phoebe with precious little to show for her life. If, she had known the true extent of Edmund's deception and ultimate betrayal Phoebe might have found it easier to move on instead of yearning for what might have been. Star crossed, lovers they were not, when all was said and done Edmund treated her very shabbily.

At least now Phoebe had Rita to brighten her old age. Even if she never found love ever again, she had Ivy, Betty, and now Rita and Rita's children, for Phoebe this was riches indeed. But what did Deirdre have? Deirdre was giving up the life she had with Rita to protect the girl from damaging revelations.

Phoebe knew she would always be in Deirdre's debt; she felt sorry for the gentle, spinster lady who had spent her life living quietly in the shadows, a woman gracious enough to walk away from the only love in her life.

"I'll look after everything for you Deirdre, I promise." Phoebe could see the possibilities the house had. The box room had a small bed pushed up against the wall, but it could easily be turned into a pretty bedroom for June, or for Deirdre, if ever Deirdre came to stay. Phoebe was beginning to see Deirdre as a true friend and ally.

"If you've got an hour to spare Phoebe then perhaps you could help me pack and sort out things in the upstairs cupboards. There are all sorts of things I need to get rid of and now's the time. I never wanted to tackle getting rid of things Mam or Da used to wear, but they're no good to anyone now, and I expect the moths will have got at most of them… this old house is rather cold and damp particularly in the winter," Deirdre smiled sadly. For all its failings it was the only house she had ever known, and it held a lot of happy memories.

"What will you do with the things you don't want Deirdre?"

"Once we've been through all the pockets and taken off the buttons, we can put the old clothes out for the rag and bone man to collect. Old Eric passes through Alma road most Fridays with his horse and cart collecting anything useful, so I'd like to have a pile of things ready for him to take this week. There's no point keeping any old clothes left in the cupboards now, most will have been eaten by the moths or blemished by mildew after years of being undisturbed, Eric will send them off to make shoddy…. He'll even offer you a goldfish if he likes what you've put out." Deirdre chuckled.

The throaty cries of "any rag bone… rag bone…" echoing through the streets brought local children running from far and wide, many a time Deirdre heard Frank and Jennifer pestering to be allowed a goldfish. Deirdre smiled at the memory and struggled to hold back a tear; *she had to be brave.*

"Of course, I'll help you sort things out Deirdre, I'm in no rush to get back. Ivy and Billy are taking June out to the park, I won't be missed."

166

Phoebe settled down to the task of snipping off shirt and blouse buttons from a pile of old garments. Quite a few of Deirdre's mother's clothes were spotted with rust and unfashionable old shoes had a bloom of mildew across the leather. As the old clothes were disturbed several spiders scuttled out causing Phoebe to shriek.

"That just shows you it's never worth keeping things stuck for years at the back of cupboards," Deirdre chortled as a huge fat spider caused Phoebe to jump onto the bed. "I should have done this job years ago, but somehow I wasn't ready to let go… but now I am," Deirdre felt calmer as the cupboards and wardrobes started to empty.

"Shall I tackle the chest of drawers?" Phoebe pointed to the small chest beside the bed, it felt strange and intrusive to be going through another person's possessions without asking permission.

"Yes please Phoebe…that used to be Edmund's drawer, I haven't checked in there, but there weren't many of his things left here once he left home to be a priest. Mam just put a few things in there he didn't take with him." Deirdre ambled over to open the chest of drawers and as she suspected there was little of note. Deirdre piled the few shirts and other items on the floor for Phoebe to retrieve the buttons. Suddenly a golden object dropped out of the clothes and bounced under the bed.

"Oh, dear Deirdre, it looks as if one button is trying to escape, it's gone under the bedstead," Phoebe said, she looked wary, reluctant to put her hands under the bed in search of the button in case some of the escaped spiders lurked there now.

"I can see it Phoebe; don't worry I'll reach under the bed and get it. I don't mind spiders and it didn't go far," Deirdre scrabbled around under the gloomy bedstead and found the small round item.

"Bingo,!" Deidre examined the golden object nestling in the palm of her hand. "Well blow me down… it's not a metal button after all Phoebe, it's a small ring of sorts!" She passed the ring to Phoebe. "I've never ever seen Edmund wear a ring, and certainly not this one." Deirdre looked puzzled.

Phoebe examined the small ring with the intricately engraved oval cartouche on the front. The roaring dragon entwined around a castle turret was a distinctive emblem. It was obviously the sort of ring a gentleman of wealth might wear on his little finger, a seal ring with the family crest, despite its size it felt heavy in Phoebe's hand. She handed it back to Deirdre.

Deirdre looked inside the ring, there was an engraving of two intertwined initials, "are you sure you didn't give this ring to Edmund Phoebe? I think those look like your initials engraved on the inside of the shank. That certainly looks like an old-fashioned P and a H to me." Deirdre passed it back to Phoebe to examine the engraving.

"Honestly Deirdre I've *never* seen this ring before in my life…and it looks like real gold too; I could never afford an expensive ring like this." Phoebe squinted at the intricate entwined initials and the penny dropped. *It wasn't a P and an H, Deirdre could see engraved inside the ring it was the letters P and L…. Piers Loxley!*

"I didn't give this to Edmund Deirdre, but I think I can guess who the ring might have belonged to. In the notebook you gave me Edmund mentioned a *close* friend who died in the trenches, he was called Piers Loxley, I suspect this might be his ring." Phoebe didn't see the point in shocking Deirdre with the true nature of Edmund's friendship with Piers Loxley, Edmund had fallen far enough in Deirdre's estimation as it was. Some secrets were best left undisturbed.

"Do you think Edmund meant to give it back to the Loxley family?" Deirdre turned the small ring over and over in the palm of her hand.

"Who is to say what he meant to do with the ring Deirdre, it might have been a dying gift from his friend Piers, or Edmund might have found it on the battlefield and picked it up meaning to return it," *or* Phoebe though to herself, *or it might have been some sort of pledge or gift between two men who loved each other.* "I think the question is what do you want to do with it now… as owner of this house and all its contents it is yours after all." Phoebe handed it back to Deirdre.

"I don't want it Phoebe… in an ideal world I would like to give it back to the young man's family, it might have been a family heirloom, or an important gift and I'm sure they would welcome this keepsake back. It doesn't seem right to just sell it or put it to the back of the drawer again now we've found it."

Deirdre was an honest woman and the thought that somewhere a grieving family years ago might have wondered what happened to their son's signet ring when he lost his life on the battlefields bothered her. She felt the only honourable thing to do would be to reunite the ring with the family who claimed the dragon and castle crest as their own.

"In Edmund's notes he said Piers Loxley came from an important family in Gloucestershire, I'm sure it must be possible to track them down, great families with long histories are usually in lots of records and this crest is quite unusual so it must be a good clue as to who the owner was." Phoebe mused. "I can try to track down the Loxley family for you if you like Deirdre?" Phoebe thought of the imposing library in the centre of Cardiff stacked with huge reference books, surely that would be the place to start looking for the mysterious wealthy Loxley family.

"Yes please Phoebe, it seems right thing to do." Deirdre handed the ring back. She knew Phoebe would try her best to find the ring's rightful owner, even after all this time it was still a ring of importance and some value.

"I'll take it with me then Deirdre and I'll try my best to track the Loxley family down. It may take me a while, but if I find out anything I'll let you know, and then we can decide what to do next. I'd best be off home now Deirdre." Just at that moment, a drumming sound began to beat on the windows, so loud it was as if someone was tossing handfuls of small pebbles up against the old panes.

"Goodness me Phoebe, just listen to that… it's starting to rain cats and dogs out there." Deirdre looked out at the lead heavy skies hovering over slate roof tops. Fat black clouds were dropping a torrent of rain, washing rubbish down into the gutters.

Rain splashed and spattered noisily on the windows. At first it was just one or two fat drops hitting the glass but within moments the downpour was cascading off the roofs and gurgling through the guttering; the bright morning weather had broken.

Chapter 29

It was the third week of January, and with Deirdre's permission, Phoebe placed some adverts for a furnished room to rent in Alma road; available from the first week of February. Phoebe placed six small white post cards in all the local tobacconist and newsagents' windows and sat back to await results. Phoebe was beginning to get to know her new patch, she spent her spare time on the weekends walking the streets around Alma road. Bag in hand she walked up and down all the busy thoroughfares which bled towards the City centre. Taking her routes through Cathays and Roath, exploring cut throughs and narrow alley ways until Phoebe started to feel she knew the area like the back of her hand. Like a cat mapping out its territory Phoebe walked miles in pursuit of knowledge; she soon recognised familiar landmarks and got to know all the shortcuts and slip throughs.

The chatty postmistress, who ran the counter in Wellfield road said rooms to rent in the area were in short supply; travelling salesmen supplying shops were often on the lookout for a base in Cardiff, she suggested Phoebe place a small advert on her notice board to attract a lodger.

Phoebe could see the Post Office was a busy one, and after adding her card she began to be hopeful of a quick result, after all she didn't have much money to last her for more than a few weeks at best. With any luck, Phoebe would soon have an income coming in, she needed pounds in her purse. She had to make a go of running the house she couldn't afford this venture to fail. She was getting too old now to be out treading the wharf in Cardiff looking for hungry eyed men ready to part with their hard-earned money for ten minutes comfort.

Over the years Phoebe had seen the older women down on the wharf, shivering in the cold when trade was slack in some of the less desirable parts of Tiger Bay. They stood forlornly with their lined faces edged out by the brassy younger women standing in the prime positions; sad careworn women existing on the margins turning tricks at a discount whilst younger plumper flesh attracted the cheeky lads with the money looking for a good time.

That was the life she used to lead in the dark alley ways of Tiger bay, just her and Betty against the world, but that was then, and now they had both left that world behind and embraced respectability. It was not the life for her now, she would never go back to it.

She had promised Deirdre she would look after the house, and she wasn't going to fail because of lack of money, she must find a lodger. Phoebe couldn't risk the shame of being caught soliciting on the wharf. Now she had people she cared about, her newly acquired good reputation was precious to her and she was not prepared to lose it no matter how much she had to tighten her belt.

Phoebe was going to be a respectable landlady running her own premises and with any luck she would be able to look forward to comfortable old age sat by the warmth of her own fire not lurking in the windy alleys and doorways of Tiger bay.

Phoebe knew she would have to be business minded, there could be no more being soft-hearted taking in waifs and strays under her wing like she did with Betty all those years ago. She decided that maybe a gentleman lodger would be best… if only she could find the right one!

It might seem hard hearted, but she didn't want history to repeat itself. Phoebe would not open her home to a young woman in trouble like she did for Betty. Living next door to her daughter Rita and the children, Phoebe wasn't going to run a disreputable household. She couldn't afford tongues to wag and curtains to twitch in respectable Alma road, she wouldn't give Rita any excuse to shun her. If she took in a woman into the house at all then she would have to be respectable woman beyond reproach.

And yet Phoebe had to admit that in her heart she felt a bit nervous at the thought of a man living upstairs next to her bedroom, *she must talk to Betty about it.*

All the thoughts about advantages and disadvantages of who she should choose as a lodger left Phoebe's head in a whirl. Betty's experiences with the devious Jimmy Benson had taught Phoebe to be wary of who she invited into her home; people lied and twisted to get what they wanted. If living in Tiger bay had taught Phoebe one thing, it was that people were rarely what they seemed to be. She didn't want to invite any trouble in her home.

Her home… it had a marvellous ring about it. In just over a weeks' time Phoebe would be sitting in her *own* sitting room, mistress of her *own* household; her heart fluttered with excitement.

171

Phoebe decide to pop into Hallit's, a small, busy newsagents and confectioners on corner of Albany road on the off chance that someone might have responded to her advert placed on the cramped noticeboard. Phoebe was so anxious to move into Alma road, just walking the streets around the area felt like a step in the right direction.

The tinkle of the corner shop bell announced Phoebe's entry, nothing got past old man Hallit or his eagle-eyed son Adrian who was usually left in charge of the shop watching for light fingered children.

"Can I help you with something missus?" A fourteen-year-old lad stood up to serve, he'd been tidying the racks of sweets in the back of the store. A newly assembled "Trebor Quality Sweets" display stood in the corner of the store awaiting stock and Adrian was sorting the shop supply of Refreshers and other Trebor items to best advantage.

"The Trebor sweet man called early today with this new stand and loads of stock, it's taken me ages to get the blessed thing put together." Adrian said by way of explanation for the mass of boxes still piled higgledy -piggledy on the shop floor.

Phoebe could see the lad was busy. "I was just checking on my advert and I noticed it has been taken down," Phoebe pointed to the gap on the shop notice board just inside the shop door.

The lad blew through his teeth, "blimey I told him not to take it down, nobody ever listens these days. I always say *don't take the cards down,* but they always do, every week we lose a few." The lad rolled his eyes in disgust, the theft of the small ads cards was a regular source of annoyance. "I'm sorry about that missus, you can put another one up if like, how long did it have left to run?"

"I had just over another week to go. I'm advertising a room to let in Alma road."

"Are you now?.... Well, that explains it, rooms to rent are like gold dust these days. People always think it will stop others getting there first if they take down the adverts. The Trebor salesman in earlier said he was looking for a room an 'all... not that I'm accusing him or nothing, 'cos I didn't see it go" Adrian added quickly. "Sometimes they whip 'em down so quick, it's gone in a blink of an eye. Tell you what, I'll put another one up for a week and.... if you like, I'll tape the card inside the door window that way it won't get taken down in a hurry, drawing pins are too easy by half." Adrian gave Phoebe the full benefit of his advice on avoiding the theft of her advert.

"Goodness me," Phoebe laughed, "it looks like I won't have any trouble finding myself a lodger, if it's that cutthroat around here. I'm beginning to think I might rent out the middle room as well." Phoebe watched as the crisp new card was secured firmly on the windowpane.

Renting out the middle room was a real possibility; she could put a small bed in the downstairs middle room as well as letting out the upstairs bedroom. The middle room was rather small and dingy, but it might suit one of those travelling salesmen the Post Office lady mentioned, especially if they only wanted a temporary set of lodgings now and again.

She might have to seriously consider it.

Chapter 30

"Phoebe's popping in for a cup of tea later on this morning Gerald." Betty called through to the sitting room. She heard Gerlad stacking up the fire for the morning, she was down on her hands and knees tidying out cupboards in the scullery, not exactly a Spring clean but as close as she was going to get on the first cold, wet week in February. The tiny lean to at the back of the house served as Betty's kitchen, it was much smaller than her old kitchen in Bute street and easier to look after, she felt it was time to have an early spring clean whilst she was in the mood. Left over brown paper from Christmas meant there was plenty to re-line and freshen the cutlery drawer, freshly washed knives, forks, and spoons were piled on the wooden draining board waiting to be replaced.

"Goodness me love," Gerald looked at the disarray gripping the kitchen, "you've certainly given yourself a job of work, don't you usually wait for spring before pulling all the cupboards to bits?" Gerald hated the house being all topsy turvy, but he knew it was more than his life's worth to criticise a woman on a mission tackling chores. His amiable late wife Janet was known to turn into a tartar when she was giving the house a good "going over" as she liked to refer to her twice yearly attack on the spidery cobwebs and mouldy corners.

"Did you say Phoebe was popping by again for a cup of tea later on?" Gerald looked hopefully at the kettle and wondered if it would be possible to step over the pile of saucepans which had made their way down from the kitchen shelf rack and make himself a cup of tea. He was parched and dying for a nice strong brew whilst he sat and read his morning newspaper. The idea of Phoebe coming over for the morning didn't exactly fill him with joy either, this was the second time this week and Phoebe only moved to Alma road on the weekend.

Now Betty's friend was living just around the corner it seemed to Gerald that Phoebe might be a rather frequent visitor in the Williams household. *Hopefully not too frequent.*

"She'll be here in about an hour, and she wants some advice…. Now she has moved into Alma road she's got to take in lodgers to help with bills; she wants us to help her make the right decision." Betty scrubbed furiously at the oilskin cloth lining the larder cupboard.

"Us?" Gerald said doubtfully.

Betty gave her husband a sideways glance, "Yes *us* Gerald…. After Jimmy Benson managed to trick his way into Bute street I thought it would be useful if you and I helped her with the decision, just chatted it through like before her mind was made up. Phoebe has promised to let the potential lodgers know her decision straight away and she wants to hear our views. I thought, being a man, you might think of something we miss." Betty gave him a winning smile and Gerald knew it was hopeless to argue.

Gerald scratched his head and left the kitchen with a glass of water; his cup of tea would have to wait until Phoebe arrived. *How on earth would he know what made a good lodger?*

*

The first day Phoebe moved into Alma road was one of the happiest days of her life. The first Saturday in February was golden and crisp, the morning air was like wine and Phoebe offered up a small prayer of thanks for the kind, sweet woman who had gifted her such joy. She hoped and prayed Deirdre Roberts was waking up to an equally sparkling morning in Porthcawl.

Phoebe took the unfamiliar keys from her purse and fumbled with the stiff front door latch, a small face, Jennifer, peeped through the net curtains next door and waved frantically at her new neighbour, her new *Aunty Phoebe.* Phoebe waved back to Jennifer Prosser and smiled; it was the perfect start to her first day. All Phoebe had to bring with her was two small brown leather suitcases and the clothes she stood up in.

It was hard to believe the house was truly hers, Phoebe had to almost pinch herself to believe she had just walked in through her own front door, and she would hang her coat and hat in her own hallway. Phoebe took a moment to drink in the delicious feeling of coming home for the first time.

The narrow hall smelled of fresh beeswax and lavender furniture polish. Before she left Deirdre cleaned the house from top to toe, tracing the house into her memory. Deirdre shed a few quiet tears as she said goodbye to the only home she'd ever known.

When Deirdre washed down the paintwork for the last time, it was almost as if she was washing herself and Edmund out of the picture. In her mind's eye she could still see her father standing by the black slate fireplace with his pipe and slippers and in the kitchen she could imagine her mother making Welsh cakes on the bakestone; the memory of the tempting aroma of cinnamon and warm cake was making her mouth water. It was all gone now, a past so distant Deirdre barely recognised herself as the carefree girl she once was.

Deirdre shook her head and the image left her, that was another life and another world away! She must not look back; she could only look forward to her new life and hope God had a purpose for her. Even in her darkest moments Deirdre still believed when God shut a door He opened a window somewhere.

She was content Phoebe was going to live in the old house now and she wished her every happiness. Deirdre knew how much Phoebe had suffered because of her foolish brother Edmund, and in her heart Deirdre wanted nothing but happiness for the woman who had, unexpectedly become her friend. Deirdre's final polishing and cleaning of the old house was a last gift to Phoebe, these walls would be hers to love and look after now.

 The colourful Victorian black, white, and ochre tiles gleamed and the stained glass in the front door let in rainbow shards of early morning sun light illuminating the cool dark interior. Phoebe stood in the hall on that first morning and the old house seemed to welcome her, she trailed her fingers over the shining banisters and headed for the kitchen to explore her new domain.

Phoebe knew money would be tight, but she was used to that. Years of penny pinching taught her how to make do and mend; thankfully, Deirdre had left her a half full coal bunker in the yard so at least she would have a fire at night. A sack of potatoes and a box of autumn apples, too heavy for Deirdre take with her, sat in the in the yard outhouse, but otherwise the larder shelves were bare.

Phoebe would need to get to the shops soon for some provisions or else there would be nothing for her supper tonight or her breakfast in the morning; whilst out shopping she might just pop into Betty's to cadge a quick cup of tea.

When Phoebe returned home from her trip to the shops clutching eggs, cheese, a loaf of bread, margarine, a pound of sugar and some tea, it was already growing dusk and the temperature was dropping rapidly. After the laughter and chat with Betty and Gerald over a cup of tea and biscuits by a warm fire, the old house in Alma road felt echoing, empty, and lifeless. Phoebe had laid the fireplace in the back parlour but decided she would save fuel and not light the fire until it was dark; she could always wear a second cardigan if it felt too chilly.

Phoebe opened every cupboard in the house and found them emptied of all the bric a brac and clutter from a lifetime of living. A few useful pots and pans and items of crockery were left for her in the kitchen, and three pairs of sheets and pillowcases had been left in the linen cupboard, but otherwise the place was a blank canvass for Phoebe to write her own narrative on. She felt daunted and excited by the prospect in equal measure.

After buying a few essential items for the larder Phoebe's purse was looking decidedly empty, a portion of her money had already been spent on small adverts and now only a few coins rattled around in the leather slots and one precious brown ten bob note nestled in the wallet part; it certainly wouldn't last long if she didn't find a source of income soon. Phoebe would have to watch the pennies until she had secured herself a lodger.

Phoebe had received four encouraging responses from her small adverts scattered around the local newsagents and three responses from the advert in the Post Office, not as many as she hoped for, but at least it gave her a choice and she needed to get those rooms let straight away. In a few days the larder would be bare, her laundry would need doing and she needed to buy some soap, starch, and blue bag. With other household items such as toothpaste and vegetables also running low, at this rate her money would soon be gone. After shivering by a small fire with just some toast and marge for her supper and toast and weak tea for breakfast, Phoebe had decided there was nothing for it; she *must* rent out the middle room as well as the one upstairs bedroom.

The more Phoebe thought about it, the more sense it made to get as much money as she could from letting out any rooms she didn't need for herself, otherwise bills would be piling up, with nothing to pay them with. She had the privacy of the front sitting room, she didn't need the middle room lying idle she told herself.

The middle room had a glazed door opening directly into the back yard so access to the outside lavatory would be easy. There was a connecting side gate from the yard which led to the service lane running behind the City road shops, so if someone kept odd hours it might suit them to use the lane.

The middle room might only be small, but it could work well as a sitting room and bedroom combined and with the access out to the yard, the house wouldn't seem too busy if a second tenant came and went through the lane entrance. Phoebe didn't want to be giving her front door keys to every Tom Dick and Harry.

Phoebe vowed to herself that she would never go back to the dingy dark alleyways of Tiger Bay no matter how tight money became. She needed to find two suitable lodgers now, not just one to fit the household, double the worry as well as double the money.

Phoebe was a little concerned at the prospect of having two men living under her roof, whilst at first she thought a gentleman lodger would be ideal, perhaps she had been too hasty to dismiss the idea of a lady lodger if the *right* sort could be found.... The best person to ask for advice on the matter would be Betty.

Luckily, Betty lived only a few streets away, Betty would not see her old friend go hungry or cold until she had found her feet. Phoebe decided to go around to Inkerman street and ask for some advice about how to pick two lodgers from the pile to invite under her roof. Strike whilst the iron is hot was Phoebe's motto, she felt sure that by the end of the day she would find her list of lodgers.

Running out of money meant returning to Tiger Bay and that was never going to happen!

Chapter 31

Ivy and Billy had settled on the last week in March to get married. Billy had visited the Registrar in County hall and completed all the documentation and now all they had to do was wait for the happy day to arrive. Anxious not to spend money they didn't have, Ivy said she didn't need a new dress for the occasion. Billy however was insistent she should look her best on their wedding day.

"Don't be soft Ivy, I'm certain we can run to a new dress, it's our wedding day for heaven's sake."

"All I'm saying Billy is that money is going to be tight without wasting money on a new dress I don't need. At this rate it's going to be a small affair anyway so there's no need to have any extra fuss and expense." Ivy knew Billy was still arguing with his parents about the wedding, Billy would get no help from them towards any wedding costs. Her Mam had offered to chip in for a modest wedding breakfast in a nearby hotel, but that still left bills to pay, and money was very tight.

"Ivy," Billy snapped, "we are *not* having some hole in the corner wedding, it's going to be the proudest day of my life and I intend to enjoy it! June will be a bridesmaid in her best frock, and you will be wearing a pretty new dress now that's the end of the matter!"

Billy didn't mean to snap but he was fed up with everyone chipping in their ten pennorth worth about this wedding and it was beginning to grind him down. His poor brother, George was caught in the middle between his wife, Alice, enthusing about how wonderful it would be to have Ivy as her sister-in-law and his parents informing George they expected him to take their side on the matter and have as little to do with Ivy and Billy as possible if the wedding did go ahead.

Billy couldn't understand why his parents had set their faces against Ivy in the way they had, it wasn't her fault her husband Jimmy had been a wrong 'un. But in his heart Billy knew that it wasn't just Ivy they had taken against it was really June they couldn't stomach… They were ashamed of the girl with the lolling tongue and almond eyes, a child they thought should be hidden away in an institution, a misfit.

His parents wanted to show off and brag about some golden new grandchild, a perfect specimen to carry on the family name, they did not want to welcome into the family a little girl who would always be different and would never grow up. Billy was disgusted with his Da, but it was his Mam who annoyed him the most. Surely his Mam as a woman and a mother should understand the love Ivy had for her child? Instead, his Mam judged Ivy for keeping June and "*parading her in public.*"

Billy could stand no more of it, he vowed that if one more person said something unkind about June then he would give them a piece of his mind, he would lay into them with both barrels to teach them a lesson. *June was not a child to be ashamed of and woe betide anyone who tried to tell him differently he was fed up to the eye balls with nasty comments and snide remarks*

Anxious to get as much money together, as he could for his new life with Ivy, Billy was working long hours at the Caroline street fish bar. He was also working the early morning shifts in Queen's wharf on the West quay as a porter delivering goods into the cavernous warehouses lining the bustling docks. The work was heavy and hard, but Billy was fit, nimble and a good worker; he moved the heavy loads around the quayside with ease.

Billy Thomas was a familiar face around the docks from the days when he went with his Da and his brother to learn about buying fish stock for the family chip shop. Many familiar old faces around the quays greeted Billy early in the mornings as he went about his business, but even Billy could see the quays were changing in character, some new faces were carving a niche for themselves, other fortunes were on the wane.

Some of the new men, fresh in on the ferries sought work with a group of Irish labourers who had set up a base on the East quay. The East quay crew was led by Paddy McGuire. Belfast men and Dubliner's looking for work sought comradeship and a friendly face amongst their own kind and the East quay docker crew grew in strength. Burly Paddy McGuire had quite a nice little racket going on the East side of the docklands and his turf was guarded jealously. Word was spreading that Paddy was looking to spread his influence across the whole of Tiger Bay.

Many blacks, and Hispanics fresh into port gravitated towards the West quay and the Kenyan gang master known as Black Harry- the imposing Kayfe Ramrakha was a man to be reckoned with, cock of the walk. But the draw of the new challenger, Paddy McGuire, was growing stronger and Paddy's reputation as a key player was building.

Black Harry's star was not in the ascendency now and the feel of the docks was changing. Other fitter, younger men such as Paddy were threatening Black Harry's power base, scuffles, and fights on the quays late at night were frequent; disputes were usually settled the old-fashioned way. But for now, Black Harry held sway and this area of Queen's wharf came under his protection and woe betide anyone who tried to encroach on his turf.

Some of Jimmy's old comrades, such as Ajo Abbas, Black Harry's right-hand man, still worked the docks too, except now they had rewritten history and distanced themselves from any links to Jimmy Benson and his mucky trade. Memories were long and Jimmy Benson's name was mud in Tiger Bay, nobody would admit to once being a close friend of Jimmy Benson.

Safe under Harry's protection, Ajo still swaggered about the quays and the busy wharfs like a top dog. That morning as Billy was stacking fish crates on a pallet, Ajo strolled through, he was busy instructing three new men in the ways of doing business on the wharf. Ajo saw Billy walk past on the far side of the fish yard and called out loudly to the three burly Poles lounging on a bench nearby... "and make sure that you stay away from him lads if you know what's good for you, that's not fish you can smell on Billy Thomas... it's Jimmy Benson's shit... he's got it smeared all over him!" Ajo pinched his nose between his thumb and forefinger and gave an exaggerated "Phwe," the three men fell about in gales of laughter.

"Phew I can smell it an' all from 'ere," one cringer said loudly eager to curry favour, "you're right Ajo he does pong!"

Billy downed his fish crate and stood to face his tormentors. Billy was not stupid; he knew there was gossip about him and Ivy getting married. He had heard the odd disobliging comment behind his back or caught a snippet of muttered gossip in a bar, the landlord at the Rose and Crown even changed the subject rapidly once when Billy went in the pub for pint of ale. But he'd never been called out and shamed like this in public and he wasn't standing for it.

"What's your problem Ajo?" Billy stared at the lean, weasel-faced, man standing in front of him. Billy stood tall and powerful, years of heavy work meant he was well muscled and a good three inches taller than the dark-skinned Moroccan smirking and swaggering on the quay.

But Ajo had the advantage of Billy, three brutish dockers with hands like lump hammers were watching his back and he could afford to be cocky. "Ain't me who's got the problem Billy," Ajo guffawed. "Seems to me you've got the problem picking up Jimmy Benson's filthy rubbish."

The three other men watched the scene and laughed uproariously. Ajo was no fighter, but nobody messed with Black Harry's man. Ajo strolled slowly towards Billy and stood within inches of Billy's face. "Seems to me Billy you're stupid," Ajo tapped his temple as if to say Billy was deficient somehow, "not only do you choose to marry Benson's bitch, but you want to bring up her retard an' all…. Women like that shouldn't be breeding." Ajo sniggered and spat in the gutter as if to say that was what he thought of Ivy and June Benson.

Fists clenched; Billy lunged towards Ajo. "You little piece of shit!" Billy exploded. Heedless of the fact he was outnumbered Billy was going deal with the grinning devil standing in front of him and wipe the smile off his smirking face. *Ajo would pay for those remarks.*

Two sets of powerful arms grabbed Billy before he could take a swing at Ajo. Billy was pinned and powerless to fight back. In the scuffle a fish crate was overturned sending a shower of slippery mackerel cascading across the greasy cobbles.

"Tsk, Tsk Billy, now look what you've gone and done…. Looks to me like you've got some more smelly stuff to pick up." Ajo kicked a spoiled fish towards Billy. "You need to be more careful Billy."

In the distance Ajo could see an irate warehouse manager sprinting over to the scene. Ajo gestured to his men to let Billy go. Ajo stood his ground and assumed an innocent expression.

"Hey… hey… what are you men playing at… that fish is going to be ruined at this rate." Alun Jones the warehouse manager yelled at the top of his voice, his feet. powered towards the group. He could see his precious stock scattered on the quay, his face was red with fury and the effort of running. *This looked like trouble brewing and he didn't need a ruckus outside his warehouse.*

"I'll have you Ajo, so help me I will," Billy seethed, his eyes glittered with rage. "Don't think you can frighten me, 'cos you ain't so brave on your own… an' you won't always have this little gang here to protect you!" Billy raged as Ajo surrounded by his men burst into gales of mocking laughter.

Ajo and the three men turned to go just as Alun Jones arrived at the scene. Ajo gave a shrug of his shoulders towards the warehouse manager as if to say *it's nothing to do with me mate* and strolled away leaving Billy to pick up the fish lying in the grit and grease.

"I'm not going to forget this you bastard," Billy shook his fist and scraped up the scattered mackerel from the cobbles.

"What the bloody hell is going on here… is this your fault Billy," Alun Jones demanded, he recognized Black Harry's man Ajo Abbas and he didn't want any trouble.

"No Mr Jones, it's *not* my fault" Billy said through gritted teeth. "Ajo barged into me on purpose… he made me spill this fish." Billy watched Ajo and his grinning acolytes stroll away, Billy could hear the jeering and sniggering as he scrabbled about on his hands and knees picking up the scattered slippery fish.

"I'll have you for this Ajo, do you hear me!" Billy shook his fist and yelled at the Moroccan's retreating back.

"No, you won't Billy," Alun Jones said hastily, "I'm not having any trouble around my warehouse, I think you'd better collect your wages and go. You're good worker, but I don't want any trouble on my patch, is that understood Billy…. Just pick up the fish and we'll say no more about it."

Billy could see the manager looked scared, he couldn't blame him, word would be all around in the quays like wildfire that Billy Thomas had threatened Ajo Abbas. Like as not no-one would give him a job in another warehouse on this side of the docks either if Black Harry had anything to say about it.

"Yes Mr Jones," Billy said glumly, he tossed the last of the mackerel back in the crate.

"I'm sorry Billy," Alun Jones, raised the palms of his hands as if to say he didn't have a choice; turned and left. *He would need to take on another man tomorrow. Alun liked Billy Thomas and he was sorry to lose him, but Black Harry could make life difficult if he chose to... Billy Thomas wasn't worth the hassle, another hungry man would be hunting for a job in the morning.*

Billy told himself he would come back early tomorrow morning and look for work elsewhere; perhaps there would be another job over on the East side with someone in Tiger bay who wasn't cowed or owned by Black Harry. Maybe the new big man Paddy McGuire might give him a chance to work on his patch. Billy needed the money, and he wasn't giving up that easily just because Ajo had caused trouble on the West quay.

*

Early the next morning Billy trailed the East side of the docks looking for work, as he cut through Queen's Wharf, he noticed the shifty glances, muttered comments and the turned backs of men who once upon a time would have shouted a cheery "good morning".

Stuff 'em, they've obviously been listening to Ajo, Billy seethed, if he couldn't find work today over on the East side then he'd check out the opportunities in the covered market. Plenty of stall holders remembered his Da with affection; he felt confident something would crop up.

As he feared, there was no work to be had that morning on the East quay. Paddy McGuire's men had it all tied up and the newcomer Billy was not needed. Mysteriously another man standing behind Billy in the waiting line did get offered a job, but Billy and the others were turned away and told to try again tomorrow.

"Blow that for a game of soldiers," Billy muttered to himself. He knew it was pointless trying to find work on the docks today if he had a black mark against his name. He decided to head for the Cardiff open market first thing the next morning, perhaps he would have better luck there. *Bloody Ajo!* Billy muttered under his breath.

Later that morning on the far Western side of the docks a hullabaloo went up. The tide was running unexpectedly low, and some discarded ropes and a large tarpaulin had managed to tangle themselves up around the small jetty leading from the main pier. The untidy ballooning tarpaulin was blocking some of the best casual moorings used by smaller fishing vessels coming into port.

Rubbish and debris thrown in from the docks or brought down from the fast-flowing Taff river upstream and it usually floated out across the bay on the fierce current crossing the dock mouth. But if debris wasn't washed straight out to sea on the retreating tide, then a mass of flotsam and jetsam would often swirl and settle near the jetty.

Once firmly entangled in the legs of the jetty, an ugly mass of detritus would build, blocking the pier, so the only option was to dislodge the obstacle and either fish it out or send it on its way before it grew into a veritable island of rubbish.

After violent winter storms, tree branches and even the occasional dead sheep swirled in a large unwieldy mass around moorings, the fishermen got used to clearing the jetty area before tying up the boats.

That morning the men on the small fishing vessels, hoping to secure their craft, had tried to move the new obstruction blocking the way with their long fishing gaffs. With a few sharp tugs of the grey tarpaulin the lifeless, battered body of the Moroccan, Ajo, bobbed up to the surface like a cork.

Shouts rang out across the docks.

Chapter 32

"So, what do *you* think I should do Betty?" Phoebe said uncertainly, apart from Betty she had never taken someone into her home before and the magnitude of the decision facing her was overwhelming. After all she had Rita to think about now, this wasn't some rough and ready street in Tiger Bay where everyone turned a blind eye to shady goings on; she needed to be certain she wasn't opening herself up to criticism from the neighbours. Phoebe had standards to maintain now. Betty's awful personal experience with the devious, smiling charm of Jimmy Benson had taught Phoebe one thing about lodgers; you certainly couldn't judge a book by its cover.

"It's not an easy decision Phoebe," Betty agreed as she nibbled her biscuit. She was intrigued to hear about the woman who had responded to an advert placed in the small Tobacconist just around the corner. Even though the advert had clearly stated a gentleman lodger was preferred, the lady had the nerve to apply and make her case.

Annoyingly Gerald was doing an excellent job of keeping out of the way this morning, so it was left up to Betty to give Phoebe advice on the tricky subject of lodgers.

Phoebe thrust the lavender coloured note paper from Miss Carol Jones towards Betty.

"It says here she's a spinster lady and that she teaches music and singing to pupils in their own homes. Sounds all right to me, at least you won't have to put up with the noise Phoebe; in fact, it makes her sound quite genteel." Betty mused. "Apparently she says since her parents died she needs to find somewhere modest to live and she thinks your room in Alma road would suit her down to the ground…. So, what's the problem here Phoebe?"

"I don't know," Phoebe wailed. "My mind is in a whirl Betty. Do you think I should take on this woman when I haven't even advertised for a woman, or do you think I should take on two men and be done with it!" Phoebe sipped her tea. Was she wrong to be suspicious of a single woman seeking lodgings?

The trouble was Phoebe knew, only too well, how hard it was for a single woman to find rooms too rent and how too often women had to lie from necessity, especially if it was a woman in trouble with a baby in her belly. What if this woman was not what she appeared to be? On the other hand, Phoebe preferred the idea of a woman upstairs in the house and a man living downstairs. *She felt in a total whirl, and she needed to make a swift decision.*

"And what are the men like who have applied," Betty looked through a few responses.

"It's hard to say from the notes they have left... the trouble is I thought it might be better if I had a travelling salesman in the middle room and only one of those has applied for the room and, annoyingly, it's that Trebor sweet representative I told you about."

"The one Adrian Hallit said he suspected removed your card from the shop notice board."

"Exactly Betty!"

"Perhaps he was just desperate Phoebe, and he won't be the only one doing it if rooms are that hard to come by," Betty said kindly, "and you only know about it because young Adrian drew it to your attention and... Adrian might have got it wrong Phoebe, it might have been the next customer who whipped it."

"True."

"Why not ask a couple of the men around you like the sound of to see what you think of them and the lady as well?... I'll be there with you if you want a bit of support." Betty offered.

"Would you please Betty? It would set my mind at rest to get a second opinion. I can't afford to have empty rooms for much longer and I need to have some money coming in P.D.Q."

It was decided, Phoebe would choose the three most suitable sounding male applicants and the woman and invite them to come to the house on Saturday, with Betty's help, she would make up her mind and, with any luck Phoebe would have her two paying lodgers before the weekend was out.

*

"Well, he was bloody awful!" Phoebe heaved a sigh of relief after the first man on her list left. "Open the back door Betty to let some air through," Phoebe stood waggling the front door to and fro to waft fresh air into the house and disperse the overpowering smell of foul body odour lingering in the hallway. It irritated Phoebe she had to sacrifice the house warmth to rid herself of the dreadful pong left behind.

"He did smell a bit like a pole cat!" Betty giggled. "I assume he will not be top of your list of lodgers!"

Phoebe rolled her eyes. She had decided to have three men to view the property in the morning with the Trebor salesman being the last on her list. Betty protested Phoebe held an unreasonable grudge against the Trebor man on the basis of nothing more than hearsay from Adrian Hallit, but Phoebe's order stayed. The only lady to apply was invited to view the room at just after lunchtime.

"If I like the first two men who view the rooms then I'll have them," Phoebe explained to Betty "and if I only like one of the men.... or none of the men then I can consider Miss Carol Jones, that's why she's coming in the afternoon." Phoebe felt there was a logic to her thinking. Betty though it was a scatty approach but held her tongue.

The second applicant fared equally badly. An elderly looking man with two missing front teeth and frayed cuffs did his best to appear like the hardworking clerk he professed to be.

"Did he say where he worked when he replied to the advert?" Betty asked sceptically.

Phoebe shook her head, she refused to believe the latest applicant could afford the room and dismissed him out of hand. "He looked down on his luck Betty, there's a lot of people losing their jobs now, and I'd lay a pound to a penny he's between jobs. He couldn't even afford a proper set of dentures for heaven's sake! I need someone who can pay the bills not a hard luck story." Phoebe frowned and felt her heart sink; this was proving harder than she thought it would be.

"Oh well Betty that just leaves the Trebor salesman this morning and then Miss Jones this afternoon, surely one of them *must* fit the bill?" Phoebe said gloomily, her earlier optimism rapidly evaporating.

"Shall we have a cup of tea whilst we wait for the next viewing Betty, the first two were over much quicker than I expected, we've got a good half an hour to spare." Phoebe led the way to the kitchen.

As Phoebe searched for cups and saucers, Betty could see the cupboards were bare. Phoebe carefully measured out two level caddy spoons of tea into the pot, she couldn't afford to run out of tea. "I haven't got any biscuits I'm afraid Betty." Phoebe frowned; the tea caddy was almost empty.

"Not to worry Phoebe, I'm getting too fat any way," Betty patted her rounded belly, she certainly had put on a few pounds recently, even her new Playtex girdle couldn't disguise the matronly bump, she really ought to cut back a bit. She had to admit Phoebe, on the other hand, was looking positively slender, work and worry must be causing the pounds to drop off her.

"So, what do we know about the Trebor salesman, other than the fact he's a post card thief?" Betty teased.

"I don't know much at all really; except he comes from a small village near Barry, and he sometimes uses a company van to do his rounds delivering boxes of sweets and confectionary all around South Wales. I think he travels all over the place, so I shouldn't see much of him if he did take the room." Phoebe said hopefully.

Adrian Hallit let slip the Trebor man also used the van to deliver a few other things on the side to local shops if he had the space in the company van, such as biscuit misshapes from contacts had in the Cardiff biscuit factory in Splott. Phoebe couldn't say she was surprised, little fiddles like that went on all the time. So long as he kept himself out of trouble, it wasn't her business to know what was kept in his van.

A vigorous triple rap echoed down the hall. "It sounds like him already Phoebe, he certainly is keen." Betty nodded towards the kitchen clock; the man was a few minutes early.

Phoebe quickly slurped the last of her tea and got up to answer the door. Her heart pounded as she headed up the hall, she needed a lodger and quick; *please God let this one be better than the last two,* she muttered under her breath.

Through the glass panels she could see the outline of a tall man waiting in the porch, she crossed her fingers and opened the door. The wind whistled down the street and sent a buzz running through the panes of the front room window.

"Good morning, I've come about the room," a slender man, sporting a striped, a dated wide lapelled suit and a broad grin doffed his hat politely. He looked about forty-five or maybe even a bit older, it was hard to tell he radiated so much energy and bounce. He looked at Phoebe expectantly.

"Good morning, you'd better come on in out of the cold." Phoebe stood aside to let the man through the door, as he walked past her she gave a deep sniff. Phoebe told herself that if this man reeked she would show him the door and tell him the room was taken, luckily the newcomer passed his first test with flying colours.

"You must be Mr Goode" Phoebe said guardedly.

"Goode by name and good by nature," Malcom Goode quipped and stretched out his hand towards Phoebe. The handshake was mercifully swift, and not clammy. "It's a nice place, you've got here." Malcolm Goode flashed her his most winning smile, deep crinkles radiated from his dancing eyes. Malcolm was used to turning on the charm when he needed to, *he was tired of trying to book accommodation in Cardiff, he had to secure the room.*

"Thank you," Phoebe kept her face impassive; she was not going to be sweet talked by Mr Goode....." this is my friend Mrs Williams. You'd better come through Mr Goode, and I will show you the middle room." Phoebe felt a little flustered, she must try keep a cool head and see through any superficial charm. She had vowed to keep her distance from the lodgers; they were not her friends as Betty had been all those years ago, this was business, and she was going to keep it that way.

Malcom Goode was probably just a typical salesman, all bounce, jovial patter, and enthusiasm but his wiry energy and rapid chatter unsettled her.

Don't judge a book by its cover Phoebe told herself.

Betty hovered in the rear of the hallway assessing the new applicant. The man looked a bit of a spiv in Betty's opinion with his slicked back hair greying at the temples, a narrow closely clipped moustache and wolfish, eager to please, lopsided grin. Betty nodded a brief hello.

Malcolm followed Phoebe through into the middle room. Thanks to help from Rita's husband George, the furniture was arranged to best advantage, a neat single bed ran along the wall, a small oak tall boy stood next to the bed and a faded armchair and side table was placed next to the disused fireplace. Phoebe could not afford to buy an electric fire for the room and the question of heating had vexed her, it was Betty who had suggested the coal option. *If he wants an electric fire then he can always buy one Phoebe, stop worrying and state your terms... tell them to take it or leave it.*

"I will not be supplying coal for the fireplace Mr Goode however you are welcome to buy your own coal and keep it in the yard if you choose to. I expect any lodger in this room will come and go through this back entrance to keep disruption to the house to a minimum."

Malcom Goode nodded and peered through the narrow French door leading to the yard.

"The room has its own access to the yard and the privy; I expect you to empty any gazunders in the privy and to use the outside tap for the rinsing pots…. You can, of course, use the upstairs bathroom and locks are fitted to all doors," Phoebe gestured to the newly acquired set of bolts on the back of the door Rita's husband fitted for her.

"Does that gate lead to a lane behind," Malcolm asked eagerly peering through the glazed door. Phoebe noticed he seemed more interested in the yard than he was in the room.

"It does Mr Goode, although it's not really a lane for the houses as it only comes off the service lane for the City road shops. This house is the only house at this end the street which comes off City road lane, it's a dead-end right behind us, all the other houses access a lane beginning at the other end of Alma road."

"A dead end? Perhaps I could park my little delivery van there then if it's not blocking the service lane?" Malcolm looked delighted by the news about the handy lane.

"I suppose so," Phoebe, said uncertainly.

"I'll take the room then, it's just the sort of thing I'm after …. If it suits you Mrs Horwat?" Malcolm smiled his best and most winning smile and extended his hand to seal the deal. *This set up would suit him down to the ground and the secluded lane to park his van away from prying eyes was an unexpected bonus.*

Phoebe glanced at Betty looking for support, *should she shake hands on the deal with Mr Goode?*

Betty gave a brief nod of approval, Phoebe couldn't afford to be too picky, cautious yes, but picky no. Betty had seen the empty cupboards and noticed the scant measure of tea, if Phoebe didn't get some money in her purse soon then she might find herself down on the wharf. Betty could help with a few hot meals but that didn't pay the rates and the bills, Phoebe needed money and she needed it quickly.

Phoebe held out her hand and shook on the agreement. "It seems like we have a deal then Mr Goode… and by the way its Miss Horwat, not Mrs."

"Marvellous *Miss* Horwat…. now when can I move in."

Malcom Good, travelling sweet salesman, was Phoebe's first new lodger. *She'd lay a pound to a penny he had taken down the postcard.*

Miss Carol Jones was late, she scurried along Alma road as fast as her short legs and sensible shoes would carry her. A slight woman grazing barely over five foot, she usually wore higher heels but today she had been teaching a singing lesson in Cathays and she needed to rush to make her two o'clock appointment in Alma road. Carol Jones had opted to wear her sensible flat walking shoes for the journey and had shrunk two inches in height.

Phoebe opened the door to a flustered and apologetic Miss Jones.

"I'm *so* sorry I'm a bit late but it was much further than I thought, and to make it worse I started at the wrong end of Alma road," Carol Jones untied her headscarf and bustled into the hallway out of the driving wind. Carol smiled sweetly, removed her gloves, and extended a delicate manicured hand towards Phoebe.

Betty gave Phoebe a slight *she looks nice* nod of the head.

Carol Jones was an attractive, well preserved looking woman who could have been any age between forty and fifty years of age. She was softly spoken, with raven hair which spoke of a little help from a bottle, plump crimson lips and a flawless porcelain complexion, if Carol had said she was of French origin, Phoebe would have believed her.

Within the hour the three women were laughing and joking in the kitchen over a cup of tea and Phoebe felt as if a huge weight had been lifted off her shoulders; she had found her second lodger.

As Betty pointed out after Carol left, Malcolm Goode shouldn't get in the way at all if he stuck to the middle room and kept himself to himself. In fact, with his job taking him here there and everywhere, Phoebe probably wouldn't even notice if Mr Goode was in the house at all. And the delightful Miss Carol Jones would fit into the household perfectly, Phoebe felt at ease with her straight away. It was a good feeling to have another woman about the place, especially one as pleasant as Carol Jones.

Now, Phoebe could relax a little and enjoy life without constantly worrying about money, for once she felt as if fate was smiling on her.

Chapter 33

Ivy had invited Karen Ashworth around to play with June for a few hours. Karen was June's only real friend and the two girls loved playing dollies together. Now all the children were free from infection they could go out and about and mix, only Gareth remained inside.

"Thank you so much for having Karen for me, Ivy, she's been so fed up with being stuck indoors for weeks on end, it will do her good to play with June for the morning." Norah cradled her bump as she sat on the settee drinking tea.

"How is Gareth now?" Ivy asked nervously. It had been over two weeks since his diagnosis of hearing loss and she knew Norah's husband Jack had refused to believe the damage to Gareth's hearing was permanent.

"Oh, he's fair to middling Ivy," Norah gave a wan smile, she felt bone achingly tired; the last few weeks looking after three sick children had drained the life out of her and to make matters worse, the baby growing inside her kept her awake half the night.

"Jack has taken it very hard, but I try to thank the Lord nothing even worse befell our Gareth. Mrs Richards in Hiles road lost her little lad Leonard because of the virus…. we could have lost him Ivy and then where would we be, it just doesn't bear thinking about." Norah tried to remain positive for Gareth's sake, but her Jack raged at the misfortune blighting his golden lad. *So many other children had escaped unscathed why did his Gareth have to lose his hearing.*

"Because Gareth used to hear he can still speak to us, but it is *so* hard for the poor lad now; he struggles to understand what people are saying to him. The doctor at the hospital said he must have a hearing aid to help in the one ear which seems to still have some sound coming through…. but it's going to look so big and bulky on the poor lad and he'll get teased to hell and back, but if it helps then he *must* wear it…." Norah started to tear up, *children could be so cruel.* The thought of her golden headed lad with a big pink plastic hearing nestled behind his ear was hard to bear.

"Of course, he must wear one if it helps him Norah…. You can't let some unkind children make his life a misery. I know with June kids will always call names and those bigger lads at the end are the worst." Ivy said hotly. "Billy has already had to have few words with those lads at the top of Wilson road, they're getting far too big for their boots bossing the little 'uns about, acting like they own the whole road…. and that lanky Jackson lad is a right one, he seems to be their ringleader."

Only the other day June ran in to Ivy crying her heart out because some of the big children in the street had called her a retard and told her she couldn't join in the games anymore. Bob Jackson had ordered June to *bugger off home.* Ivy was starting to worry that before long June would be excluded entirely from the gang of children who played from dawn until dusk out in Wilson road. Children could act like a pack, leaving the weakest on the margins.

"Don't worry too much Norah, I'm sure Gareth will always have lots of friends, he's got such a lovely way with him and after a while no-one will take any notice of his hearing aid," Ivy said kindly, unlike June, who Ivy knew would always be excluded and left out, Gareth's winning ways and talent playing football meant he was bound to still be with the in crowd what ever happened, and he had his brothers to look out for him.

Norah smiled grateful for Ivy's support. Ivy was a true friend.

"And what about the wedding…. Have Billy's parents come around to the idea yet?" Norah asked.

Ivy had confided in Norah about Billy's troubles with his family. "No not yet Norah…. I hope in time they'll accept we love each other, because Billy is adamant *nothing* is going to change his mind about getting married." Ivy smiled; Billy meant the world to her.

*

Les Thomas dashed around to the Tasty Plaice fish bar in Caroline street and hammered on the front door loud enough to wake the dead.

It was eleven o'clock in the morning and the shop would be opening soon for the lunchtime trade. Alice, still in her dressing gown, ambled towards the door and peeped through the glass. *What on earth could Les want at this time of day?*

194

"Is he here?" Les demanded and pushed through into the shop. "Is that fool Billy here?" Les barked at Alice.

George, wiping flour from his hands, came from behind the counter where he was preparing a pile of fish for frying, to see what the commotion was all about. "What's up Da?" his father had never burst into the shop before.

"Where's Billy?" his father demanded and pushed past George as if Billy might be hiding out back amongst the sacks of spuds and crates of chilled cod.

"He's working the early shift at Cardiff market today, same as he did yesterday; he left just before five o'clock this morning, but he promised to be back before we open at twelve." George looked completely at a loss, his father was steaming mad, his face florid with rage.

"Why what's up Da?" George had never seen his father look so rattled.

"*The matter* is I had constables knocking my door at eight o'clock this morning looking for Billy…. *That's* what's the matter. Two policemen standing on our doorstep in full view of all the neighbours, God knows what people are thinking!…. Your poor Mam is beside herself!" Les seethed.

His wife Pearl always kept up a good appearance; Pearl had standards. The sight of two policemen on her doorstep early in the morning was more than she could bear. At first it was the shock of two uniformed officers marching into her home and then it was the thought of the disgrace when she knew the purpose of their visit which sent her into a tailspin.

Pearl cried buckets of tears after the police left, she was not a strong woman, and she wasn't sure she could ever show her face again…. *what would the neighbours think?*

"The police!" Alice gasped.

"We've never had any trouble with the police in our family, *never ever*…. and yet as soon as he takes up with that bloody jailbird's wife Ivy Benson we have the police turning up at our door!" Les raged.

"That's not fair Les and you know it!" Alice said hotly, she could see Les was upset by a visit from the police, but it wasn't fair to accuse Ivy of being the cause of it. Ivy hadn't been Jimmy Benson's keeper and she certainly wasn't crooked like he used to be.

"Calm down Da and tell us what's the matter. Alice why don't you go and make us a quick cup of tea and then we can get to the bottom of this," George said trying to calm the tense atmosphere, he couldn't have his Da upsetting Alice, especially not in her condition, but it was obvious his father was distraught.

George looked at Alice with pleading eyes; she headed to the kitchen with a mutinous look on her face. Tea or no tea she was not going to have Les Thoms barging in throwing accusations around willy-nilly, *who did he think he was coming around in a raging fury loud enough to wake the devil himself.*

"So *why* are the police looking for Billy Da?" George tried to keep a level tone.

Les Thomas related the details of the visit and the shocking accusation that Billy was a wanted man. Billy had been overheard by several people threatening a Moroccan man on the West side of Queen's quay and now, the very same man, Ajo Abbas, was found floating near the fishing jetty as dead as a door nail with a face which spoke of a severe beating.

"No!" Alice gasped, she knew Billy could be a bit prickly, *but beating a man to death surely not?*

"You *know* Billy wouldn't do something like that Da." George said hotly.   "He came home a few days ago and told me one of Black Harry's men had been throwing his weight around and being rude about Ivy, so you can't blame Billy for losing his temper." George tried to get his father to see reason. "I wouldn't have people talking about my Alice like that either…. and Billy and Ivy are engaged to be married after all."

"Yes they are… more's the pity!" Les snarled, sweat beaded on his brow as he paced up and down.

Alice shot George a look which said his father was beyond reasoning with. She was proud of George for sticking up for his brother. As far as she could see Les Thomas was jumping to conclusions; plenty of men threw out hot headed remarks when provoked, but that didn't mean they followed through with doing something about it. They needed to hear Billy's side of things before being judge and jury.

"Well, it doesn't matter what *you* think George, because the police think he *might* have something to do with it, and they want to talk to him," Les sneered, "and you can tell him when you see him, the police have said that if Billy knows what's good for him then he'll turn himself in to the nearest police station straightaway." Les jabbed his finger in George's direction and turned to go.

"I'll tell him what you said Da…. The quicker we get this sorted the better. I don't believe our Billy would ever kill a man." George said loyally.

"I bloody well hope you're right George because if he has…. then he'll hang!" Les slammed the shop door behind him.

George's face was ashen, he couldn't believe his brother Billy would ever do such a thing… perhaps it had been some sort of terrible accident?

Trouble was the police said the man found floating in the water had been beaten to death…. *that sounded more like revenge than any sort of accident.*

"What are we going to do Alice…. This doesn't look good for Billy." George knew enough about the workings of Tiger bay to know there was a hierarchy of rule, and Black Harry was still the unofficial king of the Bay and Ajo Abbas was his man. By marrying Jimmy Benson's widow Billy was joining himself to the lowest of the low. Black Harry would show no mercy.

Alice gave her shattered husband a hug. She loved him so much, he was prepared to give Ivy a chance and Billy the benefit of the doubt, which she knew many others would not do; in her eyes George was a hero.

"I'm getting dressed George, then I'm catching the first bus over to see Ivy… some one's got to tell her about this news before the word gets out." Alice kissed George and went to get dressed. News moved quickly on the grape vine, there was no time to lose.

She knew there would be plenty of busy bodies who'd love to shatter Ivy's newfound happiness; telling dreadful tales about Billy being wanted by the police. Alice needed to make sure Ivy heard it from her first.

"If you're sure love. Then I'll wait for Billy to get back and I'll make sure he does the right thing and goes to the police station. I don't believe he's done this terrible thing; my worry is though; is he might find it hard to prove his innocence." George shook his head.

He didn't want to worry Alice any more than he had to, but he was fearful Billy might find himself a helpless pawn in a game where he didn't know the rules.

George pulled down the shop blinds and made sure the sign was turned to "Closed."

The Tasty Plaice would not be opening its doors to customers today.

Chapter 34

Eileen dared to hope she was not mistaken, and all her prayers had finally been answered. The tenderness in her breasts and her missed monthly cycle gave her reason to believe against all odds she was finally pregnant. Her heart skipped with joy, if she was right then she would have the precious baby they both longed for, a baby she feared in her darkest hours might never come.

Eileen was certain Sean would make a wonderful father and there was even talk the other evening he might try to find some work now his strength was improving. Sean was always good with machines before his accident, and he had learned to drive when he served in the army when he had been called up; he was a man with skills. Two nights earlier Norah's husband Jack had helped Sean walk to the Red Lion pub on the Grand avenue for a drink. Over a pint of Brains bitter Sean had learned about the shortage of trolley bus drivers in Cardiff. This nugget of information sparked a flicker of interest in Sean's mind.

"I bet you could do that job Sean, you can't go wrong really, it's just point and steer… after all they can't really go anywhere other than stay connected to those overhead lines they work on." Jack Ashworth joked.

"You're a cheeky sod, Jack Ashworth," Sean laughed, he was so enjoying being out and about again like any other normal man, enjoying an early evening pint and a laugh and a joke with his mates. It was good to start re-joining the real world, instead of being fussed and flapped over by doctors. This felt like living and a chance of a proper job would put the icing on the cake.

Sean knew things would never be the same as they were before the accident, but right now life was looking pretty good for a man who had been at death's door. Every day Sean felt his strength and stamina returning; muscles weakened through lack of use from months spent lying in a hospital bed were now growing stronger and he noticed he no longer collapsed with sheer exhaustion at the end of a day.

Maybe Jack was right, and maybe he really could hold down a proper job now he was back on his feet?

Eileen was bursting to tell Sean her suspicions about the baby, but she didn't want to raise his hopes and then dash them again; perhaps a visit to the doctor might be wise before letting Sean in on the secret. Eileen put on her coat and went around the corner to the Grand avenue shops to buy some chops for Sean's dinner; she decided she would pop into the doctor's surgery when she was out and about and get Dr Herbert's opinion on her condition. She knew Sean wanted to be a Da more than anything else in the world; she had to be certain of her ground before she told him.

Suddenly Alice Thomas rushed up to Eileen with scarcely time to pause for breath, "You haven't seen Ivy Benson on your travels have you Eileen," Alice gasped, "I'm looking for her and I'm not sure if she's gone out shopping yet?"

Eileen shook her head.

"If you see her around the shops will you tell her to go straight back home please… say her friend Alice has something *very* important to tell her… thanks Eileen.." Alice gasped and hurtled on her way.

Well, I wonder what that was all about? Alice was certainly in a tearing hurry to find Ivy.

Eileen watched the retreating back of Alice Thomas marching off to find Ivy in Wilson road.

*

Alice prayed Ivy would be home as she hammered on the front door, part of her prayed Billy wouldn't be there with Ivy; Alice didn't think she could cope with informing Billy he was wanted by the Cardiff police for questioning.

"Ivy are you in," Alice called through the letterbox. A small face appeared behind the glass.

"Hello Aunty Alice," June waved and giggled. It was fun playing peek-a-boo with Aunty Alice through the letter box.

"Go and get your Mammy, there's a good girl." Alice called through the letter box. *Ivy must be in… perhaps she was upstairs doing something and couldn't hear the rap of the knocker.*

June scampered off.

Within moments the door opened, and Nanna Betty stood, clad in her housecoat, wiping flour off her hands, it was obvious she had been cooking.

"Good morning Alice," Betty said brightly, "or should I say good afternoon?" she joked. "I was just making June some Welsh cakes for after tea today, come on in. I'm sure we can share your Welsh cakes with Aunty Alice can't we June?"

June looked doubtful.

"Is Ivy in Betty?" Alice panted, skipping over all the niceties and chit chat. Alice was hot and flustered from rushing about all morning, her feet ached, and she needed to sit down. The baby hung heavy in her belly.

Betty could see something was the matter, anxiety was written all over Alice's face.

"Come on in and sit yourself down Alice love and tell me what this is all about," Betty ushered Alice inside. "Ivy is upstairs washing her hair, but I'm sure she'll be down soon. What on earth is the matter?" Betty asked nervously, it was obvious Alice was not simply popping by on a social visit.

Alice didn't know what to do. She was glad Ivy's Mam was there for the morning, at least Ivy wouldn't be on her own now when she told her about Billy, but she felt she really should tell Ivy the bad news first.

"I'm sorry but I can't tell you Betty; I really *must* tell Ivy first." Alice pleaded.

"It's something about Billy isn't it?" Betty gasped; her hand flew to her mouth.

"What's this about Billy?" Ivy strolled into the sitting room with her damp hair in curlers tucked under a hair net. "Hello Alice."

Ivy could see in an instant something was wrong. Both Alice and her Mam had anxious, gloomy faces. Her knees went weak, she sat down heavily on the sofa before her legs gave way.

"Please tell me what's wrong Alice," Ivy pleaded, her heart was pounding. A wave of ice-cold terror washed over her; she couldn't bear it if something had happed to her darling Billy. Her mind was reeling with dreadful possibilities…. Perhaps Billy been involved in a dreadful accident, she knew he was being a porter to earn some extra money, *had he been injured down at the docks?* "Has Billy been involved in some sort of an accident?" Ivy gasped; the words stuck in her throat.

Alice shook her head.

"Well thank the Lord for that!" Betty muttered and crossed herself.

Ivy looked puzzled, if Billy wasn't injured, or in an accident why did Alice look like she'd lost half a crown and found a sixpence?

"I'm sorry to worry you Ivy, but this morning Les Thomas came to the fish bar, hammering on the door loud enough to wake the dead, he was looking for Billy because he said the Cardiff Police had been to his house early this morning hunting for Billy!"

"The Police!…. I'm sure there must be some sort of mistake Alice," relief flooded through Ivy, she felt her tense shoulders relax a little. Billy wasn't the sort to get in trouble.

"It *might* be a mistake Ivy, let's hope and pray it is, but nevertheless they do want to speak to Billy urgently…. he's got to turn himself in to the nearest Police station today. George is waiting for him back in Caroline street to tell him to go to the station and hand himself in I came as soon as I could to tell you what was up…. I didn't want you to hear about it from some bitchy gossip." Alice gave Ivy a hug. "Try not to worry Ivy."

"What is he supposed to have done?" Ivy said incredulously. She knew Billy was a decent, honest man, she couldn't believe he was mixed up in any sort of dodgy business…*there must be a mistake.* Billy was nothing like her late husband Jimmy; a crooked twister who was always dodging the law; her Billy was as straight as a die.

"They say Billy is wanted for questioning after some Morrocan man was found dead on the docks…. Les Thomas said Billy is a prime suspect for this man's murder as they were overheard having a vicious argument on the quay."

"Murder!" Ivy gasped. "Why on earth do they think that Billy would murder anyone…. It's ridiculous, it must be a case of mistaken identity…. Billy wouldn't do something like that!" She said hotly.

Betty could see Alice was nervous, *there must be a bit more to the story than Alice was letting on.*

202

"Do they have any proof?" Betty had lived long enough around the rough edges of Tiger bay to know that proof could be found if someone wanted it to be, and evidence could also be hidden if someone didn't want it found.

"I don't know all the details Betty, my father-in-law was in such a steaming temper when called around we couldn't get much sense out of him," Alice said smoothly, she refused to repeat Les's hateful assessment of Ivy or the blame he laid at her door.

"All we know is that a man is dead, and that Billy and the man had some big argument the day before. Some men are saying they heard Billy threatening the dead man... It's not *proof* of anything." Alice said simply.

"But Billy doesn't pick fights and arguments.... none of this makes any sense Alice." Ivy was bewildered. "He must have been provoked about something..." then the penny dropped Billy was probably fighting over her. Her hands flew to her face, *what was the matter with her, everything she touched seemed to turn out wrong. If Billy was in trouble, it was probably something to do with her...* Ivy felt tainted.

"This is my fault isn't it Alice?" Ivy wailed. "I wish I'd never agreed to Billy trying to earn some extra money for our wedding.... He should never have been down on those quays looking for work. I just know this is my fault somehow." Ivy wept.

In her heart Ivy knew Billy would defend her and June to the last, if Billy was heard having an argument with another man down on the docks she would lay a pound to a penny it was an argument over her. It was the only possible explanation which made any sense. *But Billy could never actually murder someone in a dispute over her... could he?*

"Nonsense Ivy... how can this be your fault, it's just a mistake, I'm certain of it. Men have fights and accidents down on the docks all the time." Alice wrapped her arm around Ivy's slender shoulders. "Your neighbour Sean Riley was caught up in a dreadful accident a few years ago which nearly cost him his life, this sort of thing happens, Tiger Bay is a dangerous place..... Don't fret until we know all the facts." Alice was trying to keep Ivy calm and optimistic, Billy would need them all to be strong.

Alice turned to Betty, "I must go back home now, my George will be wondering where I've got to, but as soon as I hear anything about Billy I'll let you know, I promise. The fish bar has a telephone so if I write down the number for you Betty then perhaps you could ring us from a call box in a few hours and we might have some news.... and if Billy comes here tell him to go straight back to Caroline street." Alice started to leave; she would have to hurry to get the next bus.

Betty handed Alice a scrap of paper and a pencil, "Here you are, write the number down, and I can give you the fruit and veg shop's telephone number as well. Gerald had a phone put in years ago so if you need to get hold of us urgently then you could ring the shop and ask them to take a message." Betty was trying to stay calm.

As Betty and Alice sorted out the arrangements. Ivy sat with her hands in her lap and felt as if someone had taken a sledgehammer to her heart. Her world falling apart into a million pieces, and she felt certain that, like humpty Dumpty, there would be no way of putting things back together again.

*

At four o'clock in the Cardiff City central police station, Mr William Thomas aged 26 years handed himself in and was formally cautioned and arrested for questioning on suspicion of the vicious murder of Mr Ajo Abbas on or about the twenty fifth day of February 1954.

Chapter 35

Phoebe felt a warm glow of contentment wash over her; life felt good. Both lodgers were well settled in and paying their rent and apart from a few early teething problems with Mr Goode she wasn't inconvenienced at all by having two strangers living in the house.

After the first week Phoebe had been obliged to have a few words with Mr Goode about the noises coming from his room, for some reason the man banged and thudded about in his room late at night most evenings, it was almost as if the man was moving the furniture about. At first she thought he must be re-arranging the room to his satisfaction but after three nights of bumping and thumping and dragging noises she decided to lay down the law. Enough was enough.

She banged on his door one evening at ten o'clock to have it out with him. Malcolm Goode peered around the door.

"Yes Miss Horwat," Malcolm did not ask her in.

"I can't be having you making loud noises and upsetting my neighbours late at night Mr Goode," Phoebe told him sharply, she was determined she would start as she meant to go on… her house, her rules. "Sound travels in these old houses Mr Goode, so I must insist you keep the noise down after a certain hour, there are young children living next door and I don't want any complaints. Whatever you are doing in there Mr Goode it has to stop or be done quietly." Phoebe said sternly, she drew herself up to her full five-foot two inches in height, her gold-brown eyes flashing.

"Of course, Miss Horwat, I'm sorry if I have troubled you." Malcolm Goode gave a sheepish grin. "I'm sorry for the inconvenience and I promise I won't disturb you or the neighbours again late at night." He said smoothly. *He would have to be quieter in future, he couldn't afford to be given his notice.*

"I'm glad we understand each other Mr Goode." Phoebe left no room for debate about the matter and walked off. She noted Malcolm Goode did not give any reason for the banging and thudding noises coming from his room, *still as long as they stopped it wasn't really any concern of hers.*

Phoebe was pleased to note that after her stern lecture Mr Goode did not feel the urge to bump and crash about his room late at night anymore. Any lodger must behave themselves if they wanted to stay in her home, she wouldn't have the neighbours inconvenienced by noise.

Her life was slowly, but surely, starting to become entwined with that of the Prosser family living next door. It was half term and Jennifer Prosser spent the morning with her new Aunty Phoebe making jam tarts and playing in Aunty Phoebe's kitchen. With endless patience Phoebe was teaching Jennifer how to cook some basic cakes and pastries.

"I love playing in your kitchen, Aunty Phoebe, Mam is usually too busy to let me help her." Jennifer dolloped a generous teaspoon of raspberry jam into the pastry case and patted it down with her finger.

Phoebe gave Jennifer a raised eyebrow look, as if to say, *I hope that finger was clean young lady.* Jennifer sucked the jammy finger and grinned a gappy smile. Since Phoebe settled in three weeks ago the little girl had taken to regularly popping by to talk to her new Aunty Phoebe whenever her Mam was busy. Her brother Frank was still not yet under Phoebe's spell but the lure of a few Trebor sweets courtesy of her new lodger Malcom Goode was starting to work its magic. Sweet rationing only ended the year before, and young Frank quickly developed a very sweet tooth; all his pocket money was spent on sugary treats at the corner shop, a few extra free sweets from aunty Phoebe were always welcome.

Just bide your time Phoebe he will come round eventually.

"Here you go, Angel," Phoebe handed Jennifer a teacup of cold water and a teaspoon. "You'd better add a drip of water on the top of each tart to stop the jam burning when it's cooking, just a drop mind or they'll be soggy and then I think they will be ready to go in the oven." Phoebe loaded the tray of jam tarts into the oven. Today she felt as close to being a Grandmother as she was ever going to get, and she silently thanked Deirdre for her good fortune.

"Now if you wash your hands Miss these will be done in about ten minutes, and then, when they are ready, you can take some home to Mam and your brother for their tea." Phoebe smiled, her granddaughter was a very bright and engaging little girl with two plaits of light brown hair and sparkling eyes which shifted between blue and grey. Phoebe so wanted to hug and cuddle the girl, but she had to hold back and remember they were strangers who had only recently met.

Twenty minutes later with a plateful of fresh, warm jam tarts and two packets of "Refresher" sweets tucked in her pocket, Jennifer skipped back home for her dinner.

Another reason for Phoebe's feeling of contentment that morning was she had received some crucial information from Cardiff library about origins of the mysterious gold signet ring with the entwined dragon and castle crest. The enigmatic emblem was indeed the escutcheon of the noble Loxley family.

The family entry in Debretts Peerage and Barontage listed the elderly Earl Phillip Cardew Loxley as the current incumbent of Cardew Hall, a large ancestral country house nestled in acres of rolling parkland near Frampton on Severn in Gloucestershire. The noble couple were listed as having had four children: Amy, Aurelia, Alphonse and Piers. The entry showed the Countess Marianne Loxley and her two sons, Alphonse, the eldest and Piers were all listed as deceased.

Phoebe had to pity the wealthy Loxley family who had lost both sons in the war, and from the brief entry it appeared the Loxley family was now just one elderly Earl and two daughters who could not inherit the title; soon the Loxley family would no longer be the rightful heirs to Cardew Hall. *It seems that even with all that money and privilege you can't buy happiness.* Phoebe mused.

Now Phoebe had all the information she needed she could write to the Earl with details of the ring discovered amongst Edmund's things and offer to return it. She would await instructions as to what to do now she'd traced the family who owned it. *In her heart she felt sure the family would want it back as a final memory of their youngest son.*

*

The brisk rap on the front door startled Phoebe out of her reverie. As she made her way up the passage, she could see the familiar outline of Betty through the glass panes. *How wonderful, she could share her good news about Jennifer's visits and the mysterious ring with Betty.*

Within moments of opening the door Phoebe could see Betty was agitated and worried.

"Come on in Betty…. Oh, my goodness you look like you've got the weight of the world on your shoulders," Phoebe ushered her friend through to the warm back parlour. "What on earth is the matter?"

Over a comforting cup of tea Betty related the whole sorry tale of Billy's arrest on suspicion of murder. Phoebe listened intently; she knew only too well these things could be manipulated and distorted. As far as Phoebe was concerned the question they needed to ask was not *did* Billy Williams kill Ajo Abbas? But…. *Who wanted Black Harry's man Ajo Abbas dead and why?*

"So do you know what happens next then Betty," Phoebe was very matter of fact. There was no point in everyone Billy trusted going to pieces, now was the time to pull together and fight to get Billy off the hook. "You said he's been arrested; the Police must be pretty certain they have got their man then." Phoebe was thinking out loud, on the surface of it the situation did sound dire, poor Billy…. And poor Ivy!

"That's just the point Phoebe, several witnesses have come forward saying they heard Billy shouting vicious threats at Ajo. Billy was heard yelling he would "have" him when Ajo was on his own some time, and that Ajo would "pay" for the things he said about Ivy."

It was as Phoebe feared, if witnesses were prepared to come forward and talk to the police then someone powerful was behind this. Most people working on the quays would look the other way when trouble was brewing. Men shouting the odds and issuing threats were ten a penny, nobody took that seriously and few would want to grass on a man for getting a bit hot under the collar…. If she was certain about one thing in Tiger bay anything could be bought for a price and if a patsy was needed to cover up the real killer of Ajo Abbas then witnesses could be bought ten a penny.

"What was that weasel Ajo saying about our Ivy," Phoebe felt her temper rising, she would have to try and do something. It was few years now since Phoebe had been a regular on the wharf, but she still had plenty of friends she could call on who kept an ear to the ground and would be able to find out what was really going on, friends who'd helped in the past.

Ivy was more precious to Phoebe than anything, she'd loved and helped raise Ivy since she was a babe in arms and would protect her like a vixen would defend cubs, Phoebe was determined to find out the truth behind this murder.

Some-one, with an axe to grind, was prepared to see Ivy's fiancé Billy stitched up for a murder which Phoebe would bet her life Billy didn't commit, and this person was prepared to let Billy hang for it… and all for what purpose?

Phoebe vowed to herself she would move heaven and earth until she found out the answer to the question.

"I'm going to do everything I can to get to the bottom of this Betty, I promise." Phoebe gave her old friend a hug.

"Tell Ivy not to worry, she may have to postpone that wedding of hers for a short while, but I'm going to find out who's behind all this and with any luck we should get Billy out…. Tell her to remember a man is innocent until proven guilty." Phoebe said with more positivity than she really felt.

Ivy's former husband Jimmy Benson might have hoped he too had a chance of convincing a jury of his innocence and returning home to Wilson road. That was why Phoebe had to be sure Jimmy didn't have a chance to charm the jury with his Irish good looks and bamboozle them with his oily lies. Jimmy Benson was strung up by a group of fellow remand prisoners who, for a price, were only too willing to see rough justice done to a man like Jimmy. Phoebe knew better than most that when money greases the right palms all sorts of favours can be bought.

Jimmy Benson was guilty as charged and no one cared about hearing his side of it, including Phoebe.

Betty left for Inkerman street and Phoebe sat deep in thought, she knew most of the big players down on the wharf, she also knew who ran the big business and controlled the important deals in Tiger bay. Who on earth could want Ajo dead and why did they want to frame Billy Thomas for his murder? Surely, someone must know the answer. The trouble was, if Betty was to be believed, the Police weren't even looking for anyone else in connection with murder of Ajo Abbas.

Phoebe's heart bled for Ivy, the girl had been so blissfully happy and in love, she had so many hopes and dreams of life happily married to Billy Thomas. Phoebe could only imagine how heart broken and worried Ivy must be to know the man she loved was under lock and key and possibly facing a murder charge.

209

June loved her Uncle Billy too, how would Ivy explain to June why Billy wasn't coming around to see her anymore. And when the neighbours got wind of this Ivy would face sneers and nasty comments all over again. To have one husband arrested and labelled as a criminal was bad enough but to have a fiancé tried for murder would be a stain which couldn't be erased.

People who had given Ivy the benefit of the doubt the first time would not be so forgiving a second time around. *No smoke without fire* as the saying goes.

It's a bloody awful mess, Phoebe muttered to herself. She decided to write a quick letter to the Loxley family and let them know about the signet ring and then it would be in their hands. She had other more important matters which needed her attention now.

Phoebe knew what she had to do if she was going to try and save Billy from facing trial for the murder of Ajo Abbas. If the Police weren't looking for the real culprit then Phoebe would try to uncover something which might provoke them into action.

That evening she must do what she had vowed never to do again, she would go back to the dark streets of Tiger bay, she couldn't just stand by, and watch Billy and Ivy's lives being ruined, torn apart by a lie. This time Phoebe wasn't going to be standing around on cold street corners waiting for customers to find her, tonight Phoebe would be on the hunt… on the hunt for the truth and for information. *Someone must know something.*

Outside in the hallway Phoebe could hear the click of the front door shutting and soft treads walking purposely up the stairs, Carol Jones was back from her morning music lessons. Carol kept such variable hours and was so quiet and thoughtful Phoebe barely noticed she was in the house at all. She was the ideal lodger to have about the place.

Phoebe smiled sadly. This morning life had seemed as close to perfect as she could possibly wish it to be and now, in only a space of a few hours, trouble was brewing. What was that saying in the Bible-*The Lord gives and Lord takes away.* Phoebe shook her head, for some people life seemed to be so unfair…. and Ivy seemed to be one of those people.

Chapter 36

Deirdre Roberts trailed a soft lint duster over an oval table in the centre of the bay window. The Victorian walnut table belonged to Mrs Prosser, with its attractive quartered veneers and scrolled legs the table was deeply unfashionable now, but Gwynneth loved it. It soothed her to polish and look after the treasured possessions in the bungalow, she had rearranged a few pieces of furniture to suit her but otherwise the house was as exactly as Mrs Gwyneth Prosser had left it.

Deirdre had to admit it had been more of a wrench than she anticipated to leave her home of sixty years behind, to leave all the familiar pieces of furniture and curtains that spoke of home and family. The few ornaments and personal knick knacks Deirdre brought with her from Alma road helped transform Cartref into her new home, but it still felt like a new shoe which didn't quite fit her foot and needed wearing in with time.

The sight of the motheaten old cat who strolled through the house and greeted her every morning with a rumbling purr warmed her heart. She felt at peace away from the strain of living next door to Rita in Alma road.

 She placed her Mam's special cut glass vase filled with daffodil buds in the centre of the table on a cream lace doily to protect the wood nurtured for generations by other loving hands. "There that looks better." Deirdre smiled; the cheerful yellow flowers were her Mam's favourites; in the warmth of the bay window, they would soon be in full bloom.

"Come on Bobby, it's time you had a saucer of milk and went outside to spend a penny." The elderly, once magnificent ginger and white cat lazed nonchalantly on the window ledge in his chosen sunny spot watching the world pass by. Deirdre walked over and picked him up in her arms.

Since moving into Cartref the cat had decided Deirdre was an adequate replacement for his former owner Gwyneth and deigned to grace Deirdre's lap every evening with his tatty, fluffy presence. She scratched him under the chin and the cat gave a loud contented purr.

Deirdre put the cat out. "Out you go Bobby, I've got some errands to run this morning." The cat gave Deirdre a bilious stare; decided to ignore the peace offering of a saucer of milk and stalked up the garden path to sit on the flower bed at the top of the garden bathed in early morning sunlight. Deirdre smiled, Bobby was such a character and even in the few weeks she had occupied the bungalow she had grown to love the grumpy old moggy who came with the house.

She had to admit to feeling content with her choice to move to Porthcawl. She did miss Rita of course, but in her heart she knew it was for the best she moved away. Rita promised to visit her for Easter, and she was looking forward to showing Rita and the children her new seaside home, taking them for ice creams on the prom and hunting for seashells on the shoreline. It was a new way of living and it suited her.

Deirdre was beginning to find her way around Porthcawl, it would take a little time to make new friends; she had joined the local Catholic church and the Women's Institute, before long she would find her feet.

Each morning Deirdre took the air walking along the promenade and her daily shopping trips to the bustling high street meant she was beginning to be a familiar face around and about. Shop keepers were friendly, helpful, and keen for her custom; she tried to forget the old times shopping in Wellfield road, familiar faces stopping to gossip as she wove her way from shop to shop and people asking after the family. She had no family now, certainly none she could claim as her own.

This is a new beginning and a clean slate, she told herself sternly, *hankering after how things used to be never brought anyone happiness, she must look forward to new beginnings.* Deirdre was determined to find new routines and new friends and she was going to start by getting to know her lonely neighbour in Ty Gwyrdd, the house with the strange green tiled roof.

Through her bay window Deirdre observed her neighbour James Pugh, accompanied by his dog Nero, also took a constitutional walk along the promenade each morning at about the same time. Regular as clockwork, whatever the weather James strolled in the fresh air.

At first Deirdre merely gave a brief, polite *good morning* to the man with the handsome black guide dog by his side who crossed her path most days. Her heart went out to the solitary figure walking up and down come rain or shine with only his dog for company. As the days passed they stopped to chat regularly and within days, two lonely people became friends.

Deirdre knew from Phoebe the story behind the tragic figure of James Pugh. Unlike her brother Edmund, James hadn't knowingly abandoned a girl he'd got into trouble, he didn't lie and scheme to cover up his mistakes, he'd been a victim of circumstance and the Great War; and she pitied him for it.

James was, by all accounts a decent and honourable man, and from what Phoebe said Betty and James *were* two lovers separated by events, she was determined to befriend him.

Today was a Wednesday and Deirdre was attending her first WI meeting in the local parish hall at two o'clock. In the morning however, she was meeting James Pugh in the Promenade café for a cup of tea, it was a first step towards the sort of comfortable familiarity and neighbourliness she missed from Alma road. James was good company and he appeared to enjoy her company too, it felt good to have a new friend.

Deirdre could see old Bobby snoozing at the top of the garden amongst the shrubs and locked the back door, the cat could stay out in the garden for the morning, *it would do him good to get some fresh air*. She grabbed her hat and gloves and set off to the café and her meeting with James.

James was sat waiting for her in the window seat, his dog Nero lay sleeping by his side. "Good morning Mr Pugh," Deirdre said brightly, she removed her coat and sat down at his table.

James gave a lop-sided smile, he angled his head to one side, and she knew instinctively he was trying to see her, as much as he could see, with his less damaged eye. "Please call me James Miss Roberts," James was surprised at his feelings of happiness when he heard her gentle voice. He had been worried she might not come after all.

"Thank you James... and you must call me Deirdre." Deirdre carefully unpeeled her soft leather gloves and gestured to the waitress for another pot of tea.

The view from the café window was magnificent. Set on an advantageous bend of the promenade, the café windows, when they weren't all steamed up, gave a panoramic view of the bay onwards out to the enormous Bristol channel. Nothing but a vast expanse of restless water dotted with distant fishing boats and swirling sea gulls for as far as the eye could see.

Today the water was calm as a mill pond; sparkling diamonds glittered and glinted on the crystal blue surface and gentle waves lapped against the sandy shore and sucked musically through the higher banks of rocks and pebbles.

It was such a shame James would never see this beauty. Deirdre thought to herself.

"It's incredibly beautiful out in the bay today; would you like me to describe the view to you James," she suggested shyly." Perhaps, we could go outside after we've drunk our tea and we could sit on a promenade bench, and I could describe the scene to you…. If you would like me to that is?"

"I would like that very much indeed Deirdre," James agreed. He hadn't heard such a beautiful, thoughtful remark since he'd spent time with young Lizzie…. *His darling Lizzie who always instinctively knew how to make him happy.*

Chapter 37

She thanked God it wasn't raining, the moon was well hidden behind heavy clouds which threatened rain all day, now they served to cloak the moon.

Phoebe slipped down familiar dark alleyways and cut throughs, avoiding the areas where the working girls usually stood hoping to attract passing trade; she knew better than to be seen loitering on the wharf where hard eyed woman traded themselves and defended their patches like vixens defended their cubs.

Phoebe didn't want any trouble and she didn't want to pick a fight with a mouthy madam trying to see off an interloper. She was a respectable resident of Alma road now. Phoebe couldn't be seen looking like she was up to her old tricks on West quay. Rumour had it the Port authorities had been clamping down on some of the less salubrious activities going on down on the wharfs after dark. Phoebe couldn't afford to be caught up with something; Phoebe's business was elsewhere tonight.

Phoebe knew better than to ask direct questions about Black Harry and the death of his righthand man Ajo Abbas, she needed to be careful tonight, to feel her way; only talk to people she knew she could trust. People knew her links to Ivy from when she lived in Tiger Bay, and people liked to talk, the residents of Tiger Bay had long memories and they protected their own.

Phoebe headed for the cosy bar of the Rose and Crown, it was time to buy Bill the landlord a pint and to find Jack "Cappy" Thomas. Cappy had helped her before with information, and she felt sure he might help her again.

"Well blow me…. Phoebe Horwat as I live and breathe, now what brings you to this neck of the woods… we haven't seen you in a while," Bill had a good memory for faces, Phoebe had been a regular in the saloon bar with her friend Betty before they both moved away from the area. Bill had always found Betty Jenkins a bit of a handful, especially when she had a mood on her, but he had a soft spot for Phoebe.

Phoebe waved a pound note, "nice to see you again Bill, I'll have a port and lemon and have a drink for yourself. I was actually hoping to have a word with Cappy Thomas, does he still come in here of an evening?" Phoebe knew only too well this was Cappy's local, but she didn't wish to appear to be too obvious.

"That he does Phoebe, in fact he should be in here any time now for his evening pint; he's like clockwork Cappy. He likes to stop by for a pint before he goes home to the little woman…. I won't tell his missus you're chasing after her husband though." Bill chortled and wagged his finger.

Phoebe shot him a mock glare, "now don't you go causing any trouble Bill, because that's how rumours start. I'm nearly old enough to be his mother, for heaven's sake," Phoebe chuckled and sipped her port and lemon.

"Get away with you," Bill gave her a cheeky wink, he always had a way of flirting with the ladies, especially when his wife wasn't looking. It was only ever harmless banter though; Bill knew who wore the trousers in his house and it certainly wasn't him!

Bill poured himself a half pint and gave Phoebe her change. Phoebe pushed the coins back towards Bill… "tell Cappy I'll stand him a pint when he arrives this evening."

Phoebe selected a table tucked inside a booth with a good view of the bar and waited for Cappy to come through the door. A few moments later Cappy strolled in and headed for the bar. When Bill poured him the free pint, Cappy turned to look for Phoebe and joined her with a frothing glass in his hand.

"Cheers Phoebe," he sipped the top of his pint and gave a contented sigh. "Ta very much…I needed that. Long-time no see… and to what do I owe this pleasure," he chinked his glass against hers. "This is the second time you've bought me drinks," he eyed her thoughtfully, "people might start gossiping," he joked.

Phoebe raised her glass, "cheers Cappy, it's good to see you again too, it's certainly been a while, since we last met," Phoebe waited for him to sup his ale.

He drank deeply; after a hard day's work a pint of beer slid down Cappy's gullet with ease, he wiped the froth from his top lip, "Ha I needed that," he sighed.

"Talking about hearing people gossip," Phoebe said smoothly, she sipped the syrupy mixture of port and lemon, "you've always got an ear to the ground Cappy, not much gets past you

216

does it?" Phoebe said softly, it didn't do to talk loudly about delicate matters in a pub booth, you never knew who might be earwigging on the other side of a partition

"Oh aye, so what is it you want to know this time Phoebe, I should have known you wanted something when Bill said you'd stood me a pint." Cappy raised a questioning eyebrow.

"Cappy… that's not fair, you're a good friend and I'll buy you a pint any time," Phoebe feigned outrage. She lowered her voice, "but I do want to know all the gossip on the street, I've been out of touch for a while since I moved to Ely to stay with my niece Ivy…. By the way one of our newer neighbours is your old friend Sean Riley, and he's doing very well so his wife Eileen tells me. I said I'd pass on the news when I saw you."

Cappy smiled, "that is good news Phoebe, I'm glad to hear it. He was a good mate to me, and I haven't heard about him for a while, I've often wondered how he was getting on, it's hard to keep in touch when people move away… I must go and see him now that I know where he lives." Cappy had been with Sean on the day of the accident, and it had hit him hard to see his friend so badly injured. Over the years it hadn't been easy to meet up Sean especially with the man spending so long in and out of different hospitals. He made a mental note to pay Sean and Eileen a visit soon.

Cappy sipped his pint thoughtfully, "you say you went to stay with your niece Ivy…. Is this the same Ivy who married that piece of shit Jimmy Benson?" Cappy said through gritted teeth.

Phoebe nodded.

"Hmm… I'd forgotten she was your niece Phoebe." Cappy's face hardened, when he heard what Jimmy had been mixed up in he was disgusted and ashamed he'd ever called Jimmy a friend or enjoyed his company. If ever anyone fitted the description of *a wolf in sheep's clothing* it was Jimmy Benson. Cappy and many others felt duped and used by the charismatic Irishman.

"It is the very same Ivy, and Jimmy treated her badly too Cappy. I wouldn't have treated a dog the way he used to treat her; he used her as a punch bag when the mood was on him and he was as mean as the devil to that poor little baby she had by him," Phoebe said bitterly, she needed Cappy on her side.

"The man was an animal in more ways than one Cappy and he deserved his come uppance; I for one, am glad he got what was coming to him." If Phoebe could have spat in disgust she would have done, instead she swallowed her bile with the last of the port and lemon.

"Let me get you another pint Cappy and perhaps we can trade a few stories for old time's sake."

Armed with a pint of beer and a whiskey chaser Phoebe sat a few inches closer to Cappy and started her quest for truth. When Cappy heard Ivy had been forced to marry Jimmy Benson because he had abused her and taken advantage of the innocent girl in her own home and made her pregnant he whistled with disbelief. *That certainly helped explain the stories about why quiet, mild mannered Ivy Jenkins ended up with a bad un' like Jimmy. Ivy hadn't set her cap at him as some of the nastier gossips had rumoured, he'd had his way with the poor lass.*

When Phoebe stressed that because Jimmy was drawn to children he targeted Ivy because she was an innocent young girl who looked a lot younger than her years *and* he wanted to get the new Council house in Ely Sean and Eileen had their hearts set on, Cappy swore out loud.

Bill the landlord looked across to see what the fuss was about, he liked to keep a tidy pub where harmony reigned he wasn't having shouting and swearing in his bar. He shot Cappy a warning glare.

Cappy saluted Bill an apology and lowered his voice. "The devious, disgusting piece of shit," Cappy said under his breath. "the world was a better place the day someone helped Jimmy on his way."

Phoebe raised an eyebrow.

"Oh, come on Phoebe don't pretend to be shocked, everybody knows Jimmy didn't tie that noose around his own neck whatever the official verdict was… and good riddance to bad rubbish if you ask me." Cappy growled.

"I think we can *all* agree justice was done where Jimmy Benson was concerned however it came about." Phoebe raised her glass in toast to the timely demise of Jimmy Benson.

Cappy threw back the whiskey chaser, he couldn't usually afford whiskey and certainly not whiskey and two pints, thanks to Phoebe's generosity he was starting to feel nicely mellow.

"So, as you can see Cappy my niece Ivy has been dealt a rubbishy set of cards in life and she is a decent, kind girl. She certainly doesn't deserve all the muck that has come her way in

218

life, she *deserves* a bit of happiness with a nice young man to look after her… nobody *ever* had a bad word to say about my Ivy when she worked in the pubs around here… nobody. And I'd defy anyone to say differently." Phoebe said hotly.

"Ivy has finally found love and happiness with the nicest, kindest man- Billy Thomas, who loves her to bits and wants to marry her… and now it all looks like it might be swept away because Billy has been accused of murder," Phoebe tried not to get upset, she paused to draw breath. Phoebe watched Cappy closely, he was thinking.

"You *never* ever saw Ivy flirting or slacking!" Phoebe was warming to her cause, everything she said about Ivy was true, but the girl's quiet, mild-mannered demeanour and sheltered life also meant few people in Tiger bay *knew* the real Ivy like she did. To many people hereabouts trading salacious bits of gossip on street corners, Ivy was simply Jimmy Benson's woman, and she was tainted by it.

"Well, that's true Phoebe, I do remember Ivy was always a good, hardworking girl…. And before she hooked up with Jimmy Benson she *was* well thought of" Cappy admitted as he sipped his second pint. He also remembered the jokes that Ivy Jenkins looked like she ought to be still in school and not serving behind a bar. What Phoebe said about Jimmy targeting the fresh-faced girl with the childlike figure and manipulating her for his own purposes made a lot of sense.

"So, you see Cappy, I *need* to know what the rumour on the wharf is about the death of Ajo Abbas," Phoebe tilted her head to one side to gauge the effect of her request.

Cappy lit up a cigarette and offered her one. Phoebe shook her head. He sucked deeply on the Woodbine and digested what Phoebe had to say. He knew only too well talking out of turn could be costly and dangerous, but he was a kind-hearted man and from what Phoebe said it did look like Ivy was one of Jimmy's victims too.

"Well, that puts a different complexion on it I must say." Cappy continued to draw on his cigarette, nodding as he screwed up his eyes against the smoke, deep in thought.

"I'd swear on my Mam's grave Billy didn't kill Ajo Abbas," Phoebe hissed, "but it suits someone to let the Police think he did, and most people around here don't seem to care one way or the other about the truth of the matter." Phoebe looked around her, the pub was still quiet, "if you know anything or have heard anything Cappy… and I mean *anything,* could you let me know, I'm getting pretty desperate and there isn't a lot of time before Billy will be charged with Ajo's murder." Phoebe pleaded.

Cappy tapped on his empty whiskey glass. Phoebe took the hint and nipped over to the bar to get another tot.

"Ta Phoebe… you are an angel. I can't see an innocent man hang Phoebe, but I'm a family man *and* I've got to make my living around here if you get my drift," Cappy leaned in conspiratorially, the booze was giving him courage. "Rumour has it Black Harry did it himself…. it's meant to be a warning." Cappy tapped the side of his nose with his forefinger.

"What sort of warning?"

"A warning to stay loyal."

Phoebe looked puzzled.

"Word is that Ajo was changing his allegiance to Paddy McGuire; he's the big man in charge of things over on the East side" Cappy explained, "it's said Ajo was encouraging some of Black Harry's men to go with him, to change sides and work for Paddy McGuire." Cappy paused to take a drink, he knew territories and influence on the docks gave a man respect, this was no minor squabble over a few workers seeking a better billet elsewhere, this was about power.

"Trouble is Phoebe, Ajo knows too many of Black Harry's secrets for Harry to ever allow him to work for someone else. Ajo is known all over the docks as Harry's right hand man-he could *never* leave. If there's one thing that won't be tolerated by people like Black Harry, it's disloyalty." Cappy nodded sagely.

"Rumour is the day Billy had an unfortunate run in with Ajo was the day Ajo was on his way to meet with McGuire and taking some of Harry's men with him. The three Polish guys Ajo had with him had been convinced to join with McGuire and leave Black Harry's gang… they were about to jump ship so to speak, and when Black Harry found out about it he needed to set an example to the others…. Keep a bit of discipline in the ranks."

Phoebe gasped, "Cappy are you saying those three Polish men are the same ones the Police have as witnesses to give evidence against Billy?"

"I can't possibly say one way or another Phoebe for certain, all I know is it's rumoured those three men were forced to watch Black Harry teach Ajo a lesson and then they were told to show their loyalty by throwing suspicion elsewhere if anyone came asking questions about Ajo. So, whilst I don't *know* if they are the same ones who went to the Police, I think it's a fair guess to say it's probably the truth." Cappy nodded sagely.

Cappy knew Black Harry had a reputation for always keeping his own hands clean. If Black Harry did punish Ajo with a brutal beating then he would certainly make sure some other person was framed for it if ever questions were being asked by the police about the whereabouts and fate of Ajo Abbas.

It was just Billy's bad luck the body got discovered caught up on the jetty the next day; plenty of other times Ajo's body would have simply gone out with the tide to become fish food and the matter would have been closed. Drifters like Ajo were rarely missed or mourned.

"I see…it all makes sense now Cappy, I did wonder why some witnesses were so eager to come forward and help the Police with enquiries." Phoebe felt shattered…. how on earth could she help Billy and Ivy now? She wasn't sure which way to turn next. If Black Harry heard she was stirring up trouble, who knows what might happen. She would have to be careful and tread softly.

"As I said Phoebe… the men were rumoured to be from Poland, surely that gives you a way in to find out a bit more about what really happened."

Cappy felt sure with Phoebe being half Polish herself and knowing the language, if anyone could try to talk to the close-knit community it would be Phoebe.

Cappy started to get up, "now you take care of yourself Phoebe…. People don't like questions being asked around Tiger Bay, and not everyone can be trusted. If I hear anything more I'll let you know." Cappy leant forward and gave her a peck on the cheek and whispered in her ear.

"I'm told the Poles in question usually go to the Norwegian church down on the wharf on Sundays. Quite a lot of them seem to head that way; you might find out something there to your advantage. Goodluck Phoebe and be careful!"

Phoebe squeezed Cappy's hand, her eyes started to fill with tears. At least now her suspicions of Billy's innocence had been confirmed… and now she had a flicker of hope.

"Thank you Cappy… thank you for everything."

Chapter 38

Ivy could barely drag herself out of bed she felt so miserable, just thinking about Billy being locked up in the cells at Cardiff police station was enough to bring tears to her eyes. She wasn't family so she wasn't allowed to visit Billy whilst he was held for questioning; all she could do was hope and pray he might be let out soon.

Ivy found it impossible to believe three men would maliciously point the finger of suspicion at her darling Billy. She longed to feel his arms around her, he was the only man she had ever loved and without him she felt lost. Dreadful thoughts whirled in her head and deprived her of sleep, it was torture to think Billy could end up being hung for a crime she was certain he did not commit.

Ivy lay cocooned under the blankets with the curtains closed; hugging her knees drawn up to her chest, too shattered to face the hostile world outside. It had been five days since Billy handed himself over to the Police for questioning, in less than a week his life had been turned upside down.... *And, to make matters worse she was sure that in some way she was at the root of it.*

His brother George had called around briefly to tell Ivy the latest developments but with three witnesses saying they saw Billy on the wharf shouting vicious threats at Ajo near to the place where the body was later discovered, things did indeed look bleak.

Since Aunty Phoebe moved out to her new home in Alma road in readiness for the impending wedding, June had moved rooms. At first June protested about leaving the big warm comfortable bed she shared with her Mam, and she'd wanted to stay put, but after a while the lure of her own room to play in and space for her toys had won her over. Ivy told June that Mam would be sharing a bed Uncle Billy once they were married .... but now all those happy plans and dreams were shattered. The bed felt lonely and bare.

A future which had once looked so rosy for Ivy and June, now looked so bleak.... *June would never understand.* Ivy didn't know what to say to June about the turn of events and Billy's arrest. June found the world difficult enough to comprehend at the best of times, the little girl had a simple black and white view of things and didn't deal in maybes or might haves; for

June things either were, or they were not. *It was like a knife in Ivy's heart every time she thought about trying to explain all of this to June.*

The only certain thing was there wasn't going to be a wedding; not now and if things went badly for Billy, then maybe not ever.

Ivy's heart was breaking; when she trudged down to the registry office to cancel their wedding date with bitter tears threatening to spill at any moment; she wanted to hide away from the world in shame. She knew the wedding, which was less than six weeks away, needed to be postponed but informing the snooty clerk behind the counter of the cancellation had come like a hammer blow to Ivy's heart; it was her worst nightmare come true and she didn't know how to break the terrible news to June.

Every day, oblivious to the drama unfolding around her, June chattered away happily about Uncle Billy this and Uncle Billy that, *how on earth could she tell June they might never see Uncle Billy ever again if things went badly for him?* Ivy pulled the blankets over her head and sobbed her heart out.

*

Phoebe received the letter in a smart cream envelope, thick quality paper which spoke of money. Beautiful handwriting Phoebe didn't recognise looped across the front, she was intrigued. When Phoebe slit open the envelope a small post card sized note topped with an embossed crest of a dragon encircling a castle turret lay inside. Her heart skipped a beat.

Dear Miss Horwat,

Thank you for informing us of the discovery of my late son's signet ring amongst Mr Roberts's possessions, it was a considerate and thoughtful gesture on your part to offer to return it.

My darling wife Marianne died five years ago of a broken heart, she never fully recovered from the death of our eldest, beloved son Alphonse, who died bravely serving his King and country. However, I am also certain that her untimely demise was brought on in no small way by the dissolute and reckless activities of our son Piers. Over the years, Piers caused his poor mother nothing but heartache and worry with his activities and he was a disgrace to the family name of Loxley.

Our youngest son's death in the War, whilst untimely, at least put an end to the upset he continued to give his poor mother. His name is no longer mentioned in our household.

As his father I could never forgive Piers for the hurt, shame and sorrow he brought on our family name. Consequently, I do not wish to reclaim the signet ring you mention, and you may dispose of as you see fit.

Please do not write again.

Yours- Phillip Cardew the Earl of Loxley.

His father had known what his son Piers was like, and he had disowned him because of it. Phoebe shook her head; it was so sad to think so much human misery was played out in so many families. She looked at the small gold ring in her hand; Deirdre had said if the family didn't want it back then Phoebe could keep it as a memento of Edmund, it was hers now to do as she wished with. She tucked the sad letter away in her top drawer.

Phoebe tried to imagine the owner of the ring finding a brief window of happiness with Edmund before he lost his life to a sniper's bullet on the battlefield. Edmund had obviously cherished the ring for years and kept it as a memory of a man he'd once loved.

Phoebe opened a small trinket box which sat on her dressing table and slipped the gold ring inside for safe keeping. If the Loxley family didn't want the ring back then it would stay in her possession as a reminder to grasp happiness wherever it could be found. She decided she would keep the lover's ring and never sell it unless she had to.

*

On Sunday morning Phoebe left the house early and walked to the Norwegian church. She could only guess which service might appeal to the three men she was looking for, but whatever happened she needed to track them down somehow… in the close-knit Polish community somebody would know who these men were and have the information she was seeking. All she needed was their names and then the rest would be in another's hands.

Under any other circumstances it would have felt good to have been down on the quays on a Sunday morning spotting familiar faces and chatting to old friends in the fresh sea air. The bustling cheery atmosphere of Queen's quay gladdened her heart, the salty tang of the mounds of coiled drying ropes and the familiar raucous call of the beady-eyed herring gulls wheeling overhead on the crisp morning air made her smile; it felt like coming home. Phoebe saw plenty of people she knew of old, cheery *Hellos* rang out as she mingled and jostled amongst the crowds. Phoebe nodded and smiled and exchanged a few brief greetings, but she didn't have time for chit chat today; she was looking for someone in particular this morning, and time was pressing.

Behind the tin sheds near the Norwegian church, she spotted her quarry, his familiar battered bike leaned up against a large capstan. *Things don't change much around here,* Phoebe smiled to herself.

Tomasz Nowak squatted beside the front wheel of the bike blowing up a rather deflated tyre. In truth Phoebe wasn't too sure how old Tomasz was, she remembered him as a weasel faced child with scrawny arms always wearing a hand-me-down shirt with a collar too big for his scraggy neck.

When asked Tomasz used to always reply that he was fourteen, even seven years ago he was declaring himself to be this unbelievable age, but his reply was the same. His age didn't alter for years, Tomasz remained fourteen until it suited him to be a different age; now he claimed to be seventeen if asked and would probably say he was seventeen for years yet to come, but no-one cared enough to ask anymore.

He'd been dodging and skipping the clutches of the truant man looking for children, who ought to be in school for years; nobody ever believed the barefaced lie about his true age, but Tomasz didn't seem to have any parents who cared about the niceties of going to school and reading and writing so he'd slipped through the net and lived by his wits in the alleys of Tiger Bay until the dangerous age passed.

A child of the streets, Tomasz could add up money quicker than anyone Phoebe knew and as far as the lad was concerned he had all the learning in his head he needed to get by on in life. As far as Phoebe could tell Tomasz could only be about sixteen now, but he was a wily fox, and he knew the docks like the back of his hand. Tomasz was certainly an old head on young shoulders with the uncanny ability to disappear like the early morning mist down the warren of alleyway criss-crossing Tiger Bay.

Whatever mischief Tomasz got up to, he prided himself on the fact that the police never caught him getting up to anything. Tomasz had a clean slate despite living by his wits and was determined to keep it that way.

Tomasz had been acting as a runner and go-between around the docks for as long as Phoebe could remember, on his familiar bike with a large wire basket attached to the front Tomasz could slip down alleys and navigate the cut throughs like lightening. Tomasz was trusted to pass all sorts of messages and packages for a price and more importantly he knew where people could be found or given a message. He was his own man and answered to no-one.

"Hey Tomasz, your aunty Phoebe needs a word!" Phoebe called across the cobbles in fluent Polish.

The lad stopped fettling his bike and looked up, he recognized Phoebe Horwat, she'd paid him to do jobs before.

"You ain't my aunty," the lad replied cheekily in Polish, a wide grin crossed his face and his rotten front teeth spoke of neglect. Tomasz had decided he was too old now to have a large circle of honorary aunts and uncles he was supposed to respect. Tomasz was a young man now and wanted to be treated as such.

"Cheeky monkey," Phoebe rolled her eyes and moved closer to where the lad stood. She rubbed her right finger and thumb together in the universal gesture of payment. She had a job for Tomasz, and she would pay him handsomely for conveying a message.

Tomasz noted the signal, dropped the cheeky banter, and strolled over. This was business.

"What you want Phoebe?" Tomasz lit a cigarette, he dragged deeply on the roll up before pinching it out and replacing the half-smoked gasper behind his ear. "You got a job needs doing?" He talked low in Phoebe's native language, the Poles stuck together on the docks, a close-knit club which denied outsiders entry, speaking in Polish was safer.

"I need to meet with Paddy McGuire, Tomasz." Phoebe said urgently.

"He may not want to meet with you Phoebe, Paddy is getting to be an important man over on the East side," Tomasz looked nervous. He knew Paddy was gradually gaining influence across the whole of the docklands, he couldn't see Paddy wanting to meet someone like Phoebe.

"He will want to meet with me when he hears what I've got to tell him," Phoebe said with more confidence than she really felt. Phoebe took a deep breath and placed her trust in Tomasz, "You tell him I have information which will help him take another man's crown…. Those exact words mind." Phoebe shot Tomasz a knowing look.

Tomasz squinted, "Did you say what I thought you said Phoebe?"

Phoebe handed Tomasz a crisp pound note. "I'm not paying you to think Tomasz, just give Paddy MacGuire the message and ask him for a time and a place to meet with me, tell him it's urgent. I'll wait here until you come back… remember what I said, those exact words, he should know what I mean. If you get me a meeting, there's another note in it for you."

An hour later Phoebe was being led to a deserted storeroom shed tucked behind a timber warehouse on the East quay operating as Paddy's makeshift office. Paddy, a burly Dubliner stood at over six feet, with heavily tattooed arms and fists like York hams. He was waiting for her, she recognized him from the description she'd been given; the man regarded her with interest and an amused glint in his eye.

It was a Sunday, but Paddy ruled his empire every day of the week, nothing went on the East side without Paddy's say so.

Phoebe fixed him with a steely gaze and walked into his lair. Sassy and street wise Phoebe wasn't going to be intimidated by a hard man like Paddy McGuire; the Dubliner posed a formidable figure as he lounged confidently in his chair, his fat fingers tented and a look on his face Phoebe found hard to read. She needed him to take her seriously.

Paddy cocked his head to one side and gestured to her to sit down. He'd been told a bit about Phoebe Horwat from Tomasz, just enough to whet his curiosity about a former prostitute who had once called Tiger bay her home, a woman who slipped through the shadows with ease; a woman who knew people and secrets.

"Now then, what have you got for me Phoebe that's so urgent it couldn't wait?" Paddy cut to the chase.

Phoebe took a deep breath, she didn't know this man sat in front of her, she was taking a huge gamble telling him what she knew, but she was doing it for Ivy and the thought of her precious Ivy breaking her heart over Billy made her brave. Everything she had learned from talking to Cappy and others around and about the quays was merged to paint a picture of Black Harry trying to snuff out Paddy McGuire's fast growing East quay empire.

"So, you see Mr McGuire my niece's fiancée is caught up in this mess through no fault of his own. Four men were coming to join you that day, one is dead, and three others are now in fear of their lives and being cowed into giving evidence against an innocent man." She waited for her words to sink in. "Billy Thomas was also seen joining a queue to work for you the next day, so Harry has put two and two together and Billy is conveniently taking the rap for something he didn't do."

Paddy vaguely remembered the pock marked man looking for work that day, Billy was a well-muscled chap who looked as if he could take care of himself, and he was only overlooked because Paddy knew the man behind him in the queue and had done him a favour. Paddy had no idea Billy was now being fingered for Black Harry's crime.

"I've talked to the community, and it's said many other men would also rather work for you than for Black Harry, but they are frightened especially after those three who saw Ajo beaten to death, are being threatened with the same rough justice if they join you. I can give you their names and I know they would still join you if you could protect them from Black Harry and there's other Irish lads on the West quay who feel the same way about coming over to you too." Phoebe said levelly.

If Black Harry wanted a turf war, then he was going to get one. Phoebe might be embroidering slightly but she did detect a willingness amongst the Polish workers to escape Black Harry's brutal control, if these three could be persuaded to switch allegiance then the floods gates would burst, and others would surely follow.

Phoebe had done all she could to brew the storm, she needed Paddy to fight for his turf, to be aggrieved Harry was trying to starve him out of business; to feel the slight of the Kenyan's arrogance and control.

"You say these three Poles actually *saw* Black Harry beat Ajo to death," Paddy pondered the scenario, he rubbed his chin thoughtfully, "and yet they are prepared to testify against Billy to keep in with Harry… but only because Harry is threatening them if they dare to join me?"

Phoebe nodded she could see Paddy walking a path which gave her hope. Paddy would know if the Poles testified then they and others would be bound to Black Harry for good, locked in the Kenyan's grip, tied down by fear. This was Paddy's chance to split up Harry's hold over the men, and without his men Harry would be a spent force.

"Seems to me these three men would be safer working for me. If Black Harry is going to threaten every man choosing to work for me then he needs to be taught some manners." Paddy was thinking out loud, if he could loosen the shackles of control Black Harry had over the men working on the West quays then his own star would be in the ascendency, Paddy had various fiddles operating on the East side and he needed a good team of men loyal to him.

Paddy hadn't realised until now just how much Harry was doing to choke the oxygen from his operations over on the East quay. Paddy had always been of the view that there was room enough for both him and Black Harry to operate in Tiger bay, he was obviously mistaken.

"Thank you Phoebe, you have been helpful... very helpful. I'm a persuasive man and I feel sure those three misguided men can be persuaded to change their minds about testifying against Billy." Paddy gave her a broad grin.

Phoebe felt as if a huge load was being lifted off her shoulders. It didn't mean Billy was off the hook, but *if* the men could be persuaded to retract their statements or cast doubt on the evidence then the police would have precious little to go on. Surely they couldn't hold Billy for no reason could they?

"I could do with some more good men over on the East quay and I'm sure I could reward their loyalty if they were to show it by joining me instead of cow-towing to that weasel Black Harry.... I always look after my men, especially sensible ones who learn from their mistakes." Paddy gave a grin; he was a hard man but fair, if Black Harry wanted a fight over territory then he would get one.

Phoebe and Paddy parted company, she found the man hard to read. Would he really get the men to change or retract their stories and weaken the case against Billy in time to save him?

She knew she was in Paddy McGuire's debt, she'd shown her hand, picked a side and asked for a favour- at some point in the future, maybe even years away, he would call in the favour, because that was how things worked in Tiger Bay. He knew where she lived in Alma road and Paddy would never forget she owed him something in return.

Phoebe ambled home, exhausted with the tension of the afternoon, she needed to rest. She caught sight of her reflection in a chandler's window, the woman staring back at her looked old and tired. Phoebe sighed, she was starting to feel her age, her once pretty looks which had caught the eye and drew the admiring comments on the quays were faded now and she felt herself becoming invisible.

Cheer up misery guts, just think how poor Ivy must be feeling, she chided herself.

The light was starting to fade and the call of a cosy fire and cup of tea in Alma road spurred her on. All Phoebe could do now was wait and pray she had done enough for Billy to escape the clutches of the Police.

In a power struggle with Black Harry, Paddy McGuire had to want to win, to be the top dog and after what she had told him today she believed he did. It was in Paddy's hands now.

Phoebe crossed her fingers and headed home to Alma road.

Chapter 39

"Look Nanna this potato head looks just like Uncle Billy," June giggled, she showed Nanna Betty the comical vegetable figure with a big nose and a hat.

"Nanna, where *is* Uncle Billy?" June asked with a puzzled frown.

Betty was busy washing some King Edward potatoes in the sink. June had been amusing herself all morning making Mr Potato head figures with the spuds before Nanna Betty reclaimed them for the cooking pot and dinner. Small plastic pieces were scattered on the kitchen table, June was busy selecting moustaches and noses to push into her fresh potato, Bampa Gag potato wore a big bushy moustache and now Uncle Billy was her latest creation.

Betty took a deep breath; she had been fielding June's incessant inquiries about the where abouts of Uncle Billy for days. June was a little girl who did not cope well with change and there had been far too many changes of late in the child's life.

Phoebe leaving to live in Alma road had caused a bit of a stir, but the promise of Uncle Billy moving in to live with June and Ivy had softened the blow for the child. As the days passed and Billy didn't appear as promised, June kept up a relentless drip, drip of *Where's Uncle Billy gone Nanna?*

Betty would have to have a word with Ivy about it, she couldn't keep palming June off for ever with excuses; maybe they should try to manage the child's expectations and tell her a version of the truth?

But not today.

"Uncle Billy is very busy out on a fishing boat catching fish for his fish and chip shop my angel, he might be gone a few days." Betty lied outrageously; it was her most implausible lie yet.

June's eyes widened with excitement, she loved fish and chips. "June have fish and chips too?" The little girl asked hopefully, all concerns about the absence of Uncle Billy displaced.

"We can have some nice fish and chips tomorrow my darling; I promise." Betty went back to peeling her potatoes, relieved to have changed the subject.

Betty was visiting Ivy every day now since Billy's arrest. Sadly, her daughter was going to pieces before her very eyes, as each day passed Ivy looked a bit more battered by the disaster that had landed at her door; it was as if she had given up on life.

Without Aunty Phoebe to help out around the house, it was obvious the chores were not getting done and June was getting precious little attention. Betty had stepped in, but this arrangement couldn't keep going for ever, Gerald needed her, and June needed her Mam.

Ivy drifted listlessly about the house in her dressing gown unable to face the world. Betty wanted to shake her daughter and tell her to have faith in Billy's innocence, to buck up and pull herself together, but she knew her daughter was suffering from a broken heart and no amount of jollying or chivvying was going to make a single jot of difference.

The only thing to snap Ivy out of her misery would be having some good news about Billy and it was the one thing Betty couldn't give her. As each day passed with no news of Billy Ivy sank deeper and deeper into a dark depression, sucking the life out of her and draining her of hope.

"Now you let me have those manky potatoes for the pot young lady, you've had your fun with them, and Nanna needs them for dinner; please put your play pieces away so Nanna can lay the table, there's a good girl." Betty said kindly, June was a delightful, loving child who didn't deserve to have a Mam who refused to leave her room, too scared to face the world, too miserable to give her confused little daughter a reassuring kiss and a hug.

June dutifully started putting the tiny pieces back in the box, she liked tidying up for Nanna Betty.

"When I've done with these potatoes, I'm going to take your Mam a nice cup of tea and maybe her headache might be better this morning, and perhaps she'll come downstairs and have some dinner with us today." Betty said hopefully.

Betty had told the child so many lies of late to explain away her Mam's listlessness, it couldn't go on a minute longer. It was time she said something to her daughter about it; Ivy needed to face the truth and be brave for June's sake if nothing else.

Enthralled in tidying the pieces into the correct compartments June forgot all about the Uncle Billy conundrum. Betty left June to finish the task whilst she took Ivy's tea upstairs, it was nearly midday on a Tuesday, and Betty knew Ivy hadn't left her room.

There had been no patter of feet overhead to wash in the bathroom and from the front of the house Betty could see the bedroom curtains were still closed against the world.... *this can't go on.* Betty muttered to herself crossly as she tapped the door before entering Ivy's room.

The bedroom was gloomy and subdued, the red curtains masked the weak sunlight filtering through. A smell of stale urine from the gazunder caused Betty to wrinkle her nose, Ivy had not even bothered to go downstairs to the outside toilet. *Ivy was getting worse not better she thought to herself, the girl had to pull herself together.*

"Ivy, come on love, drink this nice cup of tea I've brought you; I've put two sugars in it to give you a bit of energy." Betty drew back the curtains and picked up some dirty washing scattered on the floor. "I've had the immersion on for an hour now so there's plenty of hot water for a nice bath if you want one," Betty chattered to the mound laying enveloped in the tumble of bedding.

"Ivy, you must make an effort, for June's sake.... please darling... she doesn't understand what's going on, and she needs her Mam." Betty cajoled, willing her daughter to try.

Reluctantly Ivy sat up in bed, her eyes red-rimmed with tears, her face pale and thin through lack of sleep, her hair a greasy, unkempt mess. Betty sat on the bed beside her distraught daughter and cradled her in her arms.

"There there, my love," Betty crooned as she held Ivy close, "it's going to be all right, trust me. Always remember Ivy, nothing *good* or *bad* lasts forever. The wheel of life always turns."

"No, it's not going to be all right Mam and I know it's all my fault." Ivy sniffed miserably.

"Shh now, don't be silly none of this is your fault Ivy. Why not get up and get washed and then come down for a bit of dinner with June, she's missing her Mam, she needs you too. Afterwards we can go for a walk, get a bit of fresh air, and blow the cobwebs away; that poor child hasn't been outside for days. It will do her good to get outside." Betty tried to encourage Ivy into action.

"I don't want to go out Mam, I know everyone is talking about Billy and me behind my back… I just can't bear it." Ivy wailed.

"But you *must* bear it for Billy's sake," Betty chided. "Now get up, try to put on a brave face and I'll see you downstairs." Betty ordered. She left Ivy to get ready.

Betty padded back downstairs to the kitchen to finish preparing the sausage, cabbage and mash dinner, June had put her toys away and gone into the sitting room.

In the absence of anything entertaining to do June often spent her time looking out of the window watching the children playing in the street. "Hooray…. Hooray," June shouted and jumped up and down on the settee under the bay window.

Betty could hear June laughing excitedly at something she could view in the street. It was a blessing the little girl was so sunny natured. June could spend hours entertaining herself playing make believe with her dollies, but even so it wasn't good for the child to spend so much time on her own.

The loud rap on the front door caused Betty to jump, since Billy's arrest any unexpected knocks on the door sent a trickle of dread down Betty's spine. The kitchen clock showed twelve forty-five. *Who on earth could this be knocking the door at dinner time* Betty thought crossly?

Before she could wash and dry her hands she heard June trying open the front door.

"Hey, June don't open the door, there's a good girl… Nanna's just coming," Betty called as she wiped her wet hands.

The child pulled the door opened and there stood Uncle Billy with a grin so wide he looked like the Cheshire cat.

"Have you caught a fish Uncle Billy?" June lisped excitedly as Billy lifted her up and swung her in his arms.

"A fish my angel? Now why should Uncle Billy have a fish?" He laughed and tickled her under the arms. June squealed with delight.

Hearing the commotion in the hallway, Ivy had made it down the stairs. The sight of Billy turned her legs to jelly, unable to believe her own eyes she sat down on the stairs with a bump. Her hands flew to her face.

"Hello, my darling girl, don't I get a kiss then," Billy said with a grin as he glimpsed Ivy sitting half-way up the stairs.

"Oh, thank God, Billy, you're back!" Ivy flew into Billy's arms and hugged him as if she would never let him go.

Billy stroked Ivy's hair and kissed her. "I love you Ivy, I love you more than anything in the world." He said softly fighting back the tears. Billy's days spent languishing in the cells of Cardiff jail had made him realise he needed Ivy as sure as he needed sunlight and oxygen. She was everything to him. The thought that he might spend the rest of his life locked up or even worse had tortured him; the morning the police officer told him he was free to go it was as if all his birthdays and Christmases had come at once.

"I love you too Billy," Ivy gasped, she felt a dishevelled, scruffy mess, but Ivy had never felt happier in her entire life. *Billy had come back to her.*

"In that case I think we'd better re-book the wedding we had planned, unless you've changed your mind about marrying me," he teased and stroked the soft skin on her cheek.

"Never," Ivy grinned. Her heart felt like it would burst with happiness and when he kissed her she thought it was impossible to love anyone as much as she loved him.

On her way home to get Gerald's tea, Betty called around to Alma road to tell Phoebe the good news about Billy's release.

"He just turned up on the doorstep Phoebe, stood there as bold as brass, honestly you could have knocked me down with a feather," Betty gossiped over a cup of tea. Betty could still hardly believe Billy Thomas had been told by the Police he was a free man; all charges against him were being dropped.

"Ivy has been floating on cloud nine since Billy has turned up again, she's a changed woman Phoebe."

Phoebe smiled, *so her efforts had come to fruition, thanks to Paddy McGuire the Poles were no longer Police witnesses in the case against Billy.*

"It's a blessed miracle however it happened, Billy just said that he was told he was free to go so he came straight to Wilson road to tell Ivy. It's just as if someone has suddenly switched the light back on inside Ivy, she was like a dead woman walking before then," Betty mused recalling the ecstatic re-union between the lovestruck couple.

Within hours of Billy's arrival Ivy had separated herself from Billy's arms just long enough to spruce herself up and the girl couldn't stop smiling. It was as if the whole dreadful experience had never happened.

"True love is a fierce and wonderful thing Betty," Phoebe said wisely.

Only that morning Phoebe had another visit from Jennifer Prosser and this time her brother Frank had tagged along with her. Phoebe knew it was more than likely the lure of free Trebor sweets which brought young Frank to her door but, even so she marked it down as progress, she knew Frank would be back. *It was the start.*

"You are right Phoebe and maybe one day your time for happiness will come," Betty smiled at her friend who she loved more than life.

"Don't ever feel sorry for me Betty I am as rich as any woman could be. Thanks to the kindness of Deirdre, I have this lovely home to call my own with two lodgers who pay the rent and most importantly, I live next door to my precious daughter and grandchildren. Now Ivy's happiness is secure my cup runs over. So, let's celebrate all the good in our lives Betty and enjoy life whilst we can." Phoebe smiled.

As Phoebe spoke a small shiver ran down Betty's spine it was as if someone had walked over her grave. Betty recalled the words of comfort she'd said to Ivy earlier in the day.

Always remember that nothing good or bad lasts forever…. The wheel of life always turns. Now those same words sounded as if they were both a blessing and a curse.

Betty gave her friend a fierce hug. "You are the best friend anybody could ever have, and I will always love you Phoebe, and don't you ever forget that." Betty said with tears in her eyes.

Later as Phoebe lay in bed waiting for sleep to come she listened to the now familiar noises of the house settling down for the night. Creaks, gentle thuds and muffled stirrings percolated up through the ceiling from the middle room below her bed; at least Malcolm Goode was trying to be quiet since she had words with him about making noise late at night.

Phoebe hugged herself close and thanked everything Holy that Billy Thomas had been returned home safe and sound to Ivy's arms. She believed in her heart the truism that *when God shut a door He opened a window* so with any luck new happier opportunities would beckon for the young couple, if anyone deserved to be happy in life, it was her precious Ivy.

Now the cloud hanging over Billy had disappeared there would be a wedding to look forward to, and June would have a proper Da to love at last.

Thank You, Phoebe muttered and said a silent prayer for all those who she loved.

Just after midnight Phoebe heard soft, careful treads on the stairs and the stealthy click of the latch in the next bedroom; *it must be Carol letting herself in.*

Phoebe had noticed Miss Carol Jones was coming home rather late recently. Phoebe suspected the middle-aged woman might have a secret lover keeping her out.... *Well, if she did, then good luck to her, the more windows of opportunity opening in people's lives the better!* Phoebe smiled to herself in the inky darkness; so long as she didn't know about it then it was none of her business what Carol got up to.

A soft rain pattered gently on the sash window, outside Phoebe could hear a wind starting to get up, gusts rustled the curtains and draughts sighed their way through the cracks, it was almost as if the old house was breathing.

Phoebe lay motionless under the comforting weight of the heavy counterpane, scattered thoughts of what the future might bring tumbled and buzzed through her mind. Exhausted she willed sleep to come and deliver her some much-needed rest.

As the fat raindrops splashed and beat a soothing, gentle pitter- patter rhythm on the panes of glass Phoebe allowed her thoughts to quieten and finally she drifted off.

Enveloped in a deep and dreamless sleep Phoebe slept soundly for the first time in days; so soundly she did not hear the tiny, muffled click of the front door being closed carefully as someone stole out of the house in the early hours of the morning.

Printed in Great Britain
by Amazon